Precaution
A Novel

by

J. Fenimore Cooper

Double9
BOOKS

Precaution
A Novel
by J. Fenimore Cooper

Copyright © 2024

All Rights reserved.

ISBN: 978-93-67142-63-9

Published by

DOUBLE 9 BOOKS

2/13-B, Ansari Road
Daryaganj, New Delhi – 110002
info@double9books.com
www.double9books.com
Tel. 011-40042856

This book is under public domain

ABOUT THE AUTHOR

James Fenimore Cooper (September 15, 1789 - September 14, 1851) was an American writer of the first half of the nineteenth century, best known for his historical romances depicting colonial and indigenous characters from the 17th to the 19th centuries. He spent much of his childhood and the last fifteen years of his life at Cooperstown, New York, which was founded on land owned by his father, William Cooper. Cooper joined the Episcopal Church soon before his death and gave liberally to it. He spent three years at Yale University, where he was a member of the Linonian Society. Cooper enlisted in the United States Navy as a midshipman after a period on a commercial voyage, where he studied the mechanics of handling sailing vessels, which heavily affected many of his novels and other writings. The Spy, a story about espionage set during the American Revolutionary War and published in 1821, established his career. He also wrote American marine tales. His best-known works are the Leatherstocking Tales, a series of five historical frontier novels written between 1823 and 1841 that established the famous American frontier scout, Natty Bumppo.

CONTENTS

"Be wise to-day. It is madness to defer;
To-morrow's caution may arrive too late."

W. C. Bryant's Discourse on the Life, Genius, and Writings of James Fenimore Cooper, Delivered at Metropolitan Hall, N.Y., February 25, 1852

It is now somewhat more than a year, since the friends of James Fenimore Cooper, in this city; were planning to give a public dinner to his honor. It was intended as an expression both of the regard they bore him personally, and of the pride they took in the glory his writings had reflected on the American name. We thought of what we should say in his hearing; in what terms, worthy of him and of us, we should speak of the esteem in which we held him, and of the interest we felt in a fame which had already penetrated to the remotest nook of the earth inhabited by civilized man.

To-day we assemble for a sadder purpose: to pay to the dead some part of the honors then intended for the living. We bring our offering, but he is not here who should receive it; in his stead are vacancy and silence; there is no eye to brighten at our words, and no voice to answer. "It is an empty office that we perform," said Virgil, in his melodious verses, when commemorating the virtues of the young Marcellus, and bidding flowers be strewn, with full hands, over his early grave. We might apply the expression to the present occasion, but it would be true in part only. We can no longer do anything for him who is departed, but we may do what will not be without fruit to those who remain. It is good to occupy our thoughts with the example of great talents in conjunction with great virtues. His genius has passed away with him; but we may learn, from the history of his life, to employ the faculties we possess with useful activity and noble aims; we may copy his magnanimous frankness, his disdain of everything that wears the faintest semblance of deceit, his refusal to comply with current abuses, and the courage with which, on all occasions, he asserted what he deemed truth, and combated what he thought error.

The circumstances of Cooper's early life were remarkably suited to confirm the natural hardihood and manliness of his character, and to call forth and exercise that extraordinary power of observation, which accumulated the materials afterwards wielded and shaped by his genius. His father, while an inhabitant of Burlington, in New Jersey, on the pleasant banks of the Delaware, was the owner of large possessions on the borders of the Otsego Lake in our own state, and here, in the newly-cleared fields, he built, in 1786, the first house in Cooperstown. To this home, Cooper, who was born in Burlington, in the year 1789, was conveyed in his infancy, and here, as he informs us in his preface to the *Pioneers*, his first impressions of the external world were obtained. Here he passed his childhood, with the vast forest around him, stretching up the mountains that overlook the lake, and far beyond, in a region where the Indian yet roamed, and the white hunter, half Indian in his dress and mode of life, sought his game,--a region in which the bear and the wolf were yet hunted, and the panther, more formidable than either, lurked in the thickets, and tales of wanderings in the wilderness, and encounters with these fierce animals, beguiled the length of the winter nights. Of this place, Cooper, although early removed from it to pursue his studies, was an occasional resident throughout his life, and here his last years were wholly passed.

At the age of thirteen he was sent to Yale College, where, notwithstanding his extreme youth,--for, with the exception of the poet Hillhouse, he was the youngest of his class, and Hillhouse was afterwards withdrawn,--his progress in his studies is said to have been honorable to his talents. He left the college, after a residence of three years, and became a midshipman in the United States navy. Six years he followed the sea, and there yet wanders, among those who are fond of literary anecdote, a story of the young sailor who, in the streets of one of the English ports, attracted the curiosity of the crowd by explaining to his companions a Latin motto in some public place. That during this period he made himself master of the knowledge and the imagery which he afterwards employed to so much advantage in his romances of the sea, the finest ever written, is a common and obvious remark; but it has not been so far as I know, observed that from the discipline of a seaman's life he may have derived much of his readiness and fertility of invention, much of his skill in surrounding the personages of his novels with imaginary perils, and rescuing them by probable expedients. Of all pursuits, the life of a sailor is that which familiarizes men to danger in its most fearful shapes, most cultivates presence of mind, and most effectually calls forth the resources of a prompt and fearless dexterity by which imminent evil is avoided.

In 1811, Cooper, having resigned his post as midshipman, began the year by marrying Miss Delaney, sister of the present bishop; of the diocese of Western New York, and entered upon a domestic life happily passed to its close. He went to live at Mamaroneck, in the county of Westchester, and while here he wrote and published the first of his novels, entitled *Precaution*. Concerning the occasion of writing this work, it is related, that once, as he was reading an English novel to Mrs. Cooper, who has, within a short time past, been laid in the grave beside her illustrious husband, and of whom we may now say, that her goodness was no less eminent than his genius, he suddenly laid down the book, and said, "I believe I could write a better myself." Almost immediately he composed a chapter of a projected work of fiction, and read it to the same friendly judge, who encouraged him to finish it, and when it was completed, suggested its publication. Of this he had at the time no intention, but he was at length induced to submit the manuscript to the examination of the late Charles Wilkes, of this city, in whose literary opinions he had great confidence. Mr. Wilkes advised that it should be published, and to these circumstances we owe it that Cooper became an author.

I confess I have merely dipped into this work. The experiment was made with the first edition, deformed by a strange punctuation--a profusion of commas, and other pauses, which puzzled and repelled me. Its author, many years afterwards, revised and republished it, correcting this fault, and some faults of style also, so that to a casual inspection it appeared almost another work. It was a professed delineation of English manners, though the author had then seen nothing of English society. It had, however, the honor of being adopted by the country whose manners it described, and, being early republished in Great Britain, passed from the first for an English novel. I am not unwilling to believe what is said of it, that it contained a promise of the powers which its author afterwards put forth.

Thirty years ago, in the year 1821, and in the thirty-second of his life, Cooper published the first of the works by which he will be known to posterity, the *Spy*. It took the reading world by a kind of surprise; its merit was acknowledged by a rapid sale; the public read with eagerness and the critics wondered. Many withheld their commendations on account of defects in the plot or blemishes in the composition, arising from want of practice, and some waited till they could hear the judgment of European readers. Yet there were not wanting critics in this country, of whose good opinion any author in any part of the world might be proud, who spoke of it in terms it deserved. "Are you not delighted," wrote a literary friend to me, who has since risen to high distinction as a writer, both in verse and in prose, "are you not delighted with the *Spy*, as a work of infinite spirit and genius?" In that word genius lay the explanation of the hold which the work had taken on the minds of men. What it had of excellence was peculiar and unborrowed; its pictures of life, whether in repose or activity, were drawn, with broad lights and shadows, immediately from living originals in nature or in his own imagination. To him, whatever he described was true; it was made a reality to him by the strength with which he conceived it. His power in the delineation of character was shown in the principal personage of his story, Harvey Birch, on whom, though he has chosen to employ him in the ignoble office of a spy, and endowed him with the qualities necessary to his profession,--extreme circumspection, fertility in stratagem, and the art of concealing his real character--qualities which, in conjunction with selfishness and greediness, make the scoundrel, he has bestowed the virtues of generosity, magnanimity, an intense love of country, a fidelity not to be corrupted, and a disinterestedness beyond temptation. Out of this combination of qualities he has wrought a character which is a favorite in all nations, and with all classes of mankind.

It is said that if you cast a pebble into the ocean, at the mouth of our harbor, the vibration made in the water passes gradually on till it strikes the icy barriers of the deep at the south pole. The spread of Cooper's reputation is not confined within narrower limits. The *Spy* is read in all the written dialects of Europe, and in some of those of Asia. The French, immediately after its first appearance, gave it to the multitudes who read their far-diffused language, and placed it among the first works of its class. It was rendered into Castilian, and passed into the hands of those who dwell under the beams of the Southern Cross. At length it passed the eastern frontier of Europe, and the latest record I have seen of its progress towards absolute universality, is contained in a statement of the *International Magazine*, derived, I presume, from its author, that in 1847 it was published in a Persian translation at Ispahan. Before this time, I doubt not, they are reading it in some of the languages of Hindostan, and, if the Chinese ever translated anything, it would be in the hands of the many millions who inhabit the far Cathay.

I have spoken of the hesitation which American critics felt in admitting the merits of the *Spy*, on account of crudities in the plot or the composition, some of which, no doubt, really existed. An exception must be made in favor of the *Port Folio*, which, in a notice written by Mrs. Sarah Hall, mother of the editor of that periodical, and author of *Conversations on the Bible*, gave the work a cordial welcome; and Cooper, as I am informed, never forgot this act of timely and ready kindness.

It was perhaps favorable to the immediate success of the *Spy*, that Cooper had few American authors to divide with him the public attention. That crowd of clever men and women who now write for the magazines, who send out volumes of essays, sketches, and poems, and who supply the press with novels, biographies, and historical works, were then, for the most part, either stammering their lessons in the schools, or yet unborn. Yet it is worthy of note, that just about the time that the *Spy* made its appearance, the dawn of what we now call our literature was just breaking. The concluding number of Dana's *Idle Man*, a work neglected at first, but now numbered among the best things of the kind in our language, was issued in the same month. The *Sketch Book* was then just completed; the world was admiring it, and its author was meditating *Bracebridge Hall*. Miss Sedgwick, about the same time, made her first essay in that charming series of novels of domestic life in New England, which have gained her so high a reputation. Percival, now unhappily silent, had just put to press a volume of poems. I have a copy of an edition of Hallock's *Fanny*, published in the same year; the poem of *Yamoyden*, by Eastburn and Sands, appeared almost simultaneously with it. Livingston was putting the finishing hand to his *Report on the Penal Code of Louisiana*, a work written with such grave, persuasive eloquence, that it belongs as much to our literature as to our jurisprudence. Other contemporaneous American works there were, now less read. Paul Allen's poem of *Noah* was just laid on the counters of the booksellers. Arden published, at the same time, in this city, a translation of Ovid's *Tristia*, in heroic verse, in which the complaints of the effeminate Roman poet were rendered with great fidelity to the original, and sometimes not without beauty. If I may speak of myself, it was in that year that I timidly intrusted to the winds and waves of public opinion a small cargo of my own--a poem entitled *The Ages,* and half a dozen shorter ones, in a thin duodecimo volume, printed at Cambridge.

We had, at the same time, works of elegant literature, fresh from the press of Great Britain, which are still read and admired. Barry Cornwall, then a young suitor for fame, published in the same year his *Marcia Colonna*; Byron, in the full strength and fertility of his genius, gave the readers of English his tragedy of *Marino Faliero*, and was in the midst of his spirited controversy with Bowles concerning the poetry of Pope. The *Spy* had to sustain a comparison with Scott's *Antiquary*, published simultaneously with it, and with Lockhart's *Valerius*, which seems to me one of the most remarkable works of fiction ever composed.

In 1823, and in his thirty-fourth year, Cooper brought out his novel of the *Pioneers*, the scene of which was laid on the borders of his: own beautiful lake. In a recent survey of Mr; Cooper's works, by one of his admirers, it is intimated that the reputation of this work may have been, in some degree factitious. I cannot think so; I cannot see how such a work could fail of becoming, sooner or later, a favorite. It was several years after its first appearance that I read the *Pioneers*, and I read it with a delighted astonishment. Here, said I to myself, is the poet of rural life in this country--our Hesiod, our Theocritus, except that he writes without the restraint of numbers, and is a greater poet than they. In the *Pioneers*, as in a moving picture, are made to pass before us the hardy occupations and spirited, amusements of a prosperous settlement, in, a fertile region, encompassed for leagues around with the primeval wilderness of woods. The seasons in their different aspects, bringing with them, their different employments; forests falling before the axe; the cheerful population, with the first mild; day of spring, engaged in the sugar orchards; the chase of the deer through the deep woods, and into the lake; turkey-shooting, during the Christmas holidays, in which the Indian marksman vied for the prize of skill with the white man; swift sleigh rides under the bright winter sun, and, perilous encounters with wild animals in the forests; these, and other scenes of rural life, drawn, as Cooper knew how to draw them, in the bright and healthful coloring of which he was master are interwoven with a regular narrative of human fortunes, not unskilfully constructed; and how could such a work be otherwise than popular?

In the *Pioneers*, Leatherstocking; is first introduced--a philosopher of the woods, ignorant of books, but instructed in all that nature, without the aid of, science, could reveal to the man of quick senses and inquiring intellect, whose life has been passed under the open sky, and in companionship with a race whose animal perceptions are the acutest and most cultivated of which there is any example. But Leatherstocking has higher qualities; in him there is a genial blending of the gentlest virtues of the civilized man with the better nature of the aboriginal tribes; all that in them is noble, generous, and ideal, is adopted into his own kindly character, and all that is evil is rejected. But why should I attempt to analyse a character so familiar? Leatherstocking is acknowledged, on all hands, to be one of the noblest, as well as most striking and original creations of fiction. In some of his subsequent novels, Cooper--for he had not yet Attained to the full maturity of his powers--heightened and ennobled his first conception of the character, but in the *Pioneers* it dazzled the world with the splendor of novelty;

His next work was the *Pilot*, in which he showed how, from the vicissitudes of a life at sea, its perils and escapes, from the beauty and terrors of the great deep, from the working of a vessel on a long voyage, and from the frank, brave, and generous but peculiar character of the seaman, may be drawn materials of romance by which the minds of men may be as deeply moved as by anything in the power of romance to present. In this walk, Cooper has had many disciples but no rival. All who have since written romances of the sea have been but travellers in a country of which he was the great discoverer; and none of them all seemed to have loved a ship as Cooper loved it, or have been able so strongly to interest all classes of readers in its fortunes. Among other personages drawn with great strength in the *Pilot*, is the general favorite, Tom Coffin, the thorough seaman with all the virtues and one or two of the infirmities of his profession, superstitious, as seamen are apt to be, yet whose superstitions strike us as but an irregular growth of his devout recognition of the Power who holds the ocean in the hollow of his hand; true-hearted, gentle, full of resources, collected in danger, and at last calmly perishing at the post of duty, with the vessel he has long guided, by what I may call a great and magnanimous death. His rougher and coarser companion, Boltrope, is drawn with scarcely less skill, and with a no less vigorous hand.

The *Pioneers* is not Cooper's best tale of the American forest, nor, the *Pilot*, perhaps, in all respects, his best tale of the sea; yet, if he had ceased to write here, the measure of his fame would possibly have been scarcely less ample than it now is. Neither of them is far below the best of his productions, and in them appear the two most remarkable creations of his imagination-- two of the most remarkable characters in all fiction.

It was about this time that my acquaintance with Cooper began, an acquaintance of more than a quarter of a century, in which his deportment towards me was that of unvaried kindness. He then resided a considerable part of the year in this city, and here he had founded a weekly club, to which many of the most distinguished men of the place belonged. Of the members who have since passed away, were Chancellor Kent, the jurist; Wiley the intelligent and liberal bookseller; Henry D. Sedgwick, always active in schemes of benevolence; Jarvis, the painter, a man of infinite humor, whose jests awoke inextinguishable laughter; De Kay, the naturalist; Sands, the poet; Jacob Harvey whose genial memory is cherished by many friends. Of those who are yet living was Morse, the inventor of the electric telegraph; Durand, then, one of the first of engravers, and now no less illustrious as a painter; Henry James Anderson, whose acquirements might awaken the envy of the ripest scholars of the old world; Halleck, the poet and wit; Verplanck, who has given the world the best edition of Shakspeare for general readers; Dr. King, now at the head of Columbia College, and his two immediate predecessors in that office. I might enlarge the list with many other names of no less distinction. The army and navy contributed their proportion of members, whose names are on record in our national history. Cooper when in town was always present, and I remember being struck with the inexhaustible vivacity of his conversation and the minuteness of his knowledge, in everything which depended upon acuteness of observation and exactness of recollection. I remember, too, being somewhat startled, coming as I did from the seclusion of a country life, with a certain emphatic frankness in his manner, which, however, I came at last to like and to admire. The club met in the hotel called Washington Hall, the site of which, is now occupied by part of the circuit of Stewart's marble building.

Lionel Lincoln, which cannot be ranked among the successful productions of Cooper, was published in 1825; and in the year following appeared the Last of the Mohicans which more than recovered the ground lost by its predecessor. In this work, the construction of the narrative has signal defects, but it is one of the triumphs of the author's genius that he makes us unconscious of them while we read. It is only when we have had time to awake from the intense interest in which he has held us by the vivid reality of his narrative, and have begun to search for faults in cold blood, that we are able to find them, In the Last of the Mohicans, we have a bolder portraiture of. Leatherstocking than in the Pioneers.

This work was published in 1826, and in the same year Cooper sailed with his family for Europe. He left New York as one of the vessels of war, described in his romances of the sea, goes out of port, amidst the thunder of a parting salute from the big guns on the batteries. A dinner was given him just before his departure, attended by most of the distinguished men of the city, at which Peter A. Jay presided, and Dr. King addressed him in terms which some then thought too glowing, but which would now seem sufficiently temperate, expressing the good wishes of his friends, and dwelling on the satisfaction they promised themselves in possessing so illustrious a representative of American literature in the old world. Cooper was scarcely in France when he remembered his friends of the weekly club, and sent frequent missives to be read at its meetings; but the club missed its founder went into a decline, and not long afterwards quietly expired.

The first of Cooper's novels published after leaving America: was the Prairie, which appeared early in 1827, a work with the admirers of which I wholly agree. I read it with a certain awe, an undefined sense of sublimity, such as one experiences on entering, for the first time, upon those immense grassy deserts from which the work takes its name. The squatter and his family--that brawny old man and his large-limbed sons, living in a sort of primitive and patriarchal barbarism, sluggish on ordinary occasions, but terrible when roused, like the hurricane that sweeps the grand but monotonous wilderness in which they dwell--seem a natural growth of ancient fields of the West. Leatherstocking, a hunter in the *Pioneers*, a warrior in the *Last of the Mohicans*, and now, in his extreme old age, a trapper on the prairie, declined in strength, but undecayed in intellect, and looking to the near close of his life, and a grave under the long grass, as calmly as the laborer at sunset looks to his evening slumber, is no less in harmony with the silent desert in which he wanders. Equally so are the Indians, still his companions, copies of the American savage somewhat idealized, but not the less a part of the wild nature in which they have their haunts.

Before the year closed, Cooper had given the world another nautical tale, the *Red Rover*, which, with many, is a greater favorite than the *Pilot*, and with reason, perhaps, if we consider principally the incidents, which are conducted and described with a greater mastery over the springs of pity and terror.

It happened to Cooper while he was abroad, as it not unfrequently happens to our countrymen, to hear the United States disadvantageously compared with Europe. He had himself been a close observer of things both here and in the old world, and was conscious of being able to refute the detractors of his country in regard to many points. He published in 1828, after he had been two years in Europe, a series of letters, entitled *Notions of the Americans, by a Travelling Bachelor*, in which he gave a favorable account of the working of our institutions, and vindicated his country from various flippant and ill-natured misrepresentations of foreigners. It is rather too measured in style, but is written from a mind full of the subject, and from a memory wonderfully stored with particulars. Although twenty-four years have elapsed since its publication, but little of the vindication has become obsolete.

Cooper loved his country and was proud of her history and her institutions, but it puzzles many that he should have appeared, at different times, as her eulogist, and her censor. My friends, she is worthy both of praise and of blame, and Cooper was not the man to shrink from bestowing either, at what seemed to him the proper time. He defended her from detractors abroad; he sought to save her from flatterers at home. I will not say that he was in as good humor with his country when he wrote *Home at Found*, as when he wrote his *Notions of the Americans*, but this I will say that whether he commended or censured, he did it in the sincerity of his heart, as a true American, and in the belief that it would do good. His *Notions of the Americans* were more likely to lessen than to increase his popularity in

Europe, inasmuch as they were put forth without the slightest regard to European prejudices.

In 1829, he brought out the novel entitled the *Wept of Wishton-Wish*, one of the few of his works which we now rarely hear mentioned. He was engaged in the composition of a third nautical tale, which he afterwards published under the name of the *Water-Witch*, when the memorable revolution of the Three Days of July broke out. He saw a government, ruling by fear and in defiance of public opinion, overthrown in a few hours, with little bloodshed; he saw the French nation, far from being intoxicated with their new liberty, peacefully addressing themselves to the discussion of the institutions under which they were to live. A work which Cooper afterwards published, his *Residence in Europe*, gives the outline of a plan of government for France furnished by him at that time, to La Fayette, with whom he was in habits of close and daily intimacy. It was his idea to give permanence to the new order of things by associating two strong parties in its support, the friends of legitimacy and the republicans. He suggested that Henry V. should be called to the hereditary throne of France, a youth yet to be educated as the head of a free people, that the peerage should be abolished, and a legislature of two chambers established, with a constituency of at least a million and a half of electors; the senate to be chosen by the general vote, as the representative of the entire nation, and the members of the other house to be chosen by districts, as the representatives of the local interests. To the middle ground of politics so ostentatiously occupied by Louis Philippe at the beginning of his reign, he predicted a brief duration, believing that it would speedily be merged in despotism, or supplanted by the popular rule. His prophecy has been fulfilled more amply than he could have imagined--fulfilled in both its alternatives.

In one of the controversies of that time, Cooper bore a distinguished part. The *Revue Britannique*, a periodical published in Paris, boldly affirmed the government of the United States to be one of the most expensive in the world, and its people among the most heavily taxed of mankind. This assertion was supported with a certain show of proof, and the writer affected to have established the conclusion that a republic must necessarily be more expensive than a monarchy. The partisans of the court were delighted with the reasoning of the article, and claimed a triumph over our ancient friend La Fayette, who, during forty years, had not ceased to hold up the government of the United States as the cheapest in the world. At the suggestion of La Fayette, Cooper replied to this attack upon his country in a letter which was translated into French, and, together with, another from General Bertrand, for many years a resident in America, was laid before the people of France.

These, two letters provoked a shower of rejoinders, in which, according to Cooper, misstatements were mingled with scurrility. He commenced a series of letters on the question in dispute, which were published in the *National*, a daily sheet, and gave the first evidence of that extraordinary acuteness in controversy which was no less characteristic of his mind than the vigor of his imagination. The enemies of La Fayette pressed into their service Mr. Leavitt Harris, of New Jersey, afterwards our *chargé d'affaires* at the court of France, but Cooper replied to Mr. Harris in the *National* of May 2d, 1832, closing a discussion in which he had effectually silenced those who objected to our institutions on the score of economy. Of these letters, which would form an important chapter in political science, no entire copy, I have been told, is to be found in this country.

One of the consequences of earnest controversy is almost invariably personal ill-will. Cooper was told by one who held an official station under the French government, that the part he had taken in this dispute concerning taxation would neither be forgotten nor forgiven. The dislike he had incurred in that quarter was strengthened by his novel of the *Bravo*, published in the year 1831, while he was in the midst of his quarrel with the aristocratic party. In that work, of which he has himself justly said that it was thoroughly American in all that belonged to it, his object was to show how institutions, professedly created to prevent violence and wrong, become, when perverted from their natural destination, the instruments of injustice; and how, in every system which makes power the exclusive property of the strong, the weak are sure to be oppressed. The work is written with all the vigor and spirit of his best novels; the magnificent city of Venice, in which the scene of the story is laid, stands continually before the imagination; and from time to time the gorgeous ceremonies of the Venetian republic pass under our eyes, such as the marriage of the Doge with the Adriatic, and the, contest of the gondolas for the prize of speed. The Bravo himself and several of the other characters are strongly conceived and distinguished, but the most remarkable of them all is the spirited and generous-hearted daughter of the jailer.

It has been said by some critics, who judge of Cooper by his failures, that he had no skill in drawing female characters. By the same process, it might, I suppose, be shown that Raphael was but an ordinary painter. It must be admitted that when Cooper drew a lady of high breeding, he was apt to pay too much attention to the formal part of her character, and to make her a mere bundle of cold proprieties. But when he places his heroines in some situation in life which leaves him nothing to do but to make them natural and true, I know of nothing finer, nothing more attractive or more individual than the portraitures he has given us.

Figaro, the wittiest of the French periodicals, and at that time on the liberal side, commended the *Bravo*; the journals on the side of the government censured it. *Figaro* afterwards passed into the hands of the aristocratic party, and Cooper became the object of its attacks. He was not, however, a man to be driven from any purpose which he had formed, either by flattery or abuse, and both were tried with equal ill success. In 1832 he published his *Heidenmauer*, and in 1833 his *Headsman of Berne*, both with a political design similar to that of the *Bravo*, though neither of them takes the same high rank among his works.

In 1833, after a residence of seven years in different parts of Europe, but mostly in France, Cooper returned to his native country. The welcome which met him here was somewhat chilled by the effect of the attacks made upon him in France, and remembering with what zeal, and at what sacrifice of the universal acceptance which his works would otherwise have met, he had maintained the cause of his country against the wits and orators of the court party in France, we cannot wonder that he should have felt this coldness as undeserved. He published, shortly after his arrival in this country, *A Letter to his Countrymen* in which he complained of the censures cast upon him in the American newspapers, gave a history of the part he had taken in exposing the misstatements of the *Révue Britannique*, and warned his countrymen against the too common error of resorting, with a blind deference, to foreign authorities, often swayed by national or political prejudices, for our opinions of American authors. Going beyond this topic, he examined and reprehended the habit of applying to the interpretation of our own constitution maxims derived from the practice of other governments, particularly that of Great Britain. The importance of construing that instrument by its own principles, he illustrated by considering several points in dispute between parties of the day, on which he gave very decided opinions.

The principal effect of this pamphlet, as it seemed to me, was to awaken in certain quarters a kind of resentment that a successful writer of fiction should presume to give lessons in politics. I meddle not here with the conclusions to which he arrived, though must be allowed to say that they were stated and argued with great ability. In 1835 Cooper published *The Monnikins*, a satirical work, partly with a political aim; and in the same year appeared his *American Democrat*, a view of the civil and social relations of the United States, discussing more gravely various topics touched upon in the former work, and pointing out in what respects he deemed the American people in their practice to have fallen short of the excellence of their institutions.

He found time, however, for a more genial task--that of giving to the world his observations on foreign countries. In 1836 appeared his *Sketches of Switzerland*, a series of letters in four volumes, the second part published about two months after the first, a delightful work, written in a more fluent and flexible style than his *Notions of the Americans*. The first part of *Gleanings in Europe*, giving an account of his residence in France, followed in the same year; and the second part of the same work, containing his observations on England, was published in April, 1837. In these works, forming a series of eight volumes, he relates and describes with much of the same distinctness as in his novels; and his remarks on the manners and institutions of the different countries, often sagacious, and always peculiarly his own, derive, from their frequent reference to contemporary events, an historical interest.

In 1838 appeared *Homeward Bound* and *Home as Found*, two satirical novels, in which Cooper held up to ridicule a certain class of conductors of the newspaper press in America. These works had not the good fortune to become popular. Cooper did not, and, because he was too deeply in earnest, perhaps would not, infuse into his satirical works that gaiety without which satire becomes wearisome. I believe, however, that if they had been written by anybody else they would have met with more favor; but the world knew that Cooper was able to give them something better, and would not be satisfied with anything short of his best, Some childishly imagined that because, in the two works I have just mentioned, a newspaper editor is introduced, in whose character almost every possible vice of his profession is made to find a place, Cooper intended an indiscriminate attack upon the whole body of writers for the newspaper press, forgetting that such a portraiture was a satire only on those to whom it bore a likeness We have become less sensitive and more reasonable of late, and the monthly periodicals make sport for their readers of the follies and ignorance of the newspaper editors, without awakening the slightest resentment; but Cooper led the way in this sort of discipline, and I remember some instances of towering indignation at his audacity expressed in the journals of that time.

The next year Cooper made his appearance before the public in a new department of writing; his *Naval History of the United States* was brought out in two octavo volumes at Philadelphia, by Carey and Lea. In writing his stories of the sea, his attention had been much turned to this subject, and his mind filled with striking incidents from expeditions and battles in which our naval commanders had been engaged. This made his task the lighter; but he gathered his materials with great industry, and with a conscientious attention to exactness, for he was not a man to take a fact for granted, or allow imagination to usurp the place of inquiry He digested our naval annals into a narrative, written with spirit it is true, but with that air of sincere dealing which the reader willingly takes as a pledge of its authenticity.

An abridgment of the work was afterwards prepared and published by the author. The *Edinburgh Review,* in an article professing to examine the statements both of Cooper's work and of *The History of the English Navy,* written by Mr. James, a surgeon by profession, made a violent attack upon the American historian. Unfortunately, it took James's narrative as its sole guide, and followed it implicitly. Cooper replied in the *Democratic Review* for January, 1840, and by a masterly analysis of his statements, convicting James of self-contradiction in almost every particular in which he differed from himself, refuted both James and the reviewer. It was a refutation which admitted of no rejoinder.

Scarce anything in Cooper's life was so remarkable, or so strikingly illustrated his character, as his contest with the newspaper press. He engaged in it after provocations, many and long endured, and prosecuted it through years with great energy, perseverance, and practical dexterity, till he was left master of the field. In what I am about to say of it, I hope I shall not give offence to any one, as I shall speak without the slightest malevolence towards those with whom he waged this controversy. Over some of them, as over their renowned adversary, the grave has now closed. Yet where shall the truth be spoken, if not beside the grave?

I have already alluded to the principal causes which provoked the newspaper attacks upon Cooper. If he had never meddled with questions of government on either side of the Atlantic, and never satirized the newspaper press, I have little doubt that he would have been spared these attacks. I cannot, however, ascribe them all, or even the greater part of them, to personal malignity. One journal followed the example of another, with little reflection, I think, in most cases, till it became a sort of fashion, not merely to decry his works, but to arraign his motives.

It is related that, in 1832, while he was at Paris, an article was shown him in an American newspaper, purporting to be a criticism on one of his works, but reflecting with much asperity on his personal character. "I care nothing," he is reported to have said, "for the criticism, but I am not indifferent to the slander. If these attacks on my character should be kept up five years after my return to America, I shall resort to the New York courts for protection." He gave the newspaper press of this state the full period of forbearance on which he had fixed, but finding that forbearance seemed to encourage assault, he sought redress in the courts of law.

When these litigations were first begun, I recollect it seemed to me that Cooper had taken a step which would give him a great deal of trouble, and effect but little good. I said to myself--

"Alas! Leviathan is not so tamed!"

As he proceeded, however, I saw that he had understood the matter better than I. He put a hook into the nose of this huge monster, wallowing in his inky pool and bespattering the passers-by; he dragged him to the land and made him tractable. One suit followed another; one editor was sued, I think half-a-dozen times; some of them found themselves under a second indictment before the first was tried. In vindicating himself to his reader, against the charge of publishing one libel, the angry journalist often floundered into another. The occasions of these prosecutions seem to have been always carefully considered, for Cooper was almost uniformly successful in obtaining verdicts. In a letter of his, written in February, 1843, about five years, I think, from the commencement of the first prosecutions, he says, "I have beaten every man I have sued, who has not retracted his libels."

In one of these suits, commenced against the late William L. Stone of the *Commercial Advertiser,* and referred to the arbitration of three distinguished lawyers, he argued himself the question of the authenticity of his account of the battle of Lake Erie, which was the matter in dispute. I listened to his opening; it was clear, skilful, and persuasive, but his closing argument was said to be splendidly eloquent. "I have heard nothing like it," said a barrister to me, "since the days of Emmet."

Cooper behaved liberally towards his antagonists, so far as pecuniary damages were concerned, though some of them wholly escaped their payment by bankruptcy. After, I believe, about, six years of litigation, the newspaper press gradually subsided into a pacific disposition towards its adversary, and the contest closed with the account of pecuniary profit and loss, so far as he was concerned, nearly balanced. The occasion of these suits was far from honorable to those who provoked them, but the result was I had almost said, creditable to all parties; to him, as the courageous prosecutor, to the administration of justice in this country, and to the docility of the newspaper press, which he had disciplined into good manners.

It was while he was in the midst of these litigations, that he published, in 1840, the *Pathfinder.* People had begun to think of him as a controversialist, acute, keen, and persevering, occupied with his personal wrongs and schemes of attack and defence. They were startled from this estimate of his character by the moral duty of that glorious work--I must so call it; by the vividness and force of its delineations, by the unspoiled love of nature apparent in every page, and by the fresh and warm emotions which everywhere gave life to the narrative and the dialogue. Cooper was now in his fifty-first year, but nothing which he had produced in the earlier part of his literary life was written with so much of what might seem the generous fervor of youth, or showed the faculty of invention in higher vigor. I recollect that near the time of its appearance I was informed of an observation made upon it by one highly distinguished in the literature of our country and of the age, between whom and the author an unhappy coolness had for some years existed. As he finished the reading of the Pathfinder, he exclaimed, "They may say what they will of Cooper; the man who wrote this book is not only a great man, but a good man."

The readers of the *Pathfinder* were quickly reconciled to the fourth appearance of Leatherstocking, when they saw him made to act a different part from any which the author had hitherto assigned him--when they saw him shown as a lover, and placed in the midst of associations which invested his character with a higher and more affecting heroism. In this work are two female characters, portrayed in a masterly manner,--the corporal's daughter, Mabel Dunham, generous, resolute, yet womanly, and the young Indian woman, called by her tribe the Dew of June, a personification of female truth, affection, and sympathy, with a strong aboriginal cast, yet a product of nature as bright and pure as that from which she is named.

Mercedes of Castile, published near the close of the same year, has none of the stronger characteristics of Cooper's genius; but in the *Deerslayer*, which appeared in 1841, another of his Leatherstocking tales, he gave us a work rivalling the Pathfinder. Leatherstocking is brought before us in his early youth, in the first exercise of that keen sagacity which is blended so harmoniously with a simple and ingenuous goodness. The two daughters of the retired freebooter dwelling on the Otsego lake, inspire scarcely less interest than the principal personage; Judith, in the pride of her beauty and intellect, her good impulses contending with a fatal love of admiration, holding us fascinated with a constant interest in her fate, which, with consummate skill, we are permitted rather to conjecture than to know; and Hetty, scarcely less beautiful in person, weak-minded, but wise in the midst, of that weakness beyond the wisdom of the loftiest intellect, through the power of conscience and religion. The character of Hetty would have been a hazardous experiment in feebler hands, but in his it was admirably successful.

The *Two Admirals* and *Wing-and-Wing* were given to the public in 1842, both of them taking a high rank among Cooper's sea-tales. The first of these is a sort of naval epic in prose; the flight and chase of armed vessels hold us in breathless suspense, and the sea-fights are described with a terrible power. In the later sea-tales of Cooper, it seems to me that the mastery with which he makes his grand processions of events pass before the mind's eye is even greater than in his earlier. The next year he published the *Wyandotte or Hutted Knoll*, one of his beautiful romances of the woods, and in 1844 two more of his sea-stories, *Afloat and Ashore* and *Miles Wallingford*its sequel. The long series of his nautical tales was closed by *Jack Tier or the Florida Reef*, published in 1848, when Cooper was in his sixtieth year, and it is as full of spirit, energy, invention, life-like presentation of objects and events--

The vision and the faculty divine--

as anything he has written.

Let me pause here to say that Cooper, though not a manufacturer of verse, was in the highest sense of the word a poet; his imagination wrought nobly and grandly, and imposed its creations on the mind of the reader for realities. With him there was no withering, or decline, or disuse of the poetic faculty; as he stepped downwards from the zenith of life, no shadow or chill came over it; it was like the year of some genial climates, a perpetual season of verdure, bloom, and fruitfulness. As these works came out, I was rejoiced to see that he was unspoiled by the controversies in which he had allowed, himself to become engaged; that they had not given to these better expressions of his genius, any tinge of misanthropy, or appearance of contracting and closing sympathies any trace of an interest in his fellow-beings less large and free than in his earlier works.

Before the, appearance of his *Jack Tier*, Cooper published, in 1845 and the following year, a series of novels relating to the Anti-rent question, in which he took great interest. He thought that the disposition manifested in certain quarters to make con cessions, to what he deemed a denial of the rights of property was a first step in a most dangerous path. To discourage this disposition, he wrote *Satanstoe, The Chainbearer*, and *The Redskins*. They are didactic in their design, and want the freedom of invention which belongs to Cooper's best novels; but if they had been written by anybody but Cooper,--by a member of Congress, for example, or an eminent politician of any class,--they would have made his reputation. It was said, I am told, by a distinguished jurist of our state, that they entitled the author to as high a place in law as his other works had won for him in literature.

I had thought, in meditating the plan of this discourse, to mention all the works of Mr. Cooper, but the length to which I have found it extending has induced me to pass over several written in the last ten years of his life, and to confine myself to those which best illustrate his literary character. The last of his novels was *The Ways of the Hour*, a work in which the objections he entertained to the trial by jury in civil causes were stated in the form of a narrative.

It is a voluminous catalogue--that of Cooper's published works--but it comprises not all he wrote. He committed to the fire, without remorse, many of the fruits of his literary industry. It was understood, some years since, that he had a work ready for the press on the *Middle States of the Union*, principally illustrative of their social history; but it has not been found among his manuscripts, and the presumption is that he must have destroyed it. He had planned a work on the *Towns of Manhattan*, for the publication of which he made arrangements with Mr. Putnam of this city, and a part of which, already written, was in press at the time of his death. The printed part has since been destroyed by fire, but a portion of the manuscript was recovered. The work, I learn, will be completed by one of the family, who, within a few years past, has earned an honorable name among the authors of our country. Great as was the number of his works, and great as was the favor with which they were received, the pecuniary rewards of his success were far less than has been generally supposed--scarcely, as I am informed, a tenth part of what the common rumor made them. His fame was infinitely the largest acknowledgment which this most successful of American authors received for his labors.

The Ways of the Hour appeared in 1850. At this time his personal appearance was remarkable. He seemed in perfect health, and in the highest energy and activity of his faculties. I have scarcely seen any man at that period of life on whom his years sat more lightly. His conversation had lost none of its liveliness, though it seemed somewhat more genial and forbearing in tone, and his spirits none of their elasticity. He was contemplating, I have since been told, another Leatherstocking tale, deeming that he had not yet exhausted the character; and those who consider what new resources it yielded him in the *Pathfinder* and the *Deerslayer*, will readily conclude that he was not mistaken.

The disease, however, by which he was removed, was even then impending over him, and not long afterwards his friends here were grieved to learn that his health was declining. He came to New York so changed that they looked at him with sorrow, and after a stay of some weeks, partly for the benefits of medical advice returned to Cooperstown, to leave it no more. His complaint gradually gained strength, subdued a constitution originally robust, and finally passed into a confirmed dropsy. In August, 1851, he was visited by his excellent and learned friend, Dr. Francis, a member of the weekly club which he had founded in the early part of his literary career. He found him bearing the sufferings of his disease with manly firmness, gave him such medical counsels as the malady appeared to require, prepared him delicately for its fatal termination, and returned to New York with the most melancholy anticipations. In a few days afterwards, Cooper expired, amid the deep affliction of his family, on the 14th of September, the day before that on which he should have completed his sixty-second year. He died, apparently without pain, in peace and religious hope. The relations of man to his Maker, and to that state of being for which the present is but a preparation, had occupied much of his thoughts during his whole lifetime, and he crossed, with a serene composure, the mysterious boundary which divides this life from the next.

The departure of such a man, in the full strength of his faculties,--on whom the country had for thirty years looked as one of the permanent ornaments of its literature, and whose name had been so often associated with praise, with renown, with controversy, with blame, but never with death,--diffused a universal awe. It was as if an earthquake had shaken the ground on which we stood, and showed the grave opening by our path. In the general grief for his loss, his virtues only were remembered; and his failings forgotten.

Of his failings I have said little; such as he had were obvious to all the world; they lay on the surface of his character; those who knew him least made the most account of them. With a character so made up of positive qualities--a character so independent and uncompromising, and with a sensitiveness far more acute than he was willing to acknowledge, it is not surprising that occasions frequently arose to bring him, sometimes into friendly collision, and sometimes in to graver disagreements and misunderstandings with his fellow-men. For his infirmities, his friends found an ample counterpoise in the generous sincerity of his nature. He never thought of disguising his opinions, and he abhorred all disguise in others; he did not even deign to use that show of regard towards those of whom he did not think well, which the world tolerates, and almost demands. A manly expression of opinion, however different from his own, commanded his respect. Of his own works, he spoke with the same freedom as of the works of others; and never hesitated to express his judgment of a book for the reason that it was written by himself: yet he could bear with gentleness any dissent from the estimate lie placed on his own writings. His character was like the bark of the cinnamon, a rough and astringent rind without, and an intense sweetness within. Those who penetrated below the surface found a genial temper, warm affections, and a heart with ample place for his friends, their pursuits, their good name, their welfare. They found him a philanthropist, though not precisely after the fashion of the day; a religious man, most devout where devotion is most apt to be a feeling rather than a custom, in the household circle; hospitable, and to the extent of his means liberal-handed in acts of charity. They found, also, that though in general he would as soon have thought of giving up an old friend as of giving up an opinion, he was not proof against testimony, and could part with a mistaken opinion as one parts with an old friend who has been proved faithless and unworthy. In short, Cooper was one of those who, to be loved, must be intimately known.

Of his literary character I have spoken largely in the narrative of his life, but there are yet one or two remarks which must be made to do it justice. In that way of writing in which he excelled, it seems to me that he united, in a pre-eminent degree, those qualities which enabled him to interest the largest number of readers. He wrote not for the fastidious, the over-refined, the morbidly delicate; for these find in his genius something too robust for their liking--something by which their sensibilities are too rudely shaken; but he wrote for mankind at large--for men and women in the ordinary healthful state of feeling--and in their admiration he found his reward. It is for this class that public libraries are obliged to provide themselves with an extraordinary number of copies of his works: the number in the Mercantile Library in this city, I am told, is forty. Hence it is, that he has earned a fame, wider, I think, than any author of modern times--wider, certainly, than any author, of any age, ever enjoyed in his lifetime. All his excellences are translatable--they pass readily into languages the least allied in their genius to that in which he wrote, and in them he touches the heart and kindles the imagination with the same power as in the original English.

Cooper was not wholly without humor; it is sometimes found lurking in the dialogue of Harvey Birch, and of Leatherstocking but it forms no considerable element in his works; and if it did, it would have stood in the way of his universal popularity; since of all qualities, it is the most difficult to transfuse into a foreign language. Nor did the effect he produced upon the reader depend on any grace of style which would escape a translator of ordinary skill. With his style, it is true, he took great pains, and in his earlier works, I am told, sometimes altered the proofs sent from the printer so largely that they might be said to be written over Yet he attained no special felicity, variety, or compass of expression. His style, however, answered his purpose; it has defects, but it is manly and clear, and stamps on the mind of the reader the impression he desired to convey. I am not sure that some of the very defects of Cooper's novels do not add, by a certain force of contrast, to their power over the mind. He is long in getting at the interest of his narrative. The progress of the plot, at first, is like that of one of his own vessels of war, slowly, heavily, and even awkwardly working out of a harbor. We are impatient and weary, but when the vessel is once in the open sea, and feels the free breath of heaven in her full sheets, our delight and admiration is all the greater at the grace, the majesty, and power with which she divides and bears down the waves, and pursues her course, at will, over the great waste of waters.

Such are the works so widely read, and so universally admired, in all the zones of the globe, and by men of every kindred and every tongue; works which have made of those who dwell in remote latitudes, wanderers in our forests, and observers of our manners, and have inspired them with an interest in our history. A gentleman who had returned from Europe just before the death of Cooper, was asked what he found the people of the Continent doing. "They all are reading Cooper," he answered; "in the little kingdom of Holland, with its three millions of inhabitants, I looked into four different translations of Cooper in the language of the country." A traveller, who has seen much of the middle classes of Italy, lately said to me, "I found that all they knew of America, and that was not little, they had learned from Cooper's novels; from him they had learned the story of American liberty, and through him they had been introduced to our Washington; they had read his works till the shores of the Hudson, and the valleys of Westchester, and the banks of Otsego lake, had become to them familiar ground."

Over all the countries into whose speech this great man's works have been rendered by the labors of their scholars, the sorrow of that loss which we deplore is now diffusing itself. Here we lament the ornament of our country, there they mourn the death of him who delighted the human race. Even now, while I speak, the pulse of grief which is passing through the nations has haply just reached some remote neighborhood; the news of his death has been brought to some dwelling on the slopes of the Andes, or amidst the snowy wastes of the North, and the dark-eyed damsel of Chile, or the fair-haired maid of Norway, is sad to think that he whose stories of heroism and true love have so often kept her for hours from her pillow, lives no more.

He is gone! but the creations of his genius, fixed in living words, survive the frail material organs by which the words were first traced. They partake of a middle nature, between the deathless mind and the decaying body of which they are the common offspring, and are, therefore, destined to a duration, if not eternal, yet indefinite. The examples he has given in his glorious fictions, of heroism, honor, and truth, of large sympathies between man and man, of all that is good, great, and excellent, embodied in personages marked with so strong an individuality that we place them among our friends and favorites; his frank and generous men, his gentle and noble women, shall live through centuries to come, and only perish with our language. I have said with our language; but who shall say when it may be the fate of the English language to be numbered with the extinct forms of human speech? Who shall declare which of the present tongues of the civilized world will survive its fellows? It may be that some one of them, more fortunate than the rest, will long outlast them, in some undisturbed quarter of the globe, and in the midst of a new civilization. The creations of Cooper's genius, even now transferred to that language, may remain to be the delight of the nations through another great cycle of centuries, beginning after the English language and its contemporaneous form of civilization shall have passed away.

Preface to the New Edition

This book originally owed its existence to an accident, and it was printed under circumstances that prevented the usual supervision of the press by the author. The consequences were many defects in plot, style, and arrangement, that were entirely owing to precipitation and inexperience; and quite as many faults, of another nature, that are to be traced solely to a bad manuscript and worse proof reading. Perhaps no novel of our times was worst printed than the first edition of this work. More than a hundred periods were placed in the middle of sentences, and perhaps five times that number were omitted in places where they ought to have been inserted. It is scarcely necessary to add, that passages were rendered obscure, and that entire paragraphs were unintelligible.

Most of the faults just mentioned have now been corrected, though it would require more labor than would produce an entirely new work, to repair all the inherent defects that are attributable to haste, and to the awkwardness of a novice in the art of composing. In this respect, the work and its blemishes are probably inseparable. Still, the reader will now be better rewarded for his time, and, on the whole; the book is much more worthy of his attention.

It has been said that Precaution owes its existence to fortuitous circumstances. The same causes induced its English plot, and, in a measure, the medley of characters that no doubt will appear a mistake in the conception. It can scarcely be said that the work was commenced with any view to publication; and when it was finally put into a publisher's hands, with "all its imperfections on its head," the last thought of the writer was any expectation that it would be followed by a series of similar tales from the same pen.

More than this the public will feel no interest in knowing, and less than this the author could not consent to say on presenting to the world a reprint of a book with so few claims to notice.

Chapter I

"I wonder if we are to have a neighbor in the Deanery soon," inquired Clara Moseley, addressing herself to a small party assembled in her father's drawing-room, while standing at a window which commanded a distant view of the house in question.

"Oh yes," replied her brother, "the agent has let it to a Mr. Jarvis for a couple of years, and he is to take possession this week."

"And who is the Mr. Jarvis that is about to become so near a neighbor?" asked Sir Edward Moseley.

"Why, sir, I learn he has been a capital merchant; that he has retired from business with a large fortune; that he has, like yourself, sir, an only hope for his declining years in son, an officer in the army; and, moreover, that he has couple of fine daughters; so, sir, he is a man of family in one sense, at least, you see. But," dropping his voice, "whether he is a man of family in your sense, Jane," looking at his second sister, "is more than I could discover."

"I hope you did not take the trouble, sir, to inquire on my account," retorted Jane, coloring slightly with vexation at his speech.

"Indeed I did, my dear sis, and solely on your account," replied the laughing brother, "for you well know that no gentility, no husband; and it's dull work to you young ladies without at least a possibility of matrimony; as for Clara, she is----"

Here he was stopped by his youngest sister Emily placing her hand on his mouth, as she whispered in his ear, "John, you forget the anxiety of a certain gentleman about a fair incognita at Bath, and a list of inquiries concerning her lineage, and a few other indispensables." John, in his turn, colored, and affectionately kissing the hand which kept him silent, addressed himself to Jane, and by his vivacity and good humor soon restored her to complacency.

"I rejoice," said Lady Moseley, "that Sir William has found a tenant, however; for next to occupying it himself, it is a most desirable thing to have a good tenant in it, on account of the circle in which we live."

"And Mr. Jarvis has the great goodness of money, by John's account," caustically observed Mrs. Wilson, who was a sister of Sir Edward's.

"Let me tell you, madam," cried the rector of the parish, looking around him pleasantly, and who was pretty constant, and always a welcome visitor in the family, "that a great deal of money is a very good thing in itself, and that a great many very good things may be done with it."

"Such as paying tythes, ha! doctor," cried Mr. Haughton, a gentleman of landed property in the neighborhood, of plain exterior, but great goodness of heart, and between whom and the rector subsisted the most cordial good will.

"Aye, tythes, or halves, as the baronet did here, when he forgave old Gregson one half his rent, and his children the other."

"Well, but, my dear," said Sir Edward to his wife, "you must not starve our friends because we are to have a neighbor. William has stood with the dining-room door open these five minutes--"

Lady Moseley gave her hand to the rector, and the company followed them, without any order, to the dinner table.

The party assembled around the hospitable board of the baronet was composed, besides the before-mentioned persons, of the wife of Mr. Haughton, a woman of much good sense and modesty of deportment: their daughter, a young lady conspicuous for nothing but good nature; and the wife and son of the rector--the latter but lately admitted to holy orders himself.

The remainder of the day passed in an uninterrupted flow of pleasant conversation, the natural consequence of a unison of opinions on all leading questions, the parties having long known and esteemed each other for those qualities which soonest reconcile us to the common frailties of our nature. On parting at the usual hour, it was agreed to meet that day week at the rectory, and the doctor, on making his bow to Lady Moseley, observed, that he intended, in virtue of his office, to make an early call on the Jarvis family, and that, if possible, he would persuade them to be of the party.

Sir Edward Moseley was descended from one of the most respectable of the creations of his order by James, and had inherited, with many of the virtues of his ancestor, an estate which placed him amongst the greatest landed proprietors of the county. But, as it had been an invariable rule never to deduct a single acre from the inheritance of the eldest son, and the extravagance of his mother, who was the daughter of a nobleman, had much embarrassed the affairs of his father, Sir Edward, on coming into possession of his estate, had wisely determined to withdraw from the gay world, by renting his house in town, and retiring altogether to his respectable mansion, about a hundred miles from the metropolis. Here he hoped, by a course of systematic but liberal economy, to release himself from all embarrassments, and to make such a provision for his younger children, the three daughters already mentioned, as he conceived their birth entitled them to expect. Seventeen years enabled him to accomplish this plan; and for more than eighteen months, Sir Edward had resumed the hospitality and appearance usual in his family, and had even promised his delighted girls to take possession, the ensuing winter, of the house in St. James's Square. Nature had not qualified Sir Edward for great or continued exertions, and the prudent decision he had taken to retrieve his fortunes, was perhaps an act of as much forecast and vigor as his talents or energy would afford; it was the step most obviously for his interests, and the one that was safest both in its execution and consequences, and as such it had been adopted: but, had it required a single particle more of enterprise or calculation, it would have been beyond his powers, and the heir might have yet labored under the difficulties which distressed his more brilliant, but less prudent parent.

The baronet was warmly attached to his wife; and as she was a woman of many valuable and no obnoxious qualities, civil and attentive by habit to all around her, and perfectly disinterested in her attachments to her own family, nothing in nature could partake more of perfection in the eyes of her husband and children than the conduct of this beloved relative. Yet Lady Moseley had her failings, however, although few were disposed to view her errors with that severity which truth and a just discrimination of character render necessary. Her union had been one of love, and for a time it had been objected to by the friends of her husband, on the score of fortune; but constancy and perseverance prevailed, and the protracted and inconsequent opposition of his parents had left no other effects than an aversion in the children to the exercise of parental authority, in marrying their own descendents: an aversion which, though common to both the worthy baronet and his wife, was somewhat different in its two subjects. In the husband it was quiescent; but in the wife, it was slightly shaded with the female *esprit de corps*, of having her daughters comfortably established, and that in due season. Lady Moseley was religious, but hardly pious; she was charitable in deeds, but not always in opinions; her intentions were pure, but neither her prejudices nor her reasoning powers suffered her to be at all times consistent. Still few knew her that did not love her, and none were ever heard to say aught against her breeding, her morals, or her disposition.

The sister of Sir Edward had been married, early in life, to an officer in the army, who, spending much of his time abroad on service, had left her a prey to that solicitude to which she was necessarily a prey by her attachment to her husband. To find relief from this perpetual and life-wearing anxiety, an invaluable friend had pointed out the only true remedy of which her case admitted, a research into her own heart, and the employments of active benevolence. The death of her husband, who lost his life in battle, caused her to withdraw in a great measure from the world, and gave time and inducement for reflections, which led to impressions on religion that were sufficiently correct in themselves, and indispensable as the basis of future happiness, but which became slightly tinctured with the sternness of her vigorous mind, and possibly, at times were more unbending than was compatible with the comforts of this world; a fault, however, of manner, more than of matter. Warmly attached to her brother and his children, Mrs. Wilson, who had never been a mother herself, yielded to their earnest entreaties to become one of the family; and although left by the late General Wilson with a large income, ever since his death she had given up her own establishment, and devoted most of her time to the formation of the character of her youngest niece. Lady Moseley had submitted this child entirely to the control of the aunt; and it was commonly thought Emily would inherit the very handsome sum left at the disposal of the General's widow.

Both Sir Edward and Lady Moseley possessed a large share of personal beauty when young, and it had descended in common to all their children, but more particularly to the two youngest daughters. Although a strong family resemblance, both in person and character, existed between these closely connected relatives, yet it existed with shades of distinction that had very different effects on their conduct, and led to results which stamped their lives with widely differing degrees of happiness.

Between the families at Moseley Hall and the rectory, there had existed for many years an intimacy founded on esteem and on long intercourse. Doctor Ives was a clergyman of deep piety; and of very considerable talents; he possessed, in addition to a moderate benefice, an independent fortune in right of his wife, who was the only child of a distinguished naval officer. Both were well connected, well bred, and well disposed to their fellow creatures. They were blessed with but one child, the young divine we have mentioned, who promised to equal his father in all those qualities which had made the Doctor the delight of his friends, and almost the idol of his parishioners.

Between Francis Ives and Clara Moseley, there had been an attachment, which had grown with their years, from childhood. He had been her companion in their youthful recreations, had espoused her little quarrels, and participated in her innocent pleasures, for so many years, and with such an evident preference for each other in the youthful pair, that, on leaving college to enter on the studies of his sacred calling with his father, Francis rightly judged that none other would make his future life as happy, as the mild, the tender, the unassuming Clara. Their passion, if so gentle a feeling deserve the term, received the sanction of their parents, and the two families waited only for the establishment of the young divine, to perfect the union.

The retirement of Sir Edward's family had been uniform, with the exception of an occasional visit to an aged uncle of his wife's, and who, in return, spent much of his time with them at the Hall, and who had openly declared his intention of making the children of Lady Moseley his heirs. The visits of Mr. Benfield were always hailed with joy, and as an event that called for more than ordinary gaiety; for, although rough in manner, and somewhat infirm from years, the old bachelor, who was rather addicted to the customs in which he had indulged in his youth, and was fond of dwelling on the scenes of former days, was universally beloved where he was intimately known, for an unbounded though eccentric philanthropy.

The illness of the mother-in-law of Mrs. Wilson had called her to Bath the winter preceding the spring when our history commences, and she had been accompanied thither by her nephew and favorite niece. John and Emily, during the month of their residence in that city, were in the practice of making daily excursions in its environs. It was in one of these little drives that they were of accidental service to a very young and very beautiful woman, apparently in low health. They had taken her up in their carriage, and conveyed her to a farm-house where she resided, during a faintness which had come over her in a walk; and her beauty, air, and manner, altogether so different from those around her, had interested them both to a painful degree. They had ventured to call the following day to inquire after her welfare, and this visit led to a slight intercourse, which continued for the fortnight they remained there.

John had given himself some trouble to ascertain who she was, but in vain. They could merely learn that her life was blameless, that she saw no one but themselves, and her dialect raised a suspicion that she was not English, It was to this unknown fair Emily alluded in her playful attempt to stop the heedless rattle of her brother, who was not always restrained from uttering what he thought by a proper regard for the feelings of others.

Chapter II

The morning succeeding the day of the dinner at the Hall, Mrs. Wilson, with all her nieces and her nephew, availed herself of the fineness of the weather to walk to the rectory, where they were all in the habit of making informal and friendly visits. They had just got out of the little village of B----, which lay in their route, when a rather handsome travelling carriage and four passed them, and took the road which led to the Deanery.

"As I live," cried John, "there go our new neighbors the Jarvis's; yes, yes, that must be the old merchant muffled up in the corner; I mistook him at first for a pile of bandboxes; then the rosy-cheeked lady, with so many feathers, must be the old lady--heaven forgive me, Mrs. Jarvis I mean--aye, and the two others the belles."

"You are in a hurry to pronounce them belles, John," said Jane, pettishly; "it would be well to see more of them before you speak so decidedly."

"Oh!" replied John, "I have seen *enough* of them, and"--he was interrupted by the whirling of a tilbury and tandem followed by a couple of servants on horseback. All about this vehicle and its masters bore the stamp of decided fashion; and our party had followed it with their eyes for a short distance, when, having reached a fork in the roads, it stopped, and evidently waited the coming up of the pedestrians, as if to make an inquiry. A single glance of the eye was sufficient to apprise the gentleman on the cushion (who held the reins) of the kind of people he had to deal with, and stepping from his carriage, he met them with a graceful bow, and after handsomely apologizing for the trouble he was giving, he desired to know which road led to the Deanery. "The right," replied John, returning his salutation.

"Ask them, Colonel," cried the charioteer, "whether the old gentleman went right or not."

The Colonel, in the manner of a perfect gentleman, but with a look of compassion for his companion's want of tact, made the desired inquiry; which being satisfactorily answered, he again bowed and was retiring, as one of several pointers who followed the cavalcade sprang upon Jane, and soiled her walking dress with his dirty feet.

"Come hither, Dido," cried the Colonel, hastening to beat the dog back from the young lady; and again he apologized in the same collected and handsome manner, then turning to one of the servants, he said, "call in the dog, sir," and rejoined his companion. The air of this gentleman was peculiarly pleasant; it would not have been difficult to pronounce him a soldier had he not been addressed as such by his younger and certainly less polished companion. The Colonel was apparently about thirty, and of extremely handsome face and figure, while his driving friend appeared several years younger, and of altogether different materials.

"I wonder," said Jane, as they turned a corner which hid them from view, "who they are?"

"Who they are?" cried the brother, "why the Jarvis's to be sure; didn't you hear them ask the road to the Deanery?

"Oh! the one that drove, *he* may be a Jarvis, but not the gentleman who spoke to us--surely not, John; besides, he was called Colonel, you know."

"Yes, yes," said John, with one of his quizzing expressions, "Colonel Jarvis, that must be the alderman; they are commonly colonels of city volunteers: yes, that must have been the old gem'mun who spoke to us, and I was right after all about the bandboxes."

"You forget," said Clara, smiling, "the polite inquiry concerning the old gem'mun."

"Ah! true; who the deuce can this Colonel be then, for young Jarvis is only a captain, I know; who do you think he is, Jane?"

"How do you think I can tell you, John? But whoever he is, he owns the tilbury, although he did not drive it; and he is a gentleman both by birth and manners."

"Why, Jane, if you know so much of him, you should know more; but it is all guess with you."

"No; it is not guess--I am certain of what I say."

The aunt and sisters, who had taken little interest in the dialogue, looked at her with some surprise, which John observing, he exclaimed, "Poh: she knows no more than we all know."

"Indeed I do."

"Poh, poh, if you know, tell."

"Why, the arms were different."

John laughed as he said, "That *is* a good reason, sure enough, for the tilbury's being the colonel's property; but now for his blood; how did you discover that, sis--by his gait and actions, as we say of horses?"

Jane colored a little, and laughed faintly. "The arms on the tilbury had six quarterings."

Emily now laughed, and Mrs. Wilson and Clara smiled while John continued his teasing until they reached the rectory.

While chatting with the doctor and his wife, Francis returned from his morning ride, and told them the Jarvis family had arrived; he had witnessed an unpleasant accident to a gig, in which were Captain Jarvis, and a friend, a Colonel Egerton; it had been awkwardly driven in turning into the Deanery gate, and upset: the colonel received some injury to his ankle, nothing, however, serious he hoped, but such as to put him under the care of the young ladies, probably, for a few days. After the exclamations which usually follow such details, Jane ventured to inquire who Colonel Egerton was.

"I understood at the time, from one of the servants, that he is a nephew of Sir Edgar Egerton, and a lieutenant-colonel on half-pay, or furlough, or some such thing."

"How did he bear his misfortune, Mr. Francis?" inquired Mrs. Wilson.

"Certainly as a gentleman, madam, if not as a Christian," replied the young clergyman, slily smiling; "indeed, most men of gallantry would, I believe, rejoice in an accident which drew forth so much sympathy as both the Miss Jarvis's manifested."

"How fortunate you should all happen to be near!" said the tender-hearted Clara.

"Are the young ladies pretty?" asked Jane, with something of hesitation in her manner.

"Why, I rather think they are; but I took very little notice of their appearance, as the colonel was really in evident pain."

"This, then," cried the doctor, "affords me an additional excuse for calling on them at an early day, so I'll e'en go to-morrow."

"I trust Doctor Ives wants no apologies for performing his duty," said Mrs. Wilson.

"He is fond of making them, though," said Mrs. Ives, speaking with a benevolent smile, and for the first time in the little conversation.

It was then arranged that the rector should make his official visit, as intended by himself; and on his report, the ladies would act. After remaining at the rectory an hour, they returned to the hall, attended by Francis.

The next day the doctor drove in, and informed them the Jarvis family were happily settled, and the colonel in no danger, excepting from the fascinations of the two young ladies, who took such palpable care of him that he wanted for nothing, and they might drive over whenever they pleased, without fear of intruding unseasonably.

Mr. Jarvis received his guests with the frankness of good feelings, if not with the polish of high life; while his wife, who seldom thought of the former, would have been mortally offended with the person who could have suggested that she omitted any of the elegancies of the latter. Her daughters were rather pretty, but wanted, both in appearance and manner, the inexpressible air of *haut ton* which so eminently distinguished the easy but polished deportment of Colonel Egerton, whom they found reclining on a sofa with his leg on a chair, amply secured in numerous bandages, but unable to rise. Notwithstanding the awkwardness of his situation, he was by far the least discomposed person of the party, and having pleasantly excused himself, he appeared to think no more of the matter.

The captain, Mrs. Jarvis remarked, had gone out with his dogs to try the grounds around them, "for he seems to live only with his horses and his gun: young men, my lady, nowadays, appear to forget that there are any things in the world but themselves; now I told Harry that your ladyship and daughters would favor us with a call this morning--but no: there he went, as if Mr. Jarvis was unable to buy us a dinner, and we should all starve but for his quails and pheasants."

"Quails and pheasants," cried John, in consternation, "does Captain Jarvis shoot quails and pheasants at this time of the year?"

"Mrs. Jarvis, sir," said Colonel Egerton, with a correcting smile, "understands the allegiance due from us gentlemen to the ladies, better than the rules of sporting; my friend, the captain, has taken his fishing rod, I believe."

"It is all one, fish or birds," continued Mrs. Jarvis, "he is out of the way when he is wanted, and I believe we can buy fish as easily as birds; I wish he would take pattern after yourself, colonel, in these matters."

Colonel Egerton laughed pleasantly, but he did not blush; and Miss Jarvis observed, with a look, of something like admiration thrown on his reclining figure, "that when Harry had been in the army as long as his friend, he would know the usages of good society, she hoped, as well."

"Yes," said her mother, "the army is certainly the place to polish a young man;" and turning to Mrs. Wilson, she abruptly added, "Your husband, I believe, was in the army, ma'am?"

"I hope," said Emily hastily, "that we shall have the pleasure of seeing you soon, Miss Jarvis, at the Hall," preventing by her promptitude the necessity of a reply from her aunt. The young lady promised to make an early visit, and the subject changed to a general and uninteresting discourse on the neighborhood, the country, the weather, and other ordinary topics.

"Now, John," cried Jane in triumph, as they drove from the door, "you must acknowledge my heraldic witchcraft, as you are pleased to call it, is right for once at least."

"Oh! no doubt, Jenny," said John, who was accustomed to use that appellation to her as a provocation, when he wished what he called an enlivening scene; but Mrs. Wilson put a damper on his hopes by a remark to his mother, and the habitual respect of both the combatants kept them silent.

Jane Moseley was endowed by nature with an excellent understanding, one at least equal to that of her brother, but the wanted the more essential requisites of a well governed mind. Masters had been provided by Sir Edward for all his daughters, and if they were not acquainted with the usual acquirements of young women in their rank of life, it was not his fault: his system of economy had not embraced a denial of opportunity to any of his children, and the baronet was apt to think all *was* done, when they were put where all *might* be done. Feeling herself and parents entitled to enter into all the gaieties and splendors of some of the richer families in their vicinity, Jane, who had grown up during the temporary eclipse of Sir Edward's fortunes, had sought that self-consolation so common to people in her situation, which was to be found in reviewing the former grandeur of her house, and she had thus contracted a degree of family pride. If Clara's weaknesses were less striking than those of Jane, it was because she had less imagination, and because that in loving Francis Ives she had so long admired a character, where so little was to be found that could be censured, that she might be said to have contracted a habit of judging correctly, without being able at all times to give a reason for her conduct or her opinions.

Chapter III

The day fixed for one of the stated visits of Mr. Benfield had now arrived, and John, with Emily, who was the old bachelor's favorite niece, went in the baronet's post-chaise to the town of F----, a distance of twenty miles, to meet him, in order to accompany him in the remainder of his journey to the Hall, it being a settled rule with the old man, that his carriage horses should return to their own stables every night, where he imagined they could alone find that comfort and care to which their age and services gave them a claim. The day was uncommonly pleasant, and the young people were in high spirits with the expectation of meeting their respected relative, whose absence had been prolonged a few days by a severe fit of the gout.

"Now, Emily," cried John, as he settled himself comfortably by the side of his sister in the chaise, "let me know honestly how you like the Jarvis's, and particularly how you like the handsome colonel."

"Then, John, honestly, I neither like nor dislike the Jarvis's or the handsome colonel."

"Well, then, there is no great diversity in our sentiments, as Jane would say."

"John!"

"Emily!"

"I do not like to hear you speak so disrespectfully of out sister, whom I am sure you love as tenderly as I do myself."

"I acknowledge my error," said the brother, taking her hand and affectionately kissing it, "and will endeavor to offend no more; but this Colonel Egerton, sister, is certainly a gentleman, both by blood and in manners, as Jane"--Emily interrupted him with a laugh, which John took very good-naturedly, repeating his remark without alluding to their sister.

"Yes," said Emily, "he is genteel in his deportment, if that be what you mean; I know nothing of his family."

"Oh, I have taken a peep into Jane's Baronetage, where find him set down as Sir Edgar's heir."

"There is something about him," said Emily, musing, "that I do not much admire; he is too easy--there is no nature; I always feel afraid such people will laugh at me as soon as my back is turned, and for those very things they seem most to admire to my face. If I might be allowed to judge, I should say his manner wants one thing, without which no one can be truly agreeable."

"What's that?"

"Sincerity."

"Ah! that's my great recommendation; but I am afraid I shall have to take the poacher up, with his quails and his pheasants, indeed."

"You know the colonel explained that to be a mistake."

"What they call explaining away; but unluckily I saw the gentleman returning with his gun on his shoulder, and followed by a brace of pointers."

"There's a specimen of the colonel's manners then," said Emily, smiling; "it will do until the truth be known."

"And Jane, when she saw him also, praised his good nature and consideration, in what she was pleased to call relieving the awkwardness of my remark."

Emily finding her brother disposed to dwell on the foibles of Jane, a thing he was rather addicted to at times, was silent. They rode some distance before John, who was ever as ready to atone as he was to offend, again apologized, again promised reformation, and during the remainder of the ride only forgot himself twice more in the same way.

They reached F---- two hours before the lumbering coach of their uncle drove into the yard of the inn, and had sufficient time to refresh their own horses for the journey homewards.

Mr. Benfield was a bachelor of eighty, but retained the personal activity of a man of sixty. He was strongly attached to all the fashions and opinions of his youth, during which he had sat one term in parliament, having been a great beau and courtier in the commencement of the reign. A disappointment in an affair of the heart drove him into retirement; and for the last fifty years he had dwelt exclusively at a seat he owned within forty miles of Moseley Hall, the mistress of which was the only child of his only brother. In figure, he was tall and spare, very erect for his years, and he faithfully preserved in his attire, servants, carriages, and indeed everything around him, as much of the fashions of his youth as circumstances would allow: such then was a faint outline of the character and appearance of the old man, who, dressed in a cocked hat, bag wig, and sword, took the offered arm of John Moseley to alight from his coach.

"So," cried the old gentleman, having made good his footing on the ground, as he stopped short and stared John in the face, "you have made out to come twenty miles to meet an old cynic, have you, sir? but I thought I bid thee bring Emmy with thee."

John pointed to the window, where his sister stood anxiously watching her uncle's movements. On catching her eye, he smiled kindly, and pursued his way into the house, talking to himself.

"Aye, there she is indeed; I remember now, when I was a youngster, of going with my kinsman, old Lord Gosford, to meet his sister, the Lady Juliana, when she first came from school (this was the lady whose infidelity had driven him from the world); and a beauty she was indeed, something like Emmy there; only she was taller, and her eyes were black, and her hair too, that was black; and she was not so fair as Emmy, and she was fatter, and she stooped a little--very little; oh! they are wonderfully alike though; don't you think they were, nephew?" he stopped at the door of the room; while John, who in this description could not see a resemblance, which existed nowhere but in the old man's affections, was fain to say, "yes; but they were related, you know, uncle, and that explains the likeness."

"True, boy, true," said his uncle, pleased at a reason for a thing he wished, and which flattered his propensities. He had once before told Emily she put him in mind of his housekeeper, a woman as old as himself, and without a tooth in her head.

On meeting his niece, Mr. Benfield (who, like many others that feel strongly, wore in common the affectation of indifference and displeasure) yielded to his fondness, and folding her in his arms, kissed her affectionately, while a tear glistened in his eye; and then pushing her gently from him, he exclaimed, "Come, come, Emmy, don't strangle me, don't strangle me, girl; let me live in peace the little while I have to remain here--so," seating himself composedly in an arm chair his niece had placed for him with a cushion, "so Anne writes me, Sir William Harris has let the deanery."

"Oh, yes, uncle," cried John.

"I'll thank you, young gentleman," said Mr. Benfield, sternly, "not to interrupt me when I am speaking to a lady that is, if you please, sir. Then Sir William has let the deanery to a London merchant, a Mr. Jarvis. Now I knew three people of that name; one was a hackney coachman, when I was a member of the parliament of this realm, and drove me often to the house;

the other was *valet-de-chambre* to my Lord Gosford; and the third, I take it, is the very man who has become your neighbor. If it be the person I mean, Emmy dear, he is like--like--aye, very like old Peter, my steward."

John, unable to contain his mirth at this discovery of a likeness between the prototype of Mr. Benfield himself in leanness of figure, and the jolly rotundity of the merchant, was obliged to leave the room; Emily, though she could not forbear smiling at the comparison, quietly said, "You will meet him to-morrow, dear uncle, and then you will be able to judge for yourself."

"Yes, yes," muttered the old man, "very like old Peter, my steward; as like as two peas." The parallel was by no means as ridiculous as might be supposed; its history being as follows:

Mr. Benfield had placed twenty thousand pounds in the hands of a broker, with positive orders for him to pay it away immediately for government stock, bought by the former on his account; but disregarding this injunction, the broker had managed the transaction in such a way as to postpone the payment, until, on his failure, he had given up that and a much larger sum to Mr. Jarvis, to satisfy what he called an honorary debt. In elucidating the transaction Mr. Jarvis paid Benfield Lodge a visit, and honestly restored the bachelor his property. This act, and the high opinion he entertained of Mrs. Wilson, with his unbounded love for Emily, were the few things which prevented his believing some dreadful judgment was about to visit this world, for its increasing wickedness and follies. As his own steward was one of the honestest fellows living, he had ever after fancied that there was a personal resemblance between him and the conscientious merchant.

The horses being ready, the old bachelor was placed carefully between his nephew and niece, and in that manner they rode on quietly to the Hall, the dread of accident keeping Mr. Benfield silent most of the way. On passing, however a stately castle, about ten miles from the termination of their ride, he began one of his speeches with,

"Emmy, dear, does Lord Bolton come often to see you?"

"Very seldom, sir; his employment keeps him much of his time at St. James's, and then he has an estate in Ireland."

"I knew his father well--he was distantly connected by marriage with my friend Lord Gosford; you could not remember him, I suspect" (John rolled his eyes at this suggestion of his sister's recollection of a man who had been forty years dead); "he always voted with me in the parliament of this realm; he was a thoroughly honest man; very much such a man to look at as Peter Johnson, my steward: but I am told his son likes the good things of the ministry; well, well, William Pitt was the only minister to my mind. There was the Scotchman of whom they made a Marquis; I never could endure him--always voted against him."

"Right or wrong, uncle," cried John, who loved a little mischief in his heart.

"No, sir--right, but never wrong. Lord Gosford always voted against him too; and do you think, jackanapes, that my friend the Earl of Gosford and--and--myself were ever wrong? No, sir, men in my day were different creatures from what they are now: we were never wrong, sir; we loved our country, and had no motive for being in the wrong."

"How was it with Lord Bute, uncle?"

"Lord Bute, sir," cried the old man with great warmth, "was the minister, sir--he was the minister; aye, he was the minister, sir, and was paid for what he did."

"But Lord Chatham, was he not the minister too?"

Now, nothing vexed the old gentleman more than to hear William Pitt called by his tardy honors; and yet, unwilling to give up what he thought his political opinions, he exclaimed, with an unanswerable positiveness of argument,

"Billy Pitt, sir, was the minister, sir; but--but--but--he was *our* minister, sir."

Emily, unable to see her uncle agitated by such useless disputes, threw a reproachful glance on her brother, as she observed timidly,

"That was a glorious administration, sir, I believe."

"Glorious indeed! Emmy dear," said the bachelor, softening with the sound of her voice, and the recollections of his younger days, "we beat the French everywhere--in America--in Germany;--we took--(counting on his fingers)--we took Quebec--yes, Lord Gosford lost a cousin there; and we took all the Canadas; and we took their fleets: there was a young man killed in the battle between Hawke and Conflans, who was much attached to Lady Juliana--poor soul! how much she regretted him when dead, though she never could abide him when living--ah! she was a tender-hearted creature!"

Mr. Benfield, like many others, continued to love imaginary qualities in his mistress, long after her heartless coquetry had disgusted him with her person: a kind of feeling which springs from self-love, which finds it necessary to seek consolation in creating beauties, that may justify our follies to ourselves; and which often keeps alive the semblance of the passion, when even hope, or real admiration, is extinct.

On reaching the Hall, every one was rejoiced to see their really affectionate and worthy relative, and the evening passed in the tranquil enjoyment of the blessings which Providence had profusely scattered around the family of the baronet, but which are too often hazarded by a neglect of duty that springs from too great security, or an indolence which renders us averse to the precaution necessary to insure their continuance.

Chapter IV

"You are welcome, Sir Edward," said the venerable rector, as he took the baronet by the hand; "I was fearful a return of your rheumatism would deprive us of this pleasure, and prevent my making you acquainted with the new occupants of the deanery, who have consented to dine with us to-day, and to whom I have promised, in particular, an introduction to Sir Edward Moseley."

"I thank you, my dear doctor," rejoined the baronet; "I have not only come myself, but have persuaded Mr. Benfield to make one of the party; there he comes, leaning on Emily's arm, and finding fault with Mrs. Wilson's new-fashioned barouche, which he says has given him cold."

The rector received the unexpected guest with the kindness of his nature, and an inward smile at the incongruous assemblage he was likely to have around him by the arrival of the Jarvis's, who, at that moment, drove to his door. The introductions between the baronet and the new comers had passed, and Miss Jarvis had made a prettily worded apology on behalf of the colonel, who was not yet well enough to come out, but whose politeness had insisted on their not remaining a home on his account, as Mr. Benfield, having composedly put on his spectacles, walked deliberately up to the place where the merchant had seated himself, and having examined him through his glasses to his satisfaction, took them off, and carefully wiping them, he began to talk to himself as he put them into his pocket--"No, no; it's not Jack, the hackney coachman, nor my Lord Gosford's gentleman, but"--cordially holding out both hands, "it's the man who saved my twenty thousand pounds."

Mr. Jarvis, whom shame and embarrassment had kept silent during this examination, exchanged greetings sincerely with his old acquaintance, who now took a seat in silence by his side; while his wife, whose face had begun to kindle with indignation at the commencement of the old gentleman's soliloquy, observing that somehow or other it had not only terminated without degradation to her spouse, but with something like credit, turned complacently to Mrs. Ives, with an apology for the absence of her son.

"I cannot divine, ma'am, where he has got to; he is ever keeping us waiting for him;" and, addressing Jane, "these military men become so unsettled in their habits, that I often tell Harry he should never quit the camp."

"In Hyde Park, you should add, my dear, for he has never been in any other," bluntly observed her husband.

To this speech no reply was made, but it was evidently little relished by the ladies of the family, who were a good deal jealous of the laurels of the only hero their race had ever produced. The arrival and introduction of the captain himself changed the discourse, which turned on the comforts of their present residence.

"Pray, my lady," cried the captain, who had taken a chair familiarly by the side of the baronet's wife, "why is the house called the deanery? I am afraid I shall be taken for a son of the church, when I invite my friends to visit my father at the deanery."

"But you may add, at the same time, sir, if you please," dryly remarked Mr. Jarvis, "that it is occupied by an old man, who has been preaching and lecturing all his life; and, like others of the trade, I believe, in vain."

"You must except our good friend, the doctor here, at least, sir," said Mrs. Wilson; who, observing that her sister shrank from a familiarity she was unused to, took upon herself the office of replying to the captain's question: "The father of the present Sir William Harris held that station in the church, and although the house was his private property it took its name from the circumstance, which has been continued ever since."

"Is it not a droll life Sir William leads," cried Miss Jarvis, looking at John Moseley, "riding about all summer from one watering-place to another, and letting his house year after year in the manner he does?"

"Sir William," said Dr. Ives, gravely, "is devoted to his daughter's wishes; and since his accession to his title, has come into possession of another residence in an adjoining county, which, I believe, he retains in his own hands."

"Are you acquainted with Miss Harris?" continued the lady, addressing herself to Clara; though, without waiting for an answer, she added, "She is a great belle--all the gentlemen are dying for her."

"Or her fortune," said her sister, with a pretty toss of the head; "for my part, I never could see anything so captivating in her, although so much is said about her at Bath and Brighton."

"You know her then," mildly observed Clara.

"Why, I cannot say--we are exactly acquainted," the young lady hesitatingly answered, coloring violently.

"What do you mean by exactly acquainted, Sally?" put in the father with a laugh; "did you ever speak to or were you ever in a room with her, in your life, unless it might be at a concert or a ball?"

The mortification of Miss Sarah was too evident for concealment, and it happily was relieved by a summons to dinner.

"Never, my dear child," said Mrs. Wilson to Emily, the aunt being fond of introducing a moral from the occasional incidents of every-day life, "never subject yourself to a similar mortification, by commenting on the characters of those you don't know: ignorance makes you liable to great errors; and if they should happen to be above you in life, it will only excite their contempt, should it reach their ears, while those to whom your remarks are made will think it envy."

"Truth is sometimes blundered on," whispered John, who held his sister's arm, waiting for his aunt to precede them to the dining-room.

The merchant paid too great a compliment to the rector's dinner to think of renewing the disagreeable conversation, and as John Moseley and the young clergyman were seated next the two ladies, they soon forgot what, among themselves, they would call their father's rudeness, in receiving the attentions of a couple of remarkably agreeable young men.

"Pray, Mr. Francis, when do you preach for us?" asked Mr. Haughton; "I'm very anxious to hear you hold forth from the pulpit, where I have so often heard your father with pleasure: I doubt not you will prove orthodox, or you will be the only man, I believe, in the congregation, the rector has left in ignorance of the theory of our religion, at least."

The doctor bowed to the compliment, as he replied to the question for his son, that on the next Sunday they were to have the pleasure of hearing Frank, who had promised to assist him on that day.

"Any prospects of a living soon?" continued Mr. Haughton, helping himself bountifully to a piece of plum pudding as he spoke. John Moseley laughed aloud, and Clara blushed to the eyes, while the doctor, turning to Sir Edward, observed with an air of interest, "Sir Edward, the living of Bolton is vacant, and I should like exceedingly to obtain it for my son. The advowson belongs to the Earl, who will dispose of it only to great interest, I am afraid."

Clara was certainly, too busily occupied in picking raisins from her pudding to hear this remark, but accidentally stole, from under her long eyelashes, a timid glance at her father as he replied:

"I am sorry, my friend, I have not sufficient interest with his lordship to apply on my own account; but he is so seldom here, we are barely acquainted;" and the good baronet looked really concerned.

"Clara," said Francis Ives in a low and affectionate tone, "have you read the books I sent you?"

Clara answered him with a smile in the negative, but promised amendment as soon as she had leisure.

"Do you ride much, on horseback, Mr. Moseley?" abruptly asked Miss Sarah, turning her back on the young divine, and facing the gentleman she addressed. John, who was now hemmed in between the sisters, replied with a rueful expression that brought a smile into the face of Emily, who was placed opposite to him--

"Yes, ma'am, and sometimes I am ridden."

"Ridden, sir, what do you mean by that?"

"Oh! only my aunt there occasionally gives me a lecture."

"I understand," said the lady, pointing slily with her finger at her own father.

"Does it feel good?" John inquired, with a look of, great sympathy. But the lady, who now felt awkwardly, without knowing exactly why, shook her head in silence, and forced a faint laugh.

"Whom have we here?" cried Captain Jarvis, who was looking out at a window which commanded a view of the approach to the house--"the apothecary and his attendant judging from the equipage."

The rector threw an inquiring look on a servant, who told his master they were strangers to him.

"Have them shown up, doctor," cried the benevolent baronet, who loved to see every one as happy as himself, "and give them some of your excellent pasty, for the sake of hospitality and the credit of your cook, I beg of you."

As this request was politely seconded by others of the party, the rector ordered his servants to show in the strangers.

On opening the parlor door, a gentleman, apparently sixty years of age, appeared, leaning on the arm of a youth of five-and-twenty. There was sufficient resemblance between the two for the most indifferent observer to pronounce them father and son; but the helpless debility and emaciated figure of the former, were finely contrasted by the vigorous health and manly beauty of the latter, who supported his venerable parent into the room with a grace and tenderness that struck most of the beholders with a sensation of pleasure. The doctor and Mrs. Ives rose from their seats involuntarily, and each stood for a moment, lost in an astonishment that was mingled with grief. Recollecting himself, the rector grasped the extended hand of the senior in both his own, and endeavored to utter something, but in vain. The tears followed each other down his cheeks, as he looked on the faded and careworn figure which stood before him; while his wife, unable to control her feelings, sank back into a chair and wept aloud.

Throwing open the door of an adjoining room, and retaining the hand of the invalid, the doctor gently led the way, followed by his wife and son. The former, having recovered from the first burst of her sorrow, and regardless of everything else, now anxiously watched the enfeebled step of the stranger. On reaching the door, they both turned and bowed to the company in a manner of so much dignity, mingled with sweetness, that all, not excepting Mr. Benfield, rose from their seats to return the salutation. On passing from the dining parlor, the door was closed, leaving the company standing round the table in mute astonishment and commiseration. Not a word had been spoken, and the rector's family had left them without apology or explanation. Francis, however soon returned, and was followed in a few minutes by his mother, who, slightly apologizing for her absence, turned the discourse on the approaching Sunday, and the intention of Francis to preach on that day. The Moseleys were too well bred to make any inquiries, and the deanery family was afraid. Sir Edward retired at a very early hour, and was followed by the remainder of the party.

"Well," cried Mrs. Jarvis, as they drove from the door, "this may be good breeding, but, for my part, I think both the doctor and Mrs. Ives behaved very rudely, with the crying and sobbing."

"They are nobody of much consequence," cried her eldest daughter, casting a contemptuous glance on a plain travelling chaise which stood before the rector's stables.

"'Twas sickening," said Miss Sarah, with a shrug; while her father, turning his eyes on each speaker in succession, very deliberately helped himself to a pinch of snuff, his ordinary recourse against a family quarrel. The curiosity of the ladies was, however, more lively than they chose to avow and Mrs. Jarvis bade her maid go over to the rectory that evening, with her compliments to Mrs. Ives; she had lost a lace veil, which her maid knew, and she thought it might have been left at the rectory.

"And, Jones, when you are there, you can inquire of the servants; mind, of the servants--I would not distress Mrs. Ives for the world; how Mr.--Mr.--what's his name--Oh!--I have forgotten his name; just bring me his name too, Jones; and, as it may make some difference in our party, just find out how long they stay; and--and--- any other little thing, Jones, which can be of use, you know."

Off went Jones, and within an hour she had returned. With an important look, she commenced her narrative, the daughters being accidentally present, and it might be on purpose.

"Why, ma'am, I went across the fields, and William was good enough to go with me; so when we got there, I rang, and they showed us into the servants' room, and I gave my message, and the veil was not there. Why, ma'am, there's the veil now, on the back o' that chair."

"Very well, very well, Jones, never mind the veil," cried the impatient mistress.

"So, ma'am, while they were looking for the veil, I just asked one of the maids, what company had arrived, but"--(here Jones looked very suspicious, and shook her head ominously:) "would you think it, ma'am, not a soul of them knew! But, ma'am, there was the doctor and his son, praying and reading with the old gentleman the whole time--and"--

"And what, Jones?"

"Why, ma'am, I expect he has been a great sinner, or he wouldn't want so much praying just as he is about to die."

"Die!" cried all three at once: "will he die?"

"O yes," continued Jones, "they all agree he must die; but this praying so much, is just like the criminals. I'm sure no honest person needs so much praying, ma'am."

"No, indeed," said the mother. "No, indeed," responded the daughters, as they retired to their several rooms for the night.

Chapter V

There is something in the season of Spring which peculiarly excites the feelings of devotion. The dreariness of winter has passed, and with it, the deadened affections of our nature. New life, new vigor, arises within us, as we walk abroad and feel the genial gales of April breathe upon us; and our hopes, our wishes, awaken with the revival of the vegetable world. It is then that the heart, which has been impressed with the goodness of the Creator, feels that goodness brought, as it were, into very contact with the senses. The eye loves to wander over the bountiful provisions nature is throwing forth in every direction for our comfort, and fixes its gaze on the clouds, which, having lost the chilling thinness of winter, roll in rich volumes, amidst the clear and softened fields of azure so peculiar to the season, leading the mind insensibly, to dwell on the things of another and a better world. It was on such a day, that the inhabitants of B---- thronged toward the village church, for the double purpose of pouring out their thanksgivings, and of hearing the first efforts of their rector's son in the duties of his sacred calling.

Amongst the crowd whom curiosity or a better feeling had drawn forth, were to be seen the flaring equipage of the Jarvises, and the handsome carriages of Sir Edward Moseley and his sister. All the members of the latter family felt a lively anxiety for the success of the young divine. But knowing, as they well did, the strength of his native talents, the excellence of his education, and the fervor of his piety, it was an anxiety that partook more of hope than of fear. There was one heart, however, amongst them, that palpitated with an emotion that hardly admitted of control, as they approached the sacred edifice, for it had identified itself completely with the welfare of the rector's son. There never was a softer, truer heart, than that which now almost audibly beat within the bosom of Clara Moseley; and she had given it to the young divine with all its purity and truth.

The entrance of a congregation into the sanctuary will at all times furnish, to an attentive observer, food for much useful speculation, if it be chastened with a proper charity for the weaknesses of others; and most people are ignorant of the insight they are giving into their characters and dispositions, by such an apparently trivial circumstance as their weekly approach to the tabernacles of the Lord. Christianity, while it chastens and amends the heart, leaves the natural powers unaltered; and it cannot be doubted that its operation is, or ought to be, proportionate to the abilities and opportunities of the subject of its holy impression--"Unto whomsoever much is given, much will be required." While we acknowledge, that the thoughts might be better employed in preparing for those humiliations of the spirit and thanksgiving of the heart which are required of all, and are so necessary to all, we must be indulged in a hasty view of some of the personages of our history, as they entered the church of B----.

On the countenance of the baronet, was the dignity and composure of a mind at peace with itself and mankind. His step was rather more deliberate than common; his eye rested on the pavement, and on turning into his pew, as he prepared to kneel, in the first humble petition of our beautiful service, he raised it towards the altar with an expression of benevolence and reverence, that spoke contentment, not unmixed with faith.

In the demeanor of Lady Moseley, all was graceful and decent, while nothing could be properly said to be studied. She followed her husband with a step of equal deliberation, though it was slightly varied by a manner which, while it appeared natural to herself, might have been artificial in another: a cambric handkerchief concealed her face as she sank composedly by the side of Sir Edward, in a style which showed, that while she remembered her Maker, she had not entirely forgotten herself.

The walk of Mrs. Wilson was quicker than that of her sister. Her eye, directed before her, was fixed, as if in settled gaze, on that eternity which she was approaching. The lines of her contemplative face were unaltered, unless there might be traced a deeper shade of humility than was ordinarily seen on her pale, but expressive countenance: her petition was long; and on rising from her humble posture, the person was indeed to be seen, but the soul appeared absorbed in contemplations beyond the limits of this sphere.

There was a restlessness and varying of color, in the ordinarily placid Clara, which prevented a display of her usual manner; while Jane walked gracefully, and with a tincture of her mother's manner, by her side. She stole one hastily withdrawn glance to the deanery pew ere she kneeled, and then, on rising, handed her smelling-bottle affectionately to her elder sister.

Emily glided behind her companions with a face beaming with a look of innocence and love. As she sank in the act of supplication, the rich glow of her healthful cheek lost some of its brilliancy; but, on rising, it beamed with a renewed lustre, that plainly indicated a heart touched with the sanctity of its situation.

In the composed and sedate manner of Mr. Jarvis, as he steadily pursued his way to the pew of Sir William Harris, you might have been justified in expecting the entrance of another Sir Edward Moseley in substance, if not in externals. But the deliberate separation of the flaps of his coat, as he comfortably seated himself, when you thought him about to kneel, followed by a pinch of snuff as he threw his eye around the building, led you at once to conjecture, that what at first had been mistaken for reverence, was the abstraction of some earthly calculation; and that his attendance was in compliance with custom, and not a little depended upon the thickness of his cushions, and the room he found for the disposition of two rather unwieldy legs.

The ladies of the family followed, in garments carefully selected for the advantageous display of their persons. As they sailed into their seats, where it would seem the improvidence of Sir William's steward had neglected some important accommodation (some time being spent in preparation to be seated), the old lady, whose size and flesh really put kneeling out of the question, bent forward for a moment at an angle of eighty with the horizon, while her daughters prettily bowed their heads, with all proper precaution for the safety of their superb millinery.

At length the rector, accompanied by his son, appeared from the vestry. There was a dignity and solemnity in the manner in which this pious divine entered on the duties of his profession, which disposed the heart to listen with reverence and humility to precepts that were accompanied with so impressive an exterior. The stillness of expectation pervaded the church, when the pew opener led the way to the same interesting father and son whose entrance had interrupted the guests the preceding day, at the rectory. Every eye was turned on the emaciated parent, bending into the grave, and, as it were, kept from it by the supporting tenderness of his child. Hastily throwing open the door of her own pew, Mrs. Ives buried her face in her handkerchief; and her husband had proceeded far in the morning service before she raised it again to the view of the congregation. In the voice of the rector, there was an unusual softness and tremor that his people attributed to the feelings of a father about to witness the first efforts of an only child, but which in reality were owing to another and a deeper cause.

Prayers were ended, and the younger Ives ascended the pulpit. For a moment he paused; when, casting an anxious glance to the pew of the baronet, he commenced his sermon. He had chosen for his discourse the necessity of placing our dependence on divine grace. After having learnedly, but in the most unaffected manner, displayed the necessity of this dependence, as derived from revelation, he proceeded to paint the hope, the resignation, the felicity of a Christian's death-bed. Warmed by the subject, his animation soon lent a heightened interest to his language; and at a moment when all around him were entranced by the eloquence of the youthful divine, a sudden and deep-drawn sigh drew every eye to the rector's pew. The younger stranger sat motionless as a statue, holding in his arms the lifeless body of his parent, who had fallen that moment a corpse by his side. All was now confusion: the almost insensible young man was relieved from his burden; and, led by the rector, they left the church. The congregation dispersed in silence, or assembled in little groups, to converse on the awful event they had witnessed. None knew the deceased; he was the rector's friend, and to his residence the body was removed. The young man was evidently his child; but here all information ended. They had arrived in a private chaise, but with post horses, and without attendants. Their arrival at the parsonage was detailed by the Jarvis ladies with a few exaggerations that gave additional interest to the whole event, and which, by creating an impression with some whom gentler feelings would not have restrained, that there was something of mystery about them, prevented many distressing questions to the Ives's, that the baronet's family forbore putting, on the score of delicacy. The body left B---- at the close of the week, accompanied by Francis Ives and the unweariedly attentive and interesting son. The doctor and his wife went into deep mourning, and Clara received a short note from her lover, on the morning of their departure, acquainting her with his intended absence for a month, but throwing no light upon the affair. The London papers, however, contained the following obituary notice, and which, as it could refer to no other person, as a matter of course, was supposed to allude to the rector's friend.

"Died, suddenly, at B----, on the 20th instant, George Denbigh, Esq., aged 63."

Chapter VI

During the week of mourning, the intercourse between Moseley Hall and the rectory was confined to messages and notes of inquiry after each other's welfare: but the visit of the Moseleys to the deanery had been returned; and the day after the appearance of the obituary paragraph, the family of the latter dined by invitation at the Hall. Colonel Egerton had recovered the use of his leg, and was included in the party. Between this gentleman and Mr. Benfield there appeared, from the first moment of their introduction, a repugnance which was rather increased by time, and which the old gentleman manifested by a demeanor loaded with the overstrained ceremony of the day, and which, in the colonel, only showed itself by avoiding, when possible, all intercourse with the object of his aversion. Both Sir Edward and Lady Moseley, on the contrary, were not slow in manifesting their favorable impressions in behalf of the gentleman. The latter, in particular, having ascertained to her satisfaction that he was the undoubted heir to the title, and most probably to the estates of his uncle, Sir Edgar Egerton, felt herself strongly disposed to encourage an acquaintance she found so agreeable, and to which she could see no reasonable objection. Captain Jarvis, who was extremely offensive to her, from his vulgar familiarity, she barely tolerated, from the necessity of being civil, and keeping up sociability in the neighborhood. It is true, she could not help being surprised that a gentleman, as polished as the colonel, could find any pleasure in an associate like his friend, or even in the hardly more softened females of his family; then again, the flattering suggestion would present itself, that possibly he might have seen Emily at Bath, or Jane elsewhere, and availed himself of the acquaintance of young Jarvis to get into their neighborhood. Lady Moseley had never been vain, or much interested about the disposal of her own person, previously to her attachment to her husband: but her daughters called forth not a little of her natural pride--we had almost said of her selfishness.

The attentions of the colonel were of the most delicate and insinuating kind; and Mrs. Wilson several times turned away in displeasure at herself, for listening with too much satisfaction to nothings, uttered in an agreeable manner, or, what was worse, false sentiments supported with the gloss of language and a fascinating deportment. The anxiety of this lady on behalf of Emily kept her ever on the alert, when chance, or any chain of circumstances, threw her in the way of forming new connexions of any kind; and of late, as her charge approached the period of life her sex were apt to make that choice from which there is no retreat, her solicitude to examine the characters of the men who approached her was really painful. As to Lady Moseley, her wishes disposed her to be easily satisfied, and her mind naturally shrank from an investigation to which she felt herself unequal; while Mrs. Wilson was governed by the convictions of a sound discretion, matured by long and deep reasoning, all acting on a temper at all times ardent, and a watchfulness calculated to endure to the end.

"Pray, my lady," said Mrs. Jarvis, with a look of something like importance, "have you made any discovery about this Mr. Denbigh, who died in the church lately?"

"I did not know, ma'am," replied Lady Moseley, "there was any discovery to be made."

"You know, Lady Moseley," said Colonel Egerton, "that in town, all the little accompaniments of such a melancholy death would have found their way into the prints; and I suppose this is what Mrs. Jarvis alludes to."

"Oh yes," cried Mrs. Jarvis, "the colonel is right." But the colonel was always right with that lady.

Lady Moseley bowed her head with dignity, and the colonel had too much tact to pursue the conversation; but the captain, whom nothing had ever yet abashed, exclaimed,

"These Denbighs could not be people of much importance--I have never heard the name before."

"It is the family name of the Duke of Derwent, I believe," dryly remarked Sir Edward.

"Oh, I am sure neither the old man nor his son looked much like a duke, or so much as an officer either," exclaimed Mrs. Jarvis, who thought the latter rank the dignity in degree next below nobility.

"There sat, in the parliament of this realm, when I was a member, a General Denbigh," said Mr. Benfield, with his usual deliberation; "he was always on the same side with Lord Gosford and myself. He and his friend, Sir Peter Howell, who was the admiral that took the French squadron, in the glorious administration of Billy Pitt, and afterwards took an island with this same General Denbigh: aye, the old admiral was a hearty blade; a good deal such a looking man as my Hector would make."

Hector was Mr. Benfield's bull dog.

"Mercy," whispered John to Clara, "that's your grandfather that is to be uncle Benfield is speaking of."

Clara smiled, as she ventured to say, "Sir Peter was Mrs. Ives's father, sir."

"Indeed!" said the old gentleman, with a look of surprise, "I never knew that before; I cannot say they resemble each other much."

"Pray, uncle, does Frank look much like the family?" asked John, with an air of unconquerable gravity.

"But, sir," interrupted Emily, "were General Denbigh and Admiral Howell related?"

"Not that I ever knew, Emmy dear. Sir Frederick Denbigh did not look much like the admiral; he rather resembled (gathering himself up into an air of formality, and bowing stiffly to Colonel Egerton) this gentleman, here."

"I have not the honor of the connexion," observed the colonel, withdrawing behind the chair of Jane.

Mrs. Wilson changed the conversation to one more general; but the little that had fallen from Mr. Benfield gave reason for believing a connexion, in some way of which they were ignorant, existed between the descendants of the two veterans, and which explained the interest they felt in each other.

During dinner, Colonel Egerton placed himself next to Emily, and Miss Jarvis took the chair on the other side. He spoke of the gay world, of watering-places, novels, plays, and still finding his companion reserved, and either unwilling or unable to talk freely, he tried his favorite sentiment. He had read poetry, and a remark of his lighted up a spark of intelligence in the beautiful face of his companion that for a moment deceived him; but as he went on to point out his favorite beauties, it gave place to a settled composure, which at last led him to imagine the casket contained no gem equal to the promise of its brilliant exterior. After resting from one of his most labored displays of feeling and imagery, he accidentally caught the eyes of Jane fastened on him with an expression of no dubious import, and the soldier changed his battery. In Jane he found a more willing auditor; poetry was the food she lived on, and in works of the imagination she found her greatest delight. An animated discussion of the merits of their favorite authors now took place; to renew which, the colonel early left the dining-room for the society of the ladies; John, who disliked drinking excessively, being happy of an excuse to attend him.

The younger ladies had clustered together round a window and even Emily in her heart rejoiced that the gentlemen had come to relieve herself and sisters from the arduous task of entertaining women who appeared not to possess a single taste or opinion in common with themselves.

"You were saying, Miss Moseley," observed the colonel in his most agreeable manner, as he approached them, "you thought Campbell the most musical poet we have; I hope you will unite with me in excepting Moore."

Jane colored, as with some awkwardness she replied, "Moore was certainly very poetical."

"Has Moore written much?" innocently asked Emily.

"Not half as much as he ought," cried Miss Jarvis. "Oh! I could live on his beautiful lines."

Jane turned away in disgust; and that evening, while alone with Clara, she took a volume of Moore's songs, and very coolly consigned them to the flames. Her sister naturally asked an explanation of so extraordinary a procedure.

"Oh!" cried Jane, "I can't abide the book, since that vulgar Miss Jarvis speaks of it with so much interest. I really believe aunt Wilson is right in not suffering Emily to read such things." And Jane, who had often devoured the treacherous lines with ardor, shrank with fastidious delicacy from the indulgence of a perverted taste, when it became exposed, coupled with the vulgarity of unblushing audacity.

Colonel Egerton immediately changed the subject to one less objectionable, and spoke of a campaign he had made in Spain. He possessed the happy faculty of giving an interest to all he advanced, whether true or not; and as he never contradicted, or even opposed unless to yield gracefully, when a lady was his opponent, his conversation insensibly attracted, by putting the sex in good humor with themselves. Such a man, aided by the powerful assistants of person and manners, and no inconsiderable colloquial talents, Mrs. Wilson knew to be extremely dangerous as a companion to a youthful female heart; and as his visit was to extend to a couple of months, she resolved to reconnoitre the state of her pupil's opinion forthwith in reference to his merits. She had taken too much pains in forming the mind of Emily to apprehend she would fall a victim to the eye; but she also knew that personal grace sweetened a benevolent expression, and added force even to the oracles of wisdom. She labored a little herself under the disadvantage of what John called a didactic manner, and which, although she had not the ability, or rather taste, to amend, she had yet the sense to discern. It was the great error of Mrs. Wilson to attempt to convince, where she might have influenced; but her ardor of temperament, and great love of truth, kept her, as it were, tilting with the vices of mankind, and consequently sometimes in unprofitable combat. With her charge, however, this could never be said to be the case, Emily knew her heart, felt her love, and revered her principles too deeply, to throw away an admonition, or disregard a precept, that fell from lips she knew never spoke idly or without consideration.

John had felt tempted to push the conversation with Miss Jarvis, and he was about to utter something rapturous respecting the melodious poison of Little's poems, as the blue eye of Emily rested on him in the fulness of sisterly affection and checking his love of the ridiculous, he quietly yielded to his respect for the innocence of his sisters; and, as if eager to draw the attention of all from the hateful subject, he put question after question to Egerton concerning the Spaniards and their customs.

"Did you ever meet Lord Pendennyss in Spain, Colonel Egerton?" inquired Mrs. Wilson, with interest.

"Never, madam," he replied. "I have much reason to regret that our service lay in different parts of the country: his lordship was much with the duke, and I made the campaign under Marshal Beresford."

Emily left the group at the window, and taking a seat on the sofa by the side of her aunt, insensibly led her to forget the gloomy thoughts which had begun to steal over her; which the colonel, approaching where they sat, continued, by asking--

"Are you acquainted with the earl, madam?"

"Not in person, but by character," said Mrs. Wilson, in a melancholy manner.

"His character as a soldier was very high. He had no superior of his years in Spain, I am told."

No reply was made to this remark, and Emily endeavored anxiously to draw the mind of her aunt to reflections of a more agreeable nature. The colonel, whose vigilance to please was ever on the alert, kindly aided her, and they soon succeeded.

The merchant withdrew, with his family and guest, in proper season: and Mrs. Wilson, heedful of her duty, took the opportunity of a quarter of an hour's privacy in her own dressing-room in the evening, to touch gently on the subject of the gentlemen they had seen that day.

"How are you pleased, Emily, with your new acquaintances?" familiarly commenced Mrs. Wilson.

"Oh! aunt, don't ask me; as John says, they are *net* indeed."

"I am not sorry," continued the aunt, "to have you observe more closely than you have been used to the manners of such women as the Jarvises; they are too abrupt and unpleasant to create a dread of any imitation; but the gentlemen are heroes in very different styles."

"Different from each other, indeed."

"To which do you give the preference, my dear?"

"Preference, aunt!" said her niece, with a look of astonishment; "preference is a strong word for either; but I rather think the captain the most eligible companion of the two. I do believe you see the worst of him; and although I acknowledge it to be bad enough, he might amend; but the colonel"--

"Go on," said Mrs. Wilson.

"Why, everything about the colonel seems so seated, so ingrafted in his nature, so--so very self-satisfied, that I am afraid it would be a difficult task to take the first step in amendment--to convince him of its necessity?

"And is it then so necessary?"

Emily looked up from arranging some laces, with an expression of surprise, as he replied:

"Did you not hear him talk of those poems, and attempt to point out the beauties of several works? I thought everything he uttered was referred to taste, and that not a very natural one; at least," she added with a laugh, "it differed greatly from mine. He seemed to forget altogether there was such a thing as principle: and then he spoke of some woman to Jane, who had left her father for her lover, with so much admiration of her feelings, to take up with poverty and love, as he called it, in place of condemning her want of filial piety--I am sure, aunt, if you had heard that, you would not admire him so much."

"I do not admire him at all, child; I only want to know your sentiments, and I am happy to find them so correct. It is as you think; Colonel Egerton appears to refer nothing to principle: even the more generous feelings I am afraid are corrupted in him, from too low intercourse with the surface of society. There is by far too much pliability about him for principle of any kind, unless indeed it be a principle to please, no matter how. No one, who has deeply seated opinions of right and wrong, will ever abandon them, even in the courtesies of polite intercourse: they may be silent but never acquiescent: in short, my dear, the dread of offending our Maker ought to be so superior to that of offending our fellow creatures, that we should endeavor, I believe, to be even more unbending to the follies of the world than we are."

"And yet the colonel is what they call a good companion--I mean a pleasant one."

"In the ordinary meaning of the words, he is certainly, my dear; yet you soon tire of sentiments which will not stand the test of examination, and of a manner you cannot but see is artificial. He may do very well for a companion, but very ill for a friend; in short, Colonel Egerton has neither been satisfied to yield to his natural impressions, nor to obtain new ones from a proper source; he has copied from bad models, and his work must necessarily be imperfect."

Kissing her niece, Mrs. Wilson then retired into her own room, with the happy assurance that she had not labored in vain; but that, with divine aid, she had implanted a guide in the bosom of her charge that could not fail, with ordinary care, to lead her straight through the devious path of female duties.

Chapter VII

A month now passed in the ordinary occupations and amusements of a country life, during which both Lady Moseley and Jane manifested a desire to keep up the deanery acquaintance, that surprised Emily a little, who had ever seen her mother shrink from communications with those whose breeding subjected her own delicacy, to the little shocks she could but ill conceal. In Jane this desire was still more inexplicable; for Jane had, in a decided way very common to her, avowed her disgust of the manners of their new associates at the commencement of the acquaintance; and yet Jane would now even quit her own society for that of Miss Jarvis, especially if Colonel Egerton happened to be of the party. The innocence of Emily prevented her scanning the motives for the conduct of her sister; and she set seriously about an examination into her own deportment to find the latent cause, in order, wherever an opportunity should offer, to evince her regret, had it been her misfortune, to have erred by the tenderness of her own manner.

For a short time the colonel seemed at a loss where to make his choice; but a few days determined him, and Jane was evidently the favorite. It is true, that in the presence of the Jarvis ladies he was more guarded and general in his attentions; but as John, from a motive of charity, had taken the direction of the captain's sports into his own hands; and as they were in the frequent habit of meeting at the Hall preparatory to their morning excursion, the colonel suddenly became a sportsman. The ladies would often accompany them in their morning excursions; and as John would certainly be a baronet, and the colonel might not if his uncle married, he had the comfort of being sometimes ridden, as well as of riding.

One morning, having all prepared for an excursion on horseback, as they stood at the door ready to mount, Francis Ives drove up in his father's gig, and for a moment arrested the party. Francis was a favorite with the whole Moseley family, and their greetings were warm and sincere. He found they meant to take the rectory in their ride, and insisted that they should proceed. "Clara would take a seat with him." As he spoke, the cast of his countenance brought the color into the cheeks of his intended; she suffered herself, however, to be handed into the vacant seat in the gig, and they moved on. John, who was at the bottom good-natured, and loved both

Francis and Clara very sincerely, soon set Captain Jarvis and his sister what he called "scrub racing," and necessity, in some measure, compelled the rest of the equestrians to hard riding, in order to keep up with the sports.

"That will do, that will do," cried John, casting his eye back, and perceiving they had lost sight of the gig, and nearly so of Colonel Egerton and Jane, "why you carry it off like a jockey, captain; better than any amateur I have ever seen, unless indeed it be your sister."

The lady encouraged by his commendations, whipped on, followed by her brother and sister at half speed.

"There, Emily," said John, quietly dropping by her side "I see no reason you and I should break our necks, to show the blood of our horses. Now do you know I think we are going to have a wedding in the family soon?"

Emily looked at him in amazement.

"Frank has got a living; I saw it the moment he drove up. He came in like somebody. Yes, I dare say he has calculated the tithes already a dozen times."

John was right. The Earl of Bolton had, unsolicited, given him the desired living of his own parish; and Francis was at the moment pressing the blushing Clara to fix the day that was to put a period to his long probation. Clara, who had not a particle of coquetry about her, promised to be his as soon as he was inducted, an event that was to take place the following week; and then followed those delightful little arrangements and plans with which youthful hope is so fond of filling up the void of life.

"Doctor," said John, as he came out of the rectory to assist Clara from the gig, "the parson here is a careful driver; see, he has not turned a hair."

He kissed the burning cheek of his sister as she touched the ground, and whispered significantly.

"You need tell me nothing, my dear--I know all--I consent."

Mrs. Ives folded her future daughter to her bosom; and the benevolent smile of the good rector, together with the kind and affectionate manner of her sisters, assured Clara the approaching nuptials were anticipated, as a matter of course. Colonel Egerton offered his compliments to Francis on his preferment to the living, with the polish of high breeding, and not without an appearance of interest; and Emily thought him for the first time as handsome as he was generally reputed to be. The ladies undertook to say something civil in their turn, and John put the captain, by a hint, on the same track.

"You are quite lucky, sir," said the captain, "in getting so good a living with so little trouble; I wish you joy of it with all my heart: Mr. Moseley tells me it is a capital thing now for a gentleman of your profession. For my part. I prefer a scarlet coat to a black one, but there must be parsons you know, or how should we get married or say grace?"

Francis thanked him for his good wishes, and Egerton paid a handsome compliment to the liberality of the earl; "he doubted not he found that gratification which always attends a disinterested act;" and Jane applauded the sentiment with a smile.

The baronet, when he was made acquainted with the situation of affairs, promised Francis that no unnecessary delay should intervene, and the marriage was happily arranged for the following week. Lady Moseley, when she retired to the drawing-room after dinner, commenced a recital of the ceremony and company to be invited on the occasion. Etiquette and the decencies of life were not only the forte, but the fault of this lady; and she had gone on to the enumeration of about the fortieth personage in the ceremonials, before Clara found courage to say, that "Mr. Ives and myself both wish to be married at the altar, and to proceed to Bolton Rectory immediately after the ceremony." To this her mother warmly objected; and argument and respectful remonstrance had followed each other for some time, before Clara submitted in silence, with difficulty restraining her tears. This appeal to the better feelings of the mother triumphed; and the love of parade yielded to love of her offspring. Clara, with a lightened heart, kissed and thanked her, and accompanied by Emily left the room; Jane had risen to follow them, but catching a glimpse of the tilbury of Colonel Egerton she reseated herself.

He had merely driven over at the earnest entreaties of the ladies to beg Miss Jane would accept a seat back with him; "they had some little project on foot, and could not proceed without her assistance."

Mrs. Wilson looked gravely at her sister, as she smiled acquiescence to his wishes; and the daughter, who but the minute before had forgotten there was any other person in the world but Clara, flew for her hat and shawl, in order, as he said to herself, that the politeness of Colonel Egerton might not keep him waiting. Lady Moseley resumed her seat by the side of her sister with an air of great complacency, as she returned from the window, after having seen her daughter off. For some time each was occupied quietly with her needle, when Mrs. Wilson suddenly broke the silence by saying:

"Who is Colonel Egerton?"

Lady Moseley looked up for a moment in amazement, but recollecting herself, answered,

"The nephew and heir of Sir Edgar Egerton, sister."

This was spoken in a rather positive way, as if it were unanswerable; yet as there was nothing harsh in the reply, Mrs. Wilson continued,

"Do you not think him attentive to Jane?"

Pleasure sparkled in the still brilliant eyes of Lady Moseley, as she exclaimed--

"Do you think so?"

"I do; and you will pardon me if I say improperly so. I think you were wrong in suffering Jane to go with him this afternoon."

"Why improperly, Charlotte? If Colonel Egerton is polite enough to show Jane such attentions, should I not be wrong in rudely rejecting them?"

"The rudeness of refusing a request that is improper to grant is a very venial offence. I confess I think it improper to allow any attentions to be forced on us that may subject us to disagreeable consequences; but the attentions of Colonel Egerton are becoming marked, Anne."

"Do you for a moment doubt their being honorable, or that he dares to trifle with a daughter of Sir Edward Moseley?"

"I should hope not, certainly, although it may be well to guard even against such a misfortune. But I am of opinion it is quite as important to know whether he is *worthy* to be her husband as it is to know that he is in a situation to become so."

"On what points, Charlotte, would you wish to be more assured? You know his birth and probable fortune--you see his manners and disposition; but these latter are things for Jane to decide on; *she* is to live with him, and it is proper she should be suited in these respects."

"I do not deny his fortune or his disposition, but I complain that we give him credit for the last, and for still more important requisites, without evidence of his possessing any of them. His principles, his habits, his very character, what do we know of them? I say we, for you know, Anne, your children are as dear to me as my own would have been."

"I believe you sincerely, but the things you mention are points for Jane to decide on. If she be pleased, I have no right to complain. I am determined never to control the affections of my children."

"Had you said, never *to force* the affections of your children, you would have said enough, Anne; but to control, or rather to guide the affections of a child, especially a daughter, is, in some cases, a duty as imperative as it would be to avert any other impending calamity. Surely the proper time to do this is before the affections of the child are likely to endanger her peace of mind."

"I have seldom seen much good result from the interference of parents," said Lady Moseley, a little pertinaciously.

"True; for to be of use, unless in extraordinary cases, it should not be seen. You will pardon me, Anne, but I have often thought parents are too often in extremes--determined to make the election for their children, or leaving them entirely to their own vanity and inexperience, to govern not only their own lives, but, I may say, to leave an impression on future generations. And, after all, what is this love? In nineteen cases in twenty of what we call affairs of the heart, it would be better to term them affairs of the *imagination*."

"And is there not a great deal of imagination in all love?" inquired Lady Moseley, smiling.

"Undoubtedly, there is some; but there is one important difference: in affairs of the imagination, the admired object is gifted with all those qualities we esteem, as a matter of course, and there is a certain set of females who are ever ready to bestow this admiration on any applicant for their favors who may not be strikingly objectionable. The necessity of being courted makes our sex rather too much disposed to admire improper suitors."

"But how do you distinguish affairs of the heart, Charlotte, from those of the fancy?"

"When the heart takes the lead, it is not difficult to detect it. Such sentiments generally follow long intercourse, and opportunities of judging the real character. They are the only attachments that are likely to stand the test of worldly trials."

"Suppose Emily to be the object of Colonel Egerton's pursuit, then, sister, in what manner would you proceed to destroy the influence I acknowledge he is gaining over Jane?"

"I cannot suppose such a case," said Mrs. Wilson, gravely; and then, observing that her sister looked as if she required an explanation, she continued--

"My attention has been directed to the forming of such principles, and such a taste, if I may use the expression, under those principles, that I feel no apprehension Emily will ever allow her affections to be ensnared by a man of the opinions and views of Colonel Egerton. I am impressed with a twofold duty in watching the feelings of my charge. She has so much singleness of heart, such real strength of native feeling, that, should an improper man gain possession of her affections, the struggle between her duty and her love would be weighty indeed; and should it proceed so far as to make it her duty to love an unworthy object, I am sure she would sink under it. Emily would die in the same circumstances under which Jane would only awake from a dream, and be wretched."

"I thought you entertained a better opinion of Jane, sister," said Lady Moseley, reproachfully.

"I think her admirably calculated to make an invaluable wife and mother; but she is so much under the influence of her fancy, that she seldom gives her heart an opportunity of displaying its excellences; and again, she dwells so much upon imaginary perfections, that adulation has become necessary to her. The man who flatters her delicately will be sure to win her esteem; and every woman might love the being possessed of the qualities she will not fail to endow him with."

"I do not know that I rightly understand how you would avert all these sad consequences of improvident affections?" said Lady Moseley.

"Prevention is better than cure--I would first implant such opinions as would lessen the danger of intercourse; and as for particular attentions from improper objects, it should be my care to prevent them, by prohibiting, or rather impeding, the intimacy which might give rise to them. And least of all," said Mrs. Wilson, with a friendly smile, as she rose to leave the room, "would I suffer a fear of being impolite to endanger the happiness of a young woman intrusted to my care."

Chapter VIII

Francis, who labored with the ardor of a lover, soon completed the necessary arrangements and alterations in his new parsonage. The living was a good one, and as the rector was enabled to make a very considerable annual allowance from the private fortune his wife had brought him, and as Sir Edward had twenty thousand pounds in the funds for each of his daughters, one portion of which was immediately settled on Clara, the youthful couple had not only a sufficient, but an abundant provision for their station in life; and they entered on their matrimonial duties with as good a prospect of happiness as the ills of this world can give to health, affection, and competency. Their union had been deferred by Dr. Ives until his son was established, with a view to keep him under his own direction during the critical period of his first impressions in the priesthood; and as no objection now remained, or rather, the only one he ever felt was removed by the proximity of Bolton to his own parish, he now joyfully united the lovers at the altar of the village church, in the presence of his wife and Clara's immediate relatives. On leaving the church Francis handed his bride into his own carriage, which conveyed them to their new residence, amidst the good wishes of his parishioners, and the prayers of their relatives and friends. Dr. and Mrs. Ives retired to the rectory, to the sober enjoyment of the felicity of their only child; while the baronet and his lady felt a gloom that belied all the wishes of the latter for the establishment of her daughters. Jane and Emily acted as bridesmaids to their sister, and as both the former and her mother had insisted there should be two groomsmen as a counterpoise, John was empowered with a carte-blanche to make a provision accordingly. At first he intimated his intention of calling on Mr. Benfield, but he finally settled down, to the no small mortification of the before-mentioned ladies, into writing a note to his kinsman, Lord Chatterton, whose residence was then in London, and who in reply, after expressing his sincere regret that an accident would prevent his having the pleasure of attending, stated the intention of his mother and two sisters to pay them an early visit of congratulation, as soon as his own health would allow of his travelling. This answer arrived only the day preceding that fixed for the wedding, and at the very moment they were expecting his lordship in proper person.

"There," cried Jane, in triumph, "I told you it was silly to send so far on so sudden an occasion; now, after all, what is to be done--it will be so awkward when Clara's friends call to see her--Oh! John, John, you are a Marplot."

"Jenny, Jenny, you are a make-plot," said John, coolly taking up his hat to leave the room.

"Which way, my son?" said the baronet, who met him at the door.

"To the deanery, sir, to try to get Captain Jarvis to act as bridesmaid--I beg his pardon, groomsman, to-morrow--Chatterton has been thrown from a horse and can't come."

"John!"

"Jenny!"

"I am sure," said Jane, indignation glowing in her pretty face, "that if Captain Jarvis is to be an attendant, Clara must excuse my acting. I do not choose to be associated with Captain Jarvis."

"John," said his mother, with dignity, "your trifling is unseasonable; certainly Colonel Egerton is a more fitting person on every account, and I desire, under present circumstances, that you ask the colonel."

"Your ladyship's wishes are orders to me," said John, gaily kissing his hand as he left the room.

The colonel was but too happy in having it in his power to be of service in any manner to a gentleman he respected as much as Mr. Francis Ives. He accepted the duty, and was the only person present at the ceremony who did not stand within the bonds of consanguinity to the parties. He was invited by the baronet to dine at the hall, as a matter of course, and notwithstanding the repeated injunctions of Mrs. Jarvis and her daughters, to return immediately with an account of the dress of the bride, and with other important items of a similar nature, the invitation was accepted. On reaching the hall, Emily retired immediately to her own room, and at her reappearance when the dinner bell rang, the paleness of her cheeks and the redness of her eyes afforded sufficient proof that the translation of a companion from her own to another family was an event, however happy in itself, not unmingled with grief. The day, however, passed off tolerably well for people who are expected to be premeditatedly happy, and when, in their hearts, they are really more disposed to weep than to laugh. Jane and the colonel had most of the conversation to themselves during dinner: even the joyous and thoughtless John wearing his gaiety in a less graceful manner than usual. He was actually detected by his aunt in looking with moistened eyes at the vacant chair a servant had, from habit, placed at the table, in the spot where Clara had been accustomed to sit.

"This beef is not done, Saunders," said the baronet to his butler, "or my appetite is not as good as usual to-day. Colonel Egerton, will you allow me the pleasure of a glass of sherry?"

The wine was drunk, and the game succeeded the beef; but still Sir Edward could not eat.

"How glad Clara will be to see us all the day after to-morrow," said Mrs. Wilson; "your new housekeepers delight in their first efforts in entertaining their friends."

Lady Moseley smiled through her tears, and turning to her husband said, "We will go early, my dear, that we may see the improvements Francis has been making before we dine." The baronet nodded assent, but his heart was too full to speak; and apologizing to the colonel for his absence, on the plea of some business with his people, he left the room.

All this time, the attentions of Colonel Egerton to both mother and daughter were of the most delicate kind. He spoke of Clara as if his office of groomsman entitled him to an interest in her welfare; with John he was kind and sociable; and even Mrs. Wilson acknowledged, after he had taken his leave, that he possessed a wonderful faculty of making himself agreeable, and she began to think that, under all circumstances, he might possibly prove as advantageous a connexion as Jane could expect to form. Had any one, however, proposed him as a husband for Emily, affection would have quickened her judgment in a way that would have urged her to a very different decision.

Soon after the baronet left the room, a travelling carriage, with suitable attendants, drove to the door; the sound of the wheels drew most of the company to a window. "A baron's coronet!" cried Jane, catching a glimpse of the ornaments of the harness.

"The Chattertons," echoed her brother, running out of the room to meet them.

The mother of Sir Edward was a daughter of this family, and the sister of the grandfather of the present lord. The connexion had always been kept up with a show of cordiality between Sir Edward and his cousin, although their manner of living and habits were very different. The baron was a courtier and a placeman. His estates, which he could not alienate, produced about ten thousand a year, but the income he could and did spend; and the high perquisites of his situation under government, amounting to as much more were melted away year after year, without making the provision for his daughters that his duty and the observance of his promise to his wife's father required at his hands. He had been dead about two years, and his son found himself saddled with the support of an unjointured mother and unportioned sisters. Money was not the idol the young lord worshipped, nor even pleasure. He was affectionate to his surviving parent, and his first act was to settle, during his own life, two thousand a year on her, while he commenced setting aside as much more for each of his sisters annually. This abridged him greatly in his own expenditures; yet, as they made but one family, and the dowager was really a *managing* woman in more senses than one, they made a very tolerable figure. The son was anxious to follow the example of Sir Edward Moseley, and give up his town house, for at least a time; but his mother had exclaimed, with something like horror, at the proposal:

"Chatterton, would you give it up at the moment it can be of the most use to us?" and she threw a glance at her daughters that would have discovered her motive to Mrs Wilson, which was lost on her son; he, poor soul, thinking she found it convenient to support the interest he had been making for the place held by his father one of more emolument than service, or even honor. The contending parties were so equally matched, that this situation was kept, as it were, in abeyance, waiting the arrival of some acquisition of interest to one or other of the claimants. The interest of the peer, however, had begun to lose ground at the period of which we speak, and his careful mother saw new motives for activity in providing for her children. Mrs. Wilson herself could not be more vigilant in examining the candidates for Emily's favors than was the dowager Lady Chatterton in behalf of her daughter. It is true, the task of the former lady was by far the most arduous, for it involved a study of character and development of principle; while that of the latter would have ended with the footing of a rent-roll, provided it contained five figures. Sir Edward's was well known to contain that number, and two of them were not ciphers. Mr. Benfield was rich, and John Moseley was a very agreeable young man. Weddings are the season of love, thought the prudent dowager, and Grace is extremely pretty. Chatterton, who never refused his mother anything in his power to grant, and who was particularly dutiful when a visit to Moseley Hall was in question, suffered himself to be persuaded his shoulder was well, and they had left town the day before the wedding, thinking to be in time for all the gaieties, if not for the ceremony itself.

There existed but little similarity between the persons and manners of this young nobleman and the baronet's heir. The beauty of Chatterton was almost feminine; his skin, his color, his eyes, his teeth, were such as many a belle had sighed after; and his manners were bashful and retiring. Yet an intimacy had commenced between the boys at school, which ripened into friendship between the young men at college, and had been maintained ever since, probably as much from the contrarieties of character as from any other cause. With the baron, John was more sedate than ordinary; with John, Chatterton found unusual animation. But a secret charm which John held over the young peer was his profound respect and unvarying affection for his youngest sister, Emily. This was common ground; and no dreams of future happiness, no visions of dawning wealth, crossed the imagination of Chatterton in which Emily was not the fairy to give birth to the one, or the benevolent dispenser of the hoards of the other.

The arrival of this family was a happy relief from the oppression which hung on the spirits of the Moseleys, and their reception marked with the mild benevolence which belonged to the nature of the baronet, and that *impressement* which so eminently distinguished the manners of his wife.

The honorable Misses Chatterton were both handsome; but the younger was, if possible, a softened picture of her brother. There was the same retiring bashfulness and the same sweetness of temper as distinguished the baron, and Grace was the peculiar favorite of Emily Moseley. Nothing of the strained or sentimental nature which so often characterize what is called female friendships, however, had crept into the communications between these young women. Emily loved her sisters too well to go out of her own family for a repository of her griefs or a partaker in her joys. Had her life been chequered with such passions, her own sisters were too near her own age to suffer her to think of a confidence in which the holy ties of natural affection did not give a claim to a participation. Mrs. Wilson had found it necessary to give her charge very different views on many subjects from those which Jane and Clara had been suffered to imbibe of themselves; but in no degree had she impaired the obligations of filial piety or family concord. Emily was, if anything, more respectful to her parents, more affectionate to her friends, than any of her connexions; for in her the warmth of natural feeling was heightened by an unvarying sense of duty.

In Grace Chatterton she found, in many respects, a temper and taste resembling her own. She therefore loved her better than others who had equally general claims on her partiality, and as such a friend she now received her with cordial and sincere affection.

Jane, who had not felt satisfied with the ordering of Providence for the disposal of her sympathies, and had long felt a restlessness that prompted her to look abroad for a confiding spirit to whom to communicate her-- secrets she had none that delicacy would suffer her to reveal--but to communicate her crude opinions and reflections, she had early selected Catherine for this person. Catherine, however, had not stood the test of trial. For a short time the love of heraldry kept them together; but Jane, finding her companion's gusto limited to the charms of the coronet and supporters chiefly, abandoned the attempt in despair, and was actually on the look-out for a new candidate for the vacant station as Colonel Egerton came into the neighborhood. A really delicate female mind shrinks from the exposure of its love to the other sex, and Jane began to be less anxious to form a connexion which would either violate the sensibility of her nature, or lead to treachery to her friend.

"I regret extremely, Lady Moseley," said the dowager, as they entered the drawing-room, "that the accident which befel Chatterton should have kept us until it was too late for the ceremony: we made it a point to hasten with our congratulations, however, as soon as Astley Cooper thought it safe for him to travel."

"I feel indebted for your kindness," replied the smiling hostess. "We are always happy to have our friends around us, and none more than yourself and family. We were fortunate in finding a friend to supply your son's place, in order that the young people might go to the altar in a proper manner. Lady Chatterton, allow me to present our friend, Colonel Egerton"--adding, in a low tone, and with a little emphasis,--"heir to Sir Edgar."

The colonel bowed gracefully, and the dowager dropped a hasty courtesy at the commencement of the speech; but lower bend followed the closing remark, and a glance of the eye was thrown in quest of her daughters, as if she instinctively wished to bring them into what the sailors term "the line of battle."

Chapter IX

The following morning, Emily and Grace, declining the invitation to join the colonel and John in their usual rides, walked to the rectory, accompanied by Mrs. Wilson and Chatterton. The ladies felt a desire to witness the happiness that they so well knew reigned in the rectory, for Francis had promised his father to drive Clara over in the course of the day. Emily longed to see Clara, from whom it appeared that she had been already separated a month. Her impatience as they approached the house hurried her ahead of her companions, who waited the more sober gait of Mrs. Wilson. She entered the parlor at the rectory without meeting any one, glowing with exercise, her hair falling over her shoulders, released from the confinement of the hat she had thrown down hastily as she reached the door. In the room there stood a gentleman in deep black, with his back towards the entrance, intent on a book, and she naturally concluded it was Francis.

"Where is dear Clara, Frank?" cried the beautiful girl, faying her hand affectionately on his shoulder.

The gentleman turned suddenly, and presented to her astonished gaze the well remembered countenance of the young man whose parent's death was not likely to be forgotten at B----.

"I thought, sir," said Emily, almost sinking with confusion, "that Mr. Francis Ives--"

"Your brother 'has not yet arrived, Miss Moseley," simply replied the stranger, who felt for her embarrassment. "But I will immediately acquaint Mrs. Ives with your visit." Bowing, he delicately left the room.

Emily, who felt greatly relieved by his manner, immediately confined her hair in its proper bounds, and had recovered her composure by the time her aunt and friends joined her. She had not time to mention the incident, and laughed at her own precipitation, when the rector's wife came into the room.

Chatterton and his sister were both known to Mrs. Ives, and both were favorites. She was pleased to see them, and after reproaching the brother with compelling her son to ask a favor of a comparative stranger, she turned to Emily, and smilingly said--

"You found the parlor occupied, I believe?"

"Yes," said Emily, laughing and blushing, "I suppose Mr. Denbigh told you of my heedlessness."

"He told me of your attention in calling so soon to inquire after Clara, but said nothing more"--a servant just then telling her Francis wished to see her, she excused herself and withdrew. In the door she met Mr. Denbigh, who made way for her, saying, "your son has arrived, ma'am," and in an easy but respectful manner he took his place with the guests, no introduction passing, and none seeming necessary. His misfortunes appeared to have made him acquainted with Mrs. Wilson, and his strikingly ingenuous manner won insensibly on the confidence of those who heard him. Everything was natural, yet everything was softened by education; and the little party in the rector's parlor in fifteen minutes felt as if they had known him for years. The doctor and his son now joined them. Clara had not come, but she was looking forward in delightful expectation of to-morrow, and wished greatly for Emily as a guest at the new abode. This pleasure Mrs. Wilson promised she should have as soon as they had got over the hurry of their visit; "our friends," she added, turning to Grace, "will overlook the nicer punctilios of ceremony, where sisterly regard calls for the discharge of more important duties. Clara needs the society of Emily just now."

"Certainly," said Grace, mildly; "I hope no useless ceremony on the part of Emily would prevent her manifesting natural attachment to her sister--I should feel hurt at her not entertaining a better opinion of us than to suppose so for a moment."

"This, young ladies, is the real feeling to keep alive esteem," cried the doctor, gaily: "go on, and say and do nothing of which either can disapprove, when tried by the standard of duty, and you need never be afraid of losing a friend that is worth keeping."

It was three o'clock before the carriage of Mrs. Wilson arrived at the rectory; and the time stole away insensibly in free and friendly communications. Denbigh had joined modestly, and with the degree of interest a stranger might be supposed to feel, in the occurrences of a circle to which he was nearly a stranger; there was at times a slight display of awkwardness, however, about both him and Mrs. Ives, for which Mrs. Wilson easily accounted by recollections of his recent loss and the scene they had all witnessed in that very room. This embarrassment escaped the notice of the rest of the party. On the arrival of the carriage, Mrs. Wilson took her leave.

"I like this Mr. Denbigh greatly," said Lord Chatterton, as they drove from the door; "there is something strikingly natural and winning in his manner."

"In his matter too, judging of the little we have seen of him," replied Mrs. Wilson.

"Who is he, ma'am?"

"I rather suspect he is someway related to Mrs. Ives; her staying from Bolton to-day must be owing to Mr. Denbigh, and as the doctor has just gone he must be near enough to them to be neither wholly neglected nor yet a tax upon their politeness. I rather wonder he did not go with them."

"I heard him tell Francis," remarked Emily, "that he could not think of intruding, and he insisted on Mrs. Ives's going, but she had employments to keep her at home."

The carriage soon reached an angle in the road where the highways between Bolton Castle and Moseley Hall intersected each other, at a point on the estate of the former. Mrs. Wilson stopped a moment to inquire after an aged pensioner, who had lately met with a loss in business, which she was fearful must have greatly distressed him. In crossing a ford in the little river between his cottage and the market-town, the stream, which had been swollen unexpectedly higher than usual by heavy rains, had swept away his horse and cart loaded with the entire produce of his small field, and with much difficulty he had saved even his own life. Mrs. Wilson had not had it in her power until this moment to inquire particularly into the affair, or to offer the relief she was ever ready to bestow on proper objects. Contrary to her expectations, she found Humphreys in high spirits, showing his delighted grand-children a new cart and horse which stood at the door, and exultingly pointing out the excellent qualities of both. He ceased talking on the approach of the party, and at the request of his ancient benefactress he gave a particular account of the affair.

"And where did you get this new cart and horse, Humphreys?" inquired Mrs. Wilson, when he had ended.

"Oh, madam, I went up to the castle to see the steward, and Mr. Martin just mentioned my loss to Lord Pendennyss, ma'am, and my lord ordered me this cart, ma'am, and this noble horse, and twenty golden guineas into the bargain to put me on my legs again--God bless him for it, for ever!"

"It was very kind of his lordship, indeed," said Mrs. Wilson, thoughtfully: "I did not know he was at the castle."

"He's gone, already, madam; the servants told me that he just called to see the earl, on his way to Lon'on; but finding he'd went a few days agone to Ireland my lord went for Lon'on, without stopping the night even. Ah! madam," continued the old man, who stood leaning on a stick, with his hat in his hand, "he's a great blessing to the poor; his servants say he gives thousands every year to the poor who are in want--he is main rich, too; some people say, much richer and more great like than the earl himself. I'm sure I have need to bless him every day of my life."

Mrs. Wilson smiled mournfully as she wished Humphreys good day and put up her purse, finding the old man so well provided for; a display or competition in charity never entering into her system of benevolence.

"His lordship is munificent in his bounty," said Emily, as they drove from the door.

"Does it not savor of thoughtlessness to bestow so much where he can know so little?" Lord Chatterton ventured to inquire.

"He is," replied Mrs. Wilson, "as old Humphrey says, main rich; but the son of the old man and the father of these children is a soldier in the ----th dragoons, of which the earl is colonel, and that accounts to me for his liberality," recollecting, with a sigh, the feelings which had drawn her out of the usual circle of her charities in the case of the same man.

"Did you ever see Lord Pendennyss, aunt?"

"Never, my dear; he has been much abroad, but my letters were filled with his praises, and I confess my disappointment is great in not seeing him on this visit to Lord Bolton who is his relation; but," fixing her eyes thoughtfully on her niece, "we shall meet in London this winter, I trust."

As she spoke a cloud passed over her features, and she continued much absorbed in thought for the remainder of their drive.

General Wilson had been a cavalry officer, and he commanded the very regiment now held by Lord Pendennyss. In an excursion near the British camp he had been rescued from captivity, if not from death, by a gallant and timely interference of this young nobleman, then in command of a troop in the same corps. He had mentioned the occurrence to his wife in his letters, and from that day his correspondence was filled with the praises of the bravery and goodness to the soldiery of his young comrade. When he fell he had been supported from the field by, and he actually died in the arms of the young peer. A letter announcing his death had been received by his widow from the earl himself, and the tender and affectionate manner in which he spoke of her husband had taken a deep hold on her affections. All the circumstances together threw an interest around him that had made

Mrs. Wilson almost entertain the romantic wish he might be found worthy and disposed to solicit the hand of Emily. Her anxious inquiries into his character had been attended with such answers as flattered her wishes; but the military duties of the earl or his private affairs had never allowed a meeting; and she was now compelled to look forward to what John laughingly termed their winter campaign, as the only probable place where she could be gratified with the sight of a young man to whom she owed so much, and whose name was connected with some of the most tender though most melancholy recollections of her life.

Colonel Egerton, who now appeared to be almost domesticated in the family, was again of the party at dinner, to the no small satisfaction of the dowager, who from proper inquiries in the course of the day had learned that Sir Edgar's heir was likely to have the necessary number of figures in the sum total of his rental. While sitting in the drawing-room that afternoon she made an attempt to bring her eldest daughter and the elegant soldier together over a chess-board; a game the young lady had been required to learn because it was one at which a gentleman could be kept longer than any other without having his attention drawn away by any of those straggling charms which might be travelling a drawing-room "seeking whom they may devour." It was also a game admirably suited to the display of a beautiful hand and arm. But the mother had for a long time been puzzled to discover a way of bringing in the foot also, the young lady being particularly remarkable for the beauty of that portion of the frame. In vain her daughter hinted at dancing, an amusement of which she was passionately fond. The wary mother knew too well the effects of concentrated force to listen to the suggestion: dancing might do for every manager, but she prided herself in acting *en masse*, like Napoleon, whose tactics consisted in overwhelming by uniting his forces on a given point. After many experiments in her own person she endeavored to improve Catharine's manner of sitting, and by dint of twisting and turning she contrived that her pretty foot and ankle should be thrown forward in a way that the eye dropping from the move, should unavoidably rest on this beauteous object; giving, as it were, a Scylla and Charybdis to her daughter's charms.

John Moseley was the first person on whom she undertook to try the effect of her invention; and after comfortably seating the parties she withdrew to a little distance to watch the effect.

"Check to your king, Miss Chatterton," cried John, early in the game-- and the young lady thrust out her foot. "Check to *your* king, Mr. Moseley," echoed the damsel, and John's eyes wandered from hand to foot and foot to hand. "Check king and queen, sir."--"Check-mate."--"Did you speak?"

said John. Looking up he caught the eye of the dowager fixed on him in triumph--"Oh, ho," said the young man, internally, "Mother Chatterton, are you playing too?" and, coolly taking up his hat, he walked off, nor could they ever get him seated at the game again.

"You beat me too easily, Miss Chatterton," he would say when pressed to play, "before I have time to look up it's check-mate--excuse me."

The dowager next settled down into a more covert attack through Grace; but here she had two to contend with: her own forces rebelled, and the war had been protracted to the present hour with varied success, and at least without any material captures, on one side.

Colonel Egerton entered on the duties of his dangerous undertaking with the indifference of foolhardiness. The game was played with tolerable ability by both parties; but no emotions, no absence of mind could be discovered on the part of the gentleman. Feet and hands were in motion; still the colonel played as well as usual; he had answers for all Jane's questions, and smiles for his partner; but no check-mate could she obtain, until wilfully throwing away an advantage he suffered the lady to win the game. The dowager was satisfied nothing could be done with the colonel.

Chapter X

The first carriages that rolled over the lawn to Bolton parsonage, on the succeeding day, were those of the baronet and his sister; the latter in advance.

"There, Francis," cried Emily, who was impatiently waiting for him to remove some slight obstruction to her alighting, "thank you, thank you; that will do."

In the next moment she was in the extended arms of Clara. After pressing each other to their bosoms for a few moments in silence, Emily looked up, with a tear glistening in her eye, and first noticed the form of Denbigh, who was modestly withdrawing, as if unwilling to intrude on such pure and domestic feelings as the sisters were betraying, unconscious of the presence of a witness. Mrs. Wilson and Jane, followed by Miss Chatterton, now entered, and cordial salutes and greetings flowed upon Clara from her various friends.

The baronet's coach reached the door; it contained himself and wife, Mr. Benfield, and Lady Chatterton. Clara stood on the portico of the building, ready to receive them; her face all smiles, and tears, and blushes, and her arm locked in that of Emily.

"I wish you joy of your new abode, Mrs. Francis." Lady Moseley forgot her form, and bursting into tears, she pressed her daughter with ardor to her bosom.

"Clara, my love!" said the baronet, hastily wiping his eyes, and succeeding his wife in the embrace of their child. He kissed her, and, pressing Francis by the hand, walked into the house in silence.

"Well, well," cried the dowager, as she saluted her cousin, "all looks comfortable and genteel here, upon my word, Mrs. Ives: grapery--hot-houses--everything in good style too; and Sir Edward tells me the living is worth a good five hundred a year."

"So, girl, I suppose you expect a kiss," said Mr. Benfield who ascended the steps slowly, and with difficulty. "Kissing has gone much out of fashion lately. I remember, on the marriage of my friend, Lord Gosford, in the year fifty-eight, that all the maids and attendants were properly saluted in order. The lady Juliana was quite young then; not more than fifteen: it was there I got my first salute from her--but--so--kiss me." After which he continued, as they went into the house, "Marrying in that day was a serious business. You might visit a lady a dozen times before you could get a sight of her naked hand. Who's that?" stopping short, and looking earnestly at Denbigh, who now approached them.

"Mr. Denbigh, sir," said Clara, "my uncle, Mr. Benfield."

"Did you ever know, sir, a gentleman of your name, who sat in the parliament of this realm in the year sixty?" Mr. Benfield abruptly asked, as soon as the civilities of the introduction were exchanged. "You don't look much like him."

"That was rather before my day, sir," said Denbigh, with a smile, respectfully offering to relieve Clara, who supported him on one side, while Emily held his arm on the other.

The old gentleman was particularly averse to strangers, and Emily was in terror lest he should say something rude; but, after examining Denbigh again from head to foot, he took the offered arm, and coolly replied--

"True; very true; that was sixty years ago; you can hardly recollect as long. Ah! Mr. Denbigh, times are sadly altered since my youth. People who were then glad to ride on a pillion now drive their coaches; men who thought ale a luxury, drink their port; aye! and those who went barefoot must have their shoes and stockings, too. Luxury, sir, and the love of ease, will ruin this mighty empire. Corruption has taken hold of everything; the ministry buy the members, the members buy the ministry; everything is bought and sold. Now, sir, in the parliament in which I had the honor of a seat, there was a knot of us, as upright as posts, sir. My Lord Gosford was one, and General Denbigh was another, although I can't say he was much a favorite with me. You do not look in the least like him. How was he related to you, sir?"

"He was my grandfather," replied Denbigh, looking pleasantly at Emily, as if to tell her he understood the character of her uncle.

Had the old man continued his speech an hour longer, Denbigh would not have complained. They had stopped while talking, and he thus became confronted with the beautiful figure that supported the other arm. Denbigh contemplated in admiration the varying countenance which now blushed with apprehension, and now smiled in affection, or even with an archer expression, as her uncle proceeded in his harangue on the times. But all felicity in this world has an end, as well as misery. Denbigh retained the recollection of that speech long after Mr. Benfield was comfortably seated in the parlor, though for his life he could not recollect a word he had said.

The Haughtons, the Jarvises, and a few more of their intimate acquaintances, arrived, and the parsonage had a busy air; but John, who had undertaken to drive Grace Chatterton in his own phaeton, was yet absent. Some little anxiety had begun to be manifested, when he appeared, dashing through the gates at a great rate, and with the skill of a member of the four-in-hand.

Lady Chatterton had begun to be seriously uneasy, and she was about to speak to her son to go in quest of them, as they came in sight; but now her fears vanished, and she could only suppose that a desire to have Grace alone could keep one who had the reputation of a Jehu so much behind the rest of the party. She met them in great spirits, crying,

"Upon my word, Mr. Moseley, I began to think you had taken the road to Scotland, you stayed so long."

"Your daughter, my Lady Chatterton," said John, pithily, "would go to Scotland neither with me nor any other man, or I am greatly deceived in her character. Clara, my sister, how do you do?" He saluted the bride with great warmth and affection.

"But what detained you, Moseley?" inquired the mother.

"One of the horses was restive, and he broke the harness. We merely stopped in the village while it was mended."

"And how did Grace behave?" asked Emily, laughing.

"Oh, a thousand times better than you would, sister; as she always does, and like an angel."

The only point in dispute between Emily and her brother was her want of faith in his driving; while poor Grace, naturally timid, and unwilling to oppose any one, particularly the gentleman who then held the reins, had governed herself sufficiently to be silent and motionless. Indeed, she could hardly do otherwise had she wished it, so great was his impetuosity of character; and John felt flattered to a degree of which he was himself unconscious. Self-complacency, aided by the merit, the beauty, and the delicacy of the young lady herself, might have led to the very results her mother so anxiously wished to produce, had that mother been satisfied with letting things take their course. But managers very generally overdo their work.

"Grace *is* a good girl," said her gratified mother; "and you found her very valiant, Mr. Moseley?"

"Oh, as brave as Cæsar," answered John, carelessly, in a way that was not quite free from irony.

Grace, whose burning cheek showed but too plainly that praise from John Moseley was an incense too powerful for her resistance, now sank back behind some of the company, endeavoring to conceal the tears that almost gushed from her eyes. Denbigh was a silent spectator of the whole scene, and he now considerately observed, that he had lately seen an improvement which would obviate the difficulty Mr. Moseley had experienced. John turned to the speaker, and they were soon engaged in the discussion of curbs and buckles, when the tilbury of Colonel Egerton drove to the door, containing himself and his friend the captain.

The bride undoubtedly received congratulations that day more sincere than those which were now offered, but none were delivered in a more graceful and insinuating manner than the compliments which fell from Colonel Egerton. He passed round the room, speaking to his acquaintances, until he arrived at the chair of Jane, who was seated next her aunt. Here he stopped, and glancing his eye round, and saluting with bows and smiles the remainder of the party, he appeared fixed at the centre of all attraction.

"There is a gentleman I think I have never seen before," he observed, to Mrs. Wilson, casting his eyes on Denbigh, whose back was towards him in discourse with Mr. Benfield.

"It is Mr. Denbigh, of whom you heard us speak," replied Mrs. Wilson. While she spoke, Denbigh faced them. Egerton started as he caught a view of his face, and seemed to gaze on the countenance which was open to his inspection with an earnestness that showed an interest of some kind, but of a nature that was inexplicable to Mrs. Wilson, who was the only observer of this singular recognition; for such it evidently was. All was now natural in the colonel for the moment; his color sensibly changed, and there was an expression of doubt in his face. It might be fear, it might be horror, it might be a strong aversion; it clearly was not love. Emily sat by her aunt, and Denbigh approached them, making a cheerful remark. It was impossible for the colonel to avoid him had he wished it, and he kept his ground. Mrs. Wilson thought she would try the experiment of an introduction.

"Colonel Egerton--Mr. Denbigh."

Both gentlemen bowed, but nothing striking was seen in the deportment of either. The colonel, who was not exactly at ease, said hastily--

"Mr. Denbigh is, or has been in the army, I believe."

Denbigh was now taken by surprise in his turn: he cast a look on Egerton of fixed and settled meaning; then carelessly observed, but still as if requiring an answer:

"I am yet; but I do not recollect having had the pleasure of meeting with Colonel Egerton on service."

"Your countenance is familiar, sir," replied the colonel, coldly; "but at this moment I cannot tax my memory with the place of our meeting, though one sees so many strange faces in a campaign, that they come and go like shadows."

He then changed the conversation. It was some time, however, before either gentleman entirely recovered his ease--and many days elapsed ere anything like intercourse passed between them. The colonel attached himself during this visit to Jane, with occasional notices of the Misses Jarvis, who began to manifest symptoms of uneasiness at the decided preference he showed to a lady they now chose to look upon, in some measure, as a rival.

Mrs. Wilson and her charge, on the other hand, were entertained by the conversation of Chatterton and Denbigh, relieved by occasional sallies from the lively John. There was something in the person and manners of Denbigh that insensibly attracted those whom chance threw in his way. His face was not strikingly handsome, but it was noble; and when he smiled, or was much animated, it invariably communicated a spark of his own enthusiasm to the beholder. His figure was faultless; his air and manner, if less easy than those of Colonel Egerton, were more sincere and ingenuous; his breeding was clearly higher; his respect for others rather bordering on the old school. But in his voice there existed a charm which would make him, when he spoke, to a female ear, almost resistless: it was soft, deep, melodious, and winning.

"Baronet," said the rector, looking with a smile towards his son and daughter, "I love to see my children happy, and Mrs. Ives threatens a divorce if I go on in the manner I have commenced. She says I desert her for Bolton."

"Why, doctor, if our wives conspire against us, and prevent our enjoying a comfortable dish of tea with Clara, or a glass of wine with Frank, we must call in the higher authorities as umpires. What say you, sister? Is a parent to desert his child in any case?"

"My opinion is," said Mrs. Wilson, with a smile, yet speaking with emphasis, "that a parent is *not* to desert a child, in any case or in any manner."

"Do you hear that, my Lady Moseley?" cried the good-humored baronet.

"Do you hear that, my Lady Chatterton?" echoed John, who had just taken a seat by Grace, when her mother approached them.

"I hear it, but do not see the application, Mr. Moseley."

"No, my lady! Why, there is the honorable Miss Chatterton almost dying to play a game of her favorite chess with Mr. Denbigh. She has beaten us all but him, and her triumph will not be complete until she has him too at her feet."

And as Denbigh politely offered to meet the challenge, the board was produced, and the parties were seated. Lady Chatterton stood leaning over her daughter's chair, with a view, however, to prevent any of those consequences she was generally fond of seeing result from this amusement; every measure taken by this prudent mother being literally governed by judicious calculation.

"Umph," thought John, as he viewed the players, while listening with pleasure to the opinions of Grace, who had recovered her composure and spirits; "Kate, after all, has played one game without using her feet."

Chapter XI

Ten days or a fortnight flew swiftly by, during which Mrs. Wilson suffered Emily to give Clara a week, having first ascertained that Denbigh was a settled resident at the rectory, and thereby not likely to be oftener at the House of Francis than at the hall, where he was a frequent and welcome guest, both on his own account and as a friend of Doctor Ives. Emily had returned, and she brought the bride and groom with her; when one evening as they were pleasantly seated at their various amusements, with the ease of old acquaintances, Mr. Haughton entered. It was at an hour rather unusual for his visits; and throwing down his hat, after making the usual inquiries, he began without preface--

"I know, good people, you are all wondering what has brought me out this time of night, but the truth is, Lucy has coaxed her mother to persuade me into a ball in honor of the times; so, my lady, I have consented, and my wife and daughter have been buying up all the finery in B----, by the way, I suppose, of anticipating their friends. There is a regiment of foot come into barracks within fifteen miles of us, and to-morrow I must beat up for recruits among the officers--girls are never wanting on such occasions."

"Why," cried the baronet, "you are growing young again, my friend."
"No, Sir Edward, but my daughter is young, and life has so many cares that I am willing she should get rid of as many as she can at my expense."

"Surely you would not wish her to dance them away," said Mrs. Wilson; "such relief I am afraid will prove temporary."

"Do you disapprove of dancing, ma'am?" said Mr. Haughton, who held her opinions in great respect as well as a little dread.

"I neither approve nor disapprove of it--jumping up and down is innocent enough in itself, and if it must be done it is well it were done gracefully; as for the accompaniments of dancing I say nothing--what do you say, Doctor Ives?"

"To what, my dear madam?"

"To dancing."

"Oh let the girls dance if they enjoy it."

"I am glad you think so, doctor," cried the delighted Mr. Haughton; I was afraid I recollected your advising your son never to dance nor to play at games of chance."

"You thought right, my friend," said the doctor, laying down his newspaper; "I did give that advice to Frank, whom you will please to remember is now rector of Bolton. I do not object to dancing as not innocent in itself or as an elegant exercise; but it is like drinking, generally carried to excess: now as a Christian I am opposed to all excesses; the music and company lead to intemperance in the recreation, and they often induce neglect of duties--but so may anything else."

"I like a game of whist, doctor, greatly," said Mr. Haughton; "but observing that you never play, and recollecting your advice to Mr. Francis, I have forbidden cards when you are my guest."

"I thank you for the compliment, good sir," replied the doctor, with a smile; "still I would much rather see you play cards than hear you talk scandal, as you sometimes do."

"Scandal!" echoed Mr. Haughton.

"Ay, scandal," said the doctor, coolly, "such as the remark you made the last time, which was only yesterday, I called to see you. You accused Sir Edward of being wrong in letting that poacher off so easily; the baronet, you said, did not shoot himself, and did not know how to prize game as he ought."

"Scandal, Doctor--do you call that scandal? why I told Sir Edward so himself, two or three times."

"I know you did, and that was rude."

"Rude! I hope sincerely Sir Edward has put no such construction on it?"

The baronet smiled kindly, and shook his head.

"Because the baronet chooses to forgive your offences, it does not alter their nature," said the doctor, gravely: "no, you must repent and amend; you impeached his motives for doing a benevolent act, and that I call scandal."

"Why, doctor, I was angry the fellow should be let loose; he is a pest to all the game in the county, and every sportsman will tell you so--here, Mr. Moseley, you know Jackson, the poacher."

"Oh! a poacher is an intolerable wretch!" cried Captain Jarvis.

"Oh! a poacher," echoed John, looking drolly at Emily, "hang all poachers."

"Poacher or no poacher, does not alter the scandal," said the doctor; "now let me tell you, good sir, I would rather play at fifty games of whist than make one such speech, unless indeed it interfered with my duties; now, sir, with your leave I'll explain myself as to my son. There is an artificial levity about dancing that adds to the dignity of no man: from some it may detract: a clergyman for instance is supposed to have other things to do, and it might hurt him in the opinions of those with whom his influence is necessary, and impair his usefulness; therefore a clergyman should never dance. In the same way with cards; they are the common instruments of gambling, and an odium is attached to them on that account; women and clergymen must respect the prejudices of mankind in some cases, or lose their influence in society."

"I did hope to have the pleasure of your company, doctor, said Mr. Haughton, hesitatingly.

"And if it will give you pleasure," cried the rector, "you shall have it with all my heart, good sir; it would be a greater evil to wound the feelings of such a neighbor as Mr. Haughton, than to show my face once at a ball," and rising, he laid his hand on the shoulder of the other kindly. "Both your scandal and rudeness are easily forgiven; but I wished to show you the common error of the world which has attached odium to certain things, while it charitably overlooks others of a more heinous nature."

Mr. Haughton, who had at first been a little staggered with the attack of the doctor, recovered himself, and laying a handful of notes on the table, hoped he should have the pleasure of seeing every body. The invitation was generally accepted, and the worthy man departed, happy if his friends did but come, and were pleased.

"Do you dance, Miss Moseley?" inquired Denbigh of Emily, as he sat watching her graceful movements in netting a purse for her father.

"Oh, yes! the doctor said nothing of us girls, you know I suppose he thinks we have no dignity to lose."

"Admonitions are generally thrown away on young ladies when pleasure is in the question," said the doctor, with a look of almost paternal affection.

"I hope you do not seriously disapprove of it in moderation," said Mrs. Wilson.

"That depends, madam, upon circumstances; if it is to be made subsidiary to envy, malice, coquetry, vanity, or any other such little lady-like accomplishment, it certainly had better be let alone. But in moderation, and with the feelings of my little pet here, I should be cynical, indeed, to object."

Denbigh appeared lost in his own ruminations during this dialogue; and as the doctor ended, he turned to the captain, who was overlooking a game of chess between the colonel and Jane, of which the latter had become remarkably fond of late, playing with her hands and eyes instead of her feet--and inquired the name of the corps in barracks at F----.

"The ----th foot, sir," replied the captain, haughtily, who neither respected him, owing to his want of consequence, nor loved him, from the manner in which Emily listened to his conversation.

"Will Miss Moseley forgive a bold request," said Denbigh, with some hesitation.

Emily looked up from her work in silence, but with some little flutterings at the heart.

"The honor of her hand for the first dance," continued Denbigh, observing she was in expectation that he would proceed.

Emily laughingly said, "Certainly, Mr. Denbigh, if you can submit to the degradation."

The London papers now came in, and most of the gentlemen sat down to their perusal. The colonel, however, replaced the men for a second game, and Denbigh still kept his place beside Mrs. Wilson and her niece. The manners, the sentiments, the whole exterior of this gentleman were such as both the taste and judgment of the aunt approved of; his qualities were those which insensibly gained on the heart, and yet Mrs. Wilson noticed, with a slight uneasiness, the very evident satisfaction her niece took in his society. In Dr. Ives she had great confidence, yet Dr. Ives was a friend, and probably judged him favorably; and again, Dr. Ives was not to suppose he was introducing a candidate for the hand of Emily in every gentleman he brought to the hall. Mrs. Wilson had seen too often the ill consequences of trusting to impressions received from inferences of companionship, not to know the only safe way was to judge for ourselves: the opinions of others might be partial--might be prejudiced--and many an improper connexion had been formed by listening to the sentiments of those who spoke without interest, and consequently without examination. Not a few matches are made by this idle commendation of others, uttered by those who are respected, and which are probably suggested more by a desire to please than by reflection or even knowledge. In short Mrs. Wilson knew that as our happiness chiefly interests ourselves, so it was to ourselves, or to those few whose interest was equal to our own, we could only trust those important inquiries necessary to establish a permanent opinion of character. With Doctor Ives her communications on subjects of duty were frequent and confiding, and although she sometimes thought his benevolence disposed him to be rather too lenient to the faults of mankind, she entertained a profound respect for his judgment. It had great influence with her, if it were not always conclusive; she determined, therefore, to have an early conversation with him on the subject so near her heart, and be in a great measure regulated by his answers in the steps to be immediately taken. Every day gave her what he thought melancholy proof of the ill consequences of neglecting a duty, in the increasing intimacy of Colonel Egerton and Jane.

"Here, aunt," cried John, as he ran over a paper, "is a paragraph relating to your favorite youth, our trusty and well beloved cousin the Earl of Pendennyss."

"Read it," said Mrs. Wilson, with an interest his name never failed to excite.

"We noticed to-day the equipage of the gallant Lord Pendennyss before the gates of Annandale-house, and understand the noble earl is last from Bolton castle, Northamptonshire."

"A very important fact," said Captain Jarvis, sarcastically; "Colonel Egerton and myself got as far as the village, to pay our respects to him, when we heard he had gone on to town."

"The earl's character, both as a man and a soldier," observed the colonel, "gives him a claim to our attentions that his rank would not: on that account we would have called."

"Brother," said Mrs. Wilson, "you would oblige me greatly by asking his lordship to waive ceremony; his visits to Bolton castle will probably be frequent, now we have peace; and the owner is so much from home that we may never see him without some such invitation."

"Do you want him as a husband for Emily?" cried John, as he gaily seated himself by the side of his sister.

Mrs. Wilson smiled at an observation which reminded her of one of her romantic wishes; and as she raised her head to reply in the same tone, met the eye of Denbigh fixed on her with an expression that kept her silent. This is really an incomprehensible young man in some respects, thought the cautious widow, his startling looks on the introduction to the colonel crossing her mind at the same time; and observing the doctor opening the door that led to the baronet's library, Mrs. Wilson, who generally acted as soon as she had decided, followed him. As their conversations were known often to relate to the little offices of charity in which they both delighted, the movement excited no surprise, and she entered the library with the doctor uninterrupted.

"Doctor," said Mrs. Wilson, impatient to proceed to the point, "you know my maxim, prevention is better than cure. This young friend of yours is very interesting."

"Do you feel yourself in danger?" said the rector, smiling.

"Not very imminent," replied the lady, laughing good-naturedly. Seating herself, she continued, "Who is he? and who was his father, if I may ask?"

"George Denbigh, madam, both father and son," said the doctor, gravely.

"Ah, doctor, I am almost tempted to wish Frank had been a girl. You know what I wish to learn."

"Put your questions in order, dear madam," said the doctor, in a kind manner, "and they shall be answered."

"His principles?"

"So far as I can learn, they are good. His acts, as they have come to my notice, are highly meritorious, and I hope they originated in proper motives. I have seen but little of him of late years, however, and on this head you are nearly as good a judge as myself. His filial piety," said the doctor, dashing a tear from his eye, and speaking with fervor, "was lovely."

"His temper--his disposition?"

"His temper is under great command, although naturally ardent; his disposition eminently benevolent towards his fellow-creatures."

"His connexions?"

"Suitable," said the doctor, gravely.

His fortune was of but little moment. Emily would be amply provided, for all the customary necessaries of her station; and, thanking the divine, Mrs. Wilson returned to the parlor, easy in mind, and determined to let things take their own course for a time, but in no degree to relax the vigilance of her observation.

On her return to the room, Mrs. Wilson observed Denbigh approach Egerton, and enter into conversation of a general nature. It was the first time anything more than unavoidable courtesies had passed between them. The colonel appeared slightly uneasy under his novel situation, while, on the other hand, his companion showed an anxiety to be on a more friendly footing than heretofore. There was something mysterious in the feelings manifested by both these gentlemen that greatly puzzled the good lady; and from its complexion, she feared one or the other was not entirely free from censure. It could not have been a quarrel, or their names would have been familiar to each other. They had both served in Spain, she knew, and excesses were often committed by gentlemen at a distance from home their pride would have prevented where they were anxious to maintain a character. Gambling, and a few other prominent vices, floated through her imagination, until, wearied of conjectures where she had no data, and supposing, after all, it might be only her imagination, the turned to more pleasant reflections.

Chapter XII

The bright eyes of Emily Moseley unconsciously wandered round the brilliant assemblage at Mr. Haughton's, as she took her seat, in search of her partner. The rooms were filled with scarlet coats, and belles from the little town of F----; and if the company were not the most select imaginable, it was disposed to enjoy the passing moment cheerfully and in lightness of heart. Ere, however, she could make out to scan the countenances of the men, young Jarvis, decked in the full robes of his dignity, as captain in the ----th foot, approached and solicited the honor of her hand. The colonel had already secured her sister, and it was by the instigation of his friend, Jarvis had been thus early in his application. Emily thanked him, and pleaded her engagement. The mortified youth, who had thought dancing with the ladies a favor conferred on them, from the anxiety his sister always manifested to get partners, stood for a few moments in sullen silence; and then, as if to be revenged on the sex, he determined not to dance the whole evening. Accordingly, he withdrew to a room appropriated to the gentlemen, where he found a few of the military beaux, keeping alive the stimulus they had brought with them from the mess-table.

Clara had prudently decided to comport herself as became a clergyman's wife, and she declined dancing altogether. Catherine Chatterton was entitled to open the ball, as superior in years and rank to any who were disposed to enjoy the amusement. The dowager, who in her heart loved to show her airs upon such occasions, had chosen to be later than the rest of the family; and Lucy had to entreat her father to have patience more than once during the interregnum in their sports created by Lady Chatterton's fashion. This lady at length appeared, attended by her son, and followed by her daughters, ornamented in all the taste of the reigning fashions. Doctor Ives and his wife, who came late from choice, soon appeared, accompanied by their guest, and the dancing commenced. Denbigh had thrown aside his black for the evening, and as he approached to claim her promised hand, Emily thought him, if not as handsome, much more interesting than Colonel Egerton, who just then passed them while leading her sister to the set. Emily danced beautifully, but perfectly like a lady, as did Jane; but Denbigh, although graceful in his movements and in time, knew but little of the art; and but for the assistance of his partner, he would have more than once gone wrong in the figure. He very gravely asked her opinion of his performance as he handed her to a chair, and she laughingly told him his movements were but a better sort of march. He was about to reply, when Jarvis approached. By the aid of a pint of wine and his own reflections, the youth wrought himself into something of a passion, especially as he saw Denbigh enter, after Emily had declined dancing with himself. There was a gentleman in the corps who unfortunately was addicted to the bottle, and he had fastened on Jarvis as a man at leisure to keep him company. Wine openeth the heart, and the captain having taken a peep at the dancers, and seen the disposition of affairs, returned to his bottle companion, bursting with the indignity offered to his person. He dropped a hint, and a question or two brought the whole grievance forth.

There is a certain set of men in every service who imbibe extravagant notions that are revolting to humanity, and which too often prove to be fatal in their results. Their morals are never correct, and the little they have set loosely about them. In their own cases, their appeals to arms are not always so prompt; but in that of their friends, their perceptions of honor are intuitively keen, and their inflexibility in preserving it from reproach unbending; and such is the weakness of mankind, their "tenderness on points where the nicer feelings of a soldier are involved, that these machines of custom, these thermometers graduated to the scale of false honor, usurp the place of reason and benevolence, and become too often the arbiters of life and death to a whole corps. Such, then, was the confidant to whom Jarvis communicated the cause of his disgust, and the consequences may easily be imagined. As he passed Emily and Denbigh, he threw a look of fierceness at the latter, which he meant as an indication of his hostile intentions. It was lost on his rival, who at that moment was filled with passions of a very different kind from those which Captain Jarvis thought agitated his own bosom; for had his new friend let him alone, the captain would have gone quietly home and gone to sleep.

"Have you ever fought?" said Captain Digby coolly to his companion, as they seated themselves in his father's parlor, whither they had retired to make their arrangements for the following morning.

"Yes," said Jarvis, with a stupid look, "I fought once with Tom Halliday at school."

"At school! My dear friend, you commenced young indeed," said Digby, helping himself to another glass. "And how did it end?"

"Oh! Tom got the better, and so I cried enough," said Jarvis, surlily.

"Enough! I hope you did not flinch," eyeing him keenly "Where were you hit?"

"He hit me all over."

"All over! The d---l! Did you use small shot? How did you fight?"

"With fists," said Jarvis, yawning.

His companion, seeing how matters were, rang for his servant to put him to bed, remaining himself an hour longer to finish the bottle.

Soon after Jarvis had given Denbigh the look big with his intended vengeance, Colonel Egerton approached Emily, asking permission to present Sir Herbert Nicholson, the lieutenant-colonel of the regiment, and a gentleman who was ambitious of the honor of her acquaintance; a particular friend of his own. Emily gracefully bowed her assent. Soon after, turning her eyes on Denbigh, who had been speaking to her at the moment, she saw him looking intently on the two soldiers, who were making their way through the crowd to the place where she sat. He stammered, said something she could not understand, and precipitately withdrew; and although both she and her aunt sought his figure in the gay throng that flitted around them, he was seen no more that evening.

"Are you acquainted with Mr. Denbigh?" said Emily to her partner, after looking in vain to find his person in the crowd.

"Denbigh! Denbigh! I have known one or two of that name" replied the gentleman. "In the army there are several."

"Yes," said Emily, musing, "he is in the army;" and looking up, she saw her companion reading her countenance with an expression that brought the color to her cheeks with a glow that was painful. Sir Herbert smiled, and observed that the room was warm. Emily acquiesced in the remark, for the first time in her life conscious of a feeling she was ashamed to have scrutinized, and glad of any excuse to hide her confusion.

"Grace Chatterton is really beautiful to-night," whispered John Moseley to his sister Clara. "I have a mind to ask her to dance."

"Do, John." replied his sister, looking with pleasure on her beautiful cousin, who, observing the movements of John as he drew near where she sat, moved her face on each side rapidly, in search of some one who was apparently not to be found. Her breathing became sensibly quicker, and John was on the point of speaking to her as the dowager stepped in between them. There is nothing so flattering to the vanity of a man as the discovery of emotions in a young woman excited by himself, and which the party evidently wishes to conceal; there is nothing so touching, so sure to captivate; or, if it seem to be affected, so sure to disgust.

"Now, Mr. Moseley," cried the mother, "you shall not ask Grace to dance! She can refuse you nothing, and she has been up the last two figures."

"Your wishes are irresistible, Lady Chatterton," said John, coolly turning on his heel. On gaining the other side of the room, he turned to reconnoitre the scene. The dowager was fanning herself as violently as if *she* had been up the last two figures instead of her daughter, while Grace sat with her eyes fastened on the floor, paler than usual. "Grace," thought the young man, "would be very handsome--very sweet--very--very everything that is agreeable, if--if it were not for Mother Chatterton." He then led out one of the prettiest girls in the room.

Col. Egerton was peculiarly fitted to shine in a ball room. He danced gracefully and with spirit; was perfectly at home with all the usages of the best society, and was never neglectful of any of those little courtesies which have their charm for the moment; and Jane Moseley, who saw all those she loved around her, apparently as happy as herself, found in her judgment or the convictions of her principles, no counterpoise against the weight of such attractions, all centred as it were in one effort to please herself. His flattery was deep for it was respectful--his tastes were her tastes--his opinions her opinions. On the formation of their acquaintance they differed on some trifling point of poetical criticism, and for near a month the colonel had maintained his opinion with a show of firmness; but opportunities not wanting for the discussion, he had felt constrained to yield to her better judgment, her purer taste. The conquest of Colonel Egerton was complete, and Jane who saw in his attentions the submission of a devoted heart, began to look forward to the moment with trembling that was to remove the thin barrier that existed between the adulation of the eyes and the most delicate assiduity to please, and the open confidence of declared love. Jane Moseley had a heart to love, and to love strongly; her danger existed in her imagination: it was brilliant, unchastened by her judgment, we had almost said unfettered by her principles. Principles such as are found in every-day maxims and rules of conduct sufficient to restrain her within the bounds of perfect decorum she was furnished with in abundance; but to that principle which was to teach her submission in opposition to her wishes, to that principle that could alone afford her security against the treachery of her own passions, she was an utter stranger.

The family of Sir Edward were, among the first to retire, and as the Chattertons had their own carriage, Mrs. Wilson and her charge returned alone in the coach of the former. Emily, who had been rather out of spirits the latter-part of the evening, broke the silence by suddenly observing,

"Colonel Egerton is, or soon will be, a perfect hero!"

Her aunt somewhat surprised, both with the abruptness and with the strength of the remark, inquired her meaning.

"Oh, Jane will make him one, whether or not."

This was spoken with an air of vexation which she was unused to, and Mrs. Wilson gravely corrected her for speaking in a disrespectful manner of her sister, one whom neither her years nor situation entitled her in any measure to advise or control. There was an impropriety in judging so near and dear a relation harshly, even in thought. Emily pressed the hand of her aunt and tremulously acknowledged her error; but she added, that she felt a momentary irritation at the idea of a man of Colonel Egerton's character gaining the command over feelings such as her sister possessed. Mrs. Wilson kissed the cheek of her niece, while she inwardly acknowledged the probable truth of the very remark she had thought it her duty to censure. That the imagination of Jane would supply her lover with those qualities she most honored herself, she believed was taken as a matter of course; and that when the veil she had helped to throw before her own eyes was removed, she would cease to respect, and of course cease to love him, when too late to remedy the evil, she greatly feared. But in the approaching fate of Jane she saw new cause to call forth her own activity.

Emily Moseley had just completed her eighteenth year, and was gifted by nature with a vivacity and ardency of feeling that gave a heightened zest to the enjoyments of that happy age. She was artless but intelligent; cheerful, with a deep conviction of the necessity of piety; and uniform in her practice of all the important duties. The unwearied exertions of her aunt, aided by her own quickness of perception, had made her familiar with the attainments suitable to her sex and years. For music she had no taste, and the time which would have been thrown away in endeavoring to cultivate a talent she did not possess, was dedicated under the discreet guidance of her aunt, to works which had a tendency both to qualify her for the duties of this life, and fit her for that which comes hereafter. It might be said Emily Moseley had never read a book that contained a sentiment or inculcated an opinion improper for her sex or dangerous to her morals; and it was not difficult for those who knew the fact, to fancy they could perceive the consequences in her guileless countenance and innocent deportment. Her looks--her actions--her thoughts, wore as much of nature as the discipline of her well-regulated mind and softened manners could admit. In person she was of the middle size, exquisitely formed, graceful and elastic in her step, without, however, the least departure from her natural movements; her eye was a dark blue, with an expression of joy and intelligence; at times it seemed all soul, and again all heart; her color was rather high, but it varied with every emotion of her bosom; her feelings were strong, ardent, and devoted to those she loved. Her preceptress had never found it necessary to repeat an admonition of any kind, since her arrival at years to discriminate between the right and the wrong.

"I wish," said Doctor Ives to his wife, the evening his son had asked their permission to address Clara, "Francis had chosen my little Emily."

"Clara is a good girl," replied his wife; "she is so mild, so affectionate, that I doubt not she will make him happy--Frank might have done worse at the Hall."

"For himself he has done well, I hope," said the father, "a young woman of Clara's heart may make any man happy but a union with purity, sense, principles, like those of Emily would be more--it would be blissful."

Mrs. Ives smiled at her husband's animation. "You remind me more of the romantic youth I once knew than of the grave divine. There is but one man I know that I could wish to give Emily to; it is Lumley. If Lumley sees her, he will woo her; and if he wooes, he will win her."

"And Lumley I believe to be worthy of her," cried the rector, now taking up a candle to retire for the night.

Chapter XIII

The following day brought a large party of the military *elegants* to the Hall, in acceptance of the baronet's hospitable invitation to dinner. Lady Moseley was delighted; so long as her husband's or her children's interest had demanded a sacrifice of her love of society it had been made without a sigh, almost without a thought. The ties of affinity in her were sacred; and to the happiness, the comfort of those in which she felt an interest, there were few sacrifices of her own propensities she would not cheerfully have made: it was this very love of her offspring that made her anxious to dispose of her daughters in wedlock. Her own marriage had been so happy, that she naturally concluded it the state most likely to ensure the happiness of her children; and with Lady Moseley, as with thousands of others, who averse or unequal to the labors of investigation, jump to conclusions over the long line of connecting reasons, marriage was marriage, a husband was a husband. It is true there were certain indispensables, without which the formation of a connexion was a thing she considered not within the bounds of nature. There must be fitness in fortune, in condition, in education, and manners; there must be no glaring evil, although she did not ask for positive good. A professor of religion herself, had any one told her it was a duty of her calling to guard against a connexion with any but a Christian for her girls, she would have wondered at the ignorance that would embarrass the married state, with feelings exclusively belonging to the individual. Had any one told her it were possible to give her child to any but a gentleman, she would have wondered at the want of feeling that could devote the softness of Jane or Emily, to the association with rudeness or vulgarity. It was the misfortune of Lady Moseley to limit her views of marriage to the scene of this life, forgetful that every union gives existence to a long line of immortal beings, whose future welfare depends greatly on the force of early examples, or the strength of early impressions.

The necessity for restriction in their expenditures had ceased, and the baronet and his wife greatly enjoyed the first opportunity their secluded situation had given them, to draw around their board their fellow-creatures of their own stamp. In the former, it was pure philanthropy; the same feeling urged him to seek out and relieve distress in humble life; while in the latter it was love of station and seemliness. It was becoming the owner of Moseley

Hall, and it was what the daughters of the Benfield family had done since the conquest.

"I am extremely sorry," said the good baronet at dinner, "Mr. Denbigh declined our invitation to-day; I hope he will yet ride over in the evening."

Looks of a singular import were exchanged between Colonel Egerton and Sir Herbert Nicholson, at the mention of Denbigh's name; which, as the latter had just asked the favor of taking wine with Mrs. Wilson, did not escape her notice. Emily had innocently mentioned his precipitate retreat the night before; and he had, when reminded of his engagement to dine with them that very day, and promised an introduction to Sir Herbert Nicholson by John, in her presence, suddenly excused himself and withdrawn. With an indefinite suspicion of something wrong, she ventured, therefore, to address Sir Herbert Nicholson.

"Did you know Mr. Denbigh, in Spain?"

"I told Miss Emily Moseley, I believe, last evening, that I knew some of the name," replied the gentleman evasively; then pausing a moment, he added with great emphasis, "there is a circumstance connected with *one* of that name, I shall ever remember."

"It was creditable, no doubt, Sir Herbert," cried young Jarvis, sarcastically. The soldier affected not to hear the question, and asked Jane to take wine with him. Lord Chatterton, however, putting his knife and fork down gravely, and with a glow of animation, observed with unusual spirit,

"I have no doubt it was, sir."

Jarvis in his turn, affected not to hear this speech, and nothing farther was said, as Sir Edward saw that the name of Mr. Denbigh excited a sensation amongst his guests for which he was unable to account, and which he soon forgot himself.

After the company had retired, Lord Chatterton, however, related to the astonished and indignant family of the baronet the substance of the following scene, of which he had been a witness that morning, while on a visit to Denbigh at the rectory. They had been sitting in the parlor by themselves, over their breakfast, when a Captain Digby was announced.

"I have the honor of waiting upon you, Mr. Denbigh," said the soldier, with the stiff formality of a professed duellist, "on behalf of Captain Jarvis, but will postpone my business until you are at leisure," glancing his eye on Chatterton.

"I know of no business with Captain Jarvis," said Denbigh, politely handing the stranger a chair, "to which Lord Chatterton cannot be privy; if he will excuse the interruption. The nobleman bowed, and Captain Digby, a little awed by the rank of Denbigh's friend, proceeded in a more measured manner.

"Captain Jarvis has empowered me, sir, to make any arrangement with yourself or friend, previously to your meeting, which he hopes may be as soon as possible, if convenient to yourself," replied the soldier, coolly.

Denbigh viewed him for a moment with astonishment, in silence; when recollecting himself, he said mildly, and without the least agitation, "I cannot affect, sir, not to understand your meaning, but am at a loss to imagine what act of mine can have made Mr. Jarvis wish to make such an appeal."

"Surely Mr. Denbigh cannot think a man of Captain Jarvis's spirit can quietly submit to the indignity put upon him last evening, by your dancing with Miss Moseley, after she had declined the honor to himself," said the captain, affecting an incredulous smile. "My Lord Chatterton and myself can easily settle the preliminaries, as Captain Jarvis is much disposed to consult your wishes, sir, in this affair."

"If he consults my wishes," said Denbigh, smiling, "he will think no more about it."

"At what time, sir, will it be convenient to give him the meeting?" then, speaking with a kind of bravado gentlemen of his cast are fond of assuming, "my friend would not hurry any settlement of your affairs."

"I can never meet Captain Jarvis with hostile intentions," replied Denbigh, calmly.

"Sir!"

"I decline the combat, sir," said Denbigh, with more firmness.

"Your reasons, sir, if you please?" asked Captain Digby compressing his lips, and drawing up with an air of personal interest.

"Surely," cried Chatterton, who had with difficulty estrained his feelings, "surely Mr. Denbigh could never so far forget himself as cruelly to expose Miss Moseley by accepting this invitation."

"Your reason, my lord," said Denbigh, with interest, "would at all times have its weight; but I wish not to qualify an act of what I conceive to be principle by any lesser consideration. I cannot meet Captain Jarvis, or any other man, in private combat. There can exist no necessity for an appeal to arms in any society where the laws rule, and I am averse to bloodshed."

"Very extraordinary," muttered Captain Digby, somewhat at a loss how to act; but the calm and collected manner of Denbigh prevented a reply; and after declining a cup of tea, a liquor he never drank, he withdrew, saying he would acquaint his friend with Mr. Denbigh's singular notions.

Captain Digby had left Jarvis at an inn, about half a mile from the rectory, for the convenience of receiving early information of the result of his conference. The young man had walked up and down the room during Digby's absence, in a train of reflections entirely new to him. He was the only son of his aged father and mother, the protector of his sisters, and, he might say, the sole hope of a rising family; and then, possibly, Denbigh might not have meant to offend him--he might even have been engaged before they came to the house; or if not, it might have been inadvertence on the part of Miss Moseley. That Denbigh would offer some explanation he believed, and he had fully made up his mind to accept it, let it be what it might, as his fighting friend entered.

"Well," said Jarvis, in a tone that denoted anything but a consciousness that all *was* well.

"He says he will not meet you," dryly exclaimed his friend, throwing himself into a chair, and ordering a glass of brandy and water.

"Not meet me!" exclaimed Jarvis, in surprise. "Engaged, perhaps?"

"Engaged to his d--d conscience."

"To his conscience! I do not know whether I rightly understand you, Captain Digby," said Jarvis, catching his breath, and raising his voice a very little.

"Then, Captain Jarvis," said his friend, tossing off his brandy, and speaking with great deliberation, "he says that nothing--understand me-- *nothing* will ever make him fight a duel."

"He will not!" cried Jarvis, in a loud voice.

"No, he will not," said Digby, handing his glass to the waiter for a fresh supply.

"He shall, by----!"

"I don't know how you will make him."

"Make him! I'll--I'll post him."

"Never do that," said the captain, turning to him, as he leaned his elbows on the table. "It only makes both parties ridiculous. But I'll tell you what you may do. There's a Lord Chatterton who takes the matter up with warmth. If I were not afraid of his interests hurting my promotion, I should have resented something that fell from him myself. He will fight, I dare say, and I'll just return and require an explanation of his words on your behalf."

"No, no," said Jarvis, rather hastily; "he--*he* is related to the Moseleys, and I have views there it might injure."

"Did you think to forward your views by making the young lady the subject of a duel?" asked Captain Digby sarcastically, and eyeing his companion with contempt.

"Yes, yes," said Jarvis; "it would certainly hurt my views."

"Here's to the health of His Majesty's gallant ---- regiment of foot!" cried Captain Digby, in a tone of irony, when three-quarters drunk, at the mess-table, that evening, "and to its champion, Captain Henry Jarvis!"

One of the corps was present accidentally as a guest; and the following week, the inhabitants of F---- saw the regiment in their barracks, marching to slow time after the body of Horace Digby.

Lord Chatterton, in relating the part of the foregoing circumstances which fell under his observation, did ample justice to the conduct of Denbigh; a degree of liberality which did him no little credit, as he plainly saw in that gentleman he had, or soon would have, a rival in the dearest wish of his heart; and the smiling approbation with which his cousin Emily rewarded him for his candor almost sickened him with apprehension. The ladies were not slow in expressing their disgust at the conduct of Jarvis, or backward in their approval of Denbigh's forbearance. Lady Moseley turned with horror from a picture in which she could see nothing but murder and bloodshed; but both Mrs. Wilson and her niece secretly applauded a sacrifice of worldly feelings on the altar of duty; the former admiring the consistent refusal of admitting any collateral inducements, in explanation of his decision: the latter, while she saw the act in its true colors, could hardly help believing that a regard for *her* feelings had, in a trifling degree, its influence in inducing him to decline the meeting. Mrs. Wilson saw at once what a hold such unusual conduct would take on the feelings of her niece, and inwardly determined to increase, if possible, the watchfulness she had invariably observed on all he said or did, as likely to elucidate his real character, well knowing that the requisites to bring or to keep happiness in the married state were numerous and indispensable; and that the display of a particular excellence, however good in itself, was by no means conclusive as to character; in short, that we perhaps as often meet with a favorite principle as with a besetting sin.

Chapter XIV

Sir Edward Moseley had some difficulty in restraining the impetuosity of his son, who was disposed to resent this impertinent interference of young Jarvis with the conduct of his favorite sister; indeed, the young man only yielded to his profound respect to his father's commands, aided by a strong representation on the part of his sister of the disagreeable consequences of connecting her name with such a quarrel. It was seldom the good baronet felt himself called on to act as decidedly as on the present occasion. He spoke to the merchant in warm, but gentleman-like terms, of the consequences which might have resulted to his own child from the intemperate act of his son; exculpated Emily entirely from censure, by explaining her engagement to dance with Denbigh, previously to Captain Jarvis's application; and hinted the necessity, if the affair was not amicably terminated, of protecting the peace of mind of his daughters against any similar exposures, by declining the acquaintance of a neighbor he respected as much as Mr. Jarvis.

The merchant was a man of few words, but of great promptitude. He had made his fortune, and more than once saved it, by his decision; and assuring the baronet he should hear no more of it, he took his hat and hurried home from the village, where the conversation passed. On arriving at his own house, he found the family collected in the parlor for a morning ride, and throwing himself into a chair, he broke out on the whole party with great violence.

"So, Mrs. Jarvis," he cried, "you *would* spoil a very tolerable book-keeper, by wishing to have a soldier in your family; and there stands the puppy who would have blown out the brains of a deserving young man, if the good sense of Mr. Denbigh had not denied him the opportunity."

"Mercy!" cried the alarmed matron, on whom Newgate (for her early life had been passed near its walls), with all its horrors, floated, and a contemplation of its punishments had been her juvenile lessons of morality- -"Harry! Harry! would you commit murder?"

"Murder!" echoed her son, looking askance, as if dodging the bailiffs. "No, mother; I wanted nothing but what was fair. Mr. Denbigh would have had an equal chance to blow out my brains; I am sure everything would have been fair."

"Equal chance!" muttered his father, who had cooled himself, in some measure, by an extra pinch of snuff. "No, sir, you have no brains to lose. But I have promised Sir Edward that you shall make proper apologies to himself, to his daughter, and to Mr. Denbigh." This was rather exceeding the truth, but the alderman prided himself on performing rather more than he promised.

"Apology!" exclaimed the captain. "Why, sir, the apology is due to me. Ask Colonel Egerton if he ever heard of apologies being made by the challenger."

"No, sure," said the mother, who, having made out the truth of the matter, thought it was likely enough to be creditable to her child; "Colonel Egerton never heard of such a thing. Did you, colonel?"

"Why, madam," said the colonel, hesitatingly, and politely handing the merchant his snuff-box, which, in his agitation, had fallen on the floor, "circumstances sometimes justify a departure from ordinary measures. You are certainly right as a rule; but not knowing the particulars in the present case, it is difficult for me to decide. Miss Jarvis, the tilbury is ready."

The colonel bowed respectfully to the merchant, kissed his hand to his wife, and led their daughter to his carriage.

"Do you make the apologies?" asked Mr. Jarvis, as the door closed.

"No, sir," replied the captain, sullenly.

"Then you must make your pay answer for the next six months," cried the father, taking a signed draft on his banker from his pocket, coolly tearing it in two pieces, carefully putting the name in his mouth, and chewing it into a ball.

"Why, alderman," said his wife (a name she never used unless she had something to gain from her spouse, who loved to hear the appellation after he had relinquished the office), "it appears to me that Harry has shown nothing but a proper spirit. You are unkind--indeed you are."

"A proper spirit? In what way? Do you know anything of the matter?"

"It is a proper spirit for a soldier to fight, I suppose," said the wife, a little at a loss to explain.

"Spirit, or no spirit, apology, or ten and sixpence."

"Harry," said his mother, holding up her finger in a menacing attitude, as soon as her husband had left the room (for he had last spoken with the door in his hand), "if you *do* beg his pardon, you are no son of mine."

"No," cried Miss Sarah, "nor any brother of mine. It would be insufferably mean."

"Who will pay my debts?" asked the son, looking up at the ceiling.

"Why, I would, my child, if--if--I had not spent my own allowance."

"I would," echoed the sister; "but if we go to Bath, you know, I shall want all my money."

"Who will pay my debts?" repeated the son.

"Apology, indeed! Who is he, that you, a son of Alderman--of--Mr. Jarvis, of the deanery, B----, North 'amptonshire, should beg his pardon--a vagrant that nobody knows!"

"Who will pay my debts?" again inquired the captain drumming with his foot.

"Harry," exclaimed the mother, "do you love money better than honor--a soldier's honor?"

"No, mother; but I like good eating and drinking. Think mother; it's a cool five hundred, and that's a famous deal of money."

"Harry," cried the mother, in a rage, "you are not fit for a soldier. I wish I were in your place."

"I wish, with all my heart, you had been for an hour this morning," thought the son. After arguing for some time longer, they compromised, by agreeing to leave it to the decision of Colonel Egerton, who, the mother did not doubt, would applaud her maintaining the Jarvis dignity, a family in which he took quite as much interest as he felt for his own--so he had told her fifty times. The captain, however, determined within himself to touch the five hundred, let the colonel decide as he might; but the colonel's decision obviated all difficulties. The question was put to him by Mrs. Jarvis, on his return from the airing, with no doubt the decision would be favorable to her opinion. The colonel and herself, she said, never disagreed; and the lady was right--for wherever his interest made it desirable to convert Mrs. Jarvis to his side of the question, Egerton had a manner of doing it that never failed to succeed.

"Why, madam," said he, with one of his most agreeable smiles, "apologies are different things, at different times. You are certainly right in your sentiments, as relates to a proper spirit in a soldier; but no one can doubt the spirit of the captain, after the stand he took in this affair; if Mr. Denbigh would not meet him (a very extraordinary measure, in deed, I confess), what can your son do more? He cannot *make* a man fight against his will, you know."

"True, true," cried the matron, impatiently, "I do not want him to fight; heaven forbid! but why should he, the challenger, beg pardon? I am sure, to have the thing regular, Mr. Denbigh is the one to ask forgiveness."

The colonel felt at a little loss how to reply, when Jarvis, in whom the thoughts of the five hundred pounds had worked a revolution, exclaimed--

"You know, mother, I accused him--that is, I suspected him of dancing with Miss Moseley against my right to her; now you find that it was all a mistake, and so I had better act with dignity, and confess my error."

"Oh, by all means," cried the colonel, who saw the danger of an embarrassing rupture between the families, otherwise: "delicacy to *your* sex particularly requires that, ma'am, from your son;" and he accidentally dropped a letter as he spoke.

"From Sir Edgar, colonel?" asked Mrs. Jarvis, as he stooped to pick it up.

"From Sir Edgar, ma'am, and he begs to be remembered to yourself and all of your amiable family."

Mrs. Jarvis inclined her body, in what she intended for a graceful bend, and sighed--a casual observer might have thought, with maternal anxiety for the reputation of her child--but it was conjugal regret, that the political obstinacy of the alderman had prevented his carrying up an address, and thus becoming Sir Timothy. Sir Edgar's heir prevailed, and the captain received permission to do what he had done several hours before.

On leaving the room, after the first discussion, and before the appeal, the captain had hastened to his father with his concessions. The old gentleman knew too well the influence of five hundred pounds to doubt the effect in the present instance, and he had ordered his carriage for the excursion. It came, and to the hall they proceeded. The captain found his intended antagonist, and in a rather uncouth manner, he made the required concession. He was restored to his former favor--no great distinction--and his visits to the hall were suffered, but with a dislike Emily could never conquer, nor at all times conceal.

Denbigh was occupied with a book, when Jarvis commenced his speech to the baronet and his daughter, and was apparently too much engaged with its contents, to understand what was going on, as the captain blundered through. It was necessary, the captain saw by a glance of his father's eyes, to say something to that gentleman, who had delicately withdrawn to a distant window. His speech was consequently made here too, and Mrs. Wilson could not avoid stealing a look at them. Denbigh smiled, and bowed in silence. It is enough, thought the widow; the offence was not against him, it was against his Maker; he should not arrogate to himself, in any manner, the right to forgive, or to require apologies--the whole is consistent. The subject was never afterwards alluded to: Denbigh appeared to have forgotten it; and Jane sighed gently, as she devoutly hoped the colonel was not a duellist.

Several days passed before the deanery ladies could sufficiently forgive the indignity their family had sustained, to resume the customary intercourse. Like all other grievances, where the passions are chiefly interested, it was forgotten in time, however, and things were put in some measure on their former footing. The death of Digby served to increase the horror of the Moseleys, and Jarvis himself felt rather uncomfortable, on more accounts than one, at the fatal termination of the unpleasant business.

Chatterton, who to his friends had not hesitated to avow his attachment to his cousin, but who had never proposed for her, as his present views and fortune were not, in his estimation, sufficient for her proper support, had pushed every interest he possessed, and left no steps unattempted an honorable man could resort to, to effect his object. The desire to provide for his sisters had been backed by the ardor of a passion that had reached its crisis; and the young peer who could not, in the present state of things, abandon the field to a rival so formidable as Denbigh, even to further his views to preferment, was waiting in anxious suspense the decision on his application. A letter from his friend informed him, his opponent was likely to succeed; that, in short, all hopes of success had left him. Chatterton was in despair. On the following day, however, he received a second letter from the same friend, unexpectedly announcing his appointment. After mentioning the fact, he went on to say--"The cause of this sudden revolution in your favor is unknown to me, and unless your lordship has obtained interest I am ignorant of, it is one of the most singular instances of ministerial caprice I have ever known." Chatterton was as much at a loss as his friend, to understand the affair; but it mattered not; he could now offer to Emily--it was a patent office of great value, and a few years would amply portion his sisters. That very day, therefore, he proposed, and was refused.

Emily had a difficult task to avoid self-reproach, in regulating her deportment on this occasion. She was fond of Chatterton as a relation--as her brother's friend--as the brother of Grace, and even on his own account; but it was the fondness of a sister. His manner--his words, which, although never addressed to herself, were sometimes overheard unintentionally, and sometimes reached her through her sisters, had left her in no doubt of his attachment; she was excessively grieved at the discovery, and had innocently appealed to her aunt for directions how to proceed. Of his intentions she had no doubt, but at the same time he had not put her in a situation to dispel his hopes; as to encouragement, in the usual meaning of the term, she gave none to him, nor to any one else. There are no little attentions that lovers are fond of showing to their mistresses, and which mistresses are fond of receiving, that Emily ever permitted to any gentleman--no rides--no walks--no tête-à-têtes. Always natural and unaffected, there was a simple dignity about her that forbade the request, almost the thought, in the gentlemen of her acquaintance: she had no amusements, no pleasures of any kind in which her sisters were not her companions; and if anything was on the carpet that required an attendant, John was ever ready. He was devoted to her; the decided preference she gave him over every other man, upon such occasions, flattered his affection; and he would, at any time, leave even Grace Chatterton to attend his sister. All this too was without affectation, and generally without notice. Emily so looked the delicacy and reserve she acted with so little ostentation that not even her own sex had affixed to her conduct the epithet of squeamish; it was difficult, therefore, for her to do anything which would show Lord Chatterton her disinclination to his suit, without assuming a dislike she did not feel, or giving him slights that neither good breeding nor good nature could justify. At one time, indeed, she had expressed a wish to return to Clara; but this Mrs. Wilson thought would only protract the evil, and she was compelled to wait his own time. The peer himself did not rejoice more in his ability to make the offer, therefore, than Emily did to have it in her power to decline it. Her rejection was firm and unqualified, but uttered with a grace and a tenderness to his feelings, that bound her lover tighter than ever in her chains, and he resolved on immediate flight as his only recourse.

"I hope nothing unpleasant has occurred to Lord Chatterton," said Denbigh, with great interest, as he reached the spot where the young peer stood leaning his head against a tree, on his way from the rectory to the hall.

Chatterton raised his face as he spoke: there were evident traces of tears on it, and Denbigh, greatly shocked, was about to proceed as the other caught his arm.

"Mr. Denbigh," said the young man, in a voice almost choked with emotion, "may you never know the pain I have felt this morning. Emily--Emily Moseley--is lost to me--for ever."

For a moment the blood rushed to the face of Denbigh, and his eyes flashed with a look that Chatterton could not stand. He turned, as the voice of Denbigh, in those remarkable tones which distinguished it from every other voice he had ever heard, uttered--

"Chatterton, my lord, we are friends, I hope--I wish it; from my heart."

"Go, Mr. Denbigh--go. You were going to Miss Moseley--do not let me detain you." "I am going with *you*, Lord Chatterton, unless you forbid it," said Denbigh, with emphasis, slipping his arm through that of the peer.

For two hours they walked together in the park; and when they appeared at dinner, Emily wondered why Mr. Denbigh had taken a seat next to her mother, instead of his usual place between herself and her aunt. In the evening, he announced his intention of leaving B---- for a short time with Lord Chatterton. They were going to London together; but he hoped to return within ten days. This sudden determination caused some surprise; but, as the dowager supposed it was to secure the new situation, and the remainder of their friends thought it might be business, it was soon forgotten, though much regretted for the time. The gentlemen left the hall that night to proceed to an inn, from which they could obtain a chaise and horses; and the following morning, when the baronet's family assembled around their social breakfast, they were many miles on the road to the metropolis.

Chapter XV

Lady Chatterton, finding that little was to be expected in her present situation, excepting what she looked forward to from the varying admiration of John Moseley to her youngest daughter, determined to accept an invitation of some standing to a nobleman's seat about fifty miles from the hall, and, in order to keep things in their proper places, to leave Grace with her friends, who had expressed a wish to that effect. Accordingly, the day succeeding the departure of her son, she proceeded on her expedition, accompanied by her willing assistant in the matrimonial speculations.

Grace Chatterton was by nature retiring and delicate; but her feelings were acute, and on the subject of female propriety sensitive to a degree, that the great want of it in a relation she loved as much as her mother had possibly in some measure increased. Her affections were too single in their objects to have left her long in doubt as to their nature with respect to the baronet's son; and it was one of the most painful orders she had ever received, that which compelled her to accept her cousin's invitation. Her mother was peremptory, however, and Grace was obliged to comply. Every delicate feeling she possessed revolted at the step: the visit itself was unwished for on her part; but there did exist a reason which had reconciled her to that--the wedding of Clara. But now to remain, after all her family had gone, in the house where resided the man who had as yet never solicited those affections she had been unable to withhold, it was humiliating--it was degrading her in her own esteem, and she could scarcely endure it.

It is said that women are fertile in inventions to further their schemes of personal gratification, vanity, or even mischief. It may be it is true; but the writer of these pages is a man--one who has seen much of the other sex, and he is happy to have an opportunity of paying a tribute to female purity and female truth. That there are hearts so disinterested as to lose the considerations of self, in advancing the happiness of those they love; that there are minds so pure as to recoil with disgust from the admission of deception, indelicacy, or management, he knows; for he has seen it from long and close examination. He regrets that the very artlessness of those who are most pure in the one sex, subjects them to the suspicions of the grosser materials which compose the other. He believes that innocency, singleness of heart, ardency of feeling, and unalloyed, shrinking delicacy, sometimes exist in the female bosom, to an extent that but few men are happy enough to discover, and that most men believe incompatible with the frailties of human nature. Grace Chatterton possessed no little of what may almost be called this ethereal spirit and a visit to Bolton parsonage was immediately proposed by her to Emily. The latter, too innocent herself to suspect the motives of her cousin, was happy to be allowed to devote a fortnight to Clara, uninterrupted by the noisy round of visiting and congratulations which had attended her first week; and Mrs. Wilson and the two girls left the hall the same day with the Dowager Lady Chatterton. Francis and Clara were happy to receive them, and they were immediately domesticated in their new abode. Doctor Ives and his wife had postponed an annual visit to a relation of the former on account of the marriage of their son, and they now availed themselves of this visit to perform their own engagement. B---- appeared in some measure deserted, and Egerton had the field almost to himself. Summer had arrived, and the country bloomed in all its luxuriance of vegetation: everything was propitious to the indulgence of the softer passions; and Lady Moseley, ever a strict adherent to forms and decorum, admitted the intercourse between Jane and her admirer to be carried to as great lengths as those forms would justify. Still the colonel was not explicit; and Jane, whose delicacy dreaded the exposure of feelings that was involved in his declaration, gave or sought no marked opportunities for the avowal of his passion. Yet they were seldom separate, and both Sir Edward and his wife looked forward to their future union as a thing not to be doubted. Lady Moseley had given up her youngest child so absolutely to the government of her aunt, that she seldom thought of her future establishment. She had that kind of reposing confidence in Mrs. Wilson's proceedings that feeble minds ever bestow on those who are much superior to them; and she even approved of a system in many respects which she could not endeavor to imitate. Her affection for Emily was not, however, less than what she felt for her other children: she was, in fact, her favorite, and, had the discipline of Mrs. Wilson admitted of so weak an interference, might have been injured as such.

John Moseley had been able to find out exactly the hour they breakfasted at the deanery, the length of time it took Egerton's horses to go the distance between that house and the hall; and on the sixth morning after the departure of his aunt, John's bays were in his phaeton, and allowing ten minutes for the mile and a half to the park gates, John had got happily off his own territories, before he met the tilbury travelling eastward. I am not to know which road the colonel may turn, thought John: and after a few friendly, but rather hasty greetings, the bays were again in full trot to the parsonage.

"John," said Emily, holding out her hand affectionately, and smiling a little archly, as he approached the window where she stood, "you should take a lesson in driving from Frank; you have turned more than one hair, I believe."

"How is Clara?" cried John, hastily, taking the offered hand, with a kiss, "aye, and aunt Wilson?"

"Both well, brother, and out walking this fine morning."

"How happens it you are not with them?" inquired the brother, throwing his eyes round the room. "Have they left you alone?"

"No Grace has this moment left me."

"Well, Emily," said John, taking his seat very composedly, but keeping his eyes on the door, "I have come to dine with you. I thought I owed Clara a visit, and have managed nicely to give the colonel the go-by."

"Clara will be happy to see you, dear John, and so will aunt, and so am I"--as she drew aside his fine hair with her fingers to cool his forehead.

"And why not Grace, too?" asked John, with a look of a little alarm.

"And Grace, too, I fancy--but here she is, to answer for herself."

Grace said little on her entrance, but her eyes were brighter than usual, and she looked so contented and happy that Emily observed to her, in an affectionate manner--

"I knew the eau-de-Cologne would do your head good."

"Is Miss Chatterton unwell?" asked John, with a look of interest.

"A slight headache," said Grace, faintly, "but I feel much better."

"Want of air and exercise: my horses are at the door; phaeton will hold three easily; run, sister, for your hat," almost pushing Emily out of the room as he spoke. In a few minutes the horses might have been suffering for air, but surely not for exercise.

"I wish," cried John, with impatience, when at the distance of a couple of miles from the parsonage, "that gentleman had driven his gig out of the road."

There was a small group on one side of the road, consisting of a man, a woman, and several children. The owner of the gig had alighted, and was in the act of speaking to them, as the phaeton approached at a great rate.

"John," cried Emily, in terror, "You never can pass--you will upset us."

"There is no danger, dear Grace," said the brother, endeavoring to check his horses; he succeeded in part, but not so as to prevent his passing at a spot where the road was very narrow; a wheel hit violently against a stone, and some of his works gave way. The gentleman immediately hastened to his assistance--it was Denbigh.

"Miss Moseley!" cried he, in a voice of the tenderest interest "you are not hurt in the least, I hope."

"No," said Emily, recovering her breath, "only frightened;" and taking his hand, she sprang from the carriage.

Miss Chatterton found courage to wait quietly for the care of John. His "dear Grace," had thrilled on every nerve, and she afterwards often laughed at Emily for her terror when there was so little danger. The horses were not in the least frightened, and after a little mending, John declared all was safe. To ask Emily to enter, the carriage again, was to exact no little sacrifice of her feelings to her reason; and she stood in a suspense that too plainly showed that, the terror she had been in had not left her.

"If," said Denbigh, modestly, "if Mr. Moseley will take the ladies in my gig, I will drive the phaeton to the hall, as it is rather unsafe for so heavy a load."

"No, no, Denbigh," said John, coolly, "you are not used to such mettled nags as mine--it would be indiscreet for you to drive them: if, however, you will be good enough to take Emily into your gig--Grace Chatterton, I am sure, is not afraid to trust my driving, and we might all get back as well as ever."

Grace gave her hand almost unconsciously to John, and he handed her into the phaeton, as Denbigh stood willing to execute his part of the arrangement, but too diffident to speak. It was not a moment for affectation, if Emily had been capable of it, and blushing with the novelty of her situation, she took her place in the gig. Denbigh stopped and turned his eyes on the little group with which he had been talking, and at that moment they caught the attention of John also. The latter inquired after their situation. The tale was a piteous one, the distress evidently real. The husband had been gardener to a gentleman in a neighboring county, and he had been lately discharged, to make way, in the difficulty of the times, for a relation of the steward, who was in want of the place. Suddenly thrown on the world, with a wife and four children, with but the wages of a week for his and their support, they had travelled thus far on the way to a neighboring parish, where he said he had a right to, and must seek, public assistance. The children were crying for hunger, and the mother, who was a nurse, had been unable to walk further than where she sat, but had sunk on the ground overcome with fatigue, and weak from the want of nourishment. Neither Emily nor Grace could refrain from tears at the recital of these heavy woes; the want of sustenance was something so shocking in itself, and brought, as it were, immediately before their eyes, the appeal was irresistible. John forgot his bays--forgot even Grace, as he listened to the affecting story related by the woman, who was much revived by some nutriment Denbigh had obtained from a cottage near them, and to which they were about to proceed by his directions, as Moseley interrupted them. His hand shook, his eyes glistened as he took his purse from his pocket, and gave several guineas from it to the mendicant. Grace thought John had never appeared so handsome as the moment he handed the money to the gardener; his face glowed with unusual excitement, and his symmetry had lost the only charm he wanted in common, softness. Denbigh, after waiting patiently until Moseley had bestowed his alms, gravely repeated his directions for their proceeding to the cottage, when the carriages moved on.

Emily revolved, in her mind, during their short ride, the horrid distress she had witnessed. It had taken a strong hold on her feelings. Like her brother, she was warm-hearted and compassionate, if we may use the term, to excess; and had she been prepared with the means, the gardener would have reaped a double harvest of donations. It struck her, at the moment, unpleasantly, that Denbigh had been so backward in his liberality. The man had rather sullenly displayed half a crown as his gift, in contrast with the golden shower of John's generosity. It had been even somewhat offensive in its exhibition, and urged her brother to a more hasty departure than, under other circumstances, he would just at the moment have felt disposed to make. Denbigh, however, had taken no notice of the indignity, and continued his directions in the same mild and benevolent manner he had used during the whole interview. Half a crown was but little, thought Emily, for a family that was starving; and, unwilling to judge harshly of one she had begun to value so highly, she came to the painful conclusion, her companion was not as rich as he deserved to be. Emily had not yet to learn that charity was in proportion to the means of the donor, and a gentle wish insensibly stole over her that Denbigh might in some way become more richly endowed with the good things of this world. Until this moment her thoughts had never turned to his temporal condition. She knew he was an officer in the army, but of what rank, or even of what regiment, she was ignorant. He had frequently touched in his conversations on the customs of the different countries he had seen. He had served in Italy, in the north of Europe, in the West Indies, in Spain. Of the manners of the people, of their characters, he not unfrequently spoke, and with a degree of intelligence, a liberality, a justness of discrimination, that had charmed his auditors; but on the point of personal service he had maintained a silence that was inflexible, and not a little surprising--more particularly of that part of his history which related to the latter country; from all which she was rather inclined to think his military rank was not as high as she thought he merited, and that possibly he felt an awkwardness of putting it in contrast with the more elevated station of Colonel Egerton. The same idea had struck the whole family, and prevented any inquiries which might be painful. He was so connected with the mournful event of his father's death, that no questions could be put with propriety to the doctor's family; and if Francis had been more communicative to Clara, she was too good a wife to mention it, and her own family was possessed of too just a sense of propriety to touch upon points that might bring her conjugal fidelity in question.

Though Denbigh appeared a little abstracted during the ride, his questions concerning Sir Edward and her friends were kind and affectionate. As they approached the house he suffered his horse to walk, and, after some hesitation, he took a letter from his pocket, and handing it to her, said--

"I hope Miss Moseley will not think me impertinent in becoming the bearer of a letter from her cousin, Lord Chatterton. He requested it so earnestly, that I could not refuse taking what I am sensible is a great liberty; for it would be deception did I affect to be ignorant of his admiration, or of his generous treatment of a passion she cannot return. Chatterton," and he smiled mournfully, "is yet too true to cease his commendations."

Emily blushed painfully, but she took the letter in silence; and as Denbigh pursued the topic no further, the little distance they had to go was ridden in silence. On entering the gates, however, he said, inquiringly, and with much interest--

"I sincerely hope I have not given offence to your delicacy, Miss Moseley. Lord Chatterton has made me an unwilling confidant. I need not say the secret is sacred, on more accounts than one."

"Surely not, Mr. Denbigh," replied Emily, in a low tone; and the gig stopping, she hastened to accept the assistance of her brother to alight.

"Well, sister," cried John, laughing, "Denbigh is a disciple to Frank's system of horse-flesh. Hairs smooth enough here, I see. Grace and I thought you would never get home." Now, John fibbed a little, for neither Grace nor he had thought in the least about them, or anything else but each other, from the moment they separated until the gig arrived.

Emily made no reply to this speech, and as the gentlemen were engaged in giving directions concerning their horses, she seized an opportunity to read Chatterton's letter.

"I avail myself of the return of my friend Mr. Denbigh to that happy family from which reason requires my self-banishment to assure my amiable cousin, of my continued respect for her character, and to convince her of my gratitude for the tenderness she has manifested to feelings she cannot return. I may even venture to tell her what few women would be pleased to hear, but what I know Emily Moseley too well to doubt, for a moment, will give her unalloyed pleasure--that owing to the kind, the benevolent, the brotherly attentions of my true friend, Mr. Denbigh, I have already gained a peace of mind and resignation I once thought was lost to me for ever. Ah! Emily, my beloved cousin, in Denbigh you will find, I doubt not, a mind, principles, congenial to your own. It is impossible that he could see you without wishing to possess such a treasure; and, if I have a wish that is now uppermost in my heart, it is, that you may learn to esteem each other as you ought, when, I doubt not, you will become as happy as you both deserve to be. What greater earthly blessing can I implore upon you!

"Chatterton."

Emily, while reading this epistle, felt a confusion but little inferior to that which would have oppressed her had Denbigh himself been at her feet, soliciting that love Chatterton thought him so worthy of possessing; and when they met, she could hardly look in the face a man who, it would seem, had been so openly selected by another, as the fittest to be her partner for life. The unaltered manner of Denbigh himself, however, soon convinced her that he was entirely ignorant of the contents of the note, and it greatly relieved her from the awkwardness his presence at first occasioned.

Francis soon returned, accompanied by his wife and aunt, and was overjoyed to find the guest who had so unexpectedly arrived. His parents had not yet returned from their visit, and Denbigh, of course, would remain at his present quarters. John promised to continue with them for a couple of days: and everything was soon settled to the perfect satisfaction of the whole party. Mrs. Wilson knew the great danger of suffering young people to be inmates of the same house too well, wantonly to incur the penalties, but her visit had nearly expired, and it might give her a better opportunity of judging Denbigh's character; and Grace Chatterton, though too delicate to follow herself, was well contented to be followed, especially when John Moseley was the pursuer.

Chapter XVI

"I am sorry, aunt, Mr. Denbigh is not rich," said Emily to Mrs. Wilson, after they had retired in the evening, almost unconscious of what she uttered. The latter looked at her niece in surprise, at a remark so abrupt, and one so very different from the ordinary train of Emily's reflections, as she required an explanation. Emily, slightly coloring at the channel her thoughts had insensibly strayed into, gave her aunt an account of their adventure in the course of the morning's drive, and touched lightly on the difference in the amount of the alms of her brother and those of Mr. Denbigh.

"The bestowal of money is not always an act of charity," observed Mrs. Wilson, gravely, and the subject was dropped: though neither ceased to dwell on it in her thoughts, until sleep closed the eyes of both.

The following day Mrs. Wilson invited Grace and Emily to accompany her in a walk; the gentlemen having preceded them in pursuit of their different avocations. Francis had his regular visits of spiritual consolation; John had gone to the hall for his pointers and fowling-piece, the season for woodcock having arrived; and Denbigh had proceeded no one knew whither. On gaining the high-road, Mrs. Wilson desired her companions to lead the way to the cottage where the family of the mendicant gardener had been lodged, and thither they soon arrived. On knocking at the door, they were immediately admitted to an outer room; in which they found the wife of the laborer who inhabited the building, engaged in her customary morning employments. They explained the motives of the visit, and were told that the family they sought were in an adjoining room, but she rather thought at that moment engaged with a clergyman who had called a quarter of an hour before. "I expect, my lady, it's the new rector, who everybody says is so good to the poor and needy; but I have not found time yet to go to church to hear his reverence preach, ma'am," courtseying and handing the fresh dusted chairs to her unexpected visitors. The ladies seated themselves, too delicate to interrupt Francis in his sacred duties, and were silently waiting his appearance, when a voice was distinctly heard through the thin partition, the first note of which undeceived them as to the character of the gardener's visitor.

"It appears then, Davis, by your own confession," said Denbigh, mildly, but in a tone of reproof, "that your frequent acts of intemperance have at least given ground for the steward's procuring your discharge if it has not justified him in doing that which his duty to your common employer required."

"It is hard, sir," replied the man sullenly, "to be thrown on the world with a family like mine, to make way for a younger man with but one child."

"It may be unfortunate for your wife and children," said Denbigh, "but just, as respects yourself. I have already convinced you, that my interference or reproof is not an empty one: carry the letter to the person to whom it is directed, and I pledge you, you shall have a new trial; and should you conduct yourself soberly, and with propriety, continued and ample support; the second letter will gain you children immediate admission to the school I mentioned; and I now leave you, with an earnest injunction to remember that habits of intemperance not only disqualify you to support those who have such great claims on your protection, but inevitably lead to a loss of those powers which are necessary to insure your own eternal welfare."

"May Heaven bless your honor," cried the woman, with fervor, and evidently in tears, "both for what you have said, and what you have done. Thomas only wants to be taken from temptation, to become a sober man again--an honest one he has ever been, I am sure."

"I have selected a place for him," replied Denbigh "where there is no exposure through improper companions, and everything now depends upon himself, under Providence."

Mrs. Wilson had risen from her chair on the first intimation given by Denbigh of his intention to go, but had paused at the door to listen to this last speech; when beckoning her companions, she hastily withdrew, having first made a small present to the woman of the cottage, and requested her not to mention their having called.

"What becomes now of the comparative charity of your brother and Mr. Denbigh, Emily?" asked Mrs. Wilson, as they gained the road on their return homewards. Emily was not accustomed to hear any act of John slightly spoken of without at least manifesting some emotion, which betrayed her sisterly regard; but on the present occasion she chose to be silent; while Grace, after waiting in expectation that her cousin would speak, ventured to say timidly--

"I am sure, dear madam, Mr. Moseley was very liberal and the tears were in his eyes while he gave the money. I was looking directly at them the whole time."

"John is compassionate by nature," continued Mrs. Wilson with an almost imperceptible smile. "I have no doubt his sympathies were warmly enlisted in behalf of this family and possessing much, he gave liberally. I have no doubt he would have undergone personal privation to have relieved their distress, and endured both pain and labor, with such an excitement before him. But what is all that to the charity of Mr. Denbigh?"

Grace was unused to contend, and, least of all, with Mrs. Wilson; but, unwilling to abandon John to such censure, with increased animation, she said--

"If bestowing freely, and feeling for the distress you relieve, be not commendable, madam, I am sure I am ignorant what is."

"That compassion for the woes of others is beautiful in itself, and the want of it an invariable evidence of corruption from too much, and an ill-governed intercourse with the world, I am willing to acknowledge, my dear Grace," said Mrs. Wilson, kindly; "but the relief of misery, where the heart has not undergone this hardening ordeal, is only a relief to our own feelings: this is compassion; but Christian charity is a higher order of duty: it enters into every sensation of the heart; disposes us to judge, as well as to act, favorably to our fellow creatures; is deeply seated in the sense of our own unworthiness; keeps a single eye, in its dispensations of temporal benefits, to the everlasting happiness of the objects of its bounty; is consistent, well regulated; in short,"--and Mrs. Wilson's pale cheek glowed with an unusual richness of color--"it is an humble attempt to copy after the heavenly example of our Redeemer, in sacrificing ourselves to the welfare of others, and does and must proceed from a love of his person, and an obedience to his mandates."

"And Mr. Denbigh, aunt," exclaimed Emily, the blood mantling to her cheeks with a sympathetic glow, while she lost all consideration for John in the strength of her feelings, "his charity you think to be of this description?"

"So far, my child, as we can understand motives from the nature of the conduct, such appears to have been the charity of Mr. Denbigh."

Grace was silenced, if not convinced; and the ladies continued their walk, lost in their own reflections, until they reached a bend in the road which hid the cottage from view. Emily involuntarily turned her head as they arrived at the spot, and saw that Denbigh had approached within a few paces of them. On joining them, he commenced his complimentary address in such a way as convinced them the cottager had been true to the injunction given by Mrs. Wilson. No mention was made of the gardener, and Denbigh began a lively description of some foreign scenery, of which their present situation reminded him. The discourse was maintained with great interest by himself and Mrs. Wilson for the remainder of their walk.

It was yet early when they reached the parsonage, where they found John, who had driven to the hall to breakfast, and who, instead of pursuing his favorite amusement of shooting, laid down his gun as they entered, observing, "It is rather soon yet for the woodcocks, and I believe I will listen to your entertaining conversation, ladies, for the remainder of the morning." He threw himself upon a sofa at no great distance from Grace, and in such a position as enabled him, without rudeness, to study the features of her lovely face, while Denbigh read aloud to the ladies Campbell's beautiful description of wedded love, in Gertrude of Wyoming.

There was a chastened correctness in the ordinary manner of Denbigh which wore the appearance of the influence of his reason, and a subjection of the passions, that, if anything, gave him less interest with Emily than had it been marked by an evidence of stronger feeling. But on the present occasion, this objection was removed: his reading was impressive; he dwelt on those passages which most pleased him with a warmth of eulogium fully equal to her own undisguised sensations. In the hour occupied in the reading this exquisite little poem, and in commenting on its merits and sentiments, Denbigh gained more on her imagination than in all their former intercourse. His ideas were as pure, as chastened, and almost as vivid as those of the poet; and Emily listened to his periods with intense attention, as they flowed from him in language as glowing as his ideas. The poem had been first read to her by her brother, and she was surprised to discover how she had overlooked its beauties on that occasion. Even John acknowledged that it certainly appeared a different thing now from what he had then thought it; but Emily had taxed his declamatory power in the height of the pheasant season, and, somehow or other, John now imagined that Gertrude was just such a delicate, feminine, warm-hearted domestic girl as Grace Chatterton. As Denbigh closed the book, and entered into a general conversation with Clara and her sister, John followed Grace to a window, and speaking in a tone of unusual softness for him, he said--

"Do you know, Miss Chatterton, I have accepted your brother's invitation to go into Suffolk this summer, and that you are to be plagued with me and my pointers again?"

"Plagued, Mr. Moseley!" said Grace, in a voice even softer than his own. "I am sure--I am sure, we none of us think you or your dogs in the least a plague."

"Ah! Grace," and John was about to become what he had never been before--sentimental--- when he saw the carriage of Chatterton, containing the dowager and Catherine entering the parsonage gates.

Pshaw! *thought* John, there comes Mother Chatterton "Ah! Grace," said John, "there are your mother and sister returned already."

"Already!" said the young lady, and, for the first time in her life, she felt rather unlike a dutiful child. Five minutes could have made no great difference to her mother, and she would greatly have liked to hear what John Moseley meant to have said; for the alteration in his manner convinced her that his first "ah! Grace" was to have been continued in a somewhat different language from that in which the second "ah! Grace" was ended.

Young Moseley and her daughter, standing together at the open window, caught the attention of Lady Chatterton the moment she got a view of the house, and she entered with a good humor she had not felt since the disappointment in her late expedition in behalf of Catherine; for the gentleman she had had in view in this excursion had been taken up by another rover, acting on her own account, and backed by a little more wit and a good deal more money than what Kate could be fairly thought to possess. Nothing further in that quarter offering in the way of her occupation, she turned her horses' heads towards London, that great theatre on which there never was a loss for actors. The salutations had hardly passed before, turning to John, she exclaimed, with what she intended for a most motherly smile, "What! not shooting this fine day, Mr. Moseley? I thought you never missed a day in the season."

"It is rather early yet, my lady," said John, coolly, a little alarmed by the expression of her countenance.

"Oh!" continued the dowager, in the same strain, "I see how it is; the ladies have too many attractions for so gallant a young man as yourself." Now, as Grace, her own daughter, was the only lady of the party who could reasonably be supposed to have much influence over John's movements--a young gentleman seldom caring as much for his own as for other people's sisters, this may be fairly set down as a pretty broad hint of the opinion the dowager entertained of the real state of things; and John saw it, and Grace saw it. The former coolly replied, "Why, upon the whole, if you will excuse the neglect, I will try a shot this fine day." In five minutes, Carlo and Rover were both delighted. Grace kept her place at the window, from a feeling she could not define, and of which perhaps she was unconscious, until the gate closed, and the shrubbery hid the sportsman from her sight, and then she withdrew to her room to weep.

Had Grace Chatterton been a particle less delicate--less retiring--blessed with a managing mother, as she was, John Moseley would not have thought another moment about her. But, on every occasion when the dowager made any of her open attacks, Grace discovered so much distress, so much unwillingness to second them, that a suspicion of a confederacy never entered his brain. It is not to be supposed that Lady Chattelton's manoeuvres were limited to the direct and palpable schemes we have mentioned; no--these were the effervescence, the exuberance of her zeal; but as is generally the case, they sufficiently proved the ground-work of all her other machinations; none of the little artifices of such as placing--of leaving alone--of showing similarity of tastes:--of compliments to the gentlemen, were neglected.--This latter business she had contrived to get Catherine to take off her hands; but Grace could never pay a compliment in her life, unless changing of color, trembling, undulations of the bosom, and such natural movements can be so called; but she loved dearly to receive them from John Moseley.

"Well, my child," said the mother, as she seated herself by the side of her daughter, who hastily endeavored to conceal her tears, "when are we to have another wedding? I trust everything is settled between you and Mr. Moseley, by this time."

"Mother! Mother!" said Grace, nearly gasping for breath, "Mother, you will break my heart, indeed you will." She hid her face in the clothes of the bed by which she sat, and wept with a feeling of despair.

"Tut, my dear," replied the dowager, not noticing her anguish, or mistaking it for a girlish shame, "you young people are fools in these matters, but Sir Edward and myself will arrange everything as it should be."

The daughter now not only looked up, but sprang from her seat, her hands clasped together, her eyes fixed in horror, her cheek pale as death; but the mother had retired, and Grace sank back into her chair with a sensation of disgrace, of despair, which could not have been surpassed, had she really merited the obloquy and shame which she thought were about to be heaped upon her.

Chapter XVII

The succeeding morning, the whole party, with, the exception of Denbigh, returned to the hall. Nothing had occurred out of the ordinary course of the colonel's assiduities; and Jane, whose sense of propriety forbad the indulgence of premeditated tête-à-têtes, and such little accompaniments of every-day attachments, was rejoiced to see a sister she loved, and an aunt she respected, once more in the bosom of her family.

The dowager impatiently waited an opportunity to effect, what she intended for a master-stroke of policy in the disposal of Grace. Like all other managers, she thought no one equal to herself in devising ways and means, and was unwilling to leave anything to nature. Grace had invariably thwarted all her schemes by her obstinacy; and as she thought young Moseley really attached to her, she determined by a bold stroke to remove the impediments of false shame, and the dread of repulse, which she believed alone kept the youth from an avowal of his wishes, and get rid at once of a plague that had annoyed her not a little--her daughter's delicacy.

Sir Edward spent an hour every morning in his library, overlooking his accounts, and in other necessary employments of a similar nature, and it was here she determined to have the conference.

"My Lady Chatterton, you do me honor," said the baronet, handing her a chair on her entrance.

"Upon my word, cousin," cried the dowager, "you have a very convenient apartment here," looking around her in affected admiration of all she saw.

The baronet replied, and a short discourse on the arrangements of the whole house insensibly led to some remarks on the taste of his mother, the Honorable Lady Moseley (a Chatterton), until, having warmed the feelings of the old gentleman by some well-timed compliments of that nature, she ventured on the principal object of her visit.

"I am happy to find, Sir Edward, you are so well pleased with the family as to wish to make another selection from it. I sincerely hope it may prove as judicious as the former one."

Sir Edward was a little at a loss to understand her meaning, although he thought it might allude to his son, who he had some time suspected had views on Grace Chatterton; and willing to know the truth, and rather pleased to find John had selected a young woman he loved in his heart, he observed--

"I am not sure I rightly understand your ladyship, though I hope I do."

"No!" cried the dowager, in well-counterfeited affectation of surprise. "Perhaps, after all, maternal anxiety has deceived me, then. Mr. Moseley could hardly have ventured to proceed without your approbation."

"I have ever declined influencing any of my children, Lady Chatterton," said the baronet, "and John is not ignorant of my sentiments. I sincerely hope, however, you allude to an attachment to Grace?"

"I did certainly, Sir Edward," said the lady, hesitatingly. "I may be deceived; but you must understand the feelings of a mother, and a young woman ought not to be trifled with."

"My son is incapable of trifling, I hope," cried Sir Edward; with animation, "and, least of all, with Grace Chatterton. No; you are quite right. If he has made his choice, he should not be ashamed to avow it."

"I would not wish, on any account, to hurry matters," said the dowager; "but the report which is abroad will prevent other young men from putting in their claims, Sir Edward" (sighing). "I have a mother's feelings: if I have been hasty, your goodness will overlook it." And Lady Chatterton placed her handkerchief to her eyes, to conceal the tears that did not flow.

Sir Edward thought all this very natural, and as it should be, and he sought an early conference with his son.

"John," said the father, taking his hand kindly, "you have no reason to doubt my affection or my compliance to your wishes. Fortune is a thing out of the question with a young man of your expectations." And Sir Edward, in his eagerness to smoothe the way, went on: "You can live here, or occupy my small seat in Wiltshire. I can allow you five thousand a year, with much ease to myself. Indeed, your mother and myself would both straighten ourselves, to add to your comforts; but it is unnecessary--we have enough, and you have enough."

Sir Edward, in a few moments, would have settled everything to the dowager's perfect satisfaction, had not John interrupted him by the exclamation of--

"To what do you allude, father?"

"Allude?" said Sir Edward, simply. "Why, Grace Chatterton, my son."

"Grace Chatterton! Sir Edward. What have I to do with Grace Chatterton?"

"Her mother has made me acquainted with your proposals, and"--

"Proposals!"

"Attentions, I ought to have said; and you have no reason to apprehend anything from me, my child."

"Attentions!" said John, haughtily. "I hope Lady Chatterton does not accuse me of improper attentions to her daughter?"

"No, not improper, my son," said his father: "on the contrary, she is much pleased with them."

"She is, is she? But I am displeased that she should undertake to put constructions on my acts that no attention or words of mine will justify."

It was now Sir Edward's turn to be surprised. He had thought he was doing his son a kindness, when he had only been forwarding the dowager's schemes; but averse from contention, and wondering at his cousin's mistake, which he at once attributed to her anxiety in behalf of a favorite daughter, he told John he was sorry there had been any misapprehension, and left him.

"No, no," said Moseley, internally, as he paced up and down his father's library, "my lady dowager, you are not going to force a wife down my throat. If you do, I am mistaken; and Grace, if Grace"--John softened and began to feel unhappy a little, but anger prevailed.

From the moment Grace Chatterton conceived a dread of her mother's saying anything to Sir Edward, her whole conduct was altered. She could hardly look any of the family in the face, and it was her most ardent wish that they might depart. John she avoided as she would an adder, although it nearly broke her heart to do so.

Mr. Benfield had stayed longer than usual, and he now wished to return. John Moseley eagerly profited by this opportunity, and the very day after the conversation in the library he went to Benfield Lodge as a dutiful nephew, to see his venerable uncle safely restored once more to the abode of his ancestors.

Lady Chatterton now perceived, when too late, that she had overshot her mark, while, at the same time, she wondered at the reason of a result so strange from such well-digested and well-conducted plans. She determined, however, never again to interfere between her daughter and the baronet's heir; concluding, with a nearer approach to the truth than always accompanied her deductions, that they resembled ordinary lovers in neither their temperaments nor opinions.

Perceiving no further use in remaining any longer at the hall, she took her leave, and, accompanied by both her daughters, proceeded to the capital, where she expected to meet her son.

Dr. Ives and his wife returned to the rectory on the same day, and Denbigh immediately resumed his abode under their roof. The intercourse between the rector's family and Sir Edward's was renewed with all its former friendly confidence.

Colonel Egerton began to speak of his departure also, but hinted at intentions of visiting L---- at the period of the baronet's visit to his uncle, before he proceeded to town in the winter.

L---- was a small village on the coast, within a mile of Benfield Lodge; and from its natural convenience, it had long been resorted to by the neighboring gentry for the benefit of sea bathing. The baronet had promised Mr. Benfield his visit should be made at an earlier day than usual, in order to gratify Jane with a visit to Bath, before they went to London, at which town they were promised by Mrs. Jarvis the pleasure of her society, and that of her son and daughters.

Precaution is a word of simple meaning in itself, but various are the ways adopted by different individuals in this life to enforce its import; and not a few are the evils which it is thought necessary to guard against. To provide in season against the dangers of want; personal injury, loss of character, and a great many other such acknowledged misfortunes, has become a kind of instinctive process of our natures. The few exceptions which exist only go to prove the rule: in addition to these, almost every man has some ruling propensity to gratify, to advance which his ingenuity is ever on the alert, or some apprehended evil to avert, which calls all his prudence into activity. Yet how seldom is it exerted, in order to give a rational ground to expect permanent happiness in wedlock.

Marriage is called a lottery, and it is thought, like all other lotteries, there are more blanks than prizes; yet is it not made more precarious than it ought to be, by our neglect of that degree of precaution which we would be ridiculed for omitting in conducting our every-day concerns? Is not the standard of matrimonial felicity placed too low? Ought we not to look more to the possession of principles than to the possession of wealth? Or is it at all justifiable in a Christian to commit a child, a daughter, to the keeping of a man who wants the very essential they acknowledge most necessary to constitute a perfect character? Most men revolt at infidelity in a woman, and most men, however licentious themselves, look for, at least, the exterior of religion in their wives. The education of their children is a serious responsibility; and although seldom conducted on such rules as will stand the test of reason, it is not to be entirely shaken off: they choose their early impressions should be correct, their infant conduct at least blameless. And are not one half mankind of the male sex? Are precepts in religion, in morals, only for females? Are we to reverse the theory of the Mahommedans, and though we do not believe it, act as if *men* had no souls. Is not the example of the father as important to the son as that of the mother to the daughter? In short, is there any security against the commission of enormities, but an humble and devout dependence on the assistance of that Almighty Power, which alone is able to hold us up against temptation?

Uniformity of taste is no doubt necessary to what we call love, but is not taste acquired? Would our daughters admire a handsome deist, if properly impressed with a horror of his doctrines, sooner than they now would admire a handsome Mahommedan? We would refuse our children to a pious dissenter, to give them to impious members of the establishment: we make the substance less than the shadow.

Our principal characters are possessed of these diversified views of the evils to be averted. Mrs. Wilson considers Christianity an indispensable requisite in the husband to be *permitted* to her charge, and watches against the *possibility* of any other than a Christian's gaining the affections of Emily. Lady Chatterton considers the want of an establishment as the unpardonable sin, and directs her energies to prevent this evil; while John Moseley looks upon a free will as the birthright of an Englishman, and is, at the present moment, anxiously alive to prevent the dowager's making him the husband of Grace, the thing of all others he most strenuously desires.

Chapter XVIII

John Moseley returned from L---- within a week, and appeared as if his whole delight consisted in knocking over the inoffensive birds. His restlessness induced him to make Jarvis his companion; for although he abhorred the captain's style of pursuing the sport, being in his opinion both out of rule and without taste, yet he was a constitutional fidget, and suited his own moving propensities at the moment. Egerton and Denbigh were both frequently at the hall, but generally gave their time to the ladies, neither being much inclined to the favorite amusement of John.

There was a little arbor within the walls of the park, which for years had been a retreat from the summer heats to the ladies of the Moseley family; even so long as the youth of Mrs. Wilson it had been in vogue, and she loved it with a kind of melancholy pleasure, as the spot where she had first listened to the language of love from the lips of her late husband. Into this arbor the ladies had one day retired, during the warmth of a noon-day sun, with the exception of Lady Moseley, who had her own engagement in the house. Between Egerton and Denbigh there was maintained a kind of courtly intercourse, which prevented any disagreeable collision from their evident dislike. Mrs. Wilson thought, on the part of Denbigh, it was the forbearance of a principled indulgence to another's weakness; while the colonel's otherwise uniform good breeding was hardly able to conceal a something amounting to very near repugnance. Egerton had taken his seat on the ground, near the feet of Jane; and Denbigh was stationed on a bench placed without the arbor but so near as to have the full benefit of the shade of the noble oak, branches of which had been trained so as to compose its principal covering. It might have been accident, that gave each his particular situation; but it is certain they were so placed as not to be in sight of each other, and so placed that the colonel was ready to hand Jane her scissors, or any other little implement that she occasionally dropped, and that Denbigh could read every lineament of the animated countenance of Emily as she listened to his description of the curiosities of Egypt, a country in which he had spent a few months while attached to the army in Sicily. In this situation we will leave them for an hour, happy in the society of each other, while we trace the route of John Moseley and his companion, in their pursuit of woodcock, on the same day.

"Do you know, Moseley," said Jarvis, who began to think he was a favorite with John, now that he was admitted to his *menus plaisirs*, "that I have taken it into my head this Mr. Denbigh was very happy to plead his morals for not meeting me. He is a soldier, but I cannot find out what battles he has been in."

"Captain Jarvis," said John, coolly, "the less you say about that business the better. Call in Rover."

Now, another of Jarvis's recommendations was a set of lungs that might have been heard half a mile with great ease on a still morning.

"Why," said Jarvis, rather humbly, "I am sensible, Mr Moseley, I was very wrong as regards your sister; but don't you think it a little odd in a soldier not to fight when properly called upon?"

"I suppose Mr. Denbigh did not think himself properly called upon, or perhaps he had heard what a great shot you were."

Six months before his appearance in B----, Captain Jarvis had been a clerk in the counting-room of Jarvis, Baxter & Co., and had never held fire-arms of any kind in his hand, with the exception of an old blunderbuss, which had been a kind of sentinel over the iron chest for years. On mounting the cockade, he had taken up shooting as a martial exercise, inasmuch as the burning of gunpowder was an attendant of the recreation. He had never killed but one bird in his life, and that was an owl, of which he took the advantage of daylight and his stocking feet to knock off a tree in the deanery grounds, very early after his arrival. In his trials with John, he sometimes pulled trigger at the same moment with his companion; and as the bird generally fell, he thought he had an equal claim to the honor. He was fond of warring with crows and birds of the larger sort, and invariably went provided with small balls fitted to the bore of his fowling-piece for such accidental rencontres. He had another habit, which was not a little annoying to John, who had several times tried in vain to break him of it--that of shooting at marks. If birds were not plenty, he would throw up a chip, and sometimes his hat, by way of shooting on the wing.

As the day was excessively hot, and the game kept close, John felt willing to return from such unprofitable labor. The captain now commenced his chip firing, which in a few minutes was succeeded by his hat.

"See, Moseley, see; I have hit the band," cried the captain, delighted to find he had at last wounded his old antagonist. "I don't think you can beat that yourself."

"I am not sure I can," said John, slipping a handful of gravel in the muzzle of his piece slily, "but I can do, as you did--try."

"Do," cried the captain, pleased to get his companion down to his own level of amusements. "Are you ready?"

"Yes; throw."

Jarvis threw, and John fired: the hat fairly bounced.

"Have I hit it?" asked John, while reloading the barrel he had discharged.

"Hit it!" said the captain, looking ruefully at his hat. "It looks like a cullender; but, Moseley, your gun don't scatter well: a dozen shot have gone through in the same place."

"It does look rather like a cullender," said John, as he overlooked his companion's beaver, "and, by the *size* of some of the holes, one that has been a good deal used."

The reports of the fowling-pieces announced to the party in the arbor the return of the sportsmen, it being an invariable practice with John Moseley to discharge his gun before he came in; and Jarvis had imitated him, from a wish to be what he called in rule.

"Mr. Denbigh," said John, as he put down his gun, "Captain Jarvis has got the better of his hat at last."

Denbigh smiled without speaking; and the captain, unwilling to have anything to say to a gentleman to whom be had been obliged to apologize, went into the arbor to show the mangled condition of his head-piece to the colonel, on whose sympathies he felt a kind of claim, being of the same corps. John complained of thirst, and went to a little run of water but a short distance from them, in order to satisfy it. The interruption of Jarvis was particularly unseasonable. Jane was relating, in a manner peculiar to herself, in which was mingled that undefinable exchange of looks lovers are so fond of, some incident of her early life to the colonel that greatly interested him. Knowing the captain's foibles, he pointed, therefore, with his finger, as he said--

"There is one of your old enemies, a hawk."

Jarvis threw down his hat, and ran with boyish eagerness to drive away the intruder. In his haste, he caught up the gun of John Moseley, and loading it rapidly/threw in a ball from his usual stock; but whether the hawk saw and knew him, or whether it saw something else it liked better, it made a dart for the baronet's poultry-yard at no great distance, and was out of sight in a minute. Seeing that his foe had vanished, the captain laid the piece where he had found it, and, recovering his old train of ideas, picked up his hat again.

"John," said Emily, as she approached him affectionately, "you were too warm to drink."

"Stand off, sis," cried John, playfully, taking up the gun from against the body of the tree, and dropping it towards her.

Jarvis had endeavored to make an appeal to the commiseration of Emily in favor of the neglected beaver, and was within a few feet of them. At this moment, recoiling from the muzzle of the gun, he exclaimed, "It is loaded!" "Hold," cried Denbigh, in a voice of horror, as he sprang between John and his sister. Both were too late; the piece was discharged. Denbigh, turning to Emily, and smiling mournfully, gazed for a moment at her with an expression of tenderness, of pleasure, of sorrow, so blended that she retained the recollection of it for life, and fell at her feet.

The gun dropped from the nerveless grasp of young Moseley. Emily sank in insensibility by the side of her preserver. Mrs. Wilson and Jane stood speechless and aghast. The colonel alone retained the presence of mind necessary to devise the steps to be immediately taken. He sprang to the examination of Denbigh; the eyes of the wounded man were open, and his recollection perfect: the first were fixed in intense observation on the inanimate body which lay at his side.

"Leave me, Colonel Egerton," he said, speaking with difficulty, and pointing in the direction of the little run of water, "assist Miss Moseley--your hat--your hat will answer."

Accustomed to scenes of blood, and not ignorant that time and care were the remedies to be applied to the wounded man, Egerton flew to the stream, and returning immediately, by the help of her sister and Mrs. Wilson, soon restored Emily to life. The ladies and John had now begun to act. The tenderest assiduities of Jane were devoted to her sister; while Mrs. Wilson observing her niece to be uninjured by anything but the shock, assisted John in supporting the wounded man.

Denbigh spoke, requesting to be carried to the house; and Jarvis was despatched for help. Within half an hour, Denbigh was placed on a couch in the house of Sir Edward, and was quietly waiting for that professional aid which could only decide on his probable fate. The group assembled in the room were in fearful expectation of the arrival of the surgeons, in pursuit of whom messengers had been sent both to the barracks in F---- and to the town itself. Sir Edward sat by the side of the sufferer, holding one of his hands in his own, now turning his tearful eyes on that daughter who had so lately been rescued as it were from the certainty of death, in mute gratitude and thanksgiving; and now dwelling on the countenance of him, who, by bravely interposing his bosom to the blow, had incurred in his own person the imminent danger of a similar fate, with a painful sense of his perilous situation, and devout and earnest prayers for his safety. Emily was with her father, as with the rest of his family, a decided favorite; and no reward would have been sufficient, no gratitude lively enough, in the estimation of the baronet, to compensate the protector of such a child. She sat between her mother and Jane, with a hand held by each, pale and oppressed with a load of gratitude, of thanksgiving, of woe, that almost bowed her to the earth. Lady Moseley and Jane were both sensibly touched with the deliverance of Emily, and manifested the interest they took in her by the tenderest caresses, while Mrs. Wilson sat calmly collected within herself, occasionally giving those few directions which were necessary under the circumstances, and offering up her silent petitions in behalf of the sufferer. John had taken horse immediately for F----, and Jarvis had volunteered to go to the rectory and Bolton. Denbigh inquired frequently and with much anxiety for Dr. Ives; but the rector was absent from home on a visit to a sick parishioner, and it was late in the evening before he arrived. Within three hours of the accident, however, Dr. Black, the surgeon of the ----th, reached the hall, and immediately proceeded to examine the wound. The ball had penetrated the right breast, and gone directly through the body; it was extracted with very little difficulty, and his attendant acquainted the anxious friends of Denbigh that the heart certainly, and he hoped the lungs, had escaped uninjured. The ball was a very small one, and the principal danger to be apprehended was from fever: he had taken the usual precautions against that, and should it not set in with a violence greater than he apprehended at present, the patient might be abroad within the month.

"But," continued the surgeon, with the hardened indifference of his profession, "the gentleman has had a narrow chance in the passage of the ball itself; half an inch would have settled his accounts with this world."

This information greatly relieved the family, and orders were given to preserve a silence in the house that would favor the patient's disposition to quiet, or, if possible, sleep.

Dr. Ives now reached the hall. Mrs. Wilson had never seen the rector in the agitation, or with the want of self-command he was in, as she met him at the entrance of the house.

"Is he alive?--is there hope?--where is George?"--cried the doctor, as he caught the extended hand of Mrs. Wilson. She briefly acquainted him with the surgeon's report, and the reasonable ground there was to expect Denbigh would survive the injury.

"May God be praised," said the rector, in a suppressed voice, and he hastily withdrew into another room. Mrs. Wilson followed him slowly and in silence; but was checked on opening the door with the sight of the rector on his knees, the tears stealing down his venerable cheeks in quick succession. "Surely," thought the widow, as she drew back unnoticed, "a youth capable of exciting such affection in a man like Dr. Ives, cannot be unworthy."

Denbigh, hearing of the arrival of his friend, desired to see him alone. Their conference was short, and the rector returned from it with increased hopes of the termination of this dreadful accident. He immediately left the hall for his own house, with a promise of returning early on the following morning.

During the night, however, the symptoms became unfavorable; and before the return of Dr. Ives, Denbigh was in a state of delirium from the height of his fever, and the apprehensions of his friends were renewed with additional force.

"What, what, my good sir, do you think of him?" said the baronet to the family physician, with an emotion that the danger of his dearest child would not have exceeded, and within hearing of most of his children, who were collected in the ante-chamber of the room in which Denbigh was placed.

"It is impossible to say, Sir Edward," replied the physician: "he refuses all medicines, and unless this fever abates, there is but little hope of recovery."

Emily stood during this question and answer, motionless, pale as death, and with her hands clasped together, betraying by the workings of her fingers in a kind of convulsive motion, the intensity of her interest. She had seen the draught prepared which it was so desirable that Denbigh should take, and it now stood rejected on a table, where it could be seen through the open door of his room. Almost breathless, she glided in, and taking the draught in her hand, she approached the bed, by which sat John alone, listening with a feeling of despair to the wanderings of the sick man. Emily hesitated once or twice, as she drew near Denbigh; her face had lost the paleness of anxiety, and glowed with another emotion.

"Mr. Denbigh--dear Denbigh." said Emily, with energy, unconsciously dropping her voice into the softest notes of persuasion, "will you refuse me?--me, Emily Moseley, whose life you have saved?"

"Emily Moseley!" repeated Denbigh, and in those tones so remarkable to his natural voice. "Is she safe? I thought she was killed--dead." Then, as if recollecting himself, he gazed intently on her countenance--his eye became less fiery--his muscles relaxed--he smiled, and took, with the docility of a well-trained child, the prescribed medicines from her hand. His ideas still wandered, but his physician, profiting by the command Emily possessed over his patient, increased his care, and by night the fever had abated, and before morning the wounded man was in a profound sleep. During the whole day, it was thought necessary to keep Emily by the side of his bed; but at times it was no trifling tax on her feelings to remain there. He spoke of her by name in the tenderest manner, although incoherently, and in terms that restored to the blanched cheeks of the distressed girl more than the richness of their native color. His thoughts were not confined to Emily, however: he talked of his father, of his mother, and frequently spoke of his poor deserted Marian. The latter name he dwelt on in the language of the warmest affection, condemned his own desertion of her, and, taking Emily for her, would beg her forgiveness, tell her her sufferings had been enough, and that he would return, and never leave her again. At such moments his nurse would sometimes show, by the paleness of her cheeks, her anxiety for his health; and then, as he addressed her by her proper appellation, all her emotions appeared absorbed in the sense of shame at the praises with which he overwhelmed her. Mrs. Wilson succeeded her in the charge of the patient, and she retired to seek that repose she so greatly needed.

On the second morning after receiving the wound, Denbigh dropped into a deep sleep, from which he awoke refreshed and perfectly collected in mind. The fever had left him, and his attendants pronounced, with the usual cautions to prevent a relapse, his recovery certain. It were impossible to have communicated any intelligence more grateful to all the members of the Moseley family; for Jane had even lost sight of her own lover, in sympathy for the fate of a man who had sacrificed himself to save her beloved sister.

Chapter XIX

The recovery of Denbigh was as rapid as the most sanguine expectation of his friends could hope for, and in ten days he left his bed, and would sit an hour or two at a time in his dressing-room, where Mrs. Wilson, accompanied by Jane or Emily, came and read to him; and it was a remark of Sir Edward's gamekeeper, that the woodcocks had become so tame during the time Mr. Moseley was shut up in attendance on his friend, that Captain Jarvis was at last actually seen to bag one honestly.

As Jarvis felt something like a consciousness that but for his folly the accident would not have happened, and also something very like shame for the manner he had shrunk from the danger Denbigh had so nobly met, he pretended a recall to his regiment, then on duty near London, and left the deanery. He went off as he came in--in the colonel's tilbury, and accompanied by his friend and his pointers, John, who saw them pass from the windows of Denbigh's dressing-room, fervently prayed he might never come back again--the chip-shooting poacher!

Colonel Egerton had taken leave of Jane the evening preceding, with many assurances of the anxiety with which he should look forward to the moment of their meeting at L----, whither he intended repairing as soon as his corps had gone through its annual review. Jane had followed the bent of her natural feelings too much, during the period of Denbigh's uncertain fate, to think much of her lover, or anything else but her rescued sister and her preserver; but now the former was pronounced in safety, and the latter, by the very reaction of her grief, was, if possible, happier than ever, Jane dwelt in melancholy sadness on the perfections of the man who had taken with him the best affections (as she thought) of her heart. With him all was perfect: his morals were unexceptionable; his manners showed it; his tenderness of disposition manifest, for they had wept together over the distresses of more than one fictitious heroine; his temper, how amiable! he was never angry--she had never seen it; his opinions, his tastes, how correct! they were her own; his form, his face, how agreeable!--her eyes had seen it, and her heart acknowledged it; besides, his eyes confessed the power of her own charms; he was brave, for he was a soldier;--in short, as Emily had predicted, he was a hero--for he was Colonel Egerton.

Had Jane been possessed of less exuberance of fancy, she might have been a little at a loss to identify all these good properties with her hero: or had she possessed a matured or well-regulated judgment to control that fancy, they might possibly have assumed a different appearance. No explanation had taken place between them, however. Jane knew, both by her own feelings and by all the legends of love from its earliest days, that the moment of parting was generally a crisis in affairs of the heart, and, with a backwardness occasioned by her modesty, had rather avoided than sought an opportunity to favor the colonel's wishes. Egerton had not been over anxious to come to the point, and everything was left as heretofore: neither, however, appeared to doubt in the least the state of the other's affections; and there might be said to exist between them one of those not unusual engagements by implication which it would have been, in their own estimation, a breach of faith to recede from, but which, like all other bargains that are loosely made, are sometimes violated when convenient. Man is a creature that, as experience has sufficiently proved, it is necessary to keep in his proper place in society by wholesome restrictions; and we have often thought it a matter of regret that some well understood regulations did not exist by which it became not only customary, but incumbent on him, to proceed in his road to the temple of Hymen. We know that it is ungenerous, ignoble, almost unprecedented, to doubt the faith, the constancy, of a male paragon; yet, somehow, as the papers occasionally give us a sample of such infidelity; as we have sometimes seen a solitary female brooding over her woes in silence, and, with the seemliness of feminine decorum shrinking from the discovery of its cause, or which the grave has revealed for the first time, we cannot but wish that either the watchfulness of the parent, or a sense of self-preservation in the daughter, would, for the want of a better, cause them to adhere to those old conventional forms of courtship which require a man to speak to be understood, and a woman to answer to be committed.

There was a little parlor in the house of Sir Edward Moseley, that was the privileged retreat of none but the members of his own family. Here the ladies were accustomed to withdraw into the bosom of their domestic quietude, when occasional visitors had disturbed their ordinary intercourse; and many were the hasty and unreserved communications it had witnessed between the sisters, in their stolen flights from the graver scenes of the principal apartments. It might be said to be sacred to the pious feelings of the domestic affections. Sir Edward would retire to it when fatigued with his occupations, certain of finding some one of those he loved to draw his thoughts off from the cares of life to the little incidents of his children's happiness; and Lady Moseley, even in the proudest hours of her reviving splendor, seldom passed the door without looking in, with a smile, on the faces she might find there. It was, in fact, the room in the large mansion of the baronet, expressly devoted, by long usage and common consent, to the purest feelings of human nature. Into this apartment Denbigh had gained admission, as the one nearest to his own room and requiring the least effort of his returning strength to reach; and, perhaps, by an undefinable feeling of the Moseleys which had begun to connect him with themselves, partly from his winning manners, and partly by the sense of the obligation he had laid them under.

One warm day, John and his friend had sought this retreat, in expectation of meeting his sisters, who they found, however, on inquiry, had walked to the arbor. After remaining conversing for an hour by themselves, John was called away to attend to a pointer that had been taken ill, and Denbigh throwing a handkerchief over his head to guard against the danger of cold, quietly composed himself on one of the comfortable sofas of the room, with a disposition to sleep. Before he had entirely lost his consciousness, a light step moving near him, caught his ear; believing it to be a servant unwilling to disturb him, he endeavored to continue in his present mood, until the quick but stifled breathing of some one nearer than before roused his curiosity. He commanded himself, however, sufficiently, to remain quiet; a blind of a window near him was carefully closed; a screen drawn from a corner and placed so as sensibly to destroy the slight draught of air in which he laid himself; and other arrangements were making, but with a care to avoid disturbing him that rendered them hardly audible. Presently the step approached him again, the breathing was quicker, though gentle, the handkerchief was moved, but the hand was with drawn hastily as if afraid of itself. Another effort was successful, and Denbigh stole a glance through his dark lashes, on the figure of Emily as she stood over him in the fulness of her charms, and with a face in which glowed an interest he had never witnessed in it before. It undoubtedly was *gratitude*. For a moment she gazed on him, as her color increased in richness. His hand was carelessly thrown over an arm of the sofa; she stooped towards it with her face gently, but with an air of modesty that shone in her very figure. Denbigh felt the warmth of her breath, but her lips did not touch it. Had he been inclined to judge the actions of Emily Moseley harshly, it were impossible to mistake the movement for anything but the impulse of natural feeling. There was a pledge of innocence, of modesty in her countenance, that would have prevented any misconstruction; and he continued quietly awaiting what the preparations on her little mahogany secretary were intended for.

Mrs. Wilson entertained a great abhorrence of what is commonly called accomplishments in a woman; she knew that too much of that precious time which could never be recalled, was thrown away in endeavoring to acquire a smattering in what, if known, could never be of use to the party, and what can never be well known but to a few, whom nature and long practice have enabled to conquer. Yet as her niece had early manifested a taste for painting, and a vivid perception of the beauties of nature, her inclination had been indulged, and Emily Moseley sketched with neatness and accuracy, and with great readiness. It would have been no subject of surprise, had admiration, or some more powerful feeling, betrayed to the artist, on this occasion, the deception the young man was practising. She had entered the room from her walk, warm and careless; her hair, than which none was more beautiful, had strayed on her shoulders, freed, from the confinement of the comb, and a lock was finely contrasted to the rich color of a cheek that almost burnt with the exercise and the excitement. Her dress, white as the first snow of the winter; her looks, as she now turned them on the face of the sleeper, and betrayed by their animation the success of her art; formed a picture in itself, that Denbigh would have been content to gaze on for ever. Her back was to a window that threw its strong light on the paper--the figures of which were reflected, as she occasionally held it up to study its effect, in a large mirror so placed that Denbigh caught a view of her subject. He knew it at a glance--the arbor--the gun--himself, all were there; it appeared to have been drawn before--it must have been, from its perfect state, and Emily had seized a favorable moment to complete his own resemblance. Her touches were light and finishing, and as the picture was frequently held up for consideration, he had some time allowed for studying it. His own resemblance was strong; his eyes were turned on herself, to whom Denbigh thought she had not done ample justice, but the man who held the gun bore no likeness to John Moseley, except in dress. A slight movement of the muscles of the sleeper's mouth might have betrayed his consciousness, had not Emily been too intent on the picture, as she turned it in such a way that a strong light fell on the recoiling figure of Captain Jarvis. The resemblance was wonderful. Denbigh thought he would have known it, had he seen it in the Academy itself. The noise of some one approaching closed the portfolio; it was only a servant, yet Emily did not resume her pencil. Denbigh watched her motions, as she put the picture carefully in a private drawer of the secretary, reopened the blind, replaced the screen, and laid the handkerchief, the last thing on his face, with a movement almost imperceptible to himself.

"It is later than I thought," said Denbigh, looking at his watch; "I owe an apology, Miss Moseley, for making so free with your parlor; but I was too lazy to move."

"Apology! Mr. Denbigh," cried Emily, with a color varying with every word she spoke, and trembling at what she thought the nearness of detection, "you have no apology to make for your present debility; and surely, surely, least of all to me!"

"I understand from Mr. Moseley," continued Denbigh, with a smile, "that our obligation is at least mutual; to your perseverance and care, Miss Moseley, after the physicians had given me up, I believe I am, under Providence, indebted for my recovery."

Emily was not vain, and least of all addicted to a display of any of her acquirements; very few even of her friends knew she ever held a pencil in her hand; yet did she now unaccountably throw open her portfolio, and offer its contents to the examination of her companion. It was done almost instantaneously, and with great freedom, though not without certain flushings of the face and heavings of the bosom, that would have eclipsed Grace Chatterton in her happiest moments of natural flattery. Whatever might have been the wishes of Mr. Denbigh to pursue a subject which had begun to grow extremely interesting, both from its import and the feelings' of the parties, it would have been rude to decline viewing the contents of a lady's portfolio. The drawings were, many of them, interesting, and the exhibitor of them now appeared as anxious to remove them in haste, as she had but the moment before been to direct his attention to her performances. Denbigh would have given much to dare to ask for the paper so carefully secreted in the private drawer; but neither the principal agency he had himself in the scene, nor delicacy to his companion's wish for concealment, would allow of the request.

"Doctor Ives! how happy I am to see you," said Emily, hastily closing her portfolio, and before Denbigh had gone half through its contents; "you have become almost a stranger to us since Clara left us."

"No, no, my little friend, never a stranger, I hope, at Moseley Hall," cried the doctor, pleasantly; "George, I am happy to see you look so well-- you have even a color--there is a letter for you, from Marian."

Denbigh took the letter eagerly, and retired to a window to peruse it. His hand shook as he broke the seal, and his interest in the writer, or its contents, could not have escaped the notice of any observer, however indifferent.

"Now, Miss Emily, if you will have the goodness to order me a glass of wine and water after my ride, believe me, you will do a very charitable act," cried the doctor, as he took his seat on the sofa.

Emily was standing by the little table, deeply musing on the contents of her portfolio; for her eyes were intently fixed on the outside, as if she expected to see through the leather covering their merits and faults.

"Miss Emily Moseley," continued the doctor, gravely, "am I to die of thirst or not, this warm day?"

"Do you wish anything, Doctor Ives?"

"A servant to get me a glass of wine and water."

"Why did you not ask me, my dear sir?" said Emily, as she threw open a cellaret, and handed him what he wanted.

"There, my dear, there is a great plenty," said the doctor, with an arch expression; "I really thought I had asked you thrice--but I believe you were studying something in that portfolio."

Emily blushed, and endeavored to laugh at her own absence of mind; but she would have given the world to know who Marian was.

Chapter XX

As a month had elapsed since he received his wound, Denbigh took an opportunity, one morning at breakfast, where he was well enough now to meet his friends, to announce his intention of trespassing no longer on their kindness, but of returning that day to the rectory. The communication distressed the whole family, and the baronet turned to him in the most cordial manner, as he took one of his hands; and said with an air of solemnity--

"Mr. Denbigh, I could wish you to make this house your home; Dr. Ives may have known you longer, and may have the claim of relationship on you, but I am certain he cannot love you better; and are not the ties of gratitude as binding as those of blood?"

Denbigh was affected by the kindness of Sir Edward's manner.

"The regiment I belong to, Sir Edward, will be reviewed next week, and it has become my duty to leave here; there is one it is proper I should visit, a near connexion, who is acquainted with the escape I have met with, and wishes naturally to see me; besides, my dear Sir Edward, she has many causes of sorrow, and it is a debt I owe her affection to endeavor to relieve them."

It was the first time he had ever spoken of his family, or hardly of himself, and the silence which prevailed plainly showed the interest his listeners took in the little he uttered.

That connexion, thought Emily--I wonder if her name be Marian? But nothing further passed, excepting the affectionate regrets of her father, and the promises of Denbigh to visit them again before he left B----, and of joining them at L---- immediately after the review of which he had spoken. As soon as he had breakfasted, John drove him in his phaeton to the rectory.

Mrs. Wilson, like the rest of the baronet's family, had been too deeply impressed with the debt they owed this young man to interfere with her favorite system of caution against too great an intimacy between her niece and her preserver. Close observation and the opinion of Dr. Ives had prepared her to give him her esteem; but the gallantry, the self-devotion he had displayed to Emily was an act calculated to remove heavier objections than she could imagine as likely to exist to his becoming her husband. That he meant it, was evident from his whole deportment of late. Since the morning the portfolio was produced, Denbigh had given a more decided preference to her niece. The nice discrimination of Mrs. Wilson would not have said his feelings had become stronger, but that he labored less to conceal them. That he loved her niece she suspected from the first fortnight of their acquaintance, and it had given additional stimulus to her investigation into his character; but to doubt it, after stepping between her and death, would have been to have mistaken human nature. There was one qualification she would have wished to have been certain he possessed: before this accident, she would have made it an indispensable one; but the gratitude, the affections of Emily, she believed now to be too deeply engaged to make the strict inquiry she otherwise would have done; and she had the best of reasons for believing that if Denbigh were not a true Christian, he was at least a strictly moral man, and assuredly one who well understood the beauties of a religion she almost conceived it impossible for any impartial and intelligent man long to resist. Perhaps Mrs. Wilson, having in some measure interfered with her system, like others, had, on finding it impossible to conduct so that reason would justify all she did, began to find reasons for what she thought best to be done under the circumstances. Denbigh, however, both by his acts and his opinions, had created such an estimate of his worth in the breast of Mrs. Wilson, that there would have been but little danger of a repulse had no fortuitous accident helped him in his way to her favor.

"Who have we here?" said Lady Moseley. "A landaulet and four--the Earl of Bolton, I declare!"

Lady Moseley turned from the window with that collected grace she so well loved, and so well knew how to assume, to receive her noble visitor. Lord Bolton was a bachelor of sixty-five, who had long been attached to the court, and retained much of the manners of the old school. His principal estate was in Ireland, and most of that time which his duty at Windsor did not require he gave to the improvement of his Irish property. Thus, although on perfectly good terms with the baronet's family, they seldom met. With General Wilson he had been at college, and to his widow he always showed much of that regard he had invariably professed for her husband, The obligation he had conferred, unasked, on Francis Ives, was one conferred on all his friends, and his reception was now warmer than usual.

"My Lady Moseley," said the earl, bowing formally on her hand, "your looks do ample justice to the air of Northamptonshire. I hope you enjoy your usual health."

Then, waiting her equally courteous answer, he paid his compliments, in succession, to all the members of the family; a mode undoubtedly well adapted to discover their several conditions, but not a little tedious in its operations, and somewhat tiresome to the legs.

"We are under a debt of gratitude to your lordship," said Sir Edward, in his simple and warm-hearted way, "that I am sorry it is not in our power to repay more amply than by our thanks."

The earl was, or affected to be, surprised, as he required an explanation.

"The living at Bolton," said Lady Moseley, with dignity.

"Yes," continued her husband; "in giving the living to Frank you did me a favor, equal to what you would have done had he been my own child; and unsolicited, too, my lord, it was an additional compliment."

The earl sat rather uneasy during this speech, but the love of truth prevailed; for he had been too much round the person of our beloved sovereign not to retain all the impressions of his youth; and after a little struggle with his self-love, he answered--

"Not unsolicited, Sir Edward. I have no doubt, had nay better fortune allowed me the acquaintance of my present rector, his own merit would have obtained what a sense of justice requires I should say was granted to an applicant to whom the ear of royalty itself would not have been deaf."

It was the turn of the Moseleys now to look surprised, and Sir Edward ventured to ask an explanation.

"It was my cousin, the Earl of Pendennyss, who applied for it, as a favor done to himself; and Pendennyss is a man not to be refused anything."

"Lord Pendennyss!" exclaimed Mrs. Wilson, with animation; "and in what way came we to be under this obligation to Lord Pendennyss?"

"He did me the honor of a call during my visit to Ireland, madam," replied the earl; "and on inquiring of my steward after his old friend, Doctor Stevens, learnt his death, and the claims of Mr. Ives; but the reason he gave *me* was his interest in the widow of General Wilson," bowing with much solemnity to the lady as he spoke.

"I am gratified to find the earl yet remembers us," said Mrs. Wilson, struggling to restrain her tears. "Are we to have the pleasure of seeing him soon?"

"I received a letter from him yesterday, saying he should be here in all next week, madam." And turning pleasantly to Jane and her sister, he continued, "Sir Edward, you have here rewards fit for heavier services, and the earl is a great admirer of female charms."

"Is he not married, my lord?" asked the baronet, with great simplicity.

"No, baronet, nor engaged; but how long he will remain so after his hardihood in venturing into this neighborhood, will, I trust, depend on one of these young ladies."

Jane looked grave--for trifling on love was heresy, in her estimation; but Emily laughed, with an expression in which a skilful physiognomist might have read--if he means me, he is mistaken.

"Your cousin, Lord Chatterton, has found interest, Sir Edward," continued the peer, "to obtain his father's situation; and if reports speak truth, he wishes to become more nearly related to you, baronet."

"I do not well see how that can happen," said Sir Edward with a smile, and who had not art enough to conceal his thoughts, "unless he takes my sister here."

The cheeks of both the young ladies now vied with the rose; and the peer, observing he had touched on forbidden ground, added, "Chatterton was fortunate to find friends able to bear up against the powerful interest of Lord Haverford."

"To whom was he indebted for the place, my lord?" asked Mis. Wilson.

"It was whispered at court, madam," said the earl, sensibly lowering his voice, and speaking with an air of mystery "and a lord of the bed-chamber is fonder of discoveries than a lord of the council--that His Grace of Derwent threw the whole of his parliamentary interest into the scale on the baron's side, but you are not to suppose," raising his hand gracefully, with a wave of rejection, "that I speak from authority; only a surmise, Sir Edward, only a surmise, my lady."

"Is not the name of the Duke of Derwent, Denbigh?" inquired Mrs. Wilson, with a thoughtful manner.

"Certainly, madam, Denbigh," replied the earl, with a gravity with which he always spoke of dignities; "one of our most ancient names, and descended on the female side from the Plantagenets and Tudors."

He now rose to take his leave, and on bowing to the younger ladies, laughingly repeated his intention of bringing his cousin (an epithet he never omitted), Pendennyss, to their feet.

"Do you think, sister," said Lady Moseley, after the earl had retired, "that Mr. Denbigh is of the house of Derwent?"

"I cannot say," replied Mrs. Wilson, musing, "yet it is odd, Chatterton told me of his acquaintance with Lady Harriet Denbigh, but not with the Duke."

As this was spoken in the manner of a soliloquy, it received no answer, and was in fact but little attended to by any of the party, excepting Emily, who glanced her eye once or twice at her aunt as she was speaking, with an interest the name of Denbigh never failed to excite. Harriet was, she thought, a pretty name, but Marian was a prettier; if, thought Emily, I could know a Marian Denbigh, I am sure I could love her, and her name too.

The Moseleys now began to make their preparations for their departure to L----, and the end of the succeeding week was fixed for the period at which they were to go. Mrs. Wilson urged a delay of two or three days, in order to give her an opportunity of meeting with the Earl of Pendennyss, a young man in whom, although she had relinquished her former romantic wish of uniting him to Emily, in favor of Denbigh, she yet felt a deep interest, growing out of his connexion with the last moments of her husband, and his uniformly high character.

Sir Edward accordingly acquainted his uncle, that on the following Saturday he might expect to receive himself and family, intending to leave the hall in the afternoon of the preceding day, and reach Benfield lodge to dinner. This arrangement once made, and Mr. Benfield notified of it, was unalterable, the old man holding a variation from an engagement a deadly sin. The week succeeding the accident which had nearly proved so fatal to Denbigh, the inhabitants of the hall were surprised with the approach of a being, as singular in his manners and dress as the equipage which conveyed him to the door of the house. The latter consisted of a high-backed, old-fashioned sulky, loaded with leather and large-headed brass nails; wheels at least a quarter larger in circumference than those of the present day, and wings on each side large enough to have supported a full grown roc in the highest regions of the upper air. It was drawn by a horse, once white, but whose milky hue was tarnished through age with large and numerous red spots, and whose mane and tail did not appear to have suffered by the shears during the present reign. The being who alighted from this antiquated vehicle was tall and excessively thin, wore his own hair drawn over his almost naked head into a long thin queue, which reached half way down his back, closely cased in numerous windings of leather, or the skin of some fish. His drab coat was in shape between a frock and a close-body-

-close-body, indeed, it was; for the buttons, which were in size about equal to an old-fashioned China saucer, were buttoned to the very throat, thereby setting off his shape to peculiar advantage; his breeches were buckskin, and much soiled; his stockings blue yarn, although it was midsummer; and his shoes were provided with buckles of dimensions proportionate to the aforesaid buttons; his age might have been seventy, but his walk was quick, and the movements of his whole system showed great activity both of mind and body. He was ushered into the room where the gentlemen were sitting, and having made a low and extremely modest bow, he deliberately put on his spectacles, thrust his hand into an outside pocket of his coat, and produced from under its huge flaps a black leathern pocket-book about as large as a good-sized octavo volume; after examining the multitude of papers it contained carefully, he selected a letter, and having returned the pocket-book to its ample apartment, read aloud,

"For Sir Edward Moseley, bart. of Moseley Hall, B----, Northamptonshire--with care and speed, by the hands of Mr. Peter Johnson, steward of Benfield Lodge, Norfolk;" and dropping his sharp voice, he stalked up to the baronet, and presented the epistle, with another reverence.

"Ah, my good friend, Johnson," said Sir Edward as soon as he delivered his errand (for until he saw the contents of the letter, he had thought some accident had occurred to his uncle), "this is the first visit you have ever honored me with; come, take a glass of wine before you go to your dinner; let us drink, that it may not be the last."

"Sir Edward Moseley, and you, honorable gentlemen, will pardon me," replied the steward, in his own solemn key, "this is the first time I was ever out of his majesty's county of Norfolk, and I devoutly wish it may prove the last--Gentlemen, I drink your honorable healths."

This was the only real speech the old man made during his visit, unless an occasional monosyllabic reply to a question could be thought so. He remained, by Sir Edward's positive order, until the following day; for having delivered his message, and receiving its answer, he was about to take his departure that evening, thinking he might get a good piece on his road homewards, as it wanted half an hour to sunset. On the following morning, with the sun, he was on his way to the house in which he had been born, and which he had never left for twenty-four hours at a time in his life. In the evening, as he was ushered in by John (who had known him from his own childhood, and loved to show him attention) to the room in which he was to sleep, he broke what the young man called his inveterate silence, with, "Young Mr. Moseley--young gentleman--might I presume--to ask--to see the gentleman?"

"What gentleman?" cried John, astonished at the request, and at his speaking so much.

"That saved Miss Emmy's life, sir."

John now fully comprehended him, and led the way to Denbigh's room; he was asleep, but they were admitted to his bed-side. The steward stood for ten minutes gazing on the sleeper in silence; and John observed, as he blew his nose on regaining his own apartment, that his little grey eyes twinkled with a lustre which could not be taken for anything but a tear.

As the letter was as characteristic of the writer as its bearer was of his vocation, we may be excused giving it at length.

"Dear Sir Edward and Nephew,

"Your letter reached the lodge too late to be answered that evening, as I was about to step into my bed; but I hasten to write my congratulations, remembering the often repeated maxim of my kinsman Lord Gosford, that letters should be answered immediately; indeed, a neglect of it had very nigh brought about an affair of honor between the earl and Sir Stephens Hallett. Sir Stephens was always opposed to us in the House of Commons of this realm; and I have often thought something might have passed in the debate itself, which commenced the correspondence, as the earl certainly told him as much as if he were a traitor to his King and country.

"But it seems that your daughter Emily has been rescued from death by the grandson of General Denbigh, who sat with us in the house. Now I always had a good opinion of this young Denbigh, who reminds me, every time I look at him, of my late brother, your father-in-law that was; and I send my steward, Peter Johnson, express to the hall in order that he may see the sick man, and bring me back a true account how he fares: for should he be wanting for anything within the gift of Roderic Benfield, he has only to speak to have it; not that I suppose, nephew, you will willingly allow him to suffer for anything, but Peter is a man of close observation, although he is of few words, and may suggest something beneficial, that might escape younger heads. I pray for--that is, I hope, the young man will recover, as your letter gives great hopes; and if he should want any little matter to help him along in the army, as I take it he is not over wealthy, you have now a good opportunity to offer your assistance handsomely; and that it may not interfere with your arrangements for this winter, your draft on me for five thousand pounds will be paid at sight; for fear he may be proud, and not choose to accept your assistance, I have this morning detained Peter, while he has put a codicil to my will, leaving him ten thousand pounds. You may tell Emily she is a naughty child, or she would have written me the whole story; but, poor dear, I suppose she has other things on her mind just now. God bless Mr. ---- that is, God bless, you all, and try if you cannot get a lieutenant-colonelcy at once--the brother of Lady Juliana's friend was made a lieutenant-colonel at the first step.

"RODERIC BENFIELD."

The result of Peter's reconnoitering expedition has never reached our knowledge, unless the arrival of a servant some days after he took his leave, with a pair of enormous-goggles, and which the old gentleman assured his nephew in a note, both Peter and himself had found useful to weak eyes in their occasional sickness, might have been owing to the prudent forecast of the sagacious steward.

Chapter XXI

The morning on which Denbigh left B---- was a melancholy one to all the members of the little circle, in which he had been so distinguished for his modesty, his intelligence, and his disinterested intrepidity. Sir Edward took an opportunity solemnly to express his gratitude for the services he had rendered him, and having retired to his library, delicately and earnestly pressed his availing himself of the liberal offer of Mr. Benfield to advance his interest in the army.

"Look upon me, my dear Mr. Denbigh," said the good baronet, pressing him by the hand, while the tears stood in his eyes, "as a father, to supply the place of the one you have so recently lost. You *are* my child; I feel as a parent to you, and must be suffered to act as one."

To this affectionate offer of Sir Edward, Denbigh replied with an emotion equal to that of the baronet, though he declined, with respectful language, his offered assistance as unnecessary. He had friends powerful enough to advance his interests, without resorting to the use of money; and on taking Sir Edward's hand, as he left the apartment, he added with great warmth, "yet, my dear Sir, the day will come, I hope, when I shall ask a boon from your hands, that no act of mine or a life of service could entitle me to receive."

The baronet smiled his assent to a request he already understood, and Denbigh withdrew.

John Moseley insisted on putting the bays in requisition to carry Denbigh for the first stage, and they now stood caparisoned for the jaunt, with their master in a less joyous mood than common, waiting the appearance of his companion.

Emily delighted in their annual excursion to Benfield Lodge. She was beloved so warmly, and returned the affection of its owner so sincerely, that the arrival of the day never failed to excite that flow of spirits which generally accompanies anticipated pleasures, ere experience has proved how trifling are the greatest enjoyments the scenes of this life bestow. Yet as the day of their departure drew near, her spirits sunk in proportion; and on the morning of Denbigh's leave-taking, Emily seemed anything but excessively happy. There was a tremor in her voice and a redness about her eyes that alarmed Lady Moseley; but as the paleness of her cheeks was immediately succeeded by as fine a color as the heart could wish, the anxious mother allowed herself to be persuaded by Mrs. Wilson there was no danger, and she accompanied her sister to her own room for some purpose of domestic economy. It was at this moment Denbigh entered: he had paid his adieus to the matrons at the door, and been directed by them to the little parlor in quest of Emily.

"I have come to make my parting compliments, Miss Moseley," he said, in a tremulous voice, as he ventured to hold forth his hand. "May heaven preserve you," he continued, holding it in fervor to his bosom: then dropping it, he hastily retired, as if unwilling to trust himself any longer to utter all he felt. Emily stood a few moments, pale and almost inanimate, as the tears flowed rapidly from her eyes; and then she sought a shelter in a seat of the window. Lady Moseley, on returning, was alarmed lest the draught would increase her indisposition; but her sister, observing that the window commanded a view of the road, thought the air too mild to do her injury.

The personages who composed the society at B---- had now, in a great measure, separated, in pursuit of their duties or their pleasures. The merchant and his family left the deanery for a watering-place. Francis and Clara had gone on a little tour of pleasure in the northern counties, to take L---- in their return homeward; and the morning arrived for the commencement of the baronet's journey to the same place. The carriages had been ordered, and servants were running in various ways, busily employed in their several occupations, when Mrs. Wilson, accompanied by John and his sisters, returned from a walk they had taken to avoid the bustle of the house. A short distance from the park gates, an equipage was observed approaching, creating by its numerous horses and attendants a dust which drove the pedestrians to one side of the road. An uncommonly elegant and admirably fitted travelling barouche and six rolled by, with the graceful steadiness of an English equipage: several servants on horseback were in attendance; and our little party were struck with the beauty of the whole *establishment*.

"Can it be possible Lord Bolton drives such elegant horses?" cried John, with the ardor of a connoisseur in that noble animal. "They are the finest set in the kingdom."

Jane's eye had seen, through the clouds of dust, the armorial bearings, which seemed to float in the dark glossy panels of the carriage, and she observed, "It is an earl's coronet, but they are not the Bolton arms." Mrs. Wilson and Emily had noticed a gentleman reclining at his ease, as the owner of the gallant show; but its passage was too rapid to enable them to distinguish the features of the courteous old earl; indeed, Mrs. Wilson remarked, she thought him a younger man than her friend.

"Pray, sir," said John to a tardy groom, as he civilly walked his horse by the ladies, "who has passed in the barouche?"

"My Lord Pendennyss, sir."

"Pendennyss!" exclaimed Mrs. Wilson, with a tone of regret, "how unfortunate!"

She had seen the day named for his visit pass without his arrival, and now, as it was too late to profit by the opportunity, he had come for the second time into her neighborhood. Emily had learnt, by the solicitude of her aunt, to take an interest in the young peer's movements, and desired John to ask a question or two of the groom.

"Where does your lord stop to-night?"

"At Bolton Castle, sir; and I heard my lord tell his valet that he intended staying one day hereabouts, and the day after to-morrow he goes to Wales, your honor."

"I thank you, friend," said John; when the man spurred his horse after the cavalcade. The carriages were at the door, and Sir Edward had been hurrying Jane to enter, as a servant, in a rich livery and well mounted, galloped up and delivered a letter for Mrs. Wilson, who, on opening it, read the following:

"The Earl of Pendennyss begs leave to present his most respectful compliments to Mrs. Wilson and the family of Sir Edward Moseley. Lord Pendennyss will have the honor of paying his respects in person at any moment that the widow of his late invaluable friend, Lieutenant-General Wilson, will please to appoint.

"Bolton Castle, Friday evening."

To this note Mrs. Wilson, bitterly regretting the necessity which compelled her to forego the pleasure of meeting her paragon, wrote in reply a short letter, disliking the formality of a note.

"My LORD, "I sincerely regret that an engagement which cannot be postponed compels us to leave Moseley Hall within the hour, and must, in consequence, deprive us of the pleasure of your intended visit. But as circumstances have connected your Lordship with some of the dearest, although the most melancholy events of my life, I earnestly beg you will no longer consider us as strangers to your person, as we have long ceased to be to your character. It will afford me the greatest pleasure to hear that there will be a prospect of our meeting in town next winter, where I may find a more fitting opportunity of expressing those grateful feelings so long due to your lordship from your sincere friend,

"CHARLOTTE WILSON.

"Moseley Hall, Friday morning."

With this answer the servant was despatched, and the carriages moved on. John had induced Emily to trust herself once more to the bays and his skill; but on perceiving the melancholy of her aunt, she insisted on exchanging seats with Jane, who had accepted a place in the carriage of Mrs. Wilson. No objection being made, Mrs. Wilson and her niece rode the first afternoon together in her travelling chaise. The road ran within a quarter of a mile of Bolton Castle, and the ladies endeavored in vain to get a glimpse of the person of the young nobleman. Emily was willing to gratify her aunt's propensity to dwell on the character and history of her favorite; and hoping to withdraw her attention gradually from more unpleasant recollections, asked several trifling questions relating to those points.

"The earl must be very rich, aunt, from the style he maintains."

"Very, my dear; his family I am unacquainted with, but I understand his title is an extremely ancient one; and some one, I believe Lord Bolton, mentioned that his estates in Wales alone, exceeded fifty thousand a year."

"Much good might be done," said Emily, thoughtfully, "with such a fortune."

"Much good *is* done," cried her aunt, with fervor. "I am told by every one who knows him, his donations are large and frequent. Sir Herbert Nicholson said he was extremely simple in his habits, and it leaves large sums at his disposal every year."

"The bestowal of money is not always charity," said Emily, with an arch smile and a slight color.

Mrs. Wilson smiled in her turn as she answered, "not always, but it is charity to hope for the best."

"Sir Herbert knew him, then?" said Emily.

"Perfectly well; they were associated together in the service for several years, and he spoke of him with a fervor equal to my warmest expectations."

The Moseley arms in F---- was kept by an old butler of the family, and Sir Edward every year, in going to or coming from L----, spent a night under its roof. He was received by its master with a respect that none who ever knew the baronet well, could withhold from his goodness of heart and many virtues.

"Well, Jackson," said the baronet, kindly, as he was seated at the supper table, "how does custom increase with you--I hope you and the master of the Dun Cow are more amicable than formerly."

"Why, Sir Edward," replied the host, who had lost a little of the deference of the servant in the landlord, but none of his real respect, "Mr. Daniels and I are more upon a footing of late than we was, when your goodness enabled me to take the house; then he got all the great travellers, and for more than a twelvemonth I had not a title in my house but yourself and a great London doctor, that was called here to see a sick person in the town. He had the impudence to call me the knight barrow-knight, your honor, and we had a quarrel upon that account."

"I am glad, however, to find you are gaining in the rank of your customers, and trust, as the occasion has ceased, you will be more inclined to be good-natured to each other."

"Why, as to good-nature, Sir Edward, I lived with your honor ten years, and you must know somewhat of my temper," said Jackson, with the self-satisfaction of an approving conscience; "but Sam Daniels is a man who is never easy unless he is left quietly at the top of the ladder; however," continued the host, with a chuckle, "I have given him a dose lately."

"How so, Jackson?" inquired the baronet, willing to gratify the man's wish to relate his triumphs.

"Your honor must have heard mention made of a great lord, the Duke of Derwent; well, Sir Edward, about six weeks agone he passed through with my Lord Chatterton."

"Chatterton!" exclaimed John, interrupting him, "has he been so near us again, and so lately?"

"Yes, Mr. Moseley," replied Jackson with a look of importance: "they dashed into my yard with their chaise and four, with five servants, and would you think it, Sir Edward, they hadn't been in the house ten minutes, before Daniel's son was fishing from the servants, who they were; I told him, Sir Edward--dukes don't come every day."

"How came you to get his grace away from the Dun Cow--chance?"

"No, your honor," said the host, pointing to his sign, and bowing reverently to his old master, "the Moseley Arms did it. Mr. Daniels used to taunt me with having worn a livery, and has said more than once he could milk his cow, but that your honor's arms would never lift me into a comfortable seat for life; so I just sent him a message by the way of letting him know my good fortune, your honor."

"And what was it?"

"Only that your honor's arms had shoved a duke and a baron into my house--that's all."

"And I suppose Daniels' legs shoved your messenger out of his," said John, laughing.

"No, Mr. Moseley; Daniels would hardly dare do that: but yesterday, your honor, yesterday evening, beat everything. Daniels was seated before his door, and I was taking a pipe at mine, Sir Edward, as a coach and six, with servants upon servants, drove down the street; it got near us, and the boys were reining the horses into the yard of the Dun Cow, as the gentleman in the coach saw my sign: he sent a groom to inquire who kept the house; I got up, your honor, and told him my name, sir. 'Mr. Jackson,' said his lordship, 'my respect for the family of Sir Edward Moseley is too great not to give my custom to an old servant of his family.'"

"Indeed," said the baronet; "pray who was my lord?"

"The Earl of Pendennyss, your honor. Oh, he is a sweet gentleman, and he asked all about my living with your honor, and about Madam Wilson."

"Did his lordship stay the night?" inquired Mrs. Wilson, excessively gratified at a discovery of the disposition manifested by the earl towards her.

"Yes, madam, he left here after breakfast."

"What message did you send the Dun Cow this time, Jackson?" cried John.

Jackson looked a little foolish, but the question being repeated, he answered--"Why, sir, I was a little crowded for room, and so your honor, so I just sent Tom across the street, to know if Mr. Daniels couldn't keep a couple of the grooms."

"And Tom got his head broke."

"No, Mr. John, the tankard missed him; but if--"

"Very well," said the baronet, willing to change the conversation, "you have been so fortunate of late, you can afford to be generous; and I advise you to cultivate harmony with your neighbor, or I may take my arms down, and you may lose your noble visiters--see my room prepared."

"Yes, your honor," said the host, and bowing respectfully he withdrew.

"At least, aunt," cried John, pleasantly, "we have the pleasure of supping in the same room with the puissant earl, albeit there be twenty-four hours' difference in the time."

"I sincerely wish there had not been that difference," observed his father, taking his sister kindly by the hand.

"Such an equipage must have been a harvest indeed to Jackson," remarked the mother; as they broke up for the evening.

The whole establishment at Benfield Lodge, were drawn up to receive them on the following day in the great hall, and in the centre was fixed the upright and lank figure of its master, with his companion in leanness, honest Peter Johnson, on his right.

"I have made out, Sir Edward and my Lady Moseley, to get as far as my entrance, to receive the favor you are conferring upon me. It was a rule in my day, and one invariably practised by all the great nobility, such as Lord Gosford--and--and--his sister, the lady Juliana Dayton, always to receive and quit their guests in the country at the great entrance; and in conformity--ah, Emmy dear," cried the old gentleman, folding her in his arms as the tears rolled down his cheeks, forgetting his speech in the warmth of his feeling, "You are saved to us again; God be praised--there, that will do, let me breathe--let me breathe;" and then by the way of getting rid of his softer feelings, he turned upon John; "so, youngster, you would be playing with edge tools, and put the life of your sister in danger. No gentleman held a gun in my day; that is, no gentleman about the court. My Lord Gosford had never killed a bird in his life, or drove his horse; no sir, gentlemen then were not coachmen. Peter how old was I before I took the reins of the chaise, in driving round the estate--the time you broke your arm? it was--"

Peter, who stood a little behind his master, in modest retirement, and who had only thought his elegant form brought thither to embellish the show, when called upon, advanced a step, made a low bow, and answered in his sharp key:

"In the year 1798, your honor, and the 38th of his present majesty, and the 64th year of your life, sir, June the 12th, about meridian."

Peter dropped back as he finished; but recollecting himself, regained his place with a bow, as he added, "new style."

"How are you, old style?" cried John, with a slap on the back, that made the steward jump again.

"Mr. John Moseley--young gentleman"--a term Peter had left off using to the baronet within the last ten years, "did you think--to bring home--the goggles?"

"Oh yes," said John, gravely, producing them from his pocket. Most of the party having entered the parlor, he put them carefully on the bald head of the steward--"There, Mr Peter Johnson, you have your property again, safe and sound."

"And Mr. Denbigh said he felt much indebted to your consideration in sending them," said Emily, soothingly, as she took them off with her beautiful hands.

"Ah, Miss Emmy," said the steward, with one of his best bows, "that was--a noble act; God bless him!" then holding up his finger significantly, "the fourteenth codicil--to master's will," and Peter laid his finger alongside his nose, as he nodded his head in silence.

"I hope the thirteenth contains the name of honest Peter Johnson," said the young lady, who felt herself uncommonly well pleased with the steward's conversation.

"As witness, Miss Emmy--witness to all--but God forbid," said the steward with solemnity, "I should ever live to see the proving of them: no, Miss Emmy, master has done for me what he intended, while I had youth to enjoy it. I am rich, Miss Emmy--good three hundred a year." Emily, who had seldom heard so long a speech as the old man's gratitude drew from him, expressed her pleasure at hearing it, and shaking him kindly by the hand, left him for the parlor.

"Niece," said Mr. Benfield, having scanned the party closely with his eyes, "where is Colonel Denbigh?"

"Colonel Egerton, you mean, sir," interrupted Lady Moseley.

"No, my Lady Moseley," replied her uncle, with great formality, "I mean Colonel Denbigh. I take it he is a colonel by this time," looking expressively at the baronet; "and who is fitter to be a colonel or a general, than a man who is not afraid of gunpowder?"

"Colonels must have been scarce in your youth, sir," cried John, who had rather a mischievous propensity to start the old man on his hobby.

"No, jackanapes, gentlemen killed one another then, although they did not torment the innocent birds: honor was as dear to a gentleman of George the Second's court, as to those of his grandson's, and honesty too, sirrah--ay, honesty. I remember when we were in, there was not a man of doubtful integrity in the ministry, or on our side even; and then again, when we went out, the opposition benches were filled with sterling characters, making a parliament that was correct throughout. Can you show me such a thing at this day?"

Chapter XXII

A few days after the arrival of the Moseleys at the lodge John drove his sisters to the little village of L----, which at that time was thronged with an unusual number of visiters. It had, among other fashionable arrangements for the accommodation of its guests, one of those circulators of good and evil, a public library. Books are, in a great measure, the instruments of controlling the opinions of a nation like ours. They are an engine, alike powerful to save or to destroy. It cannot be denied, that our libraries contain as many volumes of the latter, as the former description; for we rank amongst the latter that long catalogue of idle productions, which, if they produce no other evil, lead to the misspending of time, *our own* perhaps included. But we cannot refrain expressing our regret, that such formidable weapons in the cause of morality, should be suffered to be wielded by any indifferent or mercenary dealer, who undoubtedly will consult rather the public tastes than the private good: the evil may be remediless, yet we love to express our sentiments, though we should suggest nothing new or even profitable. Into one of these haunts of the idle, then, John Moseley entered with a lovely sister leaning on either arm. Books were the entertainers of Jane, and instructors of Emily. Sir Edward was fond of reading of a certain sort--that which required no great depth of thought, or labor of research; and, like most others who are averse to contention, and disposed to be easily satisfied, the baronet sometimes found he had harbored opinions on things not exactly reconcileable with the truth, or even with each other. It is quite as dangerous to give up your faculties to the guidance of the author you are perusing, as it is unprofitable to be captiously scrutinizing every syllable he may happen to advance; and Sir Edward was, if anything, a little inclined to the dangerous propensity. Unpleasant, Sir Edward Moseley never was. Lady Moseley very seldom took a book in her hand: her opinions were established to her own satisfaction on all important points, and on the minor ones, she made it a rule to coincide with the popular feeling. Jane had a mind more active than her father, and more brilliant than her mother; and if she had not imbibed injurious impressions from the unlicensed and indiscriminate reading she practised, it was more owing to the fortunate circumstance, that the baronet's library contained nothing extremely offensive to a pure taste, nor dangerous to good morals, than to any precaution of her parents against the deadly, the irretrievable injury to be sustained from ungoverned liberty in this respect to a female mind. On the other hand, Mrs. Wilson had inculcated the necessity of restraint, in selecting the books for her perusal, so strenuously on her niece, that what at first had been the effects of obedience and submission, had now settled into taste and habit; and Emily seldom opened a book, unless in search of information; or if it were the indulgence of a less commendable spirit, it was an indulgence chastened by a taste and judgment that lessened the danger, if it did not entirely remove it.

The room was filled with gentlemen and ladies; and while John was exchanging his greetings with several of the neighboring gentry of his acquaintance, his sisters were running hastily over a catalogue of the books kept for circulation, as an elderly lady, of foreign accent and dress, entered; and depositing a couple of religious works on the counter, she inquired for the remainder of the set. The peculiarity of her idiom and her proximity to the sisters caused them both to look up at the moment, and, to the surprise of Jane, her sister uttered a slight exclamation of pleasure. The foreigner was attracted by the sound, and after a moment's hesitation, she respectfully curtsied. Emily, advancing, kindly offered her hand, and the usual inquiries after each other's welfare succeeded. To the questions asked after the friend of the matron Emily learnt, with some surprise, and no less satisfaction, that she resided in a retired cottage, about five miles from L----, where they had been for the last six months, and where they expected to remain for some time, "until she could prevail on Mrs. Fitzgerald to return to Spain; a thing, now there was peace, of which she did not despair." After asking leave to call on them in their retreat, and exchanging good wishes, the Spanish lady withdrew, and, as Jane had made her selection, was followed immediately by John Moseley and his sisters. Emily, in their walk home, acquainted her brother that the companion of their Bath incognita had been at the library, and that for the first time she had learnt that their young acquaintance was, or had been, married, and her name. John listened to his sister with the interest which the beautiful Spaniard had excited at the time they first met, and laughingly told her he could not believe their unknown friend had ever been a wife. To satisfy this doubt, and to gratify a wish they both had to renew their acquaintance with the foreigner, they agreed to drive to the cottage the following morning, accompanied by Mrs. Wilson and Jane, if she would go; but the next day was the one appointed by Egerton for his arrival at L----, and Jane, under a pretence of writing letters, declined the excursion. She had carefully examined the papers since his departure; had seen his name included in the arrivals at London; and at a later day, had read an account of the review by the commander-in-chief of the regiment to which he belonged. He had never written to any of her friends; but, judging from her own feelings, she did not in the least doubt he would be as punctual as love could make him. Mrs. Wilson listened to her niece's account of the unexpected interview in the library with pleasure, and cheerfully promised to accompany them in their morning's excursion, as she had both a wish to alleviate sorrow, and a desire to better understand the character of this accidental acquaintance of Emily's.

Mr. Benfield and the baronet had a long conversation in relation to Denbigh's fortune the morning after their arrival; and the old man was loud in his expression of dissatisfaction at the youngster's pride. As the baronet, however, in the fulness of his affection and simplicity, betrayed to his uncle his expectation of a union between Denbigh and his daughter, Mr. Benfield became contented with this reward; one fit, he thought, for any services. On the whole, "it was best, as he was to marry Emmy, he should sell out of the army; and as there would be an election soon, he would bring him into parliament--yes--- yes--it did a man so much good to sit one term in the parliament of this realm--to study human nature. All his own knowledge in that way was raised on the foundations laid in the House." To this Sir Edward cordially assented, and the gentlemen separated, happy in their arrangements to advance the welfare of two beings they so sincerely loved.

Although the care and wisdom of Mrs. Wilson had prohibited the admission of any romantic or enthusiastic expectations of happiness into the day-dreams of her charge, yet the buoyancy of health, of hope, of youth, of innocence, had elevated Emily to a height of enjoyment hitherto unknown to her usually placid and disciplined pleasures. Denbigh certainly mingled in most of her thoughts, both of the past and the future, and she stood on the threshold of that fantastic edifice in which Jane ordinarily resided. Emily was in the situation perhaps the most dangerous to a young female Christian: her heart, her affections, were given to a man, to appearance, every way worthy of possessing them, it is true but she had admitted a rival in her love to her Maker; and to keep those feelings distinct, to bend the passions in due submission to the more powerful considerations of endless duty, of unbounded gratitude, is one of the most trying struggles of Christian fortitude. We are much more apt to forget our God in prosperity than adversity. The weakness of human nature drives us to seek assistance in distress; but vanity and worldly-mindedness often induce us to imagine we control the happiness we only enjoy.

Sir Edward and Lady Moseley could see nothing in the prospect of the future but lives of peace and contentment for their children. Clara was happily settled, and her sisters were on the eve of making connexions with men of family, condition, and certain character. What more could be done for them? They must, like other people, take their chances in the lottery of life; they could only hope and pray for their prosperity, and this they did with great sincerity. Not so Mrs. Wilson: she had guarded the invaluable charge intrusted to her keeping with too much assiduity, too keen an interest, too just a sense of the awful responsibility she had undertaken, to desert her post at the moment watchfulness was most required. By a temperate, but firm and well-chosen conversation she kept alive the sense of her real condition in her niece, and labored hard to prevent the blandishments of life from supplanting the lively hope of enjoying another existence. She endeavored, by her pious example, her prayers, and her judicious allusions, to keep the passion of love in the breast of Emily secondary to the more important object of her creation; and, by the aid of a kind and Almighty Providence, her labors, though arduous, were crowned with success.

As the family were seated round the table after dinner, on the day of their walk to the library, John Moseley, awakening from a reverie, exclaimed suddenly,

"Which do you think the handsomest, Emily, Grace Chatterton or Miss Fitzgerald?"

Emily laughed, as she answered, "Grace, certainly; do you not think so, brother?"

"Yes, on the whole; but don't you think Grace looks like her mother at times?"

"Oh no, she is the image of Chatterton."

"She is very like yourself, Emmy dear," said Mr. Benfield, who was listening to their conversation.

"Me, dear uncle; I have never heard it remarked before."

"Yes, yes, she is as much like you as she can stare. I never saw as great a resemblance, excepting between you and Lady Juliana--Lady Juliana, Emmy, was a beauty in her day; very like her uncle, old Admiral Griffin-- you can't remember the admiral--he lost an eye in a battle with the Dutch, and part of his cheek in a frigate, when a young man fighting the Dons. Oh, he was a pleasant old gentleman; many a guinea has he given me when I was a boy at school."

"And he looked like Grace Chatterton, uncle, did he?" asked John, innocently.

"No, sir, he did not; who said he looked like Grace Chatterton, jackanapes?"

"Why, I thought you made it out, sir: but perhaps it was the description that deceived me--his eye and cheek, uncle."

"Did Lord Gosford leave children, uncle?" inquired Emily, throwing a look of reproach at John.

"No, Emmy dear; his only child, a son, died at school. I shall never forget the grief of poor Lady Juliana. She postponed a visit to Bath three weeks on account of it. A gentleman who was paying his addresses to her at the time, offered then, and was refused--indeed, her self-denial raised such an admiration of her in the men, that immediately after the death of young Lord Dayton, no less than seven gentlemen offered, and were refused in one week. I heard Lady Juliana say, that what between lawyers and suitors, she had not a moment's peace."

"Lawyers?" cried Sir Edward: "what had she to do with lawyers?"

"Why, Sir Edward, six thousand a year fell to her by the death of her nephew; and there were trustees and deeds to be made out--poor young woman, she was so affected, Emmy, I don't think she went out for a week--all the time at home reading papers, and attending to her important concerns. Oh! she was a woman of taste; her mourning, and liveries, and new carriage, were more admired than those of any one about the court. Yes, yes, the title is extinct; I know of none of the name now. The Earl did not survive his loss but six years, and the countess died broken-hearted, about a twelvemonth before him."

"And Lady Juliana, uncle," inquired John, "what became of her, did she marry?"

The old man helped himself to a glass of wine, and looked over his shoulder to see if Peter was at hand. Peter, who had been originally butler, and had made it a condition of his preferment, that whenever there was company, he should be allowed to preside at the sideboard, was now at his station. Mr. Benfield, seeing his old friend near him, ventured to talk on a subject he seldom trusted himself with in company.

"Why, yes--yes--she *did* marry, it's true, although she did tell me she intended to die a maid; but--hem--I suppose--hem--it was compassion for the old viscount, who often said he could not live without her; and then it gave her the power of doing so much good, a jointure of five thousand a year added to her own income: yet--hem--I confess I did not think she would have chosen such an old and infirm man--- but, Peter, give me a glass of claret." Peter handed the claret, and the old man proceeded:--"They say he was very cross to her, and that, no doubt, must have made her unhappy, she was so very tender-hearted."

How much longer the old gentleman would have continued in this strain, it is impossible to say; but he was interrupted by the opening of the parlor door, and the sudden appearance on its threshold of Denbigh. Every countenance glowed with pleasure at this unexpected return of their favorite; and but for the prudent caution of Mrs. Wilson, in handing a glass of water to her niece, the surprise might have proved too much for her. The salutations of Denbigh were returned by the different members of the family with a cordiality that must have told him how much he was valued by all its branches; and after briefly informing them that his review was over, and that he had thrown himself into a chaise and travelled post until he had rejoined them, he took his seat by Mr. Benfield, who received him with a marked preference, exceeding that which he had shown to any man who had ever entered his doors, Lord Gosford himself not excepted. Peter removed from his station behind his master's chair to one where he could face the new comer; and after wiping his eyes until they filled so rapidly with water, that at last he was noticed by the delighted John to put on the identical goggles which his care had provided for Denbigh in his illness. His laugh drew the attention of the rest to the honest steward, and when Denbigh was told this was Mr. Benfield's ambassador to the hall, he rose from his chair, and taking the old man by the hand, kindly thanked him for his thoughtful consideration for his weak eyes.

Peter took the offered hand in both his own, and after making one or two unsuccessful efforts to speak, he uttered, "Thank you, thank you; may Heaven bless you," and burst into tears. This stopped the laugh, and John followed the steward from the room, while his master exclaimed, wiping his eyes, "Kind and condescending; just such another as my old friend, the Earl of Gosford."

Chapter XXIII

At the appointed hour, the carriage of Mrs. Wilson was ready to convey herself and niece to the cottage of Mrs. Fitzgerald. John was left behind, under the pretence of keeping Denbigh company in his morning avocations, but really because Mrs. Wilson doubted the propriety of his becoming a visiting acquaintance at the house, tenanted as the cottage was represented to be. John was too fond of his friend to make any serious objections, and was satisfied for the present, by sending his compliments, and requesting his sister to ask permission for him to call in one of his morning excursions, in order to pay his personal respects.

They found the cottage a beautiful and genteel, though a very small and retired dwelling, almost hid by the trees and shrubs which surrounded it, and its mistress in its little veranda, expecting the arrival of Emily. Mrs. Fitzgerald was a Spaniard, under twenty, of a melancholy, yet highly interesting countenance; her manners were soft and retiring, but evidently bore the impression of good company, if not of high life. She was extremely pleased with this renewal of attention on the part of Emily, and expressed her gratitude to both ladies for their kindness in seeking her out in her solitude. She presented her more matronly companion to them, by the name of Donna Lorenza; and as nothing but good feeling prevailed, and useless ceremony was banished, the little party were soon on terms of friendly intercourse. The young widow (for such her dress indicated her to be), did the honors of her house with graceful ease, and conducted her visiters into her little grounds, which; together the cottage, gave evident proofs of the taste and elegance of its occupant. The establishment she supported she represented as very small; two women and an aged man servant, with occasionally a laborer for her garden and shrubbery. They never visited; it was a resolution she had made on fixing her residence here, but if Mrs. Wilson and Miss Moseley would forgive the rudeness of not returning their call, nothing would give her more satisfaction than a frequent renewal of their visits. Mrs. Wilson took so deep an interest in the misfortunes of this young female, and was so much pleased with the modest resignation of her manner, that it required little persuasion on the part of the recluse to obtain a promise of soon repeating her visit. Emily mentioned the request of John, and Mrs. Fitzgerald received it with a mournful smile, as she replied that Mr. Moseley had laid her under such an obligation in their first interview, she could not deny herself the pleasure of again thanking him for it; but she must be excused if she desired they would limit their attendants to him, as there was but one gentleman in England whose visits she admitted, and it was seldom indeed he called; he had seen her but once since she had resided in Norfolk.

After giving a promise not to suffer any one else to accompany them, and promising an early call again, our ladies returned to Benfield Lodge in season to dress for dinner. On entering the drawing-room, they found the elegant person of Colonel Egerton leaning on the back of Jane's chair. He had arrived during their absence, and immediately sought the baronet's family. His reception, if not as warm as that given to Denbigh, was cordial from all but the master of the house; and even he was in such spirits by the company around him, and the prospects of Emily's marriage (which he considered as settled), that he forced himself to an appearance of good will he did not feel. Colonel Egerton was either deceived by his manner, or too much a man of the world to discover his suspicion, and everything in consequence was very harmoniously, if not sincerely conducted between them.

Lady Moseley was completely happy. If she had the least doubts before, as to the intentions of Egerton, they were now removed. His journey to that unfashionable watering-place, was owing to his passion; and however she might at times have doubted as to Sir Edgar's heir, Denbigh she thought a man of too little consequence in the world, to make it possible he would neglect to profit by his situation in the family of Sir Edward Moseley. She was satisfied with both connexions. Mr. Benfield had told her General Sir Frederic Denbigh was nearly allied to the Duke of Derwent, and Denbigh had said the general was his grandfather. Wealth, she knew Emily would possess from both her uncle and aunt; and the services of the gentleman had their due weight upon the feelings of the affectionate mother. The greatest of her maternal anxieties was removed, and she looked forward to the peaceful enjoyment of the remnant of her days in the bosom of her descendants. John, the heir of a baronetcy, and 15,000 pounds a year, might suit himself; and Grace Chatterton, she thought, would be likely to prove the future Lady Moseley. Sir Edward, without entering so deeply into anticipations of the future as his wife, experienced an equal degree of contentment; and it would have been a difficult task to discover in the island a roof, under which there resided at the moment more happy countenances than at Benfield Lodge; for as its master had insisted on Denbigh becoming an inmate, he was obliged to extend his hospitality in an equal degree to Colonel Egerton: indeed, the subject had been fully canvassed between him and Peter the morning of his arrival, and was near being decided against his admission, when the steward, who had picked up all the incidents of the arbor scene from the servants (and of course with many exaggerations), mentioned to his master that the colonel was very active, and that he even contrived to bring water to revive Miss Emmy, a great distance, in the hat of Captain Jarvis, which was full of holes, Mr. John having blown it off the head of the captain without hurting a hair, in firing at a woodcock. This mollified the master a little, and he agreed to suspend his decision for further observation. At dinner, the colonel happening to admire the really handsome face of Lord Gosford, as delineated by Sir Joshua Reynolds, which graced the dining-room of Benfield Lodge, its master, in a moment of unusual kindness, gave the invitation; it was politely accepted, and the colonel at once domesticated.

The face of John Moseley alone, at times, exhibited evidences of care and thought, and at such moments it might be a subject of doubt whether he thought the most of Grace Chatterton or her mother: if the latter, the former was sure to lose ground in his estimation; a serious misfortune to John, not to be able to love Grace without alloy. His letters from her brother mentioned his being still at Denbigh castle, in Westmoreland, the seat of his friend the Duke of Derwent; and John thought one or two of his encomiums on Lady Harriet Denbigh, the sister of his grace, augured that the unkindness of Emily might in time be forgotten. The dowager and her daughters were at the seat of a maiden aunt in Yorkshire, where as John knew no male animal was allowed admittance, he was tolerably easy at the disposition of things. Nothing but legacy-hunting he knew would induce the dowager to submit to such a banishment from the other sex; but that was so preferable to husband-hunting he was satisfied. "I wish," said John mentally, as he finished the perusal of his letter, "mother Chatterton would get married herself, and she might let Kate and Grace manage for themselves. Kate would do very well, I dare say, and how would Grace make out!" John sighed, and whistled for Dido and Rover.

In the manners of Colonel Egerton there was the same general disposition to please, and the same unremitted attention to the wishes and amusements of Jane. They had renewed their poetical investigations, and Jane eagerly encouraged a taste which afforded her delicacy some little coloring for the indulgence of an association different from the real truth, and which, in her estimation, was necessary to her happiness. Mrs. Wilson thought the distance between the two suitors for the favor of her nieces was, if anything, increased by their short separation, and particularly noticed on the part of the colonel an aversion to Denbigh that at times painfully alarmed, by exciting apprehensions for the future happiness of the precious treasure she had prepared herself to yield to his solicitations, whenever properly proffered. In the intercourse between Emily and her preserver, as there was nothing to condemn, so there was much to admire. The attentions of Denbigh were pointed, although less exclusive than those of the colonel; and the aunt was pleased to observe that if the manners of Egerton had more of the gloss of life, those of Denbigh were certainly distinguished by a more finished delicacy and propriety. The one appeared the influence of custom and association, with a tincture of artifice; the other, benevolence, with a just perception of what was due to others, and with an air of sincerity, when speaking of sentiments and principles, that was particularly pleasing to the watchful widow. At times, however, she could not but observe an air of restraint, if not of awkwardness, about him that was a little surprising. It was most observable in mixed society, and once or twice her imagination pictured his sensations into something like alarm. These unpleasant interruptions to her admiration were soon forgotten in her just appreciation of the more solid parts of his character, which appeared literally to be unexceptionable; and when momentary uneasiness would steal over her, the remembrance of the opinion of Dr. Ives, his behavior with Jarvis, his charity, and chiefly his devotion to her niece, would not fail to drive the disagreeable thoughts from her mind. Emily herself moved about, the image of joy and innocence. If Denbigh were near her, she was happy; if absent, she suffered no uneasiness. Her feelings were so ardent, and yet so pure, that jealousy had no admission. Perhaps no circumstances existed to excite this usual attendant of the passion; but as the heart of Emily was more enchained than her imagination, her affections were not of the restless nature of ordinary attachments, though more dangerous to her peace of mind in the event of an unfortunate issue. With Denbigh she never walked or rode alone. He had never made the request, and her delicacy would have shrunk from such an open manifestation of her preference; but he read to her and her aunt; he accompanied them in their little excursions; and once or twice John noticed that she took the offered hand of Denbigh to assist her over any little impediment in their course, instead of her usual unobtrusive custom of taking his arm on such occasions. "Well, Miss Emily," thought John, "you appear to have chosen another favorite," on her doing this three times in succession in one of their walks. "How strange it is women will quit their natural friends for a face they have hardly seen." John forgot his own--"There is no danger, dear Grace," when his sister was almost dead with apprehension. But John loved Emily too well to witness her preference of another with satisfaction, even though Denbigh was the favorite; a feeling which soon wore away, however, by dint of custom and reflection. Mr. Benfield had taken it into his head that if the wedding of Emily could be solemnized while the family was at the lodge, it would render him the happiest of men; and how to compass this object, was the occupation of a whole morning's contemplation. Happily for Emily's blushes, the old gentleman harbored the most fastidious notions of female delicacy, and never in conversation made the most distant allusion to the expected connexion. He, therefore, in conformity with these feelings, could do nothing openly; all must be the effect of management; and as he thought Peter one of the best contrivers in the world, to his ingenuity he determined to refer the arrangement.

The bell rang--"Send Johnson to me, David."

In a few minutes, the drab coat and blue yarn stockings entered his dressing-room with the body of Mr. Peter Johnson snugly cased within them.

"Peter," commenced Mr. Benfield, pointing kindly to a chair, which the steward respectfully declined, "I suppose you know that Mr. Denbigh, the grandson of General Denbigh, who was in parliament with me, is about to marry my little Emmy?"

Peter smiled, as he bowed an assent.

"Now, Peter, a wedding would, of all things, make me most happy; that is, to have it here in the lodge. It would remind me so much of the marriage of Lord Gosford, and the bridemaids. I wish your opinion how to bring it about before they leave us. Sir Edward and Anne decline interfering, and Mrs. Wilson I am afraid to speak to on the subject."

Peter was not a little alarmed by this sudden requisition on his inventive faculties, especially as a lady was in the case; but, as he prided himself on serving his master, and loved the hilarity of a wedding in his heart, he cogitated for some time in silence, when, having thought a preliminary question or two necessary, he broke it with saying--

"Everything, I suppose, master, is settled between the young people?"

"Everything, I take it, Peter."

"And Sir Edward and my lady?"

"Willing; perfectly willing."

"And Madam Wilson, sir?"

"Willing, Peter, willing."

"And Mr. John and Miss Jane?"

"All willing; the whole family is willing, to the best of my belief.'"

"There is the Rev. Mr. Ives and Mrs. Ives, master?"

"They wish it, I know. Don't you think they wish others as happy as themselves, Peter?"

"No doubt they do, master. Well, then, as everybody is willing, and the young people agreeable, the only thing to be done, sir, is--"

"Is what, Peter?" exclaimed his impatient master observing him to hesitate.

"Why, sir, to send for the priest, I take it."

"Pshaw! Peter Johnson, I know that myself," replied the dissatisfied old man. "Cannot you help me to a better plan?"

"Why, master," said Peter, "I would have done as well for Miss Emmy and your honor as I would have done for myself. Now, sir, when I courted Patty Steele, your honor, in the year of our Lord one thousand seven hundred and sixty-five, I should have been married but for one difficulty, which your honor says is removed in the case of Miss Emmy."

"What was that, Peter?" asked his master, in a tender tone.

"She wasn't willing, sir."

"Very well, poor Peter," replied Mr. Benfield, mildly "you may go." And the steward, bowing low, withdrew.

The similarity of their fortunes in love was a strong link in the sympathies which bound the master and man together and the former never failed to be softened by an allusion to Patty. The want of tact in the man, on the present occasion, after much reflection, was attributed by his master to the fact that Peter had never sat in parliament.

Chapter XXIV

Mrs. Wilson and Emily, in the fortnight they had been at Benfield Lodge, paid frequent and long visits to the cottage: and each succeeding interview left a more favorable impression of the character of its mistress, and a greater certainty that she was unfortunate. The latter, however, alluded very slightly to her situation or former life; she was a Protestant, to the great surprise of Mrs. Wilson; and one that misery had made nearly acquainted with the religion she professed. Their conversations chiefly turned on the customs of her own, as contrasted with those of her adopted country, or in a pleasant exchange of opinions, which the ladies possessed in complete unison. One morning John had accompanied them and been admitted; Mrs. Fitzgerald receiving him with the frankness of an old acquaintance, though with the reserve of a Spanish lady. His visits were permitted under the direction of his aunt, but no others of the gentlemen were included amongst her guests. Mrs. Wilson had casually mentioned, in the absence of her niece, the interposition of Denbigh between her and death; and Mrs. Fitzgerald was so much pleased at the noble conduct of the gentleman, as to express a desire to see him; but the impressions of the moment appeared to have died away, a nothing more was said by either lady on the subject, and it was apparently forgotten. Mrs. Fitzgerald was found one morning, weeping over a letter she held in her hand, and the Donna Lorenza was endeavoring to console her. The situation of this latter lady was somewhat doubtful; she appeared neither wholly a friend nor a menial. In the manners of the two there was a striking difference; although the Donna was not vulgar, she was far from possessing the polish of her more juvenile friend, and Mrs. Wilson considered her to be in a station between that of a housekeeper and that of a companion. After hoping that no unpleasant intelligence occasioned the distress they witnessed, the ladies were delicately about to take their leave, when Mrs. Fitzgerald entreated them to remain.

"Your kind attention to me, dear madam, and the goodness of Miss Moseley, give you a claim to know more of the unfortunate being your sympathy has so greatly assisted to attain her peace of mind. This letter is from the gentleman of whom you have heard me speak, as once visiting me, and though it has struck me with unusual force, it contains no more than I expected to hear, perhaps no more than I deserve to hear."

"I hope your friend has not been unnecessarily harsh: severity is not the best way, always, of effecting repentance, and I feel certain that you, my young friend, can have been guilty of no offence that does not rather require gentle than stern reproof," said Mrs. Wilson.

"I thank you, dear madam, for your indulgent opinion of me, but although I have suffered much, I am willing to confess it is a merited punishment; you are, however, mistaken as to the source of my present sorrow. Lord Pendennyss is the cause of grief, I believe, to no one, much less to me."

"Lord Pendennyss!" exclaimed Emily, in surprise, unconsciously looking at her aunt.

"Pendennyss!" reiterated Mrs. Wilson, with animation "and is he your friend, too?" "Yes, madam; to his lordship I owe everything--honor--comfort--religion--and even life itself."

Mrs. Wilson's cheek glowed with an unusual color, at this discovery of another act of benevolence and virtue, in a young nobleman whose character she had so long admired, and whose person she had in vain wished to meet.

"You know the earl, then?" inquired Mrs. Fitzgerald.

"By reputation, only, my dear," said Mrs. Wilson; "but that is enough to convince me a friend of his must be a worthy character, if anything were wanting to make us your friends."

The conversation was continued for some time, and Mrs. Fitzgerald saying she did not feel equal just then to the undertaking, but the next day, if they would honor her with another call, she would make them acquainted with the incidents of her life, and the reasons she had for speaking in such terms of Lord Pendennyss. The promise to see her was cheerfully made by Mrs. Wilson, and her confidence accepted; not from a desire to gratify an idle curiosity, but a belief that it was necessary to probe a wound to cure it; and a correct opinion, that she would be a better adviser for a young and lovely woman, than even Pendennyss; for the Donna Lorenza she could hardly consider in a capacity to offer advice, much less dictation. They then took their leave, and Emily, during their ride, broke the silence with exclaiming,--

"Wherever we hear of Lord Pendennyss, aunt, we hear of him favorably."

"A certain sign, my dear, he is deserving of it. There is hardly any man who has not his enemies, and those are seldom just; but we have met with none of the earl's yet."

"Fifty thousand a year will make many friends," observed Emily, shaking her head.

"Doubtless, my love, or as many enemies; but honor, life, and religion, my child, are debts not owing to money--in this country at least."

To this remark Emily assented; and after expressing her own admiration of the character of the young nobleman, she dropped into a reverie. How many of his virtues she identified with the person of Mr. Denbigh, it is not, just now, our task to enumerate; but judges of human nature may easily determine, and that too without having sat in the parliament of this realm.

The morning this conversation occurred at the cottage, Mr. and Mrs. Jarvis, with their daughters, made their unexpected appearance at L----. The arrival of a post-chaise and four with a gig, was an event soon circulated through the little village, and the names of its owners reached the lodge just as Jane had allowed herself to be persuaded by the colonel to take her first walk with him unaccompanied by a third person. Walking is much more propitious to declarations than riding; and whether it was premeditated on the part of the colonel or not, or whether he was afraid that Mrs. Jarvis or some one else would interfere, he availed himself of this opportunity, and had hardly got out of hearing of her brother and Denbigh, before he made Jane an explicit offer of his hand. The surprise was so great, that some time elapsed before the distressed girl could reply. This she, however, at length did, but incoherently: she referred him to her parents, as the arbiters of her fate, well knowing that her wishes had long been those of her father and mother. With this the colonel was obliged to be satisfied for the present. But their walk had not ended, before he gradually drew from the confiding girl an acknowledgment that, should her parents decline his offer, she would be very little less miserable than himself; indeed, the most tenacious lover might have been content with the proofs of regard that Jane, unused to control her feelings, allowed herself to manifest on this occasion. Egerton was in raptures; a life devoted to her would never half repay her condescension; and as their confidence increased with their walk, Jane re-entered the lodge with a degree of happiness in her heart she had never before experienced. The much dreaded declaration--her own distressing acknowledgements, were made, and nothing farther remained but to live and be happy. She flew into the arms of her mother, and; hiding her blushes in her bosom, acquainted her with the colonel's offer and her own wishes. Lady Moseley, who was prepared for such a communication, and had rather wondered at its tardiness, kissed her daughter affectionately, as she promised to speak to her father, and to obtain his approbation.

"But," she added, with a degree of formality and caution which had better preceded than have followed the courtship, "we must make the usual inquiries, my child, into the fitness of Colonel Egerton as a husband for our daughter. Once assured of that, you have nothing to fear."

The baronet was requested to grant an audience to Colonel Egerton, who now appeared as determined to expedite things, as he had been dilatory before. On meeting Sir Edward, he made known his pretensions and hopes. The father, who had been previously notified by his wife of what was forthcoming, gave a general answer, similar to the speech of the mother, and the colonel bowed in acquiescence.

In the evening, the Jarvis family favored the inhabitants of the lodge with a visit, and Mrs. Wilson was struck with the singularity of their reception of the colonel. Miss Jarvis, especially, was rude to both him and Jane, and it struck all who witnessed it as a burst of jealous feeling for disappointed hopes; but to no one, excepting Mrs. Wilson, did it occur that the conduct of the gentleman could be at all implicated in the transaction. Mr. Benfield was happy to see under his roof again the best of the trio of Jarvises he had known, and something like sociability prevailed. There was to be a ball, Miss Jarvis remarked, at L----, the following day, which would help to enliven the scene a little, especially as there were a couple of frigates at anchor, a few miles off, and the officers were expected to join the party. This intelligence had but little effect on the ladies of the Moseley family; yet, as their uncle desired that, out of respect to his neighbors, if invited, they would go, they cheerfully assented. During the evening, Mrs. Wilson observed Egerton in familiar conversation with Miss Jarvis; and as she had been notified of his situation with respect to Jane, she determined to watch narrowly into the causes of so singular a change of deportment in the young lady. Mrs. Jarvis retained her respect for the colonel in full force; and called out to him across the room, a few minutes before she departed--

"Well, colonel, I am happy to tell you I have heard very lately from your uncle, Sir Edgar."

"Indeed, madam!" replied the colonel, starting. "He was well, I hope."

"Very well, the day before yesterday. His neighbor, old, Mr. Holt, is a lodger in the same house with us at L----; and as I thought you would like to hear, I made particular inquiries about the baronet." The word baronet was pronounced with emphasis and a look of triumph, as if it would say, you see *we* have baronets as well as you. As no answer was made by Egerton, excepting an acknowledging bow, the merchant and his family departed.

"Well, John," cried Emily, with a smile, "we have heard more good to-day of our trusty and well-beloved cousin, the Earl of Pendennyss."

"Indeed!" exclaimed her brother. "You must keep Emily for his lordship, positively, aunt: she is almost as great an admirer of him as yourself."

"I apprehend it is necessary she should be quite as much so, to become his wife," said Mrs. Wilson.

"Really," said Emily, more gravely, "if all one hears of him be true, or even half, it would be no difficult task to admire him."

Denbigh was standing leaning on the back of a chair, in situation where he could view the animated countenance of Emily as she spoke, and Mrs. Wilson noticed an uneasiness and a changing of color in him that appeared uncommon from so trifling a cause. Is it possible, she thought, Denbigh can harbor so mean a passion as envy? He walked away, as if unwilling to hear more, and appeared much engrossed with his own reflections for the remainder of the evening. There were moments of doubting which crossed the mind of Mrs. Wilson with a keenness of apprehension proportionate to her deep interest in Emily, with respect to certain traits in the character of Denbigh; and this, what she thought a display of unworthy feeling, was one of them. In the course of the evening, the cards for the expected ball arrived, and were accepted. As this new arrangement for the morrow interfered with their intended visit to Mrs. Fitzgerald, a servant was sent with a note of explanation in the morning and a request that on the following day the promised communication might be made. To this arrangement the recluse assented, and Emily prepared for the ball with a melancholy recollection of the consequences which grew out of the last she had attended--melancholy at the fate of Digby, and pleasure at the principles manifested by Denbigh, on the occasion. The latter, however, with a smile, excused himself from being of the party, telling Emily he was so awkward that he feared some unpleasant consequences to himself or his friends would arise from his inadvertencies, did he venture again with her into such an assembly.

Emily sighed gently, as she entered the carriage of her aunt early in the afternoon, leaving Denbigh in the door of the lodge, and Egerton absent on the execution of some business; the former to amuse himself as he could until the following morning, and the latter to join them in the dance in the evening.

The arrangement included an excursion on the water, attended by the bands from the frigates, a collation, and in the evening a ball. One of the vessels was commanded by a Lord Henry Stapleton, a fine young man, who, struck with the beauty and appearance of the sisters, sought an introduction to the baronet's family, and engaged the hand of Emily for the first dance. His frank and gentleman-like deportment was pleasing to his new acquaintances; the more so, as it was peculiarly suited to their situation at the moment. Mrs. Wilson was in unusual spirits, and maintained an animated conversation with the young sailor, in the course of which, he spoke of his cruising on the coast of Spain, and by accident he mentioned his having carried out to that country, upon one occasion, Lord Pendennyss. This was common ground between them, and Lord Henry was as enthusiastic in his praises of the earl, as Mrs. Wilson's partiality could desire. He also knew Colonel Egerton slightly, and expressed his pleasure, in polite terms, when they met in the evening in the ball-room, at being able to renew his acquaintance. The evening passed off as such evenings generally do--in gaiety, listlessness, dancing, gaping, and heartburnings, according to the dispositions and good or ill fortune of the several individuals who compose the assembly. Mrs. Wilson, while her nieces were dancing, moved her seat to be near a window, and found herself in the vicinity of two elderly gentlemen, who were commenting on the company. After making several common-place remarks, one of them inquired of the other--"Who is that military gentleman amongst the naval beaux, Holt?"

"That is the hopeful nephew of my friend and neighbor, Sir Edgar Egerton; he is here dancing, and misspending his time and money, when I know Sir Edgar gave him a thousand pounds six months ago, on express condition, he should not leave the regiment or take a card in his hand for twelvemonth."

"He plays, then?"

"Sadly; he is, on the whole, a very bad young man."

As they changed their topic, Mrs. Wilson joined her sister, dreadfully shocked at this intimation of the vices of a man so near an alliance with her brother's child. She was thankful it was not too late to avert part of the evil, and determined to acquaint Sir Edward, at once, with what she had heard, in order that an investigation might establish the colonel's innocence or guilt.

Chapter XXV

They returned to the lodge at an early hour, and Mrs Wilson, after meditating upon the course she ought to take, resolved to have a conversation with her brother that evening after supper. Accordingly, as they were among the last to retire, she mentioned her wish to detain him, and when left by themselves, the baronet taking his seat by her on a sofa, she commenced as follows, willing to avoid her unpleasant information until the last moment.

"I wished to say something to you, brother, relating to my charge: you have, no doubt, observed the attentions of Mr. Denbigh to Emily?"

"Certainly, sister, and with great pleasure; you must not suppose I wish to interfere with the authority I have so freely relinquished to you, Charlotte, when I inquire if Emily favors his views or not?"

"Neither Emily nor I, my dear brother, wish ever to question your right, not only to inquire into, but to control the conduct of your child;--she is yours, Edward, by a tie nothing can break, and we both love you too much to wish it. There is nothing you may be more certain of, than that, without the approbation of her parents, Emily would accept of no offer, however splendid or agreeable to her own wishes."

"Nay, sister, I would not wish unduly to influence my child in an affair of so much importance to herself; but my interest in Denbigh is little short of that I feel for my daughter."

"I trust," continued Mrs. Wilson, "Emily is too deeply impressed with her duty to forget the impressive mandate, 'to honor her father and mother:' yes, Sir Edward, I am mistaken if she would not relinquish the dearest object of her affections, at your request; and at the same time, I am persuaded she would, under no circumstances, approach the altar with a man she did not both love and esteem."

The baronet did not appear exactly to understand his sister's distinction, as he observed, "I am not sure I rightly comprehend the difference you make, Charlotte."

"Only, brother, that she would feel that a promise made at the altar to love a man she felt averse to, or honor one she could not esteem, as a breach of a duty, paramount to all earthly considerations," replied his sister; "but to answer your question--Denbigh has never offered, and when he does, I do not think he will be refused."

"Refused!" cried the baronet, "I sincerely hope not; I wish, with all my heart, they were married already."

"Emily is very young," said Mrs. Wilson, "and need not hurry: I was in hopes she would remain single a few years longer."

"Well," said the baronet, "you and Lady Moseley, sister, have different notions on the subject of marrying the girls."

Mrs. Wilson replied, with a good-humored smile, "you have made Anne so good a husband, Ned, that she forgets there are any bad ones in the world; *my* greatest anxiety is, that the husband of my niece may be a Christian; indeed, I know not how I can reconcile it to my conscience, as a Christian myself, to omit this important qualification,"

"I am sure, Charlotte, both Denbigh and Egerton appear to have a great respect for religion; they are punctual at church, and very attentive to the service:" Mrs. Wilson smiled as he proceeded, "but religion may come after marriage, you know."

"Yes, brother, and I know it may not come at all; no really pious woman can be happy, without her husband is in what she deems the road to future happiness himself; and it is idle--it is worse--it is almost impious to marry with a view to reform a husband: indeed, she greatly endangers her own safety thereby; for few of us, I believe, but find the temptation to err as much as we can contend with, without calling in the aid of example against us, in an object we love; indeed it appears to me, the life of such a woman must be a struggle between conflicting duties."

"Why," said the baronet, "if your plan were generally adopted, I am afraid it would give a deadly blow to matrimony."

"I have nothing to do with generals, brother, I am acting for individual happiness, and discharging individual duties: at the same time I cannot agree with you in its effects on the community. I think no man who dispassionately examines the subject, will be other than a Christian; and rather than remain bachelors, they would take even that trouble; if the strife in our sex were less for a husband, wives would increase in value."

"But how is it, Charlotte," said the baronet, pleasantly, "your sex do not use your power and reform the age?"

"The work of reformation, Sir Edward," replied his sister, gravely, "is an arduous one indeed, and I despair of seeing it general, in my day; but much, very much, might be done towards it, if those who have the guidance of youth would take that trouble with their pupils that good faith requires of them, to discharge the minor duties of life."

"Women ought to marry," observed the baronet, musing.

"Marriage is certainly the natural and most desirable state for a woman," but how few are there who, having entered it, know how to discharge its duties; more particularly those of a mother! On the subject of marrying our daughters, for instance, instead of qualifying them to make a proper choice, they are generally left to pick up such principles and opinions as they may come at, as it were by chance. It is true, if the parent be a Christian in name, certain of the externals of religion are observed; but what are these, if not enforced by a consistent example in the instructor?"

"Useful precepts are seldom lost, I believe, sister," said Sir Edward, with confidence.

"Always useful, my dear brother; but young people are more observant than we are apt to imagine, and are wonderfully ingenious in devising excuses to themselves for their conduct. I have often heard it offered as an apology, that father or mother knew it, or perhaps did it, and therefore it could not be wrong: association is all-important to a child."

"I believe no family of consequence admits of improper associates within my knowledge," said the baronet.

Mrs. Wilson smiled as she answered, "I am sure I hope not, Edward; but are the qualifications we require in companions for our daughters, always such as are most reconcileable with our good sense or our consciences; a single communication with an objectionable character is a precedent, if known and unobserved, which will be offered to excuse acquaintances with worse persons: with the other sex, especially, their acquaintance should be very guarded and select."

"You would make many old maids, sister."

"I doubt it greatly, brother; it would rather bring female society in demand. I often regret that selfishness, cupidity, and the kind of strife which prevails in our sex, on the road to matrimony, have brought celibacy into disrepute. For my part, I never see an old maid, but I am willing to think she is so from choice or principle, and although not in her proper place, serviceable, by keeping alive feelings necessary to exist, that marriages may not become curses instead of blessings."

"A kind of Eddystone, to prevent matrimonial shipwrecks," said the brother, gayly.

"Their lot may be solitary, baronet, and in some measure cheerless, but infinitely preferable to a marriage that may lead them astray from their duties, or give birth to a family which are to be turned on the world--without any religion but form--without any morals but truisms--or without even a conscience which has not been seared by indulgence. I hope that Anne, in the performance of her system, will have no cause to regret its failure."

"Clara chose for herself, and has done well, Charlotte; and so, I doubt not, will Jane and Emily: and I confess I think their mother is right."

"It is true," said Mrs. Wilson, "Clara has done well, though under circumstances of but little risk; she might have jumped into your fish-pond, and escaped with life, but the chances are she would drown: nor do I dispute the right of the girls to choose for themselves; but I say the rights extend to requiring us to qualify them to make their choice. I am sorry, Edward, to be the instigator of doubts in your breast of the worth of any one, especially as it may give you pain." Here Mrs. Wilson took her brother affectionately by the hand, and communicated what she had overheard that evening. Although the impressions of the baronet were not as vivid, or as deep as those of his sister, his parental love was too great not to make him extremely uneasy under the intelligence and after thanking her for her attention to his children's welfare, he kissed her, and withdrew. In passing to his own room, he met Egerton, that moment returned from escorting the Jarvis ladies to their lodgings; a task he had undertaken at the request of Jane, as they were without any male attendant. Sir Edward's heart was too full not to seek immediate relief, and as he had strong hopes of the innocence of the colonel, though he could give no reason for his expectation, he returned with him to the parlor, and in a few words acquainted him with the slanders which had been circulated at his expense; begging him by all means to disprove them as soon as possible. The colonel was struck with the circumstance at first, but assured Sir Edward, it was entirely untrue. He never played, as he might have noticed, and that Mr. Holt was an ancient enemy of his. He would in the morning take measures to convince Sir Edward, that he stood higher in the estimation of his uncle, than Mr. Holt had thought proper to state. Much relieved by this explanation, the baronet, forgetting that this heavy charge removed, he only stood where he did before he took time for his inquiries, assured him, that if he could convince him, or rather his sister, he did not gamble, he would receive him as a son-in-law with pleasure. The gentlemen shook hands and parted.

Denbigh had retired to his room early, telling Mr. Benfield he did not feel well, and thus missed the party at supper; and by twelve, silence prevailed in the house.

As usual after a previous day of pleasure, the party were late in assembling on the following, yet Denbigh was the last who made his appearance. Mrs. Wilson thought he threw a look round the room as he entered, which prevented his making his salutations in his usual easy and polished manner. In a few minutes, however, his awkwardness was removed, and they took their seats at the table. At that moment the door of the room was thrown hastily open, and Mr. Jarvis entered abruptly, and with a look bordering on wildness in his eye--"Is she not here?" exclaimed the merchant scanning the company closely.

"Who?" inquired all in a breath.

"Polly--my daughter--my child," said the merchant, endeavoring to control his feelings; "did she not come here this morning with Colonel Egerton?"

He was answered in the negative, and he briefly explained the cause of his anxiety. The colonel had called very early, and sent her maid up to his daughter who rose immediately. They had quitted the house together, leaving word the Miss Moseleys had sent for the young lady to breakfast, for some particular reason. Such was the latitude allowed by his wife, that nothing was suspected until one of the servants of the house said he had seen Colonel Egerton and a lady drive out of the village that morning in a post-chaise and four.

Then the old gentleman first took the alarm, and he proceeded instantly to the lodge in quest of his daughter. Of the elopement there now remained no doubt, and an examination into the state of the colonel's room, who, it had been thought, was not yet risen, gave assurance of it. Here was at once sad confirmation that the opinion of Mr. Holt was a just one. Although every heart felt for Jane during this dreadful explanation, no eye was turned on her excepting the stolen, and anxious glances of her sister; but when all was confirmed, and nothing remained but to reflect or act upon the circumstances, she naturally engrossed the whole attention of her fond parents. Jane had listened in indignation to the commencement of the narrative of Mr. Jarvis, and so firmly was Egerton enshrined in purity within her imagination, that not until it was ascertained that both his servant and clothes were missing, would she admit a thought injurious to his truth. Then indeed the feelings of Mr. Jarvis, his plain statement corroborated by this testimony, struck her at once as true; and as she rose to leave the room, she fell senseless into the arms of Emily who observing her movement and loss of color had flown to her assistance. Denbigh had drawn the merchant out in vain efforts to appease him, and happily no one witnessed this effect of Jane's passion but her nearest relatives. She was immediately removed to her own room, and in a short time was in bed with a burning fever. The bursts of her grief were uncontrolled and violent. At times she reproached herself--her friends--Egerton; in short, she was guilty of all the inconsistent sensations that disappointed hopes, accompanied by the consciousness of weakness on our part seldom fail to give rise to; the presence of her friends was irksome to her, and it was only to the soft and insinuating blandishments of Emily's love that she would at all yield. Perseverance and affection at length prevailed, and as Emily took the opportunity of some refreshments to infuse a strong soporific, Jane lost her consciousness of misery in a temporary repose. In the mean time a more searching inquiry had been able to trace out the manner and direction of the journey of the fugitives.

It appeared the colonel left the lodge immediately after his conversation with Sir Edward; he slept at a tavern, and caused his servant to remove his baggage at daylight; here he had ordered a chaise and horses, and then proceeded, as mentioned, to the lodgings of Mr. Jarvis. What arguments he used with Miss Jarvis to urge her to so sudden a flight, remained a secret; but from the remarks of Mrs. Jarvis and Miss Sarah, there was reason to believe that he had induced them to think from the commencement, that his intentions were single, and Mary Jarvis their object. How he contrived to gloss over his attentions to Jane in such a manner as to deceive those ladies, caused no little surprise; but it was obvious it had been done, and the Moseleys were not without hopes his situation with Jane would not make the noise in the world such occurrences seldom fail to excite. In the afternoon a letter was handed to Mr. Jarvis, and by him immediately communicated to the baronet and Denbigh, both of whom he considered as among his best friends. It was from Egerton, and written in a respectful manner: he apologized for his elopement, and excused it on the ground of a wish to avoid the delay of a license or the publishing of bans, as he was in hourly expectation of a summons to his regiment, and contained many promises of making an attentive husband, and an affectionate son. The fugitives were on the road to Scotland, whence they intended immediately to return to London and to wait the commands of their parents. The baronet in a voice trembling with emotion at the sufferings of his own child, congratulated the merchant that things were no worse; while Denbigh curled his lips as he read the epistle, and thought settlements were a greater inconvenience than the bans--for it was a well known fact, a maiden aunt had left the Jarvises twenty thousand pounds between them.

Chapter XXVI

Although the affections of Jane had sustained a blow, her pride had received a greater, and no persuasions of her mother or sister could induce her to leave her room. She talked little, but once or twice she yielded to the affectionate attentions of Emily, and poured out her sorrows into the bosom of her sister. At such moments she would declare her intention of never appearing in the world again. One of these paroxysms of sorrow was witnessed by her mother, and, for the first time, self-reproach mingled in the grief of the matron. Had she trusted less to appearances and to the opinions of indifferent and ill-judging acquaintances, her daughter might have been apprized in season of the character of the man who had stolen her affections. To a direct exhibition of misery Lady Moseley was always sensible, and, for the moment, she became alive to its causes and consequences; but a timely and judicious safeguard against future moral evils was a forecast neither her inactivity of mind nor abilities were equal to.

We shall leave Jane to brood over her lover's misconduct, while we regret she is without the consolation alone able to bear her up against the misfortunes of life, and return to the other personages of our history.

The visit to Mrs. Fitzgerald had been postponed in consequence of Jane's indisposition; but a week after the colonel's departure, Mrs. Wilson thought, as Jane had consented to leave her room, and Emily really began to look pale from her confinement by the side of a sick bed, she would redeem the pledge she had given the recluse on the following morning. They found the ladies at the cottage happy to see them, and anxious to hear of the health of Jane, of whose illness they had been informed by note. After offering her guests some refreshments, Mrs. Fitzgerald, who appeared laboring under a greater melancholy than usual, proceeded to make them acquainted with the incidents of her life.

The daughter of an English merchant at Lisbon had fled from the house of her father to the protection of an Irish officer in the service of his Catholic Majesty: they were united, and the colonel immediately took his bride to Madrid. The offspring of this union were a son and daughter. The former, at an early age, had entered into the service of his king, and had, as usual, been bred in the faith of his ancestors; but the Señora McCarthy had been educated, and yet remained a Protestant, and, contrary to her faith to her husband, secretly instructed her daughter in the same belief. At the age of seventeen, a principal grandee of the court of Charles sought the hand of the general's child. The Conde d'Alzada was a match not to be refused, and they were united in the heartless and formal manner in which marriages are too often entered into, in countries where the customs of society prevent an intercourse between the sexes. The Conde never possessed the affections of his wife. Of a stern and unyielding disposition, his harshness repelled her love; and as she naturally turned her eyes to the home of her childhood, she cherished all those peculiar sentiments she had imbibed from her mother. Thus, although she appeared to the world a Catholic, she lived in secret a Protestant. Her parents had always used the English language in their family, and she spoke it as fluently as the Spanish. To encourage her recollections of this strong feature, which distinguished the house of her father from the others she entered, she perused closely and constantly those books which the death of her mother placed at her disposal. These were principally Protestant works on religious subjects, and the countess became a strong sectarian, without becoming a Christian. As she was compelled to use the same books in teaching her only child, the Donna Julia, English, the consequences of the original false step of her grandmother were perpetuated in the person of this young lady. In learning English, she also learned to secede from the faith of her father, and entailed upon herself a life of either persecution or hypocrisy. The countess was guilty of the unpardonable error of complaining to their child of the treatment she received from her husband; and as these conversations were held in English, and were consecrated by the tears of the mother, they made an indelible impression on the youthful mind of Julia, who grew up with the conviction that next to being a Catholic herself, the greatest evil of life was to be the wife of one.

On her attaining her fifteenth year, she had the misfortune (if it could be termed one) to lose her mother, and within the year her father presented to her a nobleman of the vicinity as her future husband. How long the religious faith of Julia would have endured, unsupported by example in others, and assailed by the passions soliciting in behalf of a young and handsome cavalier, it might be difficult to pronounce; but as suitor was neither very young, and the reverse of very handsome, it is certain the more he wooed, the more confirmed she became in her heresy, until, in a moment of desperation, and as an only refuge against his solicitations, she candidly avowed her creed. The anger of her father was violent and lasting: she was doomed to a convent, as both a penance for her sins and a means of reformation. Physical resistance was not in her power, but mentally she determined never to yield. Her body was immured, but her mind continued unshaken and rather more settled in her belief, by the aid of those passions which had been excited by injudicious harshness. For two years she continued in her novitiate, obstinately refusing to take the vows of the order, and at the end of that period the situation of her country had called her father and uncle to the field as defenders of the rights of their lawful prince. Perhaps to this it was owing that harsher measures were not adopted in her case.

The war now raged around them in its greatest horrors, until at length a general battle was fought in the neighborhood, and the dormitories of the peaceful nuns were crowded with wounded British officers. Amongst others of his nation was a Major Fitzgerald, a young man of strikingly handsome countenance and pleasant manners. Chance threw him under the more immediate charge of Julia: his recovery was slow, and for a time doubtful, and as much owing to good nursing as science. The major was grateful, and Julia unhappy as she was beautiful. That love should be the offspring of this association, will excite no surprise. A brigade of British encamping in the vicinity of the convent, the young couple sought its protection from Spanish vengeance and Romish cruelty. They were married by the chaplain of the brigade, and for a month they were happy.

As Napoleon was daily expected in person at the seat of war, his generals were alive to their own interests, if not to that of their master. The body of troops in which Fitzgerald had sought a refuge, being an advanced party of the main army, were surprised and defeated with loss. After doing his duty as a soldier at his post, the major, in endeavoring to secure the retreat of Julia, was intercepted, and they both fell into the hands of the enemy. They were kindly treated, and allowed every indulgence their situation admitted, until a small escort of prisoners was sent to the frontiers; in this they were included, and had proceeded to the neighborhood of the Pyrenees, when, in their turn, the French were assailed suddenly, and entirely routed; and the captive Spaniards, of which the party, with the exception of our young couple, consisted, released. As the French guard made a resistance until overpowered by numbers, an unfortunate ball struck Major Fitzgerald to the earth--he survived but an hour, and died where he fell, on the open field. An English officer, the last of his retiring countrymen, was attracted by the sight of a woman weeping over the body of a fallen man, and approached them. In a few words Fitzgerald explained his situation to this gentleman, and exacted a pledge from him to guard his Julia, in safety, to his mother in England.

The stranger promised everything the dying husband required, and by the time death had closed the eyes of Fitzgerald, he had procured from some peasants a rude conveyance, into which the body, with its almost equally lifeless widow, were placed. The party which intercepted the convoy of prisoners, had been out from the British camp on other duty, but its commander hearing of the escort, had pushed rapidly into a country covered by the enemy to effect their rescue; and his service done, he was compelled to make a hasty retreat to ensure his own security. To this was owing the indifference, which left the major to the care of the Spanish peasantry who had gathered to the spot, and the retreating troops had got several miles on their return, before the widow and her protector commenced their journey. It was impossible to overtake them, and the inhabitants acquainting the gentleman that a body of French dragoons were already harassing their rear, he was compelled to seek another route to the camp. This, with some trouble and no little danger, he at last effected; and the day following the skirmish, Julia found herself lodged in a retired Spanish dwelling, several miles within the advanced posts of the British army. The body of her husband was respectfully interred, and Julia was left to mourn her irretrievable loss, uninterrupted by anything but by the hasty visits of the officer in whose care she had been left--visits which he stole from his more important duties as a soldier.

A month glided by in this melancholy manner, leaving to Mrs. Fitzgerald the only consolation she would receive--her incessant visits to the grave of her husband. The calls of her protector, however, became more frequent; and at length he announced his intended departure for Lisbon, on his way to England. A small covered vehicle, drawn by one horse, was to convey them to the city, at which place he promised to procure her a female attendant, and necessaries for the voyage home. It was no time or place for delicate punctilio; and Julia quietly, but with a heart nearly broken, prepared to submit to the wishes of her late husband. After leaving the dwelling, the manners of her guide sensibly altered; he became complimentary and assiduous to please, but in a way rather to offend than conciliate; until his attentions became so irksome, that Julia actually meditated stopping at some of the villages through which they passed, and abandoning the attempt of visiting England entirely. But the desire to comply with Fitzgerald's wish, that she would console his mother for the loss of an only child, and the dread of the anger of her relatives, determined her to persevere until they reached Lisbon, where she was resolved to separate for ever from the disagreeable and unknown guardian into whose keeping she had been thrown by chance.

The last day of their weary ride, while passing a wood, the officer so far forgot his own character and Julia's misfortunes, as to offer personal indignities. Grown desperate from her situation, Mrs. Fitzgerald sprang from the vehicle, and by her cries attracted the notice of an officer who was riding express on the same road with themselves. He advanced to her assistance at speed, but as he arrived near them, a pistol fired from the carriage brought his horse down, and the treacherous friend was enabled to escape undetected. Julia endeavored to explain her situation to her rescuer; and by her distress and appearance, satisfied him at once of its truth. Within a short time, a strong escort of light dragoons came up, and the officer despatched some for a conveyance, and others in pursuit of that disgrace to the army, the villanous guide: the former was soon obtained, but no tidings could be had of the latter. The carriage was found at a short distance, without the horse and with the baggage of Julia, but with no vestige of its owner. She never knew his name, and either accident or art had so completely enveloped him in mystery, that all efforts to unfold it then were fruitless, and had continued so ever since.

On their arrival in Lisbon, every attention was shown to the disconsolate widow the most refined delicacy could dictate, and every comfort and respect were procured for her which the princely fortune, high rank, and higher character of the Earl of Pendennyss, could command. It was this nobleman, who, on his way from head-quarters with despatches for England, had been the means of preserving Julia from a fate worse than death. A packet was in waiting for the earl, and they proceeded in her for home. The Donna Lorenza was the widow of a subaltern Spanish officer, who had fallen under the orders and near Pendennyss, and the interest he took in her brave husband had induced him to offer her, in the destruction of her little fortune by the enemy, his protection: for near two years he had maintained her at Lisbon and now, judging her a proper person, had persuaded her to accompany Mrs. Fitzgerald to England.

On the passage, which was very tedious, the earl became more intimately acquainted with the history and character of his young friend, and by a course of gentle yet powerful expedients had drawn her mind gradually from its gloomy contemplation of futurity, to a juster sense of good and evil. The peculiarity of her religious persuasion afforded an introduction to frequent discussions of the real opinions of that church, to which Julia had hitherto belonged, although ignorant of all its essential and vital truths. These conversations, which were renewed repeatedly in their intercourse while under the protection of his sister in London, laid the foundations of a faith which left her nothing to hope for but the happy termination of her earthly probation.

The mother of Fitzgerald was dead, and as he had no near relative left, Julia found herself alone in the world. Her husband had taken the precaution to make a will in season it was properly authenticated, and his widow, by the powerful assistance of Pendennyss, was put in quiet possession of a little independency. It was while waiting the decision of this affair that Mrs. Fitzgerald resided for a short time near Bath. As soon as it was terminated, the earl and his sister had seen her settled in her present abode, and once since had they visited her; but delicacy had kept him away from the cottage, although his attempts to serve her had been constant, though not always successful. He had, on his return to Spain, seen her father, and interceded with him on her behalf, but in vain. The anger of the Spaniard remained unappeased, and for a season he did not renew his efforts; out having heard that her father was indisposed, Julia had employed the earl once more to make her peace with him, without prevailing. The letter the ladies had found her weeping over was from Pendennyss, informing her of his want of success on that occasion.

The substance of the foregoing narrative was related by Mrs. Fitzgerald to Mrs. Wilson, who repeated it to Emily in their ride home. The compassion of both ladies was strongly moved in behalf of the young widow; yet Mrs. Wilson did not fail to point out to her niece the consequences of deception, and chiefly the misery which had followed from an abandonment of some of the primary duties of life--obedience and respect to her parent. Emily, though keenly alive to all the principles inculcated by her aunt, found so much to be pitied in the fate of her friend, that her failings lost their proper appearance in her eyes, and for a while she could think of nothing but Julia and her misfortunes. Previously to their leaving the cottage, Mrs. Fitzgerald, with glowing cheeks and some hesitation, informed Mrs. Wilson she had yet another important communication to make, but would postpone it until her next visit, which Mrs. Wilson promised should be on the succeeding day.

Chapter XXVII

Emily threw a look of pleasure on Denbigh, as he handed her from the carriage, which would have said, if looks could talk, "In the principles you have displayed on more than one occasion, I have a pledge of *your* worth." As he led her into the house, he laughingly informed her that he had that morning received a letter which would make his absence from L---- necessary for a short time, and that he must remonstrate against these long and repeated visits to a cottage where all attendants of the male sex were excluded, as they encroached greatly on his pleasures and improvements, bowing, as he spoke, to Mrs. Wilson. To this Emily replied, gaily, that possibly, if he conducted himself to their satisfaction; they would intercede for *his* admission. Expressing his pleasure at this promise, as Mrs. Wilson thought rather awkwardly, Denbigh changed the conversation. At dinner he repeated to the family what he had mentioned to Emily of his departure, and also his expectation of meeting with Lord Chatterton during his journey.

"Have you heard from Chatterton lately, John?" inquired Sir Edward Moseley.

"Yes, sir, to-day: he had left Denbigh Castle a fortnight since, and writes he is to meet his friend, the duke, at Bath."

"Are you connected with his grace, Mr. Denbigh?" asked Lady Moseley.

A smile of indefinite meaning played on the expressive face of Denbigh, as he answered slightly--

"On the side of my father, madam."

"He has a sister," continued Lady Moseley, willing to know more of Chatterton's friends and Denbigh's relatives.

"He has," was the brief reply.

"Her name is Harriet," observed Mrs. Wilson. Denbigh bowed his assent in silence, and Emily timidly added--

"Lady Harriet Denbigh?"

"Lady Harriet Denbigh--will you do me the favor to take wine?"

The manner of the gentleman during this dialogue had not been in the least unpleasant, but it was peculiar; it prohibited anything further on the subject; and Emily was obliged to be content without knowing who Marian was, or whether her name was to be found in the Denbigh family or not. Emily was not in the least jealous, but she wished to know all to whom her lover was dear.

"Do the Dowager and the young ladies accompany Chatterton?" asked Sir Edward, as he turned to John, who was eating his fruit in silence.

"Yes, sir--I hope--that is, I believe she will," was the answer.

"She! Who is she, my son?"

"Grace Chatterton," said John, starting from his meditations. "Did you not ask me about Grace, Sir Edward?"

"Not particularly, I believe," said the baronet, dryly.

Denbigh again smiled: it was a smile different from any Mrs. Wilson had ever seen on his countenance, and gave an entirely novel expression to his face; it was full of meaning, it was knowing--spoke more of the man of the world than anything she had before noticed in him, and left on her mind one of those vague impressions she was often troubled with, that there was something about Denbigh in character or condition, or both, that was mysterious.

The spirit of Jane was too great to leave her a pining or pensive maiden; yet her feelings had sustained a shock that time alone could cure. She appeared again amongst her friends; but the consciousness of her expectations with respect to the colonel being known to them, threw around her a hauteur and distance very foreign to her natural manner. Emily alone, whose every movement sprang from the spontaneous feelings of her heart, and whose words and actions were influenced by the finest and most affectionate delicacy, such as she was not conscious of possessing herself, won upon the better feelings of her sister so far, as to restore between them the usual exchange of kindness and sympathy. But Jane admitted no confidence; she found nothing consoling, nothing solid, to justify her attachment to Egerton; nothing indeed, excepting such external advantages as she was now ashamed to admit had ever the power over her they in reality had possessed. The marriage of the fugitives in Scotland had been announced; and as the impression that Egerton was to be connected with the Moseleys was destroyed of course, their every-day acquaintances, feeling the restraints removed that such an opinion had once imposed, were free in their comments on his character. Sir Edward and Lady Moseley were astonished to find how many things to his disadvantage were generally known; that he gambled--intrigued--and was in debt--were no secrets apparently to anybody, but to those who were most interested in knowing the truth; while Mrs. Wilson saw in these facts additional reasons for examining and judging for ourselves; the world uniformly concealing from the party and his friends their honest opinions of his character. Some of these insinuations reached the ears of Jane: her aunt having rightly judged, that the surest way to destroy Egerton's power over the imagination of her niece was to strip him of his fictitious qualities, suggested this expedient to Lady Moseley; and some of their visitors had though as the colonel had certainly been attentive to Miss Moseley, it would give her pleasure to know that her rival had not made the most eligible match in the kingdom. The project of Mrs. Wilson succeeded in a great measure; but although Egerton fell, Jane did not find she rose in her own estimation; and her friends wisely concluded that time was the only remedy that could restore her former serenity.

In the morning, Mrs. Wilson, unwilling to have Emily present at a conversation she intended to hold with Denbigh, with a view to satisfy her annoying doubts as to some minor points in his character, after excusing herself to her niece, invited that gentleman to a morning drive. He accepted her invitation cheerfully; and Mrs. Wilson saw, it was only as they drove from the door without Emily, that he betrayed the faintest reluctance to the jaunt. When they had got a short distance from the lodge she acquainted him with her intention of presenting him to Mrs. Fitzgerald, whither she had ordered the coachman to proceed. Denbigh started as she mentioned the name, and after a few moments' silence, desired Mrs. Wilson to allow him to stop the carriage; he was not very well--was sorry to be so rude-- but with her permission, he would alight and return to the house. As he requested in an earnest manner that she would proceed without him, and by no means disappoint her friend, Mrs. Wilson complied; yet, somewhat at a loss to account for his sudden illness, she turned her head to see how the sick man fared, a short time after he had left her, and was not a little surprised to see him talking very composedly with John who had met him on his way to the fields with his gun. Lovesick--thought Mrs. Wilson with a smile; and as she rode on she came to the conclusion, that as Denbigh was to leave them soon, Emily would have an important communication to make on her return.

"Well," thought Mrs. Wilson with a sigh, "if it is to happen, it may as well be done at once."

Mrs. Fitzgerald was expecting her, and appeared rather pleased than otherwise that she had come alone. After some introductory conversation, the ladies withdrew by themselves, and Julia acquainted Mrs. Wilson with a new source of uneasiness. The day the ladies had promised to visit her, but had been prevented by the arrangements for the ball, the Donna Lorenza had driven to the village to make some purchases, attended as usual by their only man-servant, and Mrs. Fitzgerald was sitting in the little parlor in momentary expectation of her friends by herself. The sound of footsteps drew her to the door, which she opened for the admission of the wretch whose treachery to her dying husband's requests had given her so much uneasiness. Horror--fear--surprise--altogether, prevented her from, making any alarm at the moment, and she sank into a chair. He stood between her and the door, as he endeavored to draw her into a conversation; he assured her she had nothing to fear; that he loved her, and her alone; that he was about to be married to a daughter of Sir Edward Moseley, but would give her up, fortune, everything, if she would consent to become his wife--that the views of her protector, he doubted not, were dishonorable--that he himself was willing to atone for his former excess of passion, by a life devoted to her.

How much longer he would have gone on, and what further he would have offered, is unknown; for Mrs. Fitzgerald, having recovered herself a little, darted to the bell on the other side of the room; he tried to prevent her ringing it, but was too late; a short struggle followed, when the sound of the footsteps of the maid compelled him to retreat precipitately. Mrs. Fitzgerald added, that his assertion concerning Miss Moseley had given her incredible uneasiness, and prevented her making the communication yesterday; but she understood this morning through her maid, that a Colonel Egerton, who had been supposed to be engaged to one of Sir Edward's daughters, had eloped with another lady. That Egerton was her persecutor, she did not now entertain a doubt; but that it was in the power of Mrs. Wilson probably to make the discovery, as in the struggle between them for the bell, a pocket-book had fallen from the breast-pocket of his coat, and his retreat was too sudden to recover it.

As she put the book into the hands of Mrs. Wilson, she desired she would take means to return it to its owner; its contents might be of value, though she had not thought it correct to examine it. Mrs. Wilson took the book, and as she dropped it into her work-bag, smiled at the Spanish punctilio of her friend in not looking into her prize under the peculiar circumstances.

A few questions as to the place and year of his first attempts, soon convinced her it was Egerton whose unlicensed passions had given so much trouble to Mrs. Fitzgerald. He had served but one campaign in Spain, and in that year, and that division of the army; and surely *his principles* were no restraint upon his conduct. Mrs. Fitzgerald begged the advice of her more experienced friend as to the steps she ought to take; to which the former asked if she had made Lord Pendennyss acquainted with the occurrence. The young widow's cheek glowed as she answered, that, at the same time she felt assured the base insinuation of Egerton was unfounded, it had created a repugnance in her to troubling the earl any more than was necessary in her affairs; and as she kissed the hand of Mrs. Wilson she added--"besides, your goodness, my dear madam, renders any other adviser unnecessary now." Mrs. Wilson pressed her hand affectionately, and assured her of her good wishes and unaltered esteem. She commended her delicacy, and plainly told the young widow, that how ever unexceptionable the character of Pendennyss might be, a female friend was the only one a woman in her situation could repose confidence in, without justly incurring the sarcasms of the world.

As Egerton was now married, and would not probably offer, for the present at least, any further molestation to Mrs. Fitzgerald, it was concluded to be unnecessary to take any immediate measures of precaution; and Mrs. Wilson thought the purse of Mr. Jarvis might be made the means of keeping him within proper bounds in future. The merchant was prompt, and not easily intimidated; and the slightest intimation of the truth would, she knew, be sufficient to engage him on their side, heart and hand.

The ladies parted, with a promise of meeting soon again, and an additional interest in each other by the communications of that and the preceding day.

Mrs. Wilson had ridden half the distance between the cottage and the lodge, before it occurred to her they had not absolutely ascertained, by the best means in their possession, the identity of Colonel Egerton with Julia's persecutor. She accordingly took the pocket-book from her bag, and opened it for examination: a couple of letters fell from it into her lap, and conceiving their direction would establish all she wished to know, as they had been read, she turned to the superscription of one of them, and saw--"George Denbigh, Esq." in the well known hand-writing of Dr. Ives.--Mrs. Wilson felt herself overcome to a degree that compelled her to lower a glass of the carriage for air. She sat gazing on the letters until the characters swam before her eyes in undistinguished confusion; and with difficulty she rallied her thoughts to the point necessary for investigation. As soon as she found herself equal to the task, she examined the letters with the closest scrutiny, and opened them both to be sure there was no mistake. She saw the dates, the "dear George" at the commencements, and the doctor's name subscribed, before she would believe they were real; it was then the truth appeared to break upon her in a flood of light. The aversion of Denbigh to speak of Spain, or of his services in that country--his avoiding Sir Herbert Nicholson, and that gentleman's observations respecting him--Colonel Egerton's and his own manners--his absence from the ball, and startling looks on the following morning, and at different times before and since--his displeasure at the name of Pendennyss on various occasions--and his cheerful acceptance of her invitation to ride until he knew her destination, and singular manner of leaving her--were all accounted for by this dreadful discovery, and Mrs. Wilson found the solution of her doubts rushing on her mind with a force and rapidity that sickened her.

The misfortunes of Mrs. Fitzgerald, the unfortunate issue to the passion of Jane, were trifles in the estimation of Mrs. Wilson, compared to the discovery of Denbigh's unworthiness. She revolved in her mind his conduct on various occasions, and wondered how one who could behave so well in common, could thus yield to temptation on a particular occasion. His recent attempts, his hypocrisy, however, proved that his villany was systematic, and she was not weak enough to hide from herself the evidence of his guilt, or of its enormity. His interposition between Emily and death, she attributed now to natural courage, and perhaps in some measure to chance; but his profound and unvarying reverence for holy things, his consistent charity, his refusing to fight, to what were they owing? And Mrs. Wilson mourned the weakness of human nature, while she acknowledged to her self, there might be men, qualified by nature, and even disposed by reason and grace, to prove ornaments to religion and the world, who fell beneath the maddening influence of their besetting sins. The superficial and interested vices of Egerton vanished before these awful and deeply seated offences of Denbigh, and the correct widow saw at a glance, that he was the last man to be intrusted with the happiness of her niece; but how to break this heartrending discovery to Emily was a new source of uneasiness to her, and the carriage stopped at the door of the lodge, ere she had determined on the first step required of her by duty.

Her brother handed her out, and, filled with the dread that Denbigh had availed himself of the opportunity of her absence to press his suit with Emily, she eagerly inquired after him. She was rejoiced to hear he had returned with John for a fowling-piece, and together they had gone in pursuit of game, although she saw in it a convincing proof that a desire to avoid Mrs. Fitzgerald, and not indisposition, had induced him to leave her.--As a last alternative, she resolved to have the pocket-book returned to him in her presence, in order to see if he acknowledged it to be his property; and, accordingly, she instructed her own man to hand it to him while at dinner, simply saying he had lost it.

The open and unsuspecting air with which her niece met Denbigh on his return gave Mrs. Wilson an additional shock, and she could hardly command herself sufficiently to extend the common courtesies of good breeding to Mr. Benfield's guest.

While sitting at the dessert, her servant handed the pocket book, as directed by his mistress, to its owner, saying, "Your pocket-book, I believe, Mr. Denbigh." Denbigh took the book, and held it in his hand for a moment in surprise, and then fixed his eye keenly on the man, as he inquired where he found it, and how he knew it was his. These were interrogatories Francis was not prepared to answer, and in his confusion he naturally turned his eyes on his mistress. Denbigh followed their direction with his own, and in encountering the looks of the lady, he asked in a stammering manner, and with a face of scarlet,

"Am I indebted to you, madam, for my property?"

"No, sir; it was given me by one who found it, to restore to you," said Mrs. Wilson, gravely, and the subject was dropped, both appearing willing to say no more. Yet Denbigh was abstracted and absent during the remainder of the repast, and Emily spoke to him once or twice without obtaining an answer. Mrs. Wilson caught his eye several times fixed on her with an inquiring and doubtful expression, that convinced her he was alarmed. If any confirmation of his guilt had been wanting, the consciousness he betrayed during this scene afforded it; and she set seriously about considering the shortest and best method of interrupting his intercourse with Emily, before he had drawn from her an acknowledgment of her love.

Chapter XXVIII

On withdrawing to her dressing-room after dinner, Mrs. Wilson commenced the disagreeable duty of removing the veil from the eyes of her niece, by recounting to her the substance of Mrs. Fitzgerald's last communication. To the innocence of Emily such persecution could excite no other sensations than surprise and horror; and as her aunt omitted the part concerning the daughter of Sir Edward Moseley, she naturally expressed her wonder as to who the wretch could be.

"Possibly, aunt," she said with an involuntary shudder, "some of the many gentlemen we have lately seen, and one who has had art enough to conceal his real character from the world."

"Concealment, my love," replied Mrs. Wilson, "would be hardly necessary. Such is the fashionable laxity of morals, that I doubt not many of his associates would laugh at his misconduct, and that he would still continue to pass with the world as an honorable man."

"And ready," cried her niece, "to sacrifice human life, in the defence of any ridiculous punctilio."

"Or," added Mrs. Wilson, striving to draw nearer to her subject, "with a closer veil of hypocrisy, wear even an affectation of principle and moral feeling that would seem to forbid such a departure from duty in favor of custom."

"Oh! no, dear aunt," exclaimed Emily, with glowing cheeks and eyes dancing with pleasure, "he would hardly dare to be so very base. It would be profanity."

Mrs. Wilson sighed heavily as she witnessed that confiding esteem which would not permit her niece even to suspect that an act which in Denbigh had been so warmly applauded, could, even in another, proceed from unworthy motives; and she found it would be necessary to speak in the plainest terms, to awaken her suspicions. Willing, however, to come gradually to the distressing truth, she replied--

"And yet, my dear, men who pride themselves greatly on their morals, nay, even some who wear the mask of religion, and perhaps deceive themselves, admit and practise this very appeal to arms. Such inconsistencies are by no means uncommon. And why, then, might there not, with equal probability, be others who would revolt at murder, and yet not hesitate being guilty of lesser enormities? This is, in some measure, the case of every man; and it is only to consider killing in unlawful encounters as murder, to make it one in point."

"Hypocrisy is so mean a vice, I should not think a brave man could stoop to it," said Emily, "and Julia admits he was brave."

"And would not a brave man revolt at the cowardice of insulting an unprotected woman? And your hero did that too," replied Mrs. Wilson, bitterly, losing her self-command in indignation.

"Oh! do not call him my hero, I beg of you, dear aunt," said Emily, starting, excited by so extraordinary an allusion, but instantly losing the unpleasant sensation in the delightful consciousness of the superiority of the man on whom she had bestowed her own admiration.

"In fact, my child," continued her aunt, "our natures are guilty of the grossest inconsistencies. The vilest wretch has generally some property or which he values himself, and the most perfect are too often frail on some tender point. Long and tried friendships are those only which can be trusted, and these oftentimes fail."

Emily looked at her aunt in surprise at hearing her utter such unusual sentiments; for Mrs. Wilson, at the same time she had, by divine assistance, deeply impressed her niece with the frailty of her nature, had withheld the disgusting representation of human vices from her view, as unnecessary to her situation and dangerous to her humility.

After a short pause, Mrs. Wilson continued, "Marriage is a fearful step in a woman, and one she is compelled, in some measure, to adventure her happiness on, without fitting opportunities of judging of the merit of the man she confides in. Jane is an instance in point, but I devoutly hope you are not to be another."

While speaking, Mrs. Wilson had taken the hand of Emily, and by her looks and solemn manner she had succeeded in alarming her niece, although Denbigh was yet furthest from the thoughts of Emily. The aunt reached her a glass of water, and willing to get rid of the hateful subject she continued, hurriedly, "Did you not notice the pocket-book Francis gave to Mr. Denbigh?" Emily fixed her inquiring eyes on her aunt, as the other added, "It was the one Mrs. Fitzgerald gave me to-day." Something like an indefinite glimpse of the facts crossed the mind of Emily; and as it most obviously involved a separation from Denbigh, she sank lifeless into the extended arms of her aunt. This had been anticipated by Mrs. Wilson, and a timely application of restoratives soon brought her back to a consciousness of misery. Mrs. Wilson, unwilling any one but herself should witness this first burst of grief, succeeded in getting her niece to her own room and in bed. Emily made no lamentations--shed no tears--asked no questions--her eye was fixed, and every faculty appeared oppressed with the load on her heart. Mrs. Wilson knew her situation too well to intrude with unseasonable consolation or useless reflections, but sat patiently by her side, waiting anxiously for the moment she could be of service. At length the uplifted eyes and clasped hands of Emily assured her she had not forgotten herself or her duty, and she was rewarded for her labor and forbearance by a flood of tears. Emily was now able to listen to a more full statement of the reasons her aunt had for believing in the guilt of Denbigh, and she felt as if her heart was frozen up for ever, as the proofs followed each other until they amounted to demonstration. As there was some indication of fever from her agitated state of mind, her aunt required she should remain in her room until morning; and Emily, feeling every way unequal to a meeting with Denbigh, gladly assented. After ringing for her maid to sit in the adjoining room, Mrs. Wilson went below, and announced to the family the indisposition of her charge, and her desire to obtain a little sleep. Denbigh looked anxious to inquire after the health of Emily, but there was a restraint on all his actions, since the return of his book, that persuaded Mrs. Wilson he apprehended that a detection of his conduct had taken place. He did venture to ask when they were to have the pleasure of seeing Miss Moseley again, hoping it would be that evening, as he had fixed the morning for his departure; and when he learnt that Emily had retired for the night, his anxiety was sensibly increased, and he instantly withdrew. Mrs. Wilson was alone in the drawing-room, and about to join her niece, as, Denbigh entered it with a letter in his hand: he approached her with a diffident and constrained manner, and commenced the following dialogue:

"My anxiety and situation will plead my apology for troubling Miss Moseley at this time--may I ask you, madam, to deliver this letter--I hardly dare ask you for your good offices."

Mrs. Wilson took the letter, and coldly replied,

"Certainly, sir; and I sincerely wish I could be of any real service to you."

"I perceive, madam," said Denbigh, like one that was choking, "I have forfeited your good opinion--that pocket book--"

"Has made a dreadful discovery," said Mrs. Wilson, shuddering.

"Will not one offence be pardoned, dear madam?" cried Denbigh, with warmth; "if you knew my circumstances--the cruel reasons--why--why did I neglect the paternal advice of Doctor Ives?"

"It is not yet too late, sir," said Mrs. Wilson, more mildly, "for your own good; as for us, your deception--"

"Is unpardonable--I see it--I feel it," cried he, in the accent of despair; "yet Emily--Emily may relent--you will at least give her my letter--anything is better than this suspense."

"You shall have an answer from Emily this evening, and one entirely unbiassed by me," said Mrs. Wilson. As she closed the door, she observed Denbigh gazing on her retiring figure with a countenance of despair, that caused a feeling of pity to mingle with her detestation of his vices.

On opening the door of Emily's room, Mrs. Wilson found her niece in tears, and her anxiety for her health was alleviated. She knew or hoped, that if she could once call in the assistance of her judgment and piety to lessen her sorrows, Emily, however she might mourn, would become resigned to her situation; and the first step to attain this was the exercise of those faculties which had been, as it were, momentarily annihilated. Mrs. Wilson kissed her niece with tenderness, as she placed the letter in her hand, and told her she would call for her answer within an hour. Employment, and the necessity of acting, would, she thought, be the surest means of reviving her energies; nor was she disappointed. When the aunt returned for the expected answer, she was informed by the maid in the ante-chamber, that Miss Moseley was up, and had been writing. On entering, Mrs. Wilson stood a moment in admiration of the picture before her. Emily was on her knees, and by her side, on the carpet, lay the letter and its answer: her face was hid by her hair, and her hands were closed in the fervent grasp of petition. In a minute she rose, and approaching her aunt with an air of profound resignation, but great steadiness, she handed her the letters, her own unsealed:

"Read them, madam, and if you approve of mine, I will thank you to deliver it."

Her aunt folded her in her arms, until Emily, finding herself yielding under the effects of sympathy, begged to be left alone. On withdrawing to her own room, Mrs. Wilson read the contents of the two letters.

"I rely greatly on the goodness of Miss Moseley to pardon the liberty I am taking, at a moment she is so unfit for such a subject; but my departure--my feelings--- must plead my apology. From the moment of my first acquaintance with you, I have been a cheerful subject to your loveliness and innocence. I feel--I know--I am not deserving of such a blessing; but since knowing you, as I do, it is impossible not to strive to win you. You have often thanked me as the preserver of your life, but you little knew the deep interest I had in its safety. Without it my own would be valueless. By accepting my offered hand, you will place me amongst the happiest, or by rejecting it, the most wretched of men."

To this note, which was unsigned, and evidently written under great agitation of mind, Emily had-penned the following reply:

"Sir--It is with much regret that I find myself reduced to the possibility of giving uneasiness to one to whom I am under such heavy obligations. It will never be in my power to accept the honor you have offered me; and I beg you to receive my thanks for the compliment conveyed in your request, as well as my good wishes for your happiness in future, and fervent prayers that you may be ever found worthy of it--Your humble servant,

"EMILY MOSELEY."

Perfectly satisfied with this answer, Mrs. Wilson went below in order to deliver it at once. She thought it probable, as Denbigh had already sent his baggage to a tavern, preparatory to his intended journey, they would not meet again; and as she felt a strong wish, both on account of Doctor Ives, and out of respect to the services of the young man himself, to conceal his conduct from the world entirely, she was in hopes that his absence might make any disclosure unnecessary. He took the letter from her with a trembling hand, and casting one of his very expressive looks at her, as if to read her thoughts, he withdrew.

Emily had fallen asleep free from fever, and Mrs. Wilson had descended to the supper-room, when Mr. Benfield was first struck with the absence of his favorite. An inquiry after Denbigh was instituted, and while they were waiting his appearance, a servant handed the old man a note.

"From whom?" cried Mr. Benfield, in surprise.

"Mr. Denbigh, sir," said the servant.

"Mr. Denbigh?" exclaimed Mr. Benfield: "no accident, I hope--I remember when Lord Gosford--here, Peter, your eyes are young; read it for me, read it aloud."

As all but Mrs. Wilson were anxiously waiting to know the meaning of this message, and Peter had many preparations to go through before his youthful eyes could make out the contents, John hastily caught the letter out of his hand, saying he would save him the trouble, and, in obedience to his uncle's wishes, he read aloud:

"Mr. Denbigh, being under the necessity of leaving L---- immediately, and unable to endure the pain of taking leave, avails himself of this means of tendering his warmest thanks to Mr. Benfield, for his hospitality, and to his amiable guests for their many kindnesses. As he contemplates leaving England, he desires to wish them all a long and an affectionate farewell."

"Farewell!" cried Mr. Benfield; "farewell--does he say farewell, John? Here, Peter, run--no, you are too old--John, run--bring my hat; I'll go myself to the village--some love-quarrel--Emmy sick--and Denbigh going away-- yes--yes, I did so myself--Lady Juliana, poor dear soul, she was a long time before she could forget it--but Peter"--Peter had disappeared the instant the letter was finished, and he was quickly followed by John. Sir Edward and Lady Moseley were lost in amazement at this sudden and unexpected movement of Denbigh, and the breast of each of the affectionate parents was filled with a vague apprehension that the peace of mind of another child was at stake. Jane felt a renewal of her woes, in the anticipation of something similar for her sister--for the fancy of Jane was yet active, and she did not cease to consider the defection of Egerton a kind of unmerited misfortune and fatality, instead of a probable consequence of want of principle. Like Mr. Benfield, she was in danger of raising an ideal idol, and of spending the remainder of her days in devotion to qualities, rarely if ever found identified with a person that never had existed. The old gentleman was entirely engrossed by a different object; and having in his own opinion decided there must have been one of those misunderstandings which sometimes had occurred to himself and Lady Juliana, he quietly composed himself to eat his salad at the supper table: on turning his head, however, in quest of his first glass of wine, he observed Peter standing quietly by the sideboard with the favorite goggles over his eyes. Now Peter was troubled with two kinds of debility about his organs of vision; one was age and natural weakness, while the other proceeded more directly from the heart. His master knew of these facts, and he took the alarm. Again the wine-glass dropped from his nerveless hand, as he said in a trembling tone,

"Peter, I thought you went"--

"Yes, master," said Peter, laconically.

"You saw him, Peter--will he return?"

Peter was busily occupied at his glasses, although no one was dry.

"Peter," repeated Mr. Benfield, rising from his seat; "is he coming in time for supper?" Peter was obliged to reply, and deliberately uncasing his eyes and blowing his nose, he was on the point of opening his mouth, as John came into the room, and threw himself into a chair with an air of great vexation. Peter pointed to the young gentleman in silence, and retired.

"John," cried Sir Edward, "where is Denbigh?"

"Gone, sir."

"Gone!"

"Yes, my dear father," said John, "gone without saying good-bye to one of us--without telling us whither, or when to return. It was cruel in him--- unkind--I'll never forgive him"--and John, whose feelings were strong, and unusually excited, hid his face between his hands on the table.--As he raised his head to reply to a question of Mr. Benfield--of "how he knew he had gone, for the coach did not go until daylight?" Mrs. Wilson saw evident marks of tears. Such proofs of emotion in one like John Moseley gave her the satisfaction of knowing that if she had been deceived, it was by a concurrence of circumstances and a depth of hypocrisy almost exceeding belief: self-reproach added less than common, therefore, to the uneasiness of the moment.

"I saw the innkeeper, uncle," said John, "who told me that Denbigh left there at eight o'clock in a post-chaise and four; but I will go to London in the morning myself." This was no sooner said than it was corroborated by acts, for the young man immediately commenced his preparations for the journey. The family separated that evening with melancholy hearts; and the host and his privy counsellor were closeted for half an hour ere they retired to their night's repose. John took his leave of them, and left the lodge for the inn, with his man, in order to be ready for the mail. Mrs. Wilson looked in upon Emily before she withdrew herself, and found her awake, but perfectly calm and composed: she said but little, appearing desirous of avoiding all allusions to Denbigh; and after her aunt had simply acquainted her with his departure, and her resolution to conceal the cause, the subject was dropped. Mrs. Wilson, on entering her own room, thought deeply on the discoveries of the day: they had interfered with her favorite system of morals, baffled her ablest calculations upon causes and effects, but in no degree had impaired her faith or reliance on Providence. She knew one exception did not destroy a rule: she was certain without principles there was no security for good conduct, and the case of Denbigh proved it. To discover these principles, might be difficult; but was a task imperiously required at her hands, as she believed, ere she yielded the present and future happiness of her pupil to the power of any man.

Chapter XXIX

The day had not yet dawned, when John Moseley was summoned to take his seat in the mail for London. Three of the places were already occupied, and John was compelled to get a seat for his man on the outside. An intercourse with strangers is particularly irksome to an Englishman, and none appeared disposed, for a long time, to break the silence. The coach had left the little village of L---- far behind it, before any of the rational beings it contained thought it prudent or becoming to bend in the least to the charities of our nature, in a communication with a fellow creature of whose name or condition he happened to be ignorant. This reserve is unquestionably characteristic of the nation; to what is it owing!--modesty? Did not national and deep personal vanity appear at once to refute the assertion, we might enter into an investigation of it. The good opinion of himself in an Englishman is more deeply seated, though less buoyant, than that of his neighbors; in them it is more of manner, in us more of feeling; and the wound inflicted on the self-love of the two is very different. The Frenchman wonders at its rudeness, but soon forgets the charge; while an Englishmam broods over it in silence and mortification. It is said this distinction in character is owing to the different estimation of principles and morals in the two nations. The solidity and purity of our ethics and religious creeds may have given a superior tone to our moral feeling; but has that man a tenable ground to value himself on either, whose respect to sacred things grows out of a respect to himself: on the other hand, is not humility the very foundation of the real Christian? For our part, we should be glad to see this national reserve lessened, if not done entirely away; we believe it is founded in pride and uncharitableness, and could wish to see men thrown accidentally together on the roads of the country, mindful that they are also travelling in company the highway of life, and that the goal of their destination is equally attainable by all.

John Moseley was occupied with thoughts very different from those of any of his fellow-travellers, as they proceeded rapidly on their route; and it was only when roused from his meditations by accidentally coming in contact with the hilt of a sword, that he looked up, and in the glimmerings of the morning's light, recognised the person of Lord Henry Stapleton: their eyes met, and--"My lord,"--"Mr. Moseley,"--were repeated in mutual surprise. John was eminently a social being, and he was happy to find recourse against his gloomy thoughts in the conversation of the dashing young sailor. The frigate of the other had entered the bay the night before, and he was going to town to the wedding of his sister; the coach of his brother the marquis was to meet him about twenty miles from town, and the ship was ordered round to Yarmouth, where he was to rejoin her.

"But how are your lovely sisters, Moseley?" cried the young sailor in a frank and careless manner. "I should have been half in love with one of them if I had time--and money; both are necessary to marriage nowadays, you know."

"As to time," said John with a laugh, "I believe that may be dispensed with, though money is certainly a different thing."

"Oh, time too," replied his lordship. "I have never time enough to do anything as it ought to be done--always hurried--I wish you could recommend to me a lady who would take the trouble off my hands."

"It might be done," said John with a smile, and the image of Kate Chatterton crossed his brain, but it was soon succeeded by that of her more lovely sister. "But how do you manage on board your ship--hurried there too?"

"Oh! never there," replied the captain gravely; "that's duty you know, and everything must be regular of course; on shore it is a different thing--there I am only a passenger. L---- has a charming society, Mr. Moseley--a week or ten days ago I was shooting, and came to a beautiful cottage about five miles from the village, that was the abode of a much more beautiful woman, a Spaniard, a Mrs. Fitzgerald--I am positively in love with her: so soft, so polished, so modest----"

"How came you acquainted with her?" inquired Moseley, interrupting him in a little surprise.

"Chance, my dear fellow, chance. I was thirsty, and approached for a drink of water; she was sitting in the veranda, and being hurried for time, you know, it saved the trouble of introduction. I fancy she is troubled with the same complaint; for she managed to get rid of me in no time, and with a great deal of politeness. I found out her name, however, at the next house."

During this rattling talk, John had fixed his eyes on the face of one of the passengers who sat opposite to him. The stranger appeared to be about fifty years of age, strongly pock-marked, with a stiff military air, and had the dress and exterior of a gentlemen. His face was much sun-burnt, though naturally very fair; and his dark keen eye was intently fixed on the sailor as he continued his remarks.

"Do you know such a lady, Moseley?"

"Yes," said John, "though very slightly; she is visited by one of my sisters, and--"

"Yourself," cried Lord Henry, with a laugh.

"Myself, once or twice, my lord, certainly," answered John, gravely; "but a lady visited by Emily Moseley and Mrs. Wilson is a proper companion for any one. Mrs. Fitzgerald is very retired in her manner of living, and chance made us acquainted; but not being, like your lordship, in want of time, we have endeavored to cultivate her society, as we have found it very agreeable."

The countenance of the stranger underwent several changes during this speech of John's, and at its close his eyes rested on him with a softer expression than generally marked its rigid and compressed muscles. Willing to change a discourse that was growing too particular for a mail-coach, John addressed himself to the opposite passengers, while his eye yet dwelt on the face of the military stranger.

"We are likely to have a fine day, gentlemen." The soldier bowed stiffly, as he smiled his assent, and the other passenger humbly answered, "Very, Mr. John," in the well known tones of honest Peter Johnson. Moseley started, as he turned his face for the first time on the lank figure which was modestly compressed into the smallest possible compass in the corner of the coach, in a way not to come in contact with any of its neighbors.

"Johnson," exclaimed John, in astonishment, "you here! Where are you going--to London?"

"To London, Mr. John," replied Peter, with a look of much importance; and then, by way of silencing further interrogatories, he added, "On my master's business, sir."

Both Moseley and Lord Henry examined him closely; the former wondering what could take the steward, at the age of seventy, for the first time in his life, into the vortex of the capital; and the latter in admiration at this figure and equipments of the old man. Peter was in full costume, with the exception of the goggles, and was in reality a subject to be gazed at; but nothing relaxed the muscles or attracted the particular notice of the soldier, who, having regained his set form of countenance, appeared drawn up in himself, waiting patiently for the moment he was expected to act. Nor did he utter more than as many words in the course of the first fifty miles of their journey. His dialect was singular, and such as put his hearers at a loss to determine his country. Lord Henry stared at him every time he spoke, as if to say, what countryman are you? until at length he suggested to John he was some officer whom the downfall of Bonaparte had driven into retirement.

"Indeed, Moseley," he added, as they were about to resume their carriage after a change of horses, "we must draw him out, and see what he thinks of his master now--delicately, you know." The soldier was, however, impervious to his lordship's attacks, until the project was finally abandoned in despair. As Peter was much too modest to talk in the presence of Mr. John Moseley and a lord, the young men had most of the discourse to themselves. At a village fifteen miles from London, a fashionable carriage and four, with the coronet of a marquis was in waiting for Lord Henry. John refused his invitation to take a seat with him to town; for he had traced Denbigh from stage to stage, and was fearful of losing sight of him, unless he persevered in the manner he had commenced. Peter and he accordingly were put down safely at an inn in the Strand, and Moseley hastened to make his inquiries after the object of his pursuit. Such a chaise had arrived an hour before, and the gentleman had ordered his trunk to a neighboring hotel. After obtaining the address, and ordering a hackney coach, he hastened to the house; but on inquiring for Mr. Denbigh, to his great mortification was told they knew of no such gentleman. John turned away from the person he was speaking to in visible disappointment, when a servant respectfully inquired if the gentleman had not come from L----, in Norfolk, that day. "He had," was the reply. "Then follow me, sir, if you please." They knocked at a door of one of the parlors, and the servant entered: he returned, and John was shown into a room, where Denbigh was sitting with his head resting on his hand, and apparently musing. On seeing who required admittance, he sprang from his seat and exclaimed--

"Mr. Moseley! Do I see aright?"

"Denbigh," cried John, stretching out his hand to him, "was this kind-- was it like yourself--to leave us so unexpectedly, and for so long a time, too, as your note mentioned?"

Denbigh waved his hand to the servant to retire, and handed a chair to his friend.

"Mr. Moseley," said he, struggling with his feelings, "you appear ignorant of my proposals to your sister."

"Perfectly," answered the amazed John.

"And her rejection of them."

"Is it possible!" cried the brother, pacing up and down the room. "I acknowledge I did expect you to offer, but not to be refused."

Denbigh placed in the other hand the letter of Emily, which, having read, John returned, with a sigh. "This, then, is the reason you left us," he continued. "Emily is not capricious--it cannot be a sudden pique--she means as she says."

"Yes, Mr. Moseley," said Denbigh, mournfully; "your sister is faultless--but I am not worthy of her--my deception"--here the door again opened to the admission of Peter Johnson. Both the gentlemen rose at this sudden interruption, and the steward advancing to the table, once more produced the formidable pocket-book, the spectacles, and a letter. He ran over its direction--"For George Denbigh, Esquire, London, by the hands of Peter Johnson, with care and speed." After the observance of these preliminaries, he delivered the missive to its lawful owner, who opened it, and rapidly perused its contents. Denbigh was much affected with whatever the latter might be, and kindly took the steward by the hand, as he thanked him for this renewed instance of the interest he took in him. If he would tell him where a letter would find him in the morning, he would send a reply to the one he had received. Peter gave his address, but appeared unwilling to go, until assured again and again that the answer would be infallibly sent. Taking a small account-book out of his pocket, and referring to its contents, the steward said, "Master has with Coutts & Co. £7,000; in the bank, £5,000. It can be easily done, sir, and never felt by us." Denbigh smiled in reply, as he assured the steward he would take proper notice of his master's offers in his own answer. The door again opened, and the military stranger was admitted to their presence. He bowed, appeared not a little surprised to find two of his mail-coach companions there, and handed Denbigh a letter, in quite as formal, although in a more silent manner than the steward. The soldier was invited to be seated, and the letter was perused with an evident curiosity on the part of Denbigh. As soon as the latter ended it, he addressed the stranger in a language which John rightly judged to be Spanish, and Peter took to be Greek. For a few minutes the conversation was maintained between them with great earnestness, his fellow travellers marvelling much at the garrulity of the soldier however, the stranger soon rose to retire, when the door thrown open for the fourth time, and a voice cried out,

"Here I am, George, safe and sound--ready to kiss the bridesmaids, if they will let me--and I can find time--- bless me, Moseley!--old marling-spike!--general!--whew, where is the coachman and guard?"--it was Lord

Henry Stapleton. The Spaniard bowed again in silence and withdrew, while Denbigh threw open the door of an adjoining room and excused himself, as he desired Lord Henry to walk in there for a few minutes.

"Upon my word," cried the heedless sailor, as he complied, "we might as well have stuck together, Moseley; we were bound to one port, it seems."

"You know Lord Henry?" said John, as he withdrew.

"Yes," said Denbigh, and he again required his address of Peter, which having been given, the steward departed. The conversation between the two friends did not return to the course it was taking when they were interrupted, as Moseley felt a delicacy in making any allusion to the probable cause of his sister's refusal. He had, however, begun to hope it was not irremovable, and with the determination of renewing his visit in the morning, he took his leave, to allow Denbigh to attend to his other guest, Lord Henry Stapleton.

About twelve on the following morning, John and the steward met at the door of the hotel where Denbigh lodged, in quest of the same person. The latter held in his hand the answer to his master's letter, but wished particularly to see its writer. On inquiring, to their mutual surprise they were told, that the gentleman had left there early in the morning, having discharged his lodgings, and that they were unable to say whither he had gone. To hunt for a man without a clew, in the city of London, is usually time misspent. Of this Moseley was perfectly sensible, and disregarding a proposition of Peter's, he returned to his own lodgings. The proposal of the steward, if it did not do much credit to his sagacity, was much in favor of his perseverance and enterprise. It was no other than that John should take one side of the street, and he the other, in order to inquire at every house in the place, until the fugitive was discovered. "Sir," said Peter, with great simplicity, "when our neighbor White lost his little girl, this was the way we found her, although we went nearly through L---- before we succeeded, Mr. John." Peter was obliged to abandon this expedient for want of an associate, and as no message was left at the lodgings of Moseley, he started with a heavy heart on his return to Benfield Lodge. But Moseley's zeal was too warm in the cause of his friend, notwithstanding his unmerited desertion, to discontinue the search for him. He sought out the town residence of the Marquess of Eltringham, the brother of Lord Henry, and was told that both the Marquess and his brother had left town early that morning for his seat in Devonshire, to attend the wedding of their sister.

"Did they go alone?" asked John musing.

"There were two chaises, the Marquess's and his Grace's"

"Who was his Grace?" inquired John.

"Why the Duke of Derwent, to be sure."

"And the Duke?--was he alone?"

"There was a gentleman with his Grace, but they did not know his name."

As nothing further could be learnt, John withdrew. A good deal of irritation mixed with the vexation of Moseley at his disappointment; for Denbigh, he thought, too evidently wished to avoid him. That he was the companion of his kinsman, the Duke of Derwent, he had now no doubt, and he entirely relinquished all expectations of finding him in London or its environs. While retracing his steps in no enviable state of mind to his lodgings, with a resolution of returning immediately to L----, his arm was suddenly taken by his friend Chatterton. If any man could have consoled John at that moment, it was the Baron. Questions and answers were rapidly exchanged between them; and with increased satisfaction, John learnt that in the next square, he could have the pleasure of paying his respects to his kinswoman, the Dowager Lady Chatterton, and her two daughters. Chatterton inquired warmly after Emily, and in a particularly kind manner concerning Mr. Denbigh, hearing with undisguised astonishment the absence of the latter from the Moseley family.

Lady Chatterton had disciplined her feelings upon the subject of Grace and John into such a state of subordination, that the fastidious jealousy of the young man now found no ground of alarm in anything she said or did. It cannot be denied the Dowager was delighted to see him again; and if it were fair to draw any conclusions from coloring, palpitations, and other such little accompaniments of female feeling, Grace was not excessively sorry. It is true, it was the best possible opportunity to ascertain all about her friend Emily and the rest of the family; and Grace was extremely happy to have intelligence of their general welfare so direct as was afforded by this visit of Mr. Moseley. Grace looked all she expressed, and possibly a little more; and John thought he looked very beautiful.

There was present an elderly gentleman, of apparently indifferent health, although his manners were extremely lively, and his dress particularly studied. A few minutes observation convinced Moseley this gentleman was a candidate for the favor of Kate; and a game of chess being soon introduced, he also saw he was one thought worthy of peculiar care and attention. He had been introduced to him as Lord Herriefield, and soon discovered by his conversation that he was a peer who promised little towards rendering the house of incurables more convalescent than it was before his admission. Chatterton mentioned him as a distant connexion of his mother; a gentleman who had lately returned from filling an official situation in the East Indies, to take his seat among the lords by the death of his brother. He was a bachelor, and reputed rich, much of his wealth being personal property, acquired by himself abroad. The dutiful son might have added, if respect and feeling had not kept him silent, that his offers of settling a large jointure upon his elder sister had been accepted, and that the following week was to make her the bride of the emaciated debauchee who now sat by her side. He might also have said, that when the proposition was made to himself and Grace, both had shrunk from the alliance with disgust: and that both had united in humble though vain remonstrances to their mother, against the sacrifice, and in petitions to their sister, that she would not be accessary to her own misery. There was no pecuniary sacrifice they would not make to her, to avert such a connexion; but all was fruitless--Kate was resolved to be a viscountess, and her mother was equally determined that she should be rich.

Chapter XXX

A day elapsed between the departure of Denbigh and the reappearance of Emily amongst her friends. An indifferent observer would have thought her much graver and less animated than usual. A loss of the rich color which ordinarily glowed on her healthful cheek might be noticed; but the placid sweetness and graceful composure which regulated her former conduct pervaded all she did or uttered. Not so with Jane: her pride had suffered more than her feelings--her imagination had been more deceived than her judgment--and although too well bred and soft by nature to become rude or captious, she was changed from a communicative, to a reserved; from a confiding, to a suspicious companion. Her parents noticed this alteration with an uneasiness that was somewhat embittered by the consciousness of a neglect of some of those duties that experience now seemed to indicate, could never be forgotten with impunity.

Francis and Clara had arrived from their northern tour, so happy in each other, and so contented with their lot, that it required some little exercise of fortitude in both Lady Moseley and her daughters, to expel unpleasant recollections while they contemplated it. Their relation of the little incidents of their tour had, however, an effect to withdraw the attention of their friends in some degree from late occurrences; and a melancholy and sympathizing kind of association had taken place of the unbounded confidence and gaiety; which so lately prevailed at Benfield Lodge. Mr. Benfield mingled with his solemnity an air of mystery; and he was frequently noticed by his relatives looking over old papers, and was apparently employed in preparations that indicated movements of more than usual importance.

The family were collected in one of the parlors on an extremely unpleasant day, the fourth after the departure of John, when the thin person of Johnson stalked in amongst them. All eyes were fixed on him in expectation of what he had to communicate, and all apparently dreading to break the silence, from an apprehension that his communication would be unpleasant. In the meantime Peter, who had respectfully left his hat at the door, proceeded to uncase his body from the multiplied defences he had taken against the inclemency of the weather. His master stood erect, with an outstretched hand, ready to receive the reply to his epistle; and Johnson having liberated his body from thraldom, produced the black leathern pocket-book, and from its contents a letter, when he read aloud--Roderic Benfield, Esq., Benfield Lodge, Norfolk; favored by Mr.--here Peter's modesty got the better of his method; he had never been called Mr. Johnson by anybody, old or young; all knew him in that neighborhood as Peter Johnson--and he had very nearly been guilty of the temerity of arrogating to himself another title in the presence of those he most respected: a degree of self-elevation from which he escaped with the loss of a small piece of his tongue. Mr. Benfield took the letter with an eagerness that plainly indicated the deep interest he took in its contents, while Emily, with a tremulous voice and flushed cheek, approached the steward with a glass of wine.

"Peter," she said, "take this; it will do you good."

"Thank you, Miss Emma," said Peter, casting his eyes from her to his master, as the latter, having finished his letter, exclaimed, with a strange mixture of consideration and disappointment--

"Johnson, you must change your clothes immediately, or you will take cold: you look now like old Moses, the Jew beggar."

Peter sighed heavily at this comparison, and saw in it a confirmation of his fears; for he well knew, that to his being the bearer of unpleasant tidings was he indebted for a resemblance to anything unpleasant to his master, and Moses was the old gentleman's aversion.

The baronet now followed his uncle from the room to his library, entering it at the same moment with the steward, who had been summoned by his master to an audience.

Pointing to a chair for his nephew, Mr. Benfield commenced the discourse with saying,

"Peter, you saw Mr. Denbigh; how did he look?"

"As usual, master," said Peter, laconically, still piqued at being likened to old Moses.

"And what did he say to the offer? did he not make any comments on it? He was not offended at it, I hope," demanded Mr. Benfield.

"He said nothing but what he has written to your honor," replied the steward, losing a little of his constrained manner in real good feeling to his master.

"May I ask what the offer was?" inquired Sir Edward.

Mr. Benfield regarding him a moment in silence, said, "Certainly, you are nearly concerned in his welfare; your daughter"--the old man stopped, turned to his letter-book, and handed the baronet a copy of the epistle he had sent to Denbigh. It read as follows:

DEAR FRIEND MR. DENBIGH,

"I have thought a great deal on the reason of your sudden departure from a house I had begun to hope you thought your own; and by calling to mind my own feelings when Lady Juliana became the heiress to her nephew's estate, take it for granted you have been governed by the same sentiments; which I know both by my own experience and that of the bearer, Peter Johnson, is a never-failing accompaniment of pure affection. Yes, my dear Denbigh, I honor your delicacy in not wishing to become indebted to a stranger, as it were, for the money on which you subsist, and that stranger your wife--who ought in reason to look up to you, instead of your looking up to her; which was the true cause Lord Gosford would not marry the countess--on account of her great wealth, as he assured me himself; notwithstanding, envious people said it was because her ladyship loved Mr Chaworth better: so in order to remove these impediments of delicacy, I have to make three propositions, namely, that I bring you into parliament the next election for my own borough--that you take possession of the lodge the day you marry Emmy, while I will live, for the little time I have to stay here, in the large cottage built by my uncle--and that I give you your legacy of ten thousand pounds down, to prevent trouble hereafter.

"As I know nothing but delicacy has driven you away from us, I make no doubt you will now find all objections removed, and that Peter will bring back the joyful intelligence of your return to us, as soon as the business you left us on, is completed.

"Your uncle, that is to be,

"RODERIC BENFIELD."

"N.B. As Johnson is a stranger to the ways of the town, I wish you to advise his inexperience, particularly against the arts of designing women, Peter being a man of considerable estate, and great modesty."

"There, nephew," cried Mr. Benfield, as the baronet finished reading the letter aloud, "is it not unreasonable to refuse my offers? Now read his answer."

"Words are wanting to express the sensations which have been excited by Mr. Benfield's letter; but it would be impossible for any man to be so base as to avail himself of such liberality: the recollection of it, together with that of his many virtues, will long continue deeply impressed on the heart of him, whom Mr. Benfield would, if within the power of man, render the happiest amongst human beings."

The steward listened eagerly to this answer, but after it was done he was as much at a loss to know its contents as before its perusal. He knew it was unfavorable to their wishes, but could not comprehend its meaning or expressions, and immediately attributed their ambiguity to the strange conference he had witnessed between Denbigh and the military stranger.

"Master," exclaimed Peter, with something of the elation of a discoverer, "I know the cause, it shows itself in the letter: there was a man talking Greek to him while he was reading your letter."

"Greek!" exclaimed Sir Edward in astonishment.

"Greek!" said the uncle. "Lord Gosford read Greek; but I believe never conversed in that language."

"Yes, Sir Edward--yes, your honor--pure wild Greek; it must have been something of that kind," added Peter, with positiveness, "that would make a man refuse such offers--Miss Emmy--the lodge--£10,000!"--and the steward shook his head with much satisfaction at having discovered the cause.

Sir Edward smiled at the simplicity of Johnson, but disliking the idea attached to the refusal of his daughter, said, "Perhaps, after all, uncle, there has been some misunderstanding between Emily and Denbigh, which may have driven him from us so suddenly."

Mr. Benfield and his steward exchanged looks, and a new idea broke upon them at the instant. They had both suffered in that way; and after all it might prove that Emily was the one whose taste or feelings had subverted their schemes. The impression, once made, soon became strong, and the party separated; the master thinking alternately on Lady Juliana and his niece, while the man, after heaving one heavy sigh to the memory of Patty Steele, proceeded to the usual occupations of his office.

Mrs. Wilson thinking a ride would be of service to Emily, and having the fullest confidence in her self-command and resignation, availed herself of a fine day to pay a visit to their friend in the cottage. Mrs. Fitzgerald received them in her usual manner, but a single glance of her eye sufficed to show the aunt that she noticed the altered appearance of Emily and her manners, although without knowing its true reason, which she did not deem it prudent to explain. Julia handed her friend a note which she said she had received the day before, and desired their counsel how to proceed in the present emergency. As Emily was to be made acquainted with its contents, her aunt read it aloud as follows:

"MY DEAR NIECE,

"Your father and myself had been induced to think you were leading a disgraceful life, with the officer your husband had consigned you to the care of; for hearing of your captivity, I had arrived with a band of Guerillas, on the spot where you were rescued, early the next morning, and there learnt of the peasants your misfortunes and retreat. The enemy pressed us too much to allow us to deviate from our route at the time; but natural affection and the wishes of your father have led me to make a journey to England, in order to satisfy our doubts as regards your conduct. I have seen you, heard your character in the neighborhood, and after much and long search have found out the officer, and am satisfied, that so far as concerns your deportment, you are an injured woman. I have therefore to propose to you, on my own behalf, and that of the Conde, that you adopt the faith of your country, and return with me to the arms of your parent, whose heiress you will be, and whose life you may be the means of prolonging. Direct your answer to me, to the care of our ambassador; and as you decide, I am your mother's brother, LOUIS M'CARTHY Y HARRISON."

"On what point do you wish my advice?" said Mrs. Wilson, kindly, after she had finished reading the letter, "and when do you expect to see your uncle?"

"Would you have me accept the offer of my father, dear madam, or am I to remain separated from him for the short residue of his life?"

Mrs. Fitzgerald was affected to tears, as she asked this question, and waited her answer, in silent dread of its nature.

"Is the condition of a change of religion, an immovable one?" inquired Mrs. Wilson, in a thoughtful manner.

"Oh! doubtless," replied Julia, shuddering; "but I am deservedly punished for my early disobedience, and bow in submission to the will of Providence. I feel now all that horror of a change of my religion, I once only affected; I must live and die a Protestant, madam."

"Certainly, I hope so, my dear," said Mrs. Wilson; "I am not a bigot, and think it unfortunate you were not, in your circumstances, bred a pious Catholic. It would have saved you much misery, and might have rendered the close of your father's life more happy; but as your present creed embraces doctrines too much at variance with the Romish church to renounce the one or to adopt the other, with your views, it will be impossible to change your church without committing a heavy offence against the opinions and practices of every denomination of Christians. I should hope a proper representation of this to your uncle would have its weight, or they might be satisfied with your being a Christian, without becoming a Catholic."

"Ah! my dear madam," answered Mrs. Fitzgerald, despairingly, "you little know the opinions of my countrymen on this subject."

"Surely, surely," cried Mrs. Wilson, "parental affection is a stronger feeling than bigotry."

Mrs. Fitzgerald shook her head in a manner which bespoke both her apprehensions and her filial regard.

"Julia ought not, must not, desert her father, dear aunt," said Emily, her face glowing with the ardency of her feelings.

"And ought she to desert her heavenly Father, my child?" asked the aunt, mildly.

"Are the duties conflicting, dearest aunt?"

"The Conde makes them so. Julia is, I trust, in sincerity a Christian, and with what face can she offer up her daily petitions to her Creator, while she wears a mask to her earthly father; or how can she profess to honor doctrines that she herself believes to be false, or practise customs she thinks improper?"

"Never, never," exclaimed Julia, with fervor; "the struggle is dreadful, but I submit to the greater duty."

"And you decide rightly, my friend," said Mrs. Wilson, soothingly; "but you need relax no efforts to convince the Conde of your wishes: truth and nature will finally conquer."

"Ah!" cried Mrs. Fitzgerald, "the sad consequences of one false step in early life!"

"Rather," added Mrs. Wilson, "the sad consequences of one false step in generations gone by. Had your grandmother listened to the voice of prudence and duty, she never would have deserted her parents for a comparative stranger, and entailed upon her descendants a train of evils which yet exist in your person."

"It will be a sad blow to my poor uncle too," said Mrs. Fitzgerald, "he who once loved me so much."

"When do you expect to see him?" inquired Emily.

Julia informed them she expected him hourly; as, fearful a written statement of her views would drive him from the country without paying her a visit before he departed, she had earnestly entreated him to see her without delay.

On taking their leave, the ladies promised to obey her summons whenever called to meet the general, as Mrs. Wilson thought she might be better able to give advice to a friend, by knowing more of the character of her relatives, than she could do with her present information,

One day intervened, and it was spent in the united society of Lady Moseley and her daughters, while Sir Edward and Francis rode to a neighboring town on business; and on the succeeding, Mrs. Fitzgerald apprised them of the arrival of General M'Carthy. Immediately after breakfast, Mrs. Wilson and Emily drove to the cottage, the aunt both wishing the latter as a companion in her ride, and believing the excitement would have a tendency to prevent her niece from indulging in reflections, alike dangerous to her peace of mind and at variance with her duties.

Our readers have probably anticipated, that the stage companion of John Moseley was the Spanish general, who had just been making those inquiries into the manner of his niece's living which terminated so happily in her acquittal. With that part of her history which relates to the injurious attempts on her before she arrived at Lisbon, he appears to have been ignorant, or his interview with Denbigh might have terminated very differently from the manner already related.

A description of the appearance of the gentleman presented to Mrs. Wilson is unnecessary, as it has been given already; and the discerning matron thought she read through the rigid and set features of the soldier, a shade of kinder feelings, which might be wrought into an advantageous intercession on behalf of Julia. The General was evidently endeavoring to keep his feelings within due bounds, before the decision of his niece might render it proper for him to indulge in that affection for her, which his eye plainly showed existed under the cover of his assumed manner.

It was an effort of great fortitude on the part of Julia to acquaint her uncle with her resolution; but as it must be done, she seized a moment after Mrs. Wilson had at some length defended her adhering to her present faith, until religiously impressed with its errors, to inform him such was her unalterable resolution. He heard her patiently, and without anger, but in visible surprise. He had construed her summons to her house into a measure preparatory to accepting his conditions; yet he betrayed no emotion, after the first expression of his wonder: he told her distinctly, a renunciation of her heresy was the only condition on which her father would own her either as his heiress or his child. Julia deeply regretted the decision, but was firm; and her friends left her to enjoy uninterruptedly for one day, the society of so near a relative. During this day every doubt as to the propriety of her conduct, if any yet remained, was removed by a relation of her little story to her uncle; and after it was completed, he expressed great uneasiness to get to London again, in order to meet a gentleman he had seen there, under a different impression as to his merits, than what now appeared to be just. Who the gentleman was, or what these impressions were, Julia was left to conjecture, taciturnity being a favorite property in the general.

Chapter XXXI

The sun had just risen on one of the loveliest vales of Caernarvonshire, as a travelling chaise and six swept up to the door of a princely mansion, so situated as to command a prospect of the fertile and extensive domains, the rental of which filled the coffers of its rich owner, having a beautiful view of the Irish channel in the distance.

Everything around this stately edifice bespoke the magnificence of its ancient possessors and the taste of its present master. It was irregular, but built of the best materials, and in the tastes of the different ages in which its various parts had been erected; and now in the nineteenth century it preserved the baronial grandeur of the thirteenth, mingled with the comforts of this later period.

The lofty turrets of its towers were tipt with the golden light of the sun, and the neighboring peasantry had commenced their daily labors, as the different attendants of the equipage we have mentioned collected around it at the great entrance to the building. The beautiful black horses, with coats as shining as the polished leather with which they were caparisoned, the elegant and fashionable finish of the vehicle, with its numerous grooms, postillions, and footmen, all wearing the livery of one master, gave evidence of wealth and rank.

In attendance there were four outriders, walking leisurely about, awaiting the appearance of those for whose comforts and pleasures they were kept to contribute; while a fifth, who, like the others, was equipped with a horse, appeared to bear a doubtful station. The form of the latter was athletic, and apparently drilled into a severer submission than could be seen in the movements of the liveried attendants: his dress was peculiar, being neither quite menial nor quite military, but partaking of both characters. His horse was heavier and better managed than those of the others, and by its side was a charger, that was prepared for the use of no common equestrian. Both were coal-black, as were all the others of the cavalcade; but the pistols of the two latter, and housings of their saddles, bore the aspect of use and elegance united.

The postillions were mounted, listlessly waiting the pleasure of their superiors; when the laughs and jokes of the menials were instantly succeeded by a respectful and profound silence, as a gentleman and lady appeared on the portico of the building. The former was a young man of commanding stature and genteel appearance; and his air, although that of one used to command, was softened by a character of benevolence and gentleness, that might be rightly supposed to give birth to the willing alacrity with which all his requests or orders were attended to.

The lady was also young, and resembled her companion both in features and expression, for both were noble, both were handsome. The former was attired for the road; the latter had thrown a shawl around her elegant form, and by her morning dress showed that a separation of the two was about to happen. Taking the hand of the gentleman with both her own, as she pressed it with fingers interlocked, the lady said, in a voice of music, and with great affection, "Then, my dear brother, I shall certainly hear from you within the week, and see you next?"

"Certainly," replied the gentleman, as he tenderly paid his adieus; then throwing himself into the chaise, it dashed from the door, like the passage of a meteor. The horsemen followed; the unridden charger, obedient to the orders of his keeper, wheeled gracefully into his station; and in an instant they were all lost amidst the wood, through which the road to the park gates conducted.

After lingering without until the last of her brother's followers had receded from her sight, the lady retired through ranks of liveried footmen and maids, whom curiosity or respect had collected.

The young traveller wore a gloom on his expressive features, amidst the pageantry that surrounded him, which showed the insufficiency of wealth and honors to fill the sum of human happiness. As his carriage rolled proudly up an eminence ere he had reached the confines of his extensive park, his eye rested, for a moment, on a scene in which meadows, forests, fields waving with golden corn, comfortable farm-houses surrounded with innumerable cottages, were seen, in almost endless variety. All these owned him for their lord, and one quiet smile of satisfaction beamed on his face as he gazed on the unlimited view. Could the heart of that youth have been read, it would at that moment have told a story very different from the feelings such a scene is apt to excite; it would have spoken the consciousness of well applied wealth, the gratification of contemplating meritorious deeds, and a heartfelt gratitude to the Being which had enabled him to become the dispenser of happiness to so many of his fellow-creatures.

"Which way, my lord, so early?" cried a gentleman in a phaeton, as he drew up, on his way to a watering place, to pay his own parting compliments.

"To Eltringham, Sir Owen, to attend the marriage of my kinsman, Mr. Denbigh, to one of the sisters of the marquess."

A few more questions and answers, and the gentlemen, exchanging friendly adieus, pursued each his own course; Sir Owen Ap Rice pushing forward for Cheltenham, and the Earl of Pendennyss proceeding to act as groomsman to his cousin.

The gates of Eltringham were open to the admission of many an equipage on the following day, and the heart of the Lady Laura beat quick, as the sound of wheels, at different times, reached her ears. At last an unusual movement in the house drew her to a window of her dressing-room, and the blood rushed to her heart as she beheld the equipages which were rapidly approaching, and through the mist which stole over her eyes she saw alight from the first, the Duke of Derwent and the bridegroom. The next contained Lord Pendennyss, and the last the Bishop of----. Lady Laura waited to see no more, but with a heart filled with terror, hope, joy, and uneasiness, she threw herself into the arms of one of her sisters.

"Ah!" exclaimed Lord Henry Stapleton, about a week after the wedding of his sister, seizing John suddenly by the arm, while the latter was taking his morning walk to the residence of the dowager Lady Chatterton, "Moseley, you dissipated youth, in town yet: you told me you should stay but a day, and here I find you at the end of a fortnight."

John blushed a little at the consciousness of his reason for sending a written, instead of carrying a verbal report, of the result of his journey, but replied,

"Yes, my friend Chatterton unexpectedly arrived, and so--and so--"

"And so you did not go, I presume you mean," cried Lord Henry, with a laugh.

"Yes," said John, "and so I stayed--but where is Denbigh?"

"Where?--why with his wife, where every well-behaved man should be, especially for the first month," rejoined the sailor, gaily.

"Wife!" echoed John, as soon as he felt able to give utterance to his words--"wife! is he married?"

"Married," cried Lord Henry, imitating his manner, "are you yet to learn that? why did you ask for him?"

"Ask for him!" said Moseley, yet lost in astonishment; "but when--how--where did he marry--my lord?"

Lord Henry looked at him for a moment with a surprise little short of his own, as he answered more gravely:

"When?--last Tuesday; how? by special license, and the Bishop of----; where?--at Eltringham:--yes, my dear fellow," continued he, with his former gaiety, "George is my brother now--and a fine fellow he is."

"I really wish your lordship much joy," said John, struggling to command his feelings.

"Thank you--thank you," replied the sailor; "a jolly time we had of it, Moseley. I wish, with all my heart, you had been there; no bolting or running away as soon as spliced, but a regularly constructed, old-fashioned wedding; all my doings. I wrote Laura that time was scarce, and I had none to throw away on fooleries; so dear, good soul, she consented to let me have everything my own way. We had Derwent and Pendennyss, the marquess, Lord William, and myself, for groomsmen, and my three sisters--ah, that was bad, but there was no helping it--Lady Harriet Denbigh, and an old maid, a cousin of ours, for bridesmaids; could not help the old maid either, upon my honor, or be quite certain I would."

How much of what he said Moseley heard, we cannot say; for had he talked an hour longer he would have been uninterrupted. Lord Henry was too much engaged with his description to notice his companion's taciturnity or surprise, and after walking a square or two together they parted; the sailor being on the wing for his frigate at Yarmouth.

John continued his course, musing on the intelligence he had just heard. That Denbigh could forget Emily so soon, he would not believe, and he greatly feared he had been driven into a step, from despair, that he might hereafter repent of. The avoiding of himself was now fully explained; but would Lady Laura Stapleton accept a man for a husband at so short a notice? and for the first time a suspicion that something in the character of Denbigh was wrong, mingled in his reflections on his sister's refusal of his offers.

Lord and Lady Herriefield were on the eve of their departure for the continent (for Catherine had been led to the altar the preceding week), a southern climate having been prescribed as necessary to the bridegroom's constitution; and the dowager and Grace were about to proceed to a seat of the baron's within a couple of miles of Bath. Chatterton himself had his own engagements, but he promised to be there in company with his friend Derwent within a fortnight; the former visit having been postponed by the marriages in their respective families.

John had been assiduous in his attentions during the season of forced gaiety which followed the nuptials of Kate; and as the dowager's time was monopolized with the ceremonials of that event, Grace had risen greatly in his estimation. If Grace Chatterton was not more miserable than usual, at what she thought was the destruction of her sister's happiness, it was owing to the presence and unconcealed affection of John Moseley.

The carriage of Lord Herriefield was in waiting when John rang for admittance. On opening the door and entering the drawing-room, he saw the bride and bridegroom, with their mother and sister, accoutred for an excursion amongst the shops of Bond street: for Kate was dying to find a vent for some of her surplus pin-money--her husband to show his handsome wife in the face of the world--the mother to display the triumph of her matrimonial schemes. And Grace was forced to obey her mother's commands, in accompanying her sister as an attendant, not to be dispensed with at all in her circumstances.

The entrance of John at that instant, though nothing more than what occurred every day at that hour, deranged the whole plan: the dowager, for a moment, forgot her resolution, and forgot the necessity of Grace's appearance, exclaiming with evident satisfaction,

"Here is Mr. Moseley come to keep you company, Grace; so, after all, you must consult your headache and stay at home. Indeed, my love, I never can consent you should go out. I not only wish, but insist you remain within this morning."

Lord Herriefield looked at his mother-in-law in some surprise, and threw a suspicious glance on his own rib at the moment, which spoke as plainly as looks can speak,

"Is it possible I have been taken in after all!"

Grace was unused to resist her mother's commands, and throwing off her hat and shawl, reseated herself with more composure than she would probably have done, had not the attentions of Moseley been more delicate and pointed of late than formerly.

As they passed the porter, Lady Chatterton observed to him significantly--"Nobody at home, Willis."--"Yes, my lady," was the laconic reply, and Lord Herriefield, as he took his seat by the side of his wife in the carriage, thought she was not as handsome as usual.

Lady Chatterton that morning unguardedly laid the foundation of years of misery for her eldest daughter; or rather the foundations were already laid in the ill-assorted, and heartless, unprincipled union she had labored with success to effect. But she, had that morning stripped the mask from her own character prematurely, and excited suspicions in the breast of her son-in-law, which time only served to confirm, and memory to brood over. Lord Herriefield had been too long in the world not to understand all the ordinary arts of match-makers and match-hunters. Like most of his own sex who have associated freely with the worst part of the other, his opinions of female excellences were by no means extravagant or romantic. Kate had pleased his eye; she was of a noble family; young, and at that moment interestingly quiet, having nothing particularly in view. She had a taste of her own, and Lord Herriefield was by no means in conformity with it; consequently, she expended none of those pretty little arts upon him which she occasionally practised, and which his experience would immediately have detected. Her disgust he had attributed to disinterestedness; and as Kate had fixed her eye on a young officer lately returned from France, and her mother on a Duke who was mourning the death of a third wife, devising means to console him with a fourth--the Viscount had got a good deal enamored with the lady, before either she or her mother took any particular notice that there was such a being in existence. His title was not the most elevated, but it was ancient. His paternal acres were not numerous, but his East-India shares were. He was not very young, but he was not very old; and as the Duke died of a fit of the gout in his stomach, and the officer ran away with a girl in her teens from a boarding-school, the dowager and her daughter, after thoroughly scanning the fashionable world, determined, for want of a better, that *he* would do.

It is not to be supposed that the mother and child held any open communications with each other to this effect. The delicacy and pride of both would have been greatly injured by such a suspicion; yet they arrived simultaneously at the same conclusion, as well as at another of equal importance to the completion of their schemes on the Viscount. It was simply to adhere to the same conduct which had made him a captive, as most likely to insure the victory.

There was such a general understanding between the two it can excite no surprise that they co-operated harmoniously as it were by signal.

For two people, correctly impressed with their duties and responsibilities, to arrive at the same conclusion in the government of their conduct, would be merely a matter of course; and so with those who are more or less under the dominion of the world. They will pursue their plans with a degree of concurrence amounting nearly to sympathy; and thus had Kate and her mother, until this morning, kept up the masquerade so well that the Viscount was as confiding as a country Corydon. When he first witnessed the dowager's management with Grace and John, however, and his wife's careless disregard of a thing which appeared too much a matter of course to be quite agreeable, his newly awakened distrust approached conviction.

Grace Chatterton both sang and played exquisitely; it was, however, seldom she could sufficiently overcome her desire, when John was an auditor, to appear to advantage.

As the party went down stairs, and Moseley had gone with them part of the way, she threw herself unconsciously in a seat, and began a beautiful song, that was fashionable at the time. Her feelings were in consonance with the words, and Grace was very happy both in execution and voice.

John had reached the back of her seat before she was at all sensible of his return, and Grace lost her self-command immediately. She rose and took a seat on a sofa, and the young man was immediately at her side.

"Ah, Grace," said John, the lady's heart beating high, "you certainly do sing as you do everything, admirably."

"I am happy you think so, Mr. Moseley," returned Grace looking everywhere but in his face.

John's eyes ran over her beauties, as with palpitating bosom and varying color she sat confused at the unusual warmth of his language and manner.

Fortunately a remarkably striking likeness of the Dowager hung directly over their heads, and John taking her unresisting hand, continued,

"Dear Grace, you resemble your brother very much in features, and what is better still, in character."

"I could wish," said Grace, venturing to look up, "to resemble your sister Emily in the latter."

"And why not to be her sister, dear Grace?" said he with ardor. "You are worthy to become her sister. Tell me, Grace, dear Miss Chatterton--can you--will you make me the happiest of men? may I present another inestimable daughter to my parents?"

As John paused for an answer, Grace looked up, and he waited her reply in evident anxiety; but she continued silent, now pale as death, and now of the color of the rose, and he added:

"I hope I have not offended you, dearest Grace; you are all that is desirable to me; my hopes, my happiness, are centred in you. Unless you consent to become my wife, I must be very wretched."

Grace burst into a flood of tears, as her lover, interested deeply in their cause, gently drew her towards him. Her head sank on his shoulder, as she faintly whispered something that was inaudible, but which he did not fail to interpret into everything he most wished to hear. John was in ecstasies. Every unpleasant feeling of suspicion had left him. Of Grace's innocence of manoeuvring he never doubted, but John did not relish the idea of being entrapped into anything, even a step which he desired. An uninterrupted communication followed; it was as confiding as their affections: and the return of the dowager and her children first recalled them to the recollection of other people.

One glance of the eye was enough for Lady Chatterton. She saw the traces of tears on the cheeks and in the eyes of Grace, and the dowager was satisfied; she knew his friends would not object; and as Grace attended her to her dressing-room, she cried on entering it, "Well, child, when is the wedding to be? You will wear me out with so much gaiety."

Grace was shocked, but did not as formerly weep over her mother's interference in agony and dread. John had opened his whole soul to her, observing the greatest delicacy towards her mother, and she now felt her happiness placed in the keeping of a man whose honor she believed much exceeded that of any other human being.

Chapter XXXII

The seniors of the party at Benfield Lodge were all assembled one morning in a parlor, when its master and the baronet were occupied in the perusal of the London papers. Clara had persuaded her sisters to accompany her and Francis in an excursion as far as the village.

Jane yet continued reserved and distant to most of her friends; while Emily's conduct would have escaped unnoticed, did not her blanched cheek and wandering looks at times speak a language not to be misunderstood. With all her relatives she maintained the affectionate intercourse she had always supported; though not even to her aunt did the name of Denbigh pass her lips. But in her most private and humble petitions to God, she never forgot to mingle with her requests for spiritual blessings on herself, fervent prayers for the conversion of the preserver of her life.

Mrs. Wilson, as she sat by the side of her sister at their needles, first discovered an unusual uneasiness in their venerable host, while he turned his paper over and over, as if unwilling or unable to comprehend some part of its contents, until he rang the bell violently, and bid the servant to send Johnson to him without a moment's delay.

"Peter," said Mr. Benfield doubtingly, "read that--your eyes are young, Peter; read that."

Peter took the paper, and after having adjusted his spectacles to his satisfaction, he proceeded to obey his master's injunctions; but the same defect of vision as suddenly seized the steward as it had affected his master. He turned the paper sideways, and appeared to be spelling the matter of the paragraph to himself. Peter would have given his three hundred a year to have had the impatient John Moseley at hand, to relieve him from his task; but the anxiety of Mr. Benfield overcoming his fear of the worst, he inquired in tremulous tone--

"Peter? hem! Peter, what do you think?"

"Why, your honor," replied the steward, stealing a look at his master, "it does seem so indeed."

"I remember," said the master, "when Lord Gosford saw the marriage of the countess announced he--"

Here the old gentleman was obliged to stop, and rising with dignity, and leaning on the arm of his faithful servant, he left the room.

Mrs. Wilson immediately took up the paper, and her eye catching the paragraph at a glance, she read aloud as follows to her expecting friends:

"Married by special license, at the seat of the Most Noble the Marquess of Eltringham, in Devonshire, by the Right Rev. Lord Bishop of ----, George Denbigh Esq., Lieutenant Colonel of his Majesty's ---- regiment of dragoons, to the Right Honorable Lady Laura Stapleton, eldest sister of the Marquess. Eltringham was honored on the present happy occasion with the presence of his grace of Derwent, and the gallant Lord Pendennyss, kinsmen of the bridegroom, and Captain Lord Henry Stapleton of the Royal Navy. We understand that the happy couple proceed to Denbigh Castle immediately after the honey-moon."

Although Mrs. Wilson had given up the expectation of ever seeing her niece the wife of Denbigh, she felt an indescribable shock as she read this paragraph. The strongest feeling was horror at the danger Emily had been in of contracting an alliance with such a man. His avoiding the ball, at which he knew Lord Henry was expected, was explained to her by this marriage; for with John, she could not believe a woman like Lady Laura Stapleton was to be won in the short space of one fortnight, or indeed less. There was too evidently a mystery yet to be developed, and she felt certain one that would not elevate his character in her opinion.

Neither Sir Edward nor Lady Moseley had given up the expectation of seeing Denbigh again, as a suitor for Emily's hand, and to both of them this certainty of his loss was a heavy blow. The baronet took up the paper, and after perusing the article, he muttered in a low tone, as he wiped the tears from his eyes, "Heaven bless him: I sincerely hope she is worthy of him." Worthy of him, thought Mrs. Wilson, with a feeling of indignation, as, taking up the paper, she retired to her own room, whither Emily, at that moment returned from her walk, had proceeded. As her niece must hear this news, she thought the sooner the better. The exercise, and the unreserved conversation of Francis and Clara, had restored in some degree the bloom to the cheek of Emily; and Mrs. Wilson felt it necessary to struggle with herself, before she could summon sufficient resolution to invade the returning peace of her charge. However, having already decided on her course, she proceeded to the discharge of what she thought to be a duty.

"Emily, my child," she whispered, pressing her affectionately to her bosom, "you have been all I could wish, and more than I expected, under your arduous struggles. But one more pang, and I trust your recollections on this painful subject will be done away."

Emily looked at her aunt in anxious expectation of what was coming, and quietly taking the paper, followed the direction of Mrs. Wilson's finger to the article on the marriage of Denbigh.

There was a momentary struggle in Emily for self-command. She was obliged to find support in a chair. The returning richness of color, excited by her walk, vanished; but recovering herself, she pressed the hand of her anxious guardian, and, gently waving her back, proceeded to her own room.

On her return to the company, the same control of her feelings which had distinguished her conduct of late, was again visible; and, although her aunt most narrowly watched her movements, looks, and speeches, she could discern no visible alteration by this confirmation of misconduct. The truth was, that in Emily Moseley the obligations of duty were so imperative, her sense of her dependence on Providence so humbling and yet so confiding, that, as soon as she was taught to believe her lover unworthy of her esteem, that moment an insuperable barrier separated them. His marriage could add nothing to the distance between them. It was impossible they could be united; and although a secret lingering of the affections over his fallen character might and did exist, it existed without any romantic expectations of miracles in his favor, or vain wishes of reformation, in which self was the prominent feeling. She might be said to be keenly alive to all that concerned his welfare or movements, if she did not harbor the passion of love; but it showed itself in prayers for his amendment of life, and the most ardent petitions for his future and eternal happiness. She had set about, seriously and with much energy, the task of erasing from her heart sentiments which, however delightful she had found it to entertain in times past, were now in direct variance with her duty. She knew that a weak indulgence of such passions would tend to draw her mind from, and disqualify her to discharge, those various calls on her time and her exertions, which could alone enable her to assist others, or effect in her own person the great purposes of her creation. It was never lost sight of by Emily Moseley, that her existence here was preparatory to an immensely more important state hereafter. She was consequently in charity with all mankind; and if grown a little more distrustful of the intentions of her fellow-creatures, it was a mistrust bottomed in a clear view of the frailties of our nature; and self-examination was amongst the not unfrequent speculations she made on this hasty marriage of her former lover.

Mrs. Wilson saw all this, and was soon made acquainted by her niece in terms, with her views of her own condition; and although she had to, and did, deeply regret, that all her caution had not been able to guard against deception, where it was most important for her to guide aright, yet she was cheered with the reflection that her previous care, with the blessings of Providence, had admirably fitted her charge to combat and overcome the consequences of their mistaken confidence.

The gloom which this little paragraph excited, extended to every individual in the family; for all had placed Denbigh by the side of John, in their affections, ever since his weighty services to Emily.

A letter from John announcing his intention of meeting them at Bath, as well as his new relation with Grace, relieved in some measure this general depression of spirit. Mr. Benfield alone found no consolation in the approaching nuptials. John he regarded as his nephew, and Grace he thought a very good sort of young woman; but neither of them were beings of the same genus with Emily and Denbigh.

"Peter," said he one day, after they had both been expending their ingenuity in vain efforts to discover the cause of this so-much-desired marriage's being so unexpectedly frustrated, "have I not often told you, that fate governed these things, in order that men might be humble in this life? Now, Peter, had the Lady Juliana wedded with a mind congenial to her own, she might have been mistress of Benfield Lodge to this very hour."

"Yes, your honor--but there's Miss Emmy's legacy."

And Peter withdrew, thinking what would have been the consequences had Patty Steele been more willing, when he wished to make her Mrs. Peter Johnson--an association by no means uncommon in the mind of the steward; for if Patty had ever a rival in his affections, it was in the person of Emily Moseley, though, indeed, with very different degrees and coloring of esteem.

The excursions to the cottage had been continued by Mrs. Wilson and Emily, and as no gentleman was now in the family to interfere with their communications, a general visit to the young widow had been made by the Moseleys, including Sir Edward and Mr. Ives.

The Jarvises had gone to London to receive their children, now penitent in more senses than one; and Sir Edward learnt with pleasure that Egerton and his wife had been admitted into the family of the merchant.

Sir Edgar had died suddenly, and the entailed estates had fallen to his successor the colonel, now Sir Harry; but the bulk of his wealth, being in convertible property, he had given by will to his other nephew, a young clergyman, and a son of a younger brother. Mary, as well as her mother, were greatly disappointed, by this deprivation, of what they considered their lawful splendor; but they found great consolation in the new dignity of Lady Egerton, whose greatest wish now was to meet the Moseleys, in order that she might precede them in or out of some place where such ceremonials are observed. The sound of "Lady Egerton's carriage stops the way," was delightful, and it never failed to be used on all occasions, although her ladyship was mistress of only a hired vehicle.

A slight insight into the situation of things amongst them may be found in the following narrative of their views, as revealed in a discussion which took place about a fortnight after the reunion of the family under one roof.

Mrs. Jarvis was mistress of a very handsome coach, the gift of her husband for her own private use. After having satisfied herself the baronet (a dignity he had enjoyed just twenty-four hours) did not possess the ability to furnish his lady, as she termed her daughter, with such a luxury, she magnanimously determined to relinquish her own, in support of the new-found elevation of her daughter. Accordingly, a consultation on the alterations which were necessary took place between the ladies--"The arms must be altered, of course," Lady Egerton observed, "and Sir Harry's, with the bloody hand and six quarterings, put in their place; then the liveries, they must be changed."

"Oh, mercy! my lady, if the arms are altered, Mr. Jarvis will be sure to notice it, and he would never forgive me; and perhaps--"

"Perhaps what?" exclaimed the new-made lady, with a disdainful toss of her head.

"Why," replied the mother, warmly, "not give me the hundred pounds he promised, to have it new-lined and painted."

"Fiddlesticks with the painting, Mrs. Jarvis," cried the *lady* with dignity: "no carriage shall be called mine that does not bear my arms and the bloody hand."

"Why, your ladyship is unreasonable, indeed you are," said Mrs. Jarvis, coaxingly; and then after a moment's thought she continued, "is it the arms or the baronetcy you want, my dear?"

"Oh, I care nothing for the arms, but I am determined, now I am a baronet's lady, Mrs. Jarvis, to have the proper emblem of my rank."

"Certainly, my lady, that's true dignity: well, then, we will put the bloody hand on your father's arms, and he will never notice it, for he never sees such things."

The arrangement was happily completed, and for a few days the coach of Mr. Jarvis bore about the titled dame, until one unlucky day the merchant, who still went on 'change when any great bargain in the stocks was to be made, arrived at his own door suddenly, to procure a calculation he had made on the leaf of his prayer-book the last Sunday during sermon. This he obtained after some search. In his haste he drove to his broker's in the carriage of his wife, to save time, it happening to be in waiting at the moment, and the distance not great. Mr. Jarvis forgot to order the man to return, and for an hour the vehicle stood in one of the most public places in the city. The consequence was, that when Mr. Jarvis undertook to examine into his gains, with the account rendered of the transaction by his broker, he was astonished to read, "Sir Timothy Jarvis, Bart., in account with John Smith, Dr." Sir Timothy examined the account in as many different ways as Mr. Benfield had examined the marriage of Denbigh, before he would believe his eyes; and when assured of the fact, he immediately caught up his hat, and went to find the man who had dared to insult him, as it were, in defiance of the formality of business. He had not proceeded one square in the city before he met a friend, who spoke to him by the title; an explanation of the mistake followed, and the quasi baronet proceeded to his stables. Here by actual examination he detected the fraud. An explanation with his consort followed; and the painter's brush soon effaced the emblem of dignity from the panels of the coach. All this was easy but with his waggish companions on 'Change and in the city (where, notwithstanding his wife's fashionable propensities, he loved to resort) he was Sir Timothy still.

Mr. Jarvis, though a man of much modesty, was one of great decision, and he determined to have the laugh on his side. A newly purchased borough of his sent up an address flaming with patriotism, and it was presented by his own hands. The merchant seldom kneeled to his Creator, but on this occasion he humbled himself dutifully before his prince, and left the presence with a legal right to the appellation which his old companions had affixed to him sarcastically.

The rapture of Lady Jarvis may be more easily imagined than faithfully described, the Christian name of her husband alone throwing any alloy into the enjoyment of her elevation: but by a license of speech she ordered, and addressed in her own practice, the softer and more familiar appellation of Sir Timo. Two servants were discharged the first week, because, unused to titles, they had addressed her as mistress; and her son, the captain, then at a watering-place, was made acquainted by express with the joyful intelligence.

All this time Sir Henry Egerton was but little seen amongst his new relatives. He had his own engagements and haunts, and spent most of his time at a fashionable gaming house in the West End. As, however, the town was deserted, Lady Jarvis and her daughters, having condescended to pay a round of city visits, to show off her airs and dignity to her old friends, persuaded Sir Timo that the hour for their visit to Bath had arrived, and they were soon comfortably settled in that city.

Lady Chatterton and her youngest daughter had arrived at the seat of her son, and John Moseley, as happy as the certainty of love returned and the approbation of his friends could make him, was in lodgings in the town. Sir Edward notified his son of his approaching visit to Bath, and John took proper accommodations for the family, which he occupied for a few days by himself as *locum tenens*.

Lord and Lady Herriefield had departed for the south of France; and Kate, removed from the scenes of her earliest enjoyments and the bosom of her own family, and under the protection of a man she neither loved nor respected, began to feel the insufficiency of a name or of a fortune to constitute felicity. Lord Herriefield was of a suspicious and harsh temper, the first propensity being greatly increased by his former associations, and the latter not being removed by the humility of his eastern dependants. But the situation of her child gave no uneasiness to the managing mother, who thought her in the high-road to happiness, and was gratified at the result of her labors. Once or twice, indeed, her habits had overcome her caution so much as to endeavor to promote, a day or two sooner than had been arranged, the wedding of Grace; but her imprudence was checked instantly by the recoiling of Moseley from her insinuations in disgust; and the absence of the young man for twenty-four hours gave her timely warning of the danger of such an interference with one of such fastidious feelings. John punished himself as much as the dowager on these occasions; but the smiling face of Grace, with her hand frankly placed in his own at his return, never failed to do away the unpleasant sensations created by her mother's care.

The Chatterton and Jarvis families met in the rooms, soon after the arrival of the latter, when the lady of the knight, followed by both her daughters, approached the dowager with a most friendly salute of recognition. Lady Chatterton, really forgetful of the persons of her B---- acquaintance, and disliking the vulgarity of her air, drew up into an appearance of great dignity, as she hoped the lady was well. The merchant's wife felt the consciousness of rank too much to be repulsed in this manner, and believing that the dowager had merely forgotten her face, she added, with a simpering smile, in imitation of what she had seen better bred people practise with success--

"Lady Jarvis--my lady--your ladyship don't remember me--Lady Jarvis of the Deanery, B----, Northamptonshire, and my daughters, Lady Egerton and Miss Jarvis." Lady Egerton bowed stiffly to the recognising smile the dowager now condescended to bestow; but Sarah, remembering a certain handsome lord in the family, was more urbane, determining at the moment to make the promotion of her mother and sister stepping-stones to greater elevation for herself.

"I hope my lord is well," continued the city lady. "I regret that Sir Timo, and Sir Harry, and Captain Jarvis, are not here this morning to pay their respects to your ladyship; but as we shall see naturally a good deal of each other, it must be deferred to a more fitting opportunity."

"Certainly, madam," replied the dowager, as, passing her compliments with those of Grace, she drew back from so open a conversation with creatures of such doubtful standing in the fashionable world.

Chapter XXXIII

On taking leave of Mrs. Fitzgerald, Emily and her aunt settled a plan of correspondence; the deserted situation of this young woman having created great interest in the breasts of her new friends. General M'Carthy had returned to Spain without receding from his original proposal, and his niece was left to mourn her early departure from one of the most solemn duties of life.

Mr. Benfield, thwarted in one of his most favorite schemes of happiness for the residue of his life, obstinately refused to make one of the party at Bath; and Ives and Clara having returned to Bolton, the remainder of the Moseleys arrived at the lodgings of John a very few days after the interview of the preceding chapter, with hearts ill qualified to enter into the gaieties of the place, though, in obedience to the wishes of Lady Moseley, to see and to be seen once more on that great theatre of fashionable amusement.

The friends of the family who had known them in times past were numerous, and were glad to renew their acquaintance with those they had always esteemed; so that they found themselves immediately surrounded by a circle of smiling faces and dashing equipages.

Sir William Harris, the proprietor of the deanery, and a former neighbor, with his showy daughter, were amongst the first to visit them. Sir William was a man of handsome estate and unexceptionable character, but entirely governed by the whims and desires of his only child. Caroline Harris wanted neither sense nor beauty, but expecting a fortune, she had placed her views too high. She at first aimed at the peerage; and while she felt herself entitled to suit her taste as well as her ambition, had failed of her object by ill-concealed efforts to attain it. She had justly acquired the reputation of the reverse of a coquette or yet of a prude; still she had never received an offer, and at the age of twenty-six, had now begun to lower her thoughts to the commonalty. Her fortune would have easily obtained her husband here, but she was determined to pick amongst the lower supporters of the aristocracy of the nation. With the Moseleys she had been early acquainted, though some years their senior; a circumstance, however, to which she took care never to allude unnecessarily.

The meeting between Grace and the Moseleys was tender and sincere. John's countenance glowed with delight, as he saw his future wife folded successively in the arms of those he loved, and Grace's tears and blushes added twofold charms to her native beauty. Jane relaxed from her reserve to receive her future sister, and determined with herself to appear in the world, in order to show Sir Henry Egerton that she did not feel the blow he had inflicted as severely as the truth might have proved.

The Dowager found some little occupation, for a few days, in settling with Lady Moseley the preliminaries of the wedding; but the latter had suffered too much through her youngest daughters, to enter into these formalities with her ancient spirit. All things were, however, happily settled; and Ives making a journey for the express purpose, John and Grace were united privately at the altar of one of the principal churches in Bath. Chatterton had been summoned on the occasion; and the same paper which announced the nuptials, contained, amongst the fashionable arrivals, the names of the Duke of Derwent and his sister, the Marquess of Eltringham and sisters, amongst whom was to be found Lady Laura Denbigh. Lady Chatterton carelessly remarked, in presence of her friends, the husband of the latter was summoned to the death-bed of a relative, from whom he had great expectations. Emily's color did certainly change as she listened to this news, but not allowing her thoughts to dwell on the subject, she was soon enabled to recall her serenity of appearance.

But Jane and Emily were delicately placed. The lover of the former, and the wives of the lovers of both, were in the way of daily, if not hourly rencounters; and it required all the energies of the young women to appear with composure before them. The elder was supported by pride, the younger by principle. The first was restless, haughty, distant, and repulsive. The last mild, humble, reserved, but eminently attractive. The one was suspected by all around her; the other was unnoticed by any, but by her nearest and dearest friends.

The first rencounter with these dreaded guests occurred at the rooms one evening, where the elder ladies had insisted on the bride's making her appearance. The Jarvises were there before them, and at their entrance caught the eyes of the group. Lady Jarvis approached immediately, filled with exultation--her husband with respect. The latter was received with cordiality--the former politely, but with distance. The young ladies and Sir Henry bowed distantly, and the gentleman soon drew off into another part of the room: his absence alone kept Jane from fainting. The handsome figure of Egerton standing by the side of Mary Jarvis, as her acknowledged husband, was near proving too much for her pride, notwithstanding all her efforts; and he looked so like the imaginary being she had set up as the object of her worship, that her heart was also in danger of rebelling.

"Positively, Sir Edward and my lady, both Sir Timo and myself, and, I dare say, Sir Harry and Lady Egerton too, are delighted to see you comfortably at Bath among us. Mrs. Moseley, I wish you much happiness; Lady Chatterton too. I suppose your ladyship recollects me now; I am Lady Jarvis. Mr. Moseley, I regret, for your sake, that my son Captain Jarvis is not here; you were so fond of each other, and both so loved your guns."

"Positively, my Lady Jarvis," said Moseley, drily, "my feelings on the occasion are as strong as your own; but I presume the captain is much too good a shot for me by this time."

"Why, yes; he improves greatly in most things he undertakes," rejoined the smiling dame, "and I hope he will soon learn, like you, to shoot with the *h*arrows of Cupid. I hope the Honorable Mrs. Moseley is well."

Grace bowed mildly, as she answered to the interrogatory, and smiled at the thought of Jarvis put in competition with her husband in this species of archery, when a voice immediately behind where they sat caught the ears of the whole party; all it said was--

"Harriet, you forgot to show me Marian's letter."

"Yes, but I will to-morrow," was the reply.

It was the tone of Denbigh. Emily almost fell from her seat as it first reached her, and the eyes of all but herself were immediately turned in quest of the speaker. He had approached within a very few feet of them, supporting a lady on each arm. A second look convinced the Moseleys that they were mistaken. It was not Denbigh, but a young man whose figure, face, and air resembled him strongly, and whose voice possessed the same soft melodious tones which had distinguished that of Denbigh. This party seated themselves within a very short distance of the Moseleys, and they continued their conversation.

"You heard from the Colonel to-day, too, I believe," continued the gentleman, turning to the lady who sat next to Emily.

"Yes, he is a very punctual correspondent; I hear every other day."

"How is his uncle, Laura?" inquired her female companion.

"Rather better; but I will thank your grace to find the Marquess and Miss Howard."

"Bring them to us," rejoined the other.

"Yes," said the former lady, with a laugh, "and Eltringham will thank you too, I dare say."

In an instant the duke returned, accompanied by a gentleman of thirty and an elderly lady, who might have been safely taken for fifty without offence to anybody but herself.

During these speeches their auditors had listened with almost breathless interest. Emily had stolen a glance which satisfied her it was not Denbigh himself and it greatly relieved her; but was startled at discovering that she was actually seated by the side of his young and lovely wife. When an opportunity offered, she dwelt on the amiable, frank countenance of her rival with melancholy satisfaction: at least, she thought, he may yet be happy, and I hope penitent.

It was a mixture of love and gratitude which prompted this wish, both sentiments not easily got rid of when once ingrafted in our better feelings. John eyed the strangers with a displeasure for which he could not account at once, and saw, in the ancient lady, the bridesmaid Lord Henry had so unwillingly admitted to that distinction.

Lady Jarvis was astounded with her vicinity to so much nobility, and she drew back to her family to study its movements to advantage; while Lady Chatterton sighed heavily, as she contemplated the fine figures of an unmarried Duke and Marquess, and she without a single child to dispose of. The remainder of the party continued to view them with curiosity, and listened with interest to what they said.

Two or three young ladies had now joined the strangers, attended by a couple of gentlemen, and the conversation became general. The ladies declined dancing entirely, but appeared willing to throw away an hour in comments on their neighbors.

"William," said one of the young ladies, "there is your old messmate, Col. Egerton."

"Yes, I observe him," replied her brother, "I see him;" but, smiling significantly, he continued, "we are messmates no longer."

"He is a sad character," said the Marquess, with a shrug. "William, I would advise you to be cautious of his acquaintance."

"I thank you," replied Lord William, "but I believe I understand him thoroughly."

Jane manifested strong emotion during these remarks, while Sir Edward and his wife averted their faces from a simultaneous feeling of self-reproach. Their eyes met, and mutual concessions were contained in the glance; yet their feelings were unnoticed by their companions, for over the fulfilment of her often repeated forewarnings of neglect and duty to our children, Mrs. Wilson had mourned in sincerity, but she had forgotten to triumph.

"When are we to see Pendennyss?" inquired the Marquess; "I hope he will be here with George--I have a mind to beat up his quarters in Wales this season--what say you, Derwent?"

"I intend it, if I can persuade Lady Harriet to quit the gaieties of Bath so soon--what say *you*, sister--will you be in readiness to attend me so early?"

This question was asked in an arch tone, and drew the eyes of her friends on the person to whom it was addressed.

"I am ready now, Frederick, if you wish it," answered the sister hastily, and coloring excessively as she spoke.

"But where is Chatterton? I thought he was here--he had a sister married here last week," inquired Lord William Stapleton, addressing no one in particular.

A slight movement in their neighbors attracted the attention of the party.

"What a lovely young woman," whispered the duke to Lady Laura, "your neighbor is!"

The lady smiled her assent, and as Emily overheard it, she rose with glowing cheeks, and proposed a walk round the room.

Chatterton soon after entered. The young peer had acknowledged to Emily that, deprived of hope as he had been by her firm refusal of his hand, his efforts had been directed to the suppression of a passion which could never be successful; but his esteem, his respect, remained in full force. He did not touch at all on the subject of Denbigh, and she supposed that he thought his marriage was a step that required justification.

The Moseleys had commenced their promenade round the room as Chatterton came in. He paid his compliments to them as soon as he entered, and walked with their party. The noble visitors followed their example, and the two parties met. Chatterton was delighted to see them, the Duke was particularly fond of him; and, had one been present of sufficient observation, the agitation of his sister, the Lady Harriet Denbigh, would have accounted for the doubts of her brother as respects her willingness to leave Bath.

A few words of explanation passed; the duke and his friends appeared to urge something on Chatterton, who acted as their ambassador, and the consequence was, an introduction of the two parties to each other. This was conducted with the ease of the present fashion--it was general, and occurred, as it were incidentally, in the course of the evening.

Both Lady Harriet and Lady Laura Denbigh were particularly attentive to Emily. They took their seats by her, and manifested a preference for her conversation that struck Mrs. Wilson as remarkable. Could it be that the really attractive manners and beauty of her niece had caught the fancy of these ladies, or was there a deeper seated cause for the desire to draw Emily out, that both of them evinced? Mrs. Wilson had heard a rumor that Chatterton was thought attentive to Lady Harriet, and the other was the wife of Denbigh; was it possible the quondam suitors of her niece had related to their present favorites the situation they had stood in as regarded Emily? It was odd, to say no more; and the widow dwelt on the innocent countenance of the bride with pity and admiration. Emily herself was not a little abashed at the notice of her new acquaintances, especially Lady Laura's; but as their admiration appeared sincere, as well as their desire to be on terms of intimacy with the Moseleys, they parted, on the whole, mutually pleased.

The conversation several times was embarrassing to the baronet's family, and at moments distressingly so to their daughters.

At the close of the evening they all formed one group at a little distance from the rest of the company, and in a situation to command a view of it.

"Who is that vulgar-looking woman," said Lady Sarah Stapleton, "seated next to Sir Henry Egerton, brother?"

"No less a personage than my Lady Jarvis," replied the marquess, gravely, "and the mother-in-law of Sir Harry, and the wife to Sir Timo--;" this was said, with a look of drollery that showed the marquess was a bit of a quiz.

"Married!" cried Lord William, "mercy on the woman who is Egerton's wife. He is the greatest latitudinarian amongst the ladies, of any man in England--nothing--no, nothing would tempt me to let such a man marry a sister of mine!"

Ah, thought Mrs. Wilson, how we may be deceived in character, with the best intentions, after all! In what are the open vices of Egerton worse than the more hidden ones of Denbigh?

These freely expressed opinions on the character of Sir Henry were excessively awkward to some of the listeners, to whom they were connected with unpleasant recollections of duties neglected, and affections thrown away.

Sir Edward Moseley was not disposed to judge his fellow-creatures harshly; and it was as much owing to his philanthropy as to his indolence, that he had been so remiss in his attention to the associates of his daughters.

But the veil once removed, and the consequences brought home to him through his child, no man was more alive to the necessity of caution on this important particular; and Sir Edward formed many salutary resolutions for the government of his future conduct in relation to those whom an experience nearly fatal in its results had now greatly qualified to take care of themselves. But to resume our narrative--Lady Laura had maintained with Emily a conversation, which was enlivened by occasional remarks from the rest of the party, in the course of which the nerves as well as the principles of Emily were put to a severe trial.

"My brother Henry," said Lady Laura, "who is a captain in the navy, once had the pleasure of seeing you, Miss Moseley, and in some measure made me acquainted with you before we met."

"I dined with Lord Henry at L----, and was much indebted to his polite attentions in an excursion on the water," replied Emily, simply.

"Oh, I am sure his attentions were exclusive," cried the sister; "indeed, he told us that nothing but want of time prevented his being deeply in love--he had even the audacity to tell Denbigh it was fortunate for me he had never seen you, or I should have been left to lead apes."

"And I suppose you believe him now," cried Lord William, laughing, as he bowed to Emily.

His sister laughed in her turn, but shook her head, in the confidence of conjugal affection.

"It is all conjecture, for the Colonel said he had never enjoyed the pleasure of meeting Miss Moseley, so I will not boast of what my powers might have done; Miss Moseley," continued Lady Laura, blushing slightly at her inclination to talk of an absent husband, so lately her lover, "I hope to have the pleasure of presenting Colonel Denbigh to you soon."

"I think," said Emily, with a strong horror of deception, and a mighty struggle to suppress her feelings, "Colonel Denbigh was mistaken in saying that we had never met; he was of material service to me once, and I owe him a debt of gratitude that I only wish I could properly repay."

Lady Laura listened in surprise; but as Emily paused, she could not delicately, as his wife, remind her further of the obligation, by asking what the service was, and hesitating a moment, continued--

"Henry quite made you the subject of conversation amongst us; Lord Chatterton too, who visited us for a day, was equally warm in his eulogiums. I really thought they created a curiosity in the Duke and Pendennyss to behold their idol."

"A curiosity that would be ill rewarded in its indulgence," said Emily, abashed by the personality of the discourse.

"So says the modesty of Miss Moseley," said the Duke of Derwent, in the peculiar tone which distinguished the softer keys of Denbigh's voice. Emily's heart beat quick as she heard them, and she was afterwards vexed to remember with how much pleasure she had listened to this opinion of the duke. Was it the sentiment, or was it the voice? She, however, gathered strength to answer, with a dignity that repressed further praises:--

"Your grace is willing to divest me of what little I possess."

"Pendennyss is a man of a thousand," continued Lady Laura, with the privilege of a married woman. "I do wish he would join us at Bath--is there no hope, duke?"

"I am afraid not," replied his grace: "he keeps himself immured in Wales with his sister, who is as much of a hermit as he is himself."

"There was a story of an inamorata in private somewhere," cried the marquess; "why at one time it was even said he was privately married to her."

"Scandal, my lord," said the duke, gravely: "Pendennyss is of unexceptionable morals, and the lady you mean is the widow of Major Fitzgerald, whom you knew. Pendennyss never sees her, though by accident he was once of very great service to her."

Mrs. Wilson breathed freely again, as she heard this explanation, and thought if the Marquess knew all, how differently would he judge Pendennyss, as well as others.

"Oh! I have the highest opinion of Lord Pendennyss," cried the Marquess.

The Moseleys were not sorry that the usual hour of retiring put an end to the conversation and their embarrassment.

Chapter XXXIV

During the succeeding fortnight, the intercourse between the Moseleys and their new acquaintances increased daily. It was rather awkward at first on the part of Emily; and her beating pulse and changing color too often showed the alarm of feelings not yet overcome, when any allusions were made to the absent husband of one of the ladies. Still, as her parents encouraged the acquaintance, and her aunt thought the best way to get rid of the remaining weakness with respect to Denbigh was not to shrink from even an interview with the gentleman himself, Emily succeeded in conquering her reluctance; and as the high opinion entertained by Lady Laura of her husband was expressed in a thousand artless ways, an interest was created in her that promised in time to weaken if not destroy the impression that had been made by Denbigh himself.

On the other hand, Egerton carefully avoided all collision with the Moseleys. Once, indeed, he endeavored to renew his acquaintance with John, but a haughty repulse almost produced a quarrel.

What representations Egerton had thought proper to make to his wife, we are unable to say; but she appeared to resent something, as she never approached the dwelling or persons of her quondam associates, although in her heart she was dying to be on terms of intimacy with their titled friends. Her incorrigible mother was restrained by no such or any other consideration, and contrived to fasten on the Dowager and Lady Harriet a kind of bowing acquaintance, which she made great use of at the rooms.

The Duke sought out the society of Emily wherever he could obtain it; and Mrs. Wilson thought her niece admitted his approaches with less reluctance than that of any other of the gentlemen around her. At first she was surprised, but a closer observation betrayed to her the latent cause.

Derwent resembled Denbigh greatly in person and voice, although there were distinctions easily to be made on an acquaintance. The Duke had an air of command and hauteur that was never to be seen in his cousin. But his admiration of Emily he did not attempt to conceal; and, as he ever addressed her in the respectful language and identical voice of Denbigh, the observant widow easily perceived, that it was the remains of her attachment to the one that induced her niece to listen, with such evident pleasure, to the conversation of the other.

The Duke of Derwent wanted many of the indispensable requisites of a husband, in the eyes of Mrs. Wilson; yet, as she thought Emily out of all danger at the present of any new attachment, she admitted the association, under no other restraint than the uniform propriety of all that Emily said or did.

"Your niece will one day be a Duchess, Mrs. Wilson," whispered Lady Laura, as Derwent and Emily were running over a new poem one morning, in the lodgings of Sir Edward; the former reading a fine extract aloud so strikingly in the air and voice of Denbigh, as to call all the animation of the unconscious Emily into her expressive face.

Mrs. Wilson sighed, as she reflected on the strength of those feelings which even principles and testimony had not been able wholly to subdue, as she answered--

"Not of Derwent, I believe. But how wonderfully the Duke resembles your husband at times," she added, entirely thrown off her guard.

Lady Laura was evidently surprised.

"Yes, at times he does; they are brothers' children, you know: the voice in all that connexion is remarkable. Pendennyss, though a degree further off in blood, possesses it; and Lady Harriet, you perceive, has the same characteristic; there has been some syren in the family, in days past."

Sir Edward and Lady Moseley saw the attention of the Duke with the greatest pleasure. Though not slaves to the ambition of wealth and rank, they were certainly no objections in their eyes; and a proper suitor Lady Moseley thought the most probable means of driving the recollection of Denbigh from the mind of her daughter. The latter consideration had great weight in inducing her to cultivate an acquaintance so embarrassing on many accounts.

The Colonel, however, wrote to his wife the impossibility of his quitting his uncle while he continued so unwell, and it was settled that the bride should join him, under the escort of Lord William.

The same tenderness distinguished Denbigh on this occasion that had appeared so lovely when exercised to his dying father. Yet, thought Mrs. Wilson, how insufficient are good feelings to effect what can only be the result of good principles.

Caroline Harris was frequently of the parties of pleasure, walks, rides, and dinners, which the Moseleys were compelled to join in; and as the Marquess of Eltringham had given her one day some little encouragement, she determined to make an expiring effort at the peerage, before she condescended to enter into an examination of the qualities of Capt. Jarvis, who, his mother had persuaded her, was an Apollo, that had great hopes of being one day a Lord, as both the Captain and herself had commenced laying up a certain sum quarterly for the purpose of buying a title hereafter--an ingenious expedient of Jarvis's to get into his hands a portion of the allowance of his mother.

Eltringham was strongly addicted to the ridiculous; and without committing himself in the least, drew the lady out on divers occasions, for the amusement of himself and the Duke--who enjoyed, without practising, that species of joke.

The collisions between ill-concealed art and as ill-concealed irony had been practised with impunity by the Marquess for a fortnight, and the lady's imagination began to revel in the delights of a triumph, when a really respectable offer was made to Miss Harris by a neighbor of her father's in the country--one she would rejoice to have received a few days before, but which, in consequence of hopes created by the following occurrence, she haughtily rejected.

It was at the lodgings of the Baronet that Lady Laura exclaimed one day,--

"Marriage is a lottery, certainly, and neither Sir Henry nor Lady Egerton appears to have drawn a prize."

Here Jane stole from the room.

"Never, sister," cried the Marquess. "I will deny that. Any man can select a prize from your sex, if he only knows his own taste."

"Taste is a poor criterion, I am afraid," said Mrs. Wilson, gravely, "on which to found matrimonial felicity."

"To what would you refer the decision, my dear madam?" inquired the Lady Laura.

"Judgment."

Lady Laura shook her hear doubtingly.

"You remind me so much of Lord Pendennyss! Everything he wishes to bring under the subjection of judgment and principles."

"And is he wrong, Lady Laura?" asked Mrs. Wilson, pleased to find such correct views existed in one of whom she thought so highly.

"Not wrong, my dear madam, only impracticable. What do you think, Marquess, of choosing a wife in conformity to your principles, and without consulting your tastes?"

Mrs. Wilson shook her head with a laugh, and disclaimed any such statement of the case; but the Marquess, who disliked one of John's didactic conversations very much, gaily interrupted her by saying--

"Oh! taste is everything with me. The woman of my heart against the world, if she suits my fancy, and satisfies my judgment."

"And what may this fancy of your Lordship be?" said Mrs. Wilson, willing to gratify the trifling. "What kind of a woman do you mean to choose? How tall for instance?"

"Why, madam," cried the Marquess, rather unprepared for such a catechism, and looking around him until the outstretched neck and the eager attention of Caroline Harris caught his eye, when he added with an air of great simplicity--"about the height of Miss Harris."

"How old?" asked Mrs. Wilson with a smile.

"Not too young, ma'am, certainly. I am thirty-two--my wife must be five or six and twenty. Am I old enough, do you think, Derwent?" he added in a whisper to the Duke.

"Within ten years," was the reply.

Mrs. Wilson continued--

"She must read and write, I suppose?"

"Why, faith," said the Marquess, "I am not fond of a bookish sort of a woman, and least of all a scholar."

"You had better take Miss Howard," whispered his brother. "She is old enough--never reads--and is just the height."

"No, no, Will," rejoined the brother. "Rather too old that. Now, I admire a woman who has confidence in herself. One that understands the proprieties of life, and has, if possible, been at the head of an establishment before she is to take charge of mine."

The delighted Caroline wriggled about in her chair, and, unable to contain herself longer, inquired:--

"Noble blood of course, you would require, my Lord?"

"Why no! I rather think the best wives are to be found in a medium. I would wish to elevate my wife myself. A Baronet's daughter for instance."

Here Lady Jarvis, who had entered during the dialogue, and caught a clue to the topic they were engaged in, drew near, and ventured to ask if he thought a simple knight too low. The Marquess, who did not expect such an attack, was a little at a loss for an answer; but recovering himself answered gravely, under the apprehension of another design on his person, that "he did think that would be forgetting his duty to his descendants."

Lady Jarvis sighed, and fell back in disappointment; while Miss Harris, turning to the nobleman, in a soft voice, desired him to ring for her carriage. As he handed her down, she ventured to inquire if his lordship had ever met with such a woman as he described.

"Oh, Miss Harris," he whispered, as he handed her into the coach, "how can you ask me such a question? You are very cruel. Drive on, coachman."

"How, cruel, my Lord?" said Miss Harris eagerly. "Stop, John. How, cruel, my Lord?" and she stretched her neck out of the window as the Marquess, kissing his hand to her, ordered the man to proceed.

"Don't you hear your lady, sir?"

Lady Jarvis had followed them down, also with a view to catch anything which might be said, having apologized for her hasty visit; and as the Marquess handed her politely into her carriage, she also begged "he would favor Sir Timo and Sir Henry with a call;" which being promised, Eltringham returned to the room.

"When am I to salute a Marchioness of Eltringham?" cried Lady Laura to her brother, "one on the new standard set up by your Lordship."

"Whenever Miss Harris can make up her mind to the sacrifice," replied the brother very gravely. "Ah me! how very considerate some of your sex are, for the modesty of ours."

"I wish you joy with all my heart, my Lord Marquess," exclaimed John Moseley. "I was once favored with the notice of that same lady for a week or two, but a viscount saved me from capture."

"I really think, Moseley," said the Duke innocently, but speaking with animation, "an intriguing daughter worse than a managing mother."

John's gravity for a moment vanished, as he replied in a lowered key,

"Oh, much worse."

Grace's heart was in her throat, until, by stealing a glance at her husband, she saw the cloud passing over his fine brow; and happening to catch her affectionate smile; his face was at once lighted into a look of pleasantry.

"I would advise caution, my Lord. Caroline Harris has the advantage of experience in her trade, and was expert from the first."

"John--John," said Sir Edward with warmth, "Sir William is my friend, and his daughter must be respected."

"Then, baronet," cried the Marquess, "she has one recommendation I was ignorant of, and as such I am silent: but ought not Sir William to teach his daughter to respect herself? I view these husband-hunting ladies as pirates on the ocean of love, and lawful objects for any roving cruiser like myself to fire at. At one time I was simple enough to retire as they advanced, but you know, madam," turning to Mrs. Wilson with a droll look, "flight only encourages pursuit, so I now give battle in self-defence."

"And I hope successfully, my Lord," observed the Lady. "Miss Harris, brother, does appear to have grown desperate in her attacks, which were formerly much more masked than at present. I believe it is generally the case, when a young worman throws aside the delicacy and feelings which ought to be the characteristics of her sex, and which teach her studiously to conceal her admiration, that she either becomes in time cynical and disagreeable to all around her from disappointment, or persevering in her efforts, as it were, runs a muck for a husband. Now in justice to the gentlemen, I must say, baronet, there are strong symptoms of the Malay about Caroline Harris."

"A muck, a muck," cried the marquess, as, in obedience to the signal of his sister, he rose to withdraw.

Jane had retired to her own room in a mortification of spirit she could ill conceal during this conversation, and she felt a degree of humiliation which almost drove her to the desperate resolution of hiding herself for ever from the world. The man she had so fondly enshrined in her heart proving to be so notoriously unworthy as to be the subject of unreserved censure in general company, was a reproach to her delicacy, her observation, her judgment, that was the more severe, from being true; and she wept in bitterness over her fallen happiness.

Emily had noticed the movement of Jane, and waited anxiously for the departure of the visitors to hasten to her room. She knocked two or three times before her sister replied to her request for admittance.

"Jane, my dear Jane," said Emily, soothingly, "will you not admit me?"

Jane could not resist any longer the affection of her sister, and the door was opened; but as Emily endeavored to take her hand, she drew back coldly, and cried--

"I wonder you, who are so happy, will leave the gay scene below for the society of an humbled wretch like me;" and overcome with the violence of her emotion, she burst into tears.

"Happy!" repeated Emily, in a tone of anguish, "happy, did you say, Jane? Oh, little do you know my sufferings, or you would never speak so cruelly!"

Jane, in her turn, surprised at the strength of Emily's language, considered her weeping sister with commiseration; and then her thoughts recurring to her own case, she continued with energy--

"Yes, Emily, happy; for whatever may have been the reason of Denbigh's conduct, he is respected; and if you do or did love him, he was worthy of it. But I," said Jane, wildly, "threw away my affections on a wretch--*a mere impostor*--and I am miserable for ever."

"No, dear Jane," rejoined Emily, having recovered her self-possession, "not miserable--nor for ever. You have many, very many sources of happiness yet within your reach, even in this world. I--I do think, even our strongest attachments may be overcome by energy and a sense of duty. And oh! how I wish I could see you make the effort."

For a moment the voice of the youthful moralist had failed her; but anxiety in behalf of her sister overcame her feelings, and she ended the sentence with earnestness.

"Emily," said Jane, with obstinacy, and yet in tears, "you don't know what blighted affections are. To endure the scorn of the world, and see the man you once thought near being your husband married to another, who is showing herself in triumph before you, wherever you go!"

"Hear me, Jane, before you reproach me further, and then judge between us." Emily paused a moment to acquire nerve to proceed, and then related to her astonished sister the little history of her own disappointments. She did not affect to conceal her attachment for Denbigh. With glowing cheeks she acknowledged, that she found a necessity for all her efforts to keep her rebellious feelings yet in subjection; and as she recounted generally his conduct to Mrs. Fitzgerald, she concluded by saying, "But, Jane, I can see enough to call forth my gratitude; and although, with yourself, I feel at this moment as if my affections were sealed for ever, I wish to make no hasty resolutions, nor act in any manner as if I were unworthy of the lot Providence has assigned me."

"Unworthy? no!--you have no reasons for self-reproach. If Mr. Denbigh has had the art to conceal his crimes from you, he did it to the rest of the world also, and has married a woman of rank and character. But how differently are we situated! Emily--I--I have no such consolation."

"You have the consolation, my sister, of knowing there is an interest made for you where we all require it most, and it is there I endeavor to seek my support," said Emily, in a low and humble tone. "A review of our own errors takes away the keenness of our perception of the wrongs done us, and by placing us in charity with the rest of the world, disposes us to enjoy calmly the blessings within our reach. Besides, Jane, we have parents whose happiness is locked up in that of their children, and we should--we must overcome the feelings which disqualify us for our common duties, on their account."

"Ah!" cried Jane, "how can I move about in the world, while I know the eyes of all are on me, in curiosity to discover how I bear my disappointments. But you, Emily, are unsuspected. It is easy for you to affect a gaiety you do not feel."

"I neither affect nor feel any gaiety," said her sister, mildly. "But are there not the eyes of One on us, of infinitely more power to punish or reward than what may be found in the opinions of the world? Have we no duties? For what is our wealth, our knowledge, our time given us, but to improve for our own and for the eternal welfare of those around us? Come then, my sister, we have both been deceived--let us endeavor not to be culpable."

"I wish, from my soul, we could leave Bath," cried Jane. "The place, the people are hateful to me!"

"Jane," said Emily, "rather say you hate their vices, and wish for their amendment: but do not indiscriminately condemn a whole community for the wrongs you have sustained from one of its members."

Jane allowed herself to be consoled, though by no means convinced, by this effort of her sister; and they both found a relief by thus unburdening their hearts to each other, that in future brought them more nearly together, and was of mutual assistance in supporting them in the promiscuous circles in which they were obliged to mix.

With all her fortitude and principle, one of the last things Emily would have desired was an interview with Denbigh, and she was happily relieved from the present danger of it by the departure of Lady Laura and her brother, to go to the residence of the Colonel's sick uncle.

Both Mrs. Wilson and Emily suspected that a dread of meeting them had detained him from his intended journey to Bath; and neither was sorry to perceive, what they considered as latent signs of grace--a grace of which Egerton appeared entirely to be without.

"He may yet see his errors, and make a kind and affectionate husband," thought Emily; and then, as the image of Denbigh rose in her imagination, surrounded with the domestic virtues, she roused herself from the dangerous reflection to the exercise of the duties in which she found a refuge from unpardonable wishes.

Chapter XXXV

Nothing material occurred for a fortnight after the departure of Lady Laura, the Moseleys entering soberly into the amusements of the place, and Derwent and Chatterton becoming more pointed every day in their attentions--the one to Emily, and the other to Lady Harriet; when the dowager received a pressing entreaty from Catherine to hasten to her at Lisbon, where her husband had taken up his abode for a time, after much doubt and indecision as to his place of residence. Lady Herriefield stated generally in her letter, that she was miserable, and that without the support of her mother she could not exist under the present grievances; but what was the cause of those grievances, or what grounds she had for her misery, she left unexplained.

Lady Chatterton was not wanting in maternal regard, and she promptly determined to proceed to Portugal in the next packet. John felt inclined for a little excursion with his bride; and out of compassion to the baron, who was in a dilemma between his duty and his love (for Lady Harriet about that time was particularly attractive), he offered his services.

Chatterton allowed himself to be persuaded by the good-natured John, that his mother could safely cross the ocean under the protection of the latter. Accordingly, at the end of the before mentioned fortnight, the dowager, John, Grace, and Jane, commenced their journey to Falmouth.

Jane had offered to accompany Grace, as a companion in her return (it being expected Lady Chatterton would remain in the country with her daughter); and her parents appreciating her motives, permitted the excursion, with a hope it would draw her thoughts from past events.

Although Grace shed a few tears at parting with Emily and her friends, it was impossible for Mrs. Moseley to be long unhappy, with the face of John smiling by her side; and they pursued their route uninterruptedly. In due season they reached the port of embarkation.

The following morning the packet got under weigh, and a favorable breeze soon wafted them out of sight of their native shores. The ladies were too much indisposed the first day to appear on the deck; but the weather becoming calm and the sea smooth, Grace and Jane ventured out of the confinement of their state-rooms, to respire the fresh air above.

There were but few passengers, and those chiefly ladies--the wives of officers on foreign stations, on their way to join their husbands. As these had been accustomed to moving in the world, their disposition to accommodate soon removed the awkwardness of a first meeting, and our travellers began to be at home in their novel situation.

While Grace stood leaning on the arm of her husband, and clinging to his support, both from affection and a dread of the motion of the vessel, Jane ventured with one of the ladies to attempt a walk round the deck of the ship. Unaccustomed to such an uncertain foothold, the walkers were prevented falling by the kind interposition of a gentleman, who for the first time had shown himself among them at that moment. The accident, and their situation, led to a conversation which was renewed at different times during their passage, and in some measure created an intimacy between our party and the stranger. He was addressed by the commander of the vessel as Mr. Harland; and Lady Chatterton exercised her ingenuity in the investigation of his history, by which she made the following discovery:

The Rev. and Hon. Mr. Harland was the younger son of an Irish earl, who had early embraced his sacred profession in that church, in which he held a valuable living in the gift of his father's family. His father was yet alive, and then at Lisbon with his mother and sister, in attendance on his elder brother, who had been sent there in a deep decline a couple of months before. It had been the wish of his parents to have taken all their children with them; but a sense of duty had kept the young clergyman in the exercise of his holy office, until a request of his dying brother, and the directions of his father, caused him to hasten abroad to witness the decease of the one, and to afford all the solace within his power to the others.

It may be easily imagined that the discovery of the rank of their accidental acquaintance, with the almost certainty that existed of his being the heir of his father's honors, in no degree impaired his consequence in the eyes of the dowager; and it is certain, his visible anxiety and depressed spirits, his unaffected piety, and disinterested hopes for his brother's recovery, no less elevated him in the opinions of her companions.

There was, at the moment, a kind of sympathy between Harland and Jane, notwithstanding the melancholy which gave rise to it proceeding from such very different causes and as the lady, although with diminished bloom, retained all her personal charms, rather heightened than otherwise by the softness of low spirits, the young clergyman sometimes relieved his apprehensions of his brother's death by admitting the image of Jane among his more melancholy reflections.

The voyage was tedious, and some time before it was ended the dowager had given Grace an intimation of the probability there was of Jane's becoming, at some future day, a countess. Grace sincerely hoped that whatever she became she would be as happy as she thought all allied to John deserved to be.

They entered the bay of Lisbon early in the morning; and as the ship had been expected for some days, a boat came alongside with a note for Mr. Harland, before they had anchored. It apprised him of the death of his brother. The young man threw himself precipitately into it, and was soon employed in one of the loveliest offices of his vocation, that of healing the wounds of the afflicted.

Lady Herriefield received her mother in a sort of sullen satisfaction, and her companions with an awkwardness she could ill conceal. It required no great observation in the travellers to discover, that their arrival was entirely unexpected by the viscount, if it were not equally disagreeable; indeed, one day's residence under his roof assured them all that no great degree of domestic felicity was an inmate of the dwelling.

From the moment Lord Herriefield became suspicious that he had been the dupe of the management of Kate and her mother, he viewed every act of his wife with a prejudiced eye. It was easy, with his knowledge of human nature, to detect her selfishness and worldly-mindedness; for as these were faults she was unconscious of possessing, so she was unguarded in her exposure of them. But her designs, in a matrimonial point of view, having ended with her marriage, had the viscount treated her with any of the courtesies due her sex and station, she might, with her disposition, have been contented in the enjoyment of rank and in the possession of wealth; but their more private hours were invariably rendered unpleasant, by the overflowings of her husband's resentment at having been deceived in his judgment of the female sex.

There is no point upon which men are more tender than their privilege of suiting themselves in a partner for life, although many of both sexes are influenced in this important selection more by the wishes and whims of others than is usually suspected; yet, as all imagine what is the result of contrivance and management is the election of free will and taste, so long as they are ignorant, they are contented. Lord Herriefield wanted this bliss of ignorance; and, with contempt for his wife, was mingled anger at his own want of foresight.

Very few people can tamely submit to self-reproach; and as the cause of this irritated state of mind was both not only constantly present, but completely within his power, the viscount seemed determined to give her as little reason to exult in the success of her plans as possible. Jealous he was, from temperament, from bad associations, and a want of confidence in the principles of his wife, the freedom of foreign manners having an additional tendency to excite this baneful passion to an unusual degree. Abridged in her pleasures, reproached with motives she was incapable of harboring, and disappointed in all those enjoyments her mother had ever led her to believe the invariable accompaniments of married life, where proper attention had been paid to the necessary qualifications of riches and rank, Kate had written to the dowager with the hope her presence might restrain, or her advice teach her, successfully to oppose the unfeeling conduct of the viscount.

Lady Chatterton never having implanted any of her favorite systems in her daughter, so much by precept as by the force of example in her own person, as well as by indirect eulogiums on certain people who were endowed with those qualities and blessings she most admired, on the present occasion Catherine did not unburden herself in terms to her mother; but by a regular gradation of complaints, aimed more at the world than at her husband, she soon let the knowing dowager see their application, and in the end completely removed the veil from her domestic grievances.

The example of John and Grace for a short time awed the peer into dissembling his disgust for his spouse; but the ice once broken, their presence soon ceased to affect either the frequency or the severity of his remarks, when under its influence.

From such exhibitions of matrimonial discord, Grace shrank timidly into the retirement of her room, and Jane, with dignity, would follow her example; while John at times became a listener, with a spirit barely curbed within the bounds of prudence, and at others, he sought in the company of his wife and sister, relief from the violence of his feelings.

John never admired nor respected Catherine, for she wanted those very qualities he chiefly loved in her sister; yet, as she was a woman, and one nearly connected with him, he found it impossible to remain a quiet spectator of the unmanly treatment she often received from her husband; he therefore made preparations for his return to England by the first packet, abridging his intended residence in Lisbon more than a month.

Lady Chatterton endeavored all within her power to heal the breach between Kate and her husband, but it greatly exceeded her abilities. It was too late to implant such principles in her daughter, as by a long course of self-denial and submission might have won the love of the viscount, had the mother been acquainted with them herself; so that having induced her child to marry with a view to obtaining precedence and a jointure, she once more set to work to undo part of her former labors, by bringing about a decent separation between the husband and wife, in such a manner as to secure to her child the possession of her wealth, and the esteem of the world. The latter, though certainly a somewhat difficult undertaking, was greatly lessened by the assistance of the former.

John and his wife determined to seize the opportunity to examine the environs of the city. In one of these daily rides, they met their fellow traveller, Mr. now Lord Harland. He was rejoiced to see them again, and hearing of their intended departure, informed them of his being about to return to England in the same vessel--his parents and sister contemplating ending the winter in Portugal.

The intercourse between the two families was kept up with a show of civilities between the noblemen, and much real good-will on the part of the juniors of the circle, until the day arrived for the sailing of the packet.

Lady Chatterton was left behind with Catherine, as yet unable to circumvent her schemes with prudence; it being deemed by the world a worse offence to separate, than to join together one's children in the bands of wedlock.

The confinement of a vessel is very propitious to those intimacies which lead to attachments. The necessity of being agreeable is a check upon the captious, and the desire to lessen the dulness of the scene a stimulus to the lively; and though the noble divine and Jane could not possibly be ranked in either class, the effect was the same. The noble man was much enamored, and Jane unconsciously gratified. It is true, love had never entered her thoughts in its direct and unequivocal form; but admiration is so consoling to those laboring under self-condemnation, and flattery of a certain kind so very soothing to all, it is not to be wondered that she listened with increasing pleasure to the interesting conversation of Harland on all occasions, and more particularly, as often happened, when exclusively addressed to herself.

Grace had of late reflected more seriously on the subject of her eternal welfare than she had been accustomed to do in the house of her mother; and the example of Emily, with the precepts of Mrs. Wilson, had not been thrown away upon her. It is a singular fact, that more women feel a disposition to religion soon after marriage than at any other period of life; and whether it is, that having attained the most important station this life affords the sex, they are more willing to turn their thoughts to a provision for the next, or whether it be owing to any other cause, Mrs. Moseley was included in the number. She became sensibly touched with her situation, and as Harland was both devout and able as well as anxious to instruct, one of the party, at least, had cause to rejoice in the journey for the remainder of her days. But precisely as Grace increased in her own faith, so did her anxiety after the welfare of her husband receive new excitement; and John, for the first time, became the cause of sorrow to his affectionate companion.

The deep interest Harland took in the opening conviction of Mrs. Moseley, did not so entirely engross his thoughts as to prevent the too frequent contemplation of the charms of her friend for his own peace of mind; and by the time the vessel reached Falmouth, he had determined to make a tender of his hand and title to the acceptance of Miss Moseley. Jane did not love Egerton; on the contrary, she despised him; but the time had been, when all her romantic feelings, every thought of her brilliant imagination, had been filled with his image, and Jane felt it a species of indelicacy to admit the impression of another so soon, or even at all. These objections would, in time, have been overcome, as her affections became more and more enlisted on behalf of Harland, had she admitted his addresses; but there was an impediment that Jane considered insurmountable to a union with any man.

She had once communicated her passion to its object. There had been the confidence of approved love; and she had now no heart for Harland, but one that had avowedly been a slave to another. To conceal this from him would be unjust, and not reconcilable to good faith; to confess it, humiliating, and without the pale of probability. It was the misfortune of Jane to keep the world too constantly before her, and to lose sight too much of her really depraved nature, to relish the idea of humbling herself so low in the opinion of a fellow-creature. The refusal of Harland's offer was the consequence, although she had begun to feel an esteem for him, that would no doubt have given rise to an attachment in time, far stronger and more deeply seated than her passing fancy for Colonel Egerton had been.

If the horror of imposing on the credulity of Harland a wounded heart, was creditable to Jane, and showed an elevation of character that under proper guidance would have placed her in the first ranks of her sex; the pride which condemned her to a station nature did not design her for was irreconcilable with the humility a just view of her condition could not fail to produce; and the second sad consequence of the indulgent weakness of her parents, was confirming their child in passions directly at variance with the first duties of a Christian.

We have so little right to value ourselves on anything, that pride is a sentiment of very doubtful service, and one certainly, that is unable to effect any useful results which will not equally flow from good principles.

Harland was disappointed and grieved, but prudently judging that occupation and absence would remove recollections which could not be very deep, they parted at Falmouth, and our travellers proceeded on their journey for B----, whither, during their absence, Sir Edward's family had returned to spend a month, before they removed to town for the residue of the winter.

The meeting of the two parties was warm and tender, and as Jane had many things to recount, and John as many to laugh at, their arrival threw a gaiety around Moseley Hall to which it had for months been a stranger.

One of the first acts of Grace, after her return, was to enter strictly into the exercise of all those duties and ordinances required by her church, and the present state of her mind, and from the hands of Dr. Ives she received her first communion at the altar.

As the season had now become far advanced, and the fashionable world had been some time assembled in the metropolis, the Baronet commenced his arrangements to take possession of his town-house, after an interval of nineteen years. John proceeded to the capital first; and the necessary domestics procured, furniture supplied, and other arrangements usual to the appearance of a wealthy family in the world having been completed, he returned with the information that all was ready for their triumphal entrance.

Sir Edward, feeling that a separation for so long a time, and at such an unusual distance, in the very advanced age of Mr. Benfield, would be improper, paid him a visit, with the intention of persuading him to make one of his family for the next four months. Emily was his companion, and their solicitations were happily crowned with a success they had not anticipated. Averse to be deprived of Peter's society, the honest steward was included in the party.

"Nephew," said Mr. Benfield, beginning to waver in his objections to the undertaking, as the arguments pro and con were produced, "there are instances of gentlemen, not in parliament, going to town in the winter, I know. You are one yourself; and old Sir John Cowel, who never could get in, although he ran for every city in the kingdom, never missed his winter in Soho. Yes, yes--the thing is admissible--but had I known your wishes before, I would certainly have kept my borough if it were only for the appearance of the thing--besides," continued the old man, shaking his head, "his majesty's ministers require the aid of some more experienced members in these critical times; for what should an old man like me do in Westminster, unless it were to aid his country with his advice?"

"Make his friends happy with his company, dear uncle," said Emily, taking his hand between both her own, and smiling affectionately on the old gentleman as she spoke.

"Ah! Emmy dear!" cried Mr. Benfield, looking on her with melancholy pleasure, "you are not to be resisted--just such another as the sister of my old friend Lord Gosford; she could always coax me out of anything. I remember now, I heard the earl tell her once he could not afford to buy a pair of diamond ear-rings; and she looked--only looked--did not speak! Emmy!--that I bought them with intent to present them to her myself."

"And did she take them, uncle?" asked his niece, in a little surprise.

"Oh yes! When I told her if she did not I would throw them into the river, as no one else should wear what had been intended for her; poor soul! how delicate and unwilling she was. I had to convince her they cost three hundred pounds, before she would listen to it; and then she thought it such a pity to throw away a thing of so much value. It would have been wicked, you know, Emmy, dear; and she was much opposed to wickedness and sin in any shape."

"She must have been a very unexceptionable character indeed," cried the Baronet, with a smile, as he proceeded to make the necessary orders for their journey. "But we must return to the party left at Bath."

Chapter XXXVI

The letters of Lady Laura informed her friends, that she and Colonel Denbigh had decided to remain with his uncle until the recovery of the latter was complete, and then to proceed to Denbigh Castle, to meet the Duke and his sister during the approaching holidays.

Emily was much relieved by this postponement of an interview which she would gladly have avoided for ever; and her aunt sincerely rejoiced that her niece was allowed more time to eradicate impressions, which, she saw with pain, her charge had yet a struggle to overcome.

There were so many points to admire in the character of Denbigh; his friends spoke of him with such decided partiality; Dr. Ives, in his frequent letters, alluded to him with so much affection; that Emily frequently detected herself in weighing the testimony of his guilt, and indulging the expectation that circumstances had deceived them all in their judgment of his conduct. Then his marriage would cross her mind; and with the conviction of the impropriety of admitting him to her thoughts at all, would come the mass of circumstantial testimony which had accumulated against him.

Derwent served greatly to keep alive the recollections of his person, however; and as Lady Harriet seemed to live only in the society of the Moseleys, not a day passed without giving the Duke some opportunity of indirectly preferring his suit.

Emily not only appeared, but in fact was, unconscious of his admiration; and entered into their amusements with a satisfaction that was increased by the belief that the unfortunate attachment her cousin Chatterton had once professed for herself, was forgotten in the more certain enjoyments of a successful love.

Lady Harriet was a woman of manners and character very different from Emily Moseley; yet had she in a great measure erased the impressions made by the beauty of his kinswoman from the bosom of the baron.

Chatterton, under the depression of his first disappointment, it will be remembered, had left B---- in company with Mr. Denbigh. The interest of the duke had been unaccountably exerted to procure him the place he had so long solicited in vain, and gratitude required his early acknowledgments for the favor. His manner, so very different from a successful applicant for a valuable office, had struck both Derwent and his sister as singular. Before, however, a week's intercourse had passed between them, his own frankness had made them acquainted with the cause; and a double wish prevailed in the bosom of Lady Harriet, to know the woman who could resist the beauty of Chatterton, and to relieve him from the weight imposed on his spirits by disappointed affection.

The manners of Lady Harriet Denbigh were not in the least forward or masculine; but they had the freedom of high rank, mingled with a good deal of the ease of fashionable life. Mrs. Wilson noticed, moreover, in her conduct to Chatterton, a something exceeding the interest of ordinary communications in their situation, which might possibly have been attributed more to feeling than to manner. It is certain, one of the surest methods to drive Emily from his thoughts, was to dwell on the perfections of some other lady; and Lady Harriet was so constantly before him in his visit into Westmoreland, so soothing, so evidently pleased with his presence, that the baron made rapid advances in attaining his object.

He had alluded, in his letter to Emily, to the obligation he was under to the services of Denbigh, in erasing his unfortunate partiality for her: but what those services were, we are unable to say, unless they were the usual arguments of the plainest good sense, enforced in the singularly insinuating and kind manner which distinguished that gentleman. In fact, Lord Chatterton was not formed by nature to love long, deprived of hope, or to resist long the flattery of a preference from such a woman as Harriet Denbigh.

On the other hand, Derwent was warm in his encomiums on Emily to all but herself; and Mrs. Wilson again thought it prudent to examine into the state of her feelings, in order to discover if there was any danger of his unremitted efforts drawing Emily into a connexion that neither her religion nor prudence could wholly approve.

Derwent was a man of the world--a Christian only in name; and the cautious widow determined to withdraw in season, should she find grounds for her apprehensions.

About ten days after the departure of the Dowager and her companions, Lady Harriet exclaimed, in one of her morning visits--

"Lady Moseley! I have now hopes of presenting to you soon the most polished man in the United Kingdom!"

"As a husband! Lady Harriet?" inquired the other, with a smile.

"Oh, no! only as a cousin, a second cousin! madam!" replied Lady Harriet, blushing a little, and looking in the opposite direction to the one in which Chatterton was placed.

"But his name? You forget our curiosity! What is his name?" cried Mrs. Wilson, entering into the trifling for the moment.

"Pendennyss, to be sure, my dear madam: whom else can I mean?"

"And you expect the earl at Bath?" Mrs. Wilson eagerly inquired.

"He has given us such hopes, and Derwent has written him to-day, pressing the journey."

"You will be disappointed, I am afraid, sister," said the duke. "Pendennyss has become so fond of Wales of late, that it is difficult to get him out of it."

"But," said Mrs. Wilson, "he will take his seat in parliament during the winter, my lord?"

"I hope he will, madam; though Lord Eltringham holds his proxies, in my absence, in all important questions before the house."

"Your grace will attend, I trust," said Sir Edward. "The pleasure of your company is among my expected enjoyments in the town."

"You are very good, Sir Edward," replied the duke, looking at Emily. "It will somewhat depend on circumstances, I believe."

Lady Harriet smiled, and the speech seemed understood by all but the lady most concerned in it.

"Lord Pendennyss is a universal favorite, and deservedly so," cried the duke. "He has set an example to the nobility, which few are equal to imitate. An only son, with an immense estate, he has devoted himself to the profession of a soldier, and gained great reputation by it in the world; nor has he neglected any of his private duties as a man----"

"Or a Christian, I hope," said Mrs. Wilson, delighted with the praises of the earl.

"Nor of a Christian, I believe," continued the duke; "he appears consistent, humble, and sincere--three requisites, I believe, for that character."

"Does not your grace know?" said Emily, with a benevolent smile.

Derwent colored slightly as he answered--

"Not as well as I ought; but"--lowering his voice for her ear alone, he added, "under proper instruction I think I might learn."

"Then I would recommend that book to you, my lord," rejoined Emily, with a blush, pointing to a pocket Bible which lay near her, though still ignorant of the allusion he meant to convey.

"May I ask the honor of an audience of Miss Moseley," said Derwent, in the same low tone, "whenever her leisure will admit of her granting the favor?"

Emily was surprised; but from the previous conversation and the current of her thoughts at the moment, supposing his communication had some reference to the subject before them, she rose from her chair, and unobtrusively, but certainly with an air of perfect innocence and composure, she went into the adjoining room, the door of which was open very near them.

Caroline Harris had abandoned all ideas of a coronet with the departure of the Marquess of Eltringham and his sisters for their own seat; and as a final effort of her fading charms, had begun to calculate the capabilities of Captain Jarvis, who had at this time honored Bath with his company.

It is true, the lady would have greatly preferred her father's neighbor, but that was an irretrievable step. He had retired, disgusted with her haughty dismissal of his hopes, and was a man who, although he greatly admired her fortune, was not to be recalled by any beck or smile which might grow out of caprice.

Lady Jarvis had, indeed, rather magnified the personal qualifications of her son; but the disposition they had manifested, to devote some of their surplus wealth to purchasing a title, had great weight, for Miss Harris would cheerfully, at any time, have sacrificed one half her own fortune to be called my lady. Jarvis would make but a shabby-looking lord, 'tis true; but then what a lord's wife would she not make herself! His father was a merchant, to be sure, but then merchants were always immensely rich, and a few thousand pounds, properly applied, might make the merchant's son a baron. She therefore resolved to inquire, the first opportunity, into the condition of the sinking fund of his plebeianism, and had serious thoughts of contributing her mite towards the advancement of the desired object, did she find it within the bounds of probable success.

An occasion soon offered, by the invitation of the Captain to accompany him in an excursion in the tilbury of his brother-in-law.

In this ride they passed the equipages of Lady Harriet and Mrs. Wilson, with their respective mistresses, taking an airing. In passing the latter, Jarvis bowed (for he had renewed his acquaintance at the rooms, without daring to visit at the lodgings of Sir Edward), and Miss Harris saw both parties as they dashed by them.

"You know the Moseleys, Caroline?" said Jarvis, with the freedom her manners had established between them.

"Yes," replied the lady, drawing her head back from a view of the carriages; "what fine arms those of the Duke's are--and the coronet, it is so noble--so rich--I am sure if I were a man," laying great emphasis on the word--"I would be a Lord."

"If you could, you mean," cried the captain.

"Could--why money will buy a title, you know--only most people are fonder of their cash than of honor."

"That's right," said the unreflecting captain; "money is the thing, after all. Now what do you suppose our last mess-bill came to?"

"Oh, don't talk of eating and drinking," cried Miss Harris, in affected aversion; "is it beneath the consideration of nobility."

"Then any one may be a lord for me," said Jarvis, drily "if they are not to eat and drink; why, what do they live for, but such sort of things!"

"A soldier lives to fight and gain honor and distinction"--for his wife--Miss Harris would have added, had she spoken all she thought.

"A poor way that of spending a man's time," said the Captain. "Now there is Captain Jones in our regiment; they say he loves fighting as much as eating: if he do, he is a bloodthirsty fellow."

"You know how intimate I am with your dear mother," continued the lady, bent on the principal object; "she has made me acquainted with her greatest wish."

"Her greatest wish!" cried the Captain, in astonishment; "why, what can that be?--a new coach and horses?"

"No, I mean one much dearer to us--I should say, to her, than any such trifles: she has told me of the *plan*."

"Plan!" said Jarvis, still in wonder, "what plan?"

"About the fund for the peerage, you know. Of course, the thing is sacred with me, as, indeed, I am equally interested with you all in its success."

Jarvis eyed her with a knowing look, and as she concluded, rolling his eyes in an expression of significance, he said--

"What, serve Sir William some such way, eh?"

"I will assist a little, if it be necessary, Henry," said the lady, tenderly, "although my mite cannot amount to a great deal."

During this speech, the Captain was wondering what she could mean; but, having had a suspicion, from something that had fallen from his mother, that the lady was intended for him as a wife, and that she might be as great a dupe as Lady Jarvis herself, he was resolved to know the whole, and to act accordingly.

"I think it might be made to do," he replied, evasively in order to discover the extent of his companion's information.

"Do!", cried Miss Harris, with fervor, "it cannot fail! How much do you suppose will be wanting to buy a barony, for instance?"

"Hem!" said Jarvis; "you mean more than we have already?"

"Certainly."

"Why, about a thousand pounds, I think, will do it, with what we have," said Jarvis, affecting to calculate.

"Is that all?" cried the delighted Caroline; and the captain grew in an instant, in her estimation, three inches higher;--quite noble in his air, and, in short, very tolerably handsome.

From that moment, Miss Harris, in her own mind, had fixed the fate of Captain Jarvis, and had determined to be his wife, whenever she could persuade him to offer himself; a thing she had no doubt of accomplishing with comparative ease. Not so the Captain. Like all weak men, there was nothing of which he stood more in terror than of ridicule. He had heard the manoeuvres of Miss Harris laughed at by many of the young men in Bath, and was by no means disposed to add himself to the food for mirth of these wags; and, indeed, had cultivated her acquaintance with a kind of bravado to some of his bottle companions, in order to show his ability to oppose all her arts, when most exposed to them: for it is one of the greatest difficulties to the success of this description of ladies, that their characters soon become suspected, and do them infinitely more injury than all their skill in their vocation.

With these views in the respective champions the campaign opened, and the lady, on her return, acquainted his mother with the situation of the privy purse, that was to promote her darling child to the enviable distinction of the peerage. Lady Jarvis was for purchasing a baronetcy on the spot, with what they had, under the impression that when ready for another promotion they would only have to pay the difference, as they did in the army when he received his captaincy. As, however, the son was opposed to any arrangement that might make the producing the few hundred pounds he had obtained from his mother's folly necessary, she was obliged to postpone the wished-for day, until their united efforts could compass the means of effecting the main point. As an earnest, however, of her spirit in the cause, she gave him a fifty pound note, that morning obtained from her husband, and which the Captain lost at one throw of the dice to his brother-in-law the same evening.

During the preceding events, Egerton had either studiously avoided all collision with the Moseleys, or his engagements had confined him to such very different scenes, that they never met.

The Baronet had felt his presence a reproach, and Lady Moseley rejoiced that Egerton yet possessed sufficient shame to keep him from insulting her with his company.

It was a month after the departure of Lady Chatterton that Sir Edward returned to B----, as related in the preceding chapter, and that the arrangements for the London winter were commenced.

The day preceding their leaving Bath, the engagement of Chatterton with Lady Harriet was made public amongst their mutual friends, and an intimation was given that their nuptials would be celebrated before the family of the Duke left his seat for the capital.

Something of the pleasure that she had for a long time been a stranger to, was felt by Emily Moseley, as the well remembered tower of the village church of B---- struck her sight on their return from their protracted excursion. More than four months had elapsed since they had commenced their travels, and in that period what changes of sentiments had she not witnessed in others; of opinions of mankind in general, and of one individual in particular, had she not experienced in her own person. The benevolent smiles, the respectful salutations they received, in passing the little group of houses which, clustered round the church, had obtained the name of "the village," conveyed a sensation of delight that can only be felt by the deserving and virtuous; and the smiling faces, in several instances glistening with tears, which met them at the Hall, gave ample testimony to the worth of both the master and his servants.

Francis and Clara were in waiting to receive them, and a very few minutes elapsed before the rector and Mrs. Ives, having heard they had passed, drove in also. In saluting the different members of the family, Mrs. Wilson noticed the startled look of the doctor, as the change in Emily's appearance first met his eyes. Her bloom, if not gone, was greatly diminished; and it was only when under the excitement of strong emotions, that her face possessed that radiance which had so eminently distinguished it before her late journey.

"Where did you last see my friend George?" said the Doctor to Mrs. Wilson, in the course of the first afternoon, as he took a seat by her side, apart from the rest of the family.

"At L----," said Mrs. Wilson, gravely.

"L----!" cried the doctor, in evident amazement. "Was he not at Bath then during your stay there?"

"No; I understand he was in attendance on some sick relative, which detained him from his friends," said Mrs. Wilson, wondering why the doctor chose to introduce so delicate a topic. Of his guilt in relation to Mrs. Fitzgerald he was doubtless ignorant, but surely not of his marriage.

"It is now some time since I heard from him," continued the doctor, regarding Mrs. Wilson expressively, but to which the lady only replied with a gentle inclination of the body; and the Rector, after pausing a moment, continued:

"You will not think me impertinent if I am bold enough to ask, has George ever expressed a wish to become connected with your niece by other ties than those of friendship?"

"He did," answered the widow, after a little hesitation.

"He did, and--"

"Was refused," continued Mrs. Wilson, with a slight feeling for the dignity of her sex, which for a moment caused her to lose sight of justice to Denbigh.

Dr. Ives was silent; but manifested by his dejected countenance the interest he had taken in this anticipated connexion, and as Mrs. Wilson had spoken with ill-concealed reluctance on the subject at all, the Rector did not attempt a renewal of the disagreeable.

Chapter XXXVII

"Samvenson has returned, and I certainly must hear from Harriet," exclaimed the sister of Pendennyss, as she stood at a window watching the return of a servant from the neighboring post-office.

"I am afraid," rejoined the Earl, who was seated by the breakfast table, waiting the leisure of the lady to give him his cup of tea--"You find Wales very dull, sister. I sincerely hope both Derwent and Harriet will not forget their promise of visiting us this month."

The lady slowly took her seat at the table, engrossed in her own reflections, when the man entered with his budget of news; and having deposited sundry papers and letters he respectfully withdrew. The Earl glanced his eyes over the directions of the epistles, and turning to his servants said, "Answer the bell when called." Three or four liveried footmen deposited their silver salvers and different implements of servitude, and the peer and his sister were left to themselves.

"Here is one from the Duke to me, and one for you from his sister," said the brother; "I propose they be read aloud for our mutual advantage." To this proposal the lady, whose curiosity to hear the contents of Derwent's letter greatly exceeded her interest in that of his sister, cheerfully acquiesced, and her brother first broke the seal of his own epistle, and read its contents as follow:

"Notwithstanding my promise of seeing you this month in Caernarvonshire, I remain here yet, my dear Pendennyss, unable to tear myself from the attractions I have found in this city, although the pleasure of their contemplation has been purchased at the expense of mortified feelings and unrequited affections. It is a truth (though possibly difficult to be believed), that this mercenary age has produced a female disengaged, young, and by no means very rich, who has refused a jointure of six thousand a year, with the privilege of walking at a coronation within a dozen of royalty itself."

Here the accidental falling of a cup from the hands of the fair listener caused some little interruption to the reading of the brother; but as the lady, with a good deal of trepidation and many blushes, apologized hastily for the confusion her awkwardness had made, the Earl continued to read.

"I could almost worship her independence: for I know the wishes of both her parents were for my success. I confess to you freely, that my vanity has been a good deal hurt, as I really thought myself agreeable to her. She certainly listened to my conversation, and admitted my approaches, with more satisfaction than those of any other of the men around her; and when I ventured to hint to her this circumstance, as some justification for my presumption, she frankly acknowledged the truth of my impression, and, without explaining the reasons for her conduct, deeply regretted the construction I had been led to place upon the circumstance. Yes, my lord, I felt it necessary to apologize to Emily Moseley for presuming to aspire to the honor of possessing so much loveliness and virtue. The accidental advantages of rank and wealth lose all their importance, when opposed to her delicacy, ingenuousness, and unaffected principles.

"I have heard it intimated lately, that George Denbigh was in some way or other instrumental in saving her life once; and that to her gratitude, and to my resemblance to the colonel, am I indebted to a consideration with Miss Moseley, which, although it has been the means of buoying me up with false hopes, I can never regret, from the pleasure her society has afforded me. I have remarked, on my mentioning his name to her, that she showed unusual emotion; and as Denbigh is already a husband, and myself rejected, the field is now fairly open to you. You will enter on your enterprise with great advantage, as you have the same flattering resemblance, and, if anything, the voice, which, I am told, is our greatest recommendation with the ladies, in higher perfection than either George or your humble servant."

Here the reader stopped of his own accord, and was so intently absorbed in his meditations, that the almost breathless curiosity of his sister was obliged to find relief by desiring him to proceed. Roused by the sound of her voice, the earl changed color sensibly, and continued:

"But to be serious on a subject of great importance to my future life (for I sometimes think her negative will make Denbigh a duke), the lovely girl did not appear happy at the time of our interview, nor do I think she enjoys at any time the spirits nature has evidently given her. Harriet is nearly as great an admirer of Miss Moseley, and takes her refusal to heart as much as myself; she even attempted to intercede with her in my behalf. But the charming girl though mild, grateful, and delicate, was firm and unequivocal, and left no grounds for the remotest expectation of success from perseverance on my part.

"As Harriet had received an intimation that both Miss Moseley and her aunt entertained extremely rigid notions on the score of religion, she took occasion to introduce the subject in her conference with the former, and was told in reply, 'that other considerations would have determined her to decline the honor I intended her; but that, under any circumstances, a more intimate knowledge of my principles would be necessary before she could entertain a thought of accepting my hand, or, indeed, that of any other man.' Think of that, Pendennyss! The principles of a duke!--now, a dukedom and forty thousand a year would furnish a character, with most people, for a Nero.

"I trust the important object I have had in view here is a sufficient excuse for my breach of promise to you; and I am serious when I wish you (unless the pretty Spaniard has, as I sometimes suspect, made you a captive) to see, and endeavor to bring me in some degree connected with, the charming family of Sir Edward Moseley.

"The aunt, Mrs. Wilson, often speaks of you with the greatest interest, and, from some cause or other, is strongly enlisted in your favor, and Miss Moseley hears your name mentioned with evident pleasure. Your religion or principles cannot be doubted. You can offer larger settlements, as honorable if not as elevated a title, a far more illustrious name, purchased by your own services, and personal merit greatly exceeding the pretensions of your assured friend and relative,

"DERWENT."

Both brother and sister were occupied with their own reflections for several minutes after the letter was ended, and the silence was broken first, by the latter saying with a low tone to her brother,--

"You must endeavor to become acquainted with Mrs. Wilson; she is, I know, very anxious to see you, and your friendship for the general requires it of you."

"I owe General Wilson much," replied the brother, in a melancholy voice; "and when we go to Annerdale House, I wish you to make the acquaintance of the ladies of the Moseley family, should they be in town this winter;--but you have yet the letter of Harriet to read."

After first hastily running over its contents, the lady commenced the fulfilment of her part of the engagement.

"Frederick has been so much engrossed of late with his own affairs, that he has forgotten there is such a creature in existence as his sister, or, indeed, any one else but a Miss Emily Moseley, and consequently I have been unable to fulfil my promise of making you a visit, for want of a proper escort, and--and--perhaps some other considerations, not worth mentioning in a letter I know you will read to the earl.

"Yes, my dear cousin, Frederick Denbigh has supplicated the daughter of a country baronet to become a duchess; and, hear it, ye marriage-seeking nymphs and marriage-making dames! has supplicated in vain!

"I confess to you, when the thing was first in agitation, my aristocratic blood roused itself a little at the anticipated connexion; but finding on examination that Sir Edward was of no doubtful lineage, and that the blood of the Chattertons runs in his veins, and finding the young lady everything I could wish in a sister, my scruples soon disappeared, with the folly that engendered them.

"There was no necessity for any alarm, for the lady very decidedly refused the honor offered her by Derwent, and what makes the matter worse, refused the solicitations of his sister also.

"I have fifty times been surprised at my own condescension, and to this moment am at a loss to know whether it was to the lady's worth, my brother's happiness, or the Chatterton blood, that I finally yielded. Heigho! this Chatterton is certainly much too handsome for a man; but I forget you have never seen him." (Here an arch smile stole over the features of the listener, as his sister continued)--"To return to my narration, I had half a mind to send for a Miss Harris there is here, to learn the most approved fashion of a lady preferring a suit, but as fame said she was just now practising on a certain hero ycleped Captain Jarvis, heir to Sir Timo of that name, it struck me her system might be rather too abrupt, so I was fain to adopt the best plan--that of trusting to nature and my own feelings for words.

"Nobility is certainly a very pretty thing (for those who have it), but I would defy the old Margravine of ---- to keep up the semblance of superiority with Emily Moseley. She is so very natural, so very beautiful, and withal at times a little arch, that one is afraid to set up any other distinctions than such as can be fairly supported.

"I commenced with hoping her determination to reject the hand of Frederick was not an unalterable one. (Yes, I called him Frederick, what I never did out of my own family before in my life.) There was a considerable tremor in the voice of Miss Moseley, as she replied, 'I now perceive, when too late, that my indiscretion has given reason to my friends to think that I have entertained intentions towards his grace, of which I entreat you to believe me, Lady Harriet, I am innocent. Indeed--indeed, as anything more than an agreeable acquaintance I have never allowed myself to think of your brother:' and from my soul I believe her. We continued our conversation for half an hour longer, and such was the ingenuousness, delicacy, and high religious feeling displayed by the charming girl, that if I entered the room with a spark of regret that I was compelled to solicit another to favor my brother's love, I left it with a feeling that my efforts had been unsuccessful. Yes! thou peerless sister of the more peerless Pendennyss! I once thought of your ladyship as a wife for Derwent--"

A glass of water was necessary to enable the reader to clear her voice, which grew husky from speaking so long.

"But I now openly avow, neither your birth, your hundred thousand pounds, nor your merit, would put you on a footing, in my estimation, with my Emily. You may form some idea of her power to captivate, and of her indifference to her conquests, when I mention that she once refused--but I forget, you don't know him, and therefore cannot be a judge. The thing is finally decided, and we shortly go into Westmoreland, and next week, the Moseleys return to Northamptonshire. I don't know when I shall be able to visit you, and think I may *now* safely invite you to Denbigh Castle, although a month ago I might have hesitated. Love to the earl, and kind assurance to yourself of unalterable regard.

"HARRIET DENBIGH."

"P.S. I believe I forgot to mention that Mrs. Moseley, a sister of Lord Chatterton, has gone to Portugal, and that the peer himself is to go into the country with us: there is, I suppose, a fellow-feeling between *them* just now, though I do not think Chatterton looks so very miserable as he might. Adieu."

On ending this second epistle the same silence which had succeeded the reading of the first prevailed, until the lady with an arch expression, interrupted it by saying,

"Harriet will, I think, soon grace the peerage."

"And happily, I trust," replied the brother.

"Do you know Lord Chatterton?"

"I do; he is very amiable, and admirably calculated to contrast with the lively gaiety of Harriet Denbigh."

"You believe in loving our opposites, I see," rejoined the lady; and then affectionately stretching out her hand to him, she added, "but, Pendennyss, you must give me for a sister one as nearly like yourself as possible."

"That might please your affections," answered the earl with a smile, "but how would it comport with my tastes? Will you suffer me to describe the kind of man *you* are to select for your future lord, unless, indeed, you have decided the point already?"

The lady colored violently, and appearing anxious to change the subject, she tumbled over two or three unopened letters, as she cried eagerly--

"Here is one from the Donna Julia." The earl instantly broke the seal and read aloud; no secrets existing between them in relation to their mutual friend.

"My Lord,

"I hasten to write you what I know it will give you pleasure to hear, concerning my future prospects in life. My uncle, General M'Carthy, has written me the cheerful tidings, that my father has consented to receive his only child, without any other sacrifice than a condition of attending the service of the Catholic Church without any professions on my side, or even an understanding that I am conforming to its peculiar tenets. This may be, in some measure, irksome at times, and possibly distressing; but the worship of God with a proper humiliation of spirit, I have learnt to consider as a privilege to us here, and I owe a duty to my earthly father of penitence and care in his later years that will justify the measure in the eyes of my heavenly One. I have, therefore, acquainted my uncle in reply, that I am willing to attend the Conde's summons at any moment he will choose to make them; and I thought it a debt due your care and friendship to apprise your lordship of my approaching departure from this country; indeed, I have great reasons for believing that your kind and unremitted efforts to attain this object have already prepared you to expect this result.

"I feel it will be impossible to quit England without seeing you and your sister, to thank you for the many, very many favors, of both a temporal and eternal nature, you have been the agents of conferring on me. The cruel suggestions which I dreaded, and which it appears had reached the ears of my friends in Spain, have prevented my troubling your lordship of late unnecessarily with my concerns. The consideration of a friend to your character (Mrs. Wilson) has removed the necessity of applying for your advice; she and her charming niece, Miss Emily Moseley, have been, next to yourselves, the greatest solace I have had in my exile, and united you will be remembered in my prayers. I will merely mention here, deferring the explanation until I see you in London, that I have been visited by the wretch from whom you delivered me in Portugal, and that the means of ascertaining his name have fallen into my hands. You will be the best judge of the proper steps to be taken; but I wish, by all means, something may be done to prevent his attempting to see me in Spain. Should it be discovered to my relations there that he has any such intentions, it would certainly terminate in his death, and possibly in my disgrace. Wishing you and your kind sister all possible happiness, I remain,

"Your Lordship's obliged friend,

"JULIA FITZGERALD."

"Oh!" cried the sister as she concluded the letter, "we must certainly see her before she goes. What a wretch that persecutor of hers must be! how persevering in his villainy!"

"He does exceed my ideas of effrontery," said the earl, in great warmth--"but he may offend too far; the laws shall interpose their power to defeat his schemes, should he ever repeat them."

"He attempted to take your life, brother," said the lady shuddering, "if I remember the tale aright."

"Why, I have endeavored to free him from that imputation," rejoined the brother, musing, "he certainly fired a pistol, but the latter hit my horse at such a distance from myself, that I believe his object was to disable me and not murder. His escape has astonished me; he must have fled by himself into the woods, as Harmer was but a short distance behind me, admirably mounted, and the escort was up and in full pursuit within ten minutes. After all it may be for the best he was not taken; for I am persuaded the dragoons would have sabred him on the spot, and he may have parents of respectability, or a wife to kill by the knowledge of his misconduct."

"This Emily Moseley must be a faultless being," cried the sister, as she ran over the contents of Julia's letter. "Three different letters, and each containing her praises!"

The earl made no reply, but opening the duke's letter again, he appeared to be studying its contents. His color slightly changed as he dwelt on its passages, and turning to his sister he inquired if she had a mind to try the air of Westmoreland for a couple of weeks or a month.

"As you say, my Lord," replied the lady, with cheeks of scarlet.

"Then I say we will go. I wish much to see Derwent and I think there will be a wedding during our visit."

He rang the bell, and the almost untasted breakfast was removed in a few minutes. A servant announced that his horse was in readiness. The earl wished his sister a friendly good morning, and proceeded to the door, where was standing one of the noble black horses before mentioned, held by a groom, and the military-looking attendant ready mounted on another.

Throwing himself into the saddle, the young peer rode gracefully from the door, followed by his attendant horseman. During this ride, the master suffered his steed to take whatever course most pleased himself, and his follower looked up in surprise more than once, to see the careless manner in which the Earl of Pendennyss, confessedly one of the best horsemen in England, managed the noble animal. Having, however, got without the gates of his own park, and into the vicinity of numberless cottages and farm-houses, the master recovered his recollection, and the man ceased to wonder.

For three hours the equestrians pursued their course through the beautiful vale which opened gracefully opposite one of the fronts of the castle; and if faces of smiling welcome, inquiries after his own and his sister's welfare, which evidently sprang from the heart, or the most familiar but respectful representations of their own prosperity or misfortunes, gave any testimony of the feelings entertained by the tenantry of this noble estate for their landlord, the situation of the young nobleman might be justly considered envied.

As the hour for dinner approached, they turned the heads of their horses towards home; and on entering the park, removed from the scene of industry and activity without, the earl relapsed into his fit of musing. A short distance from the house he suddenly called, "Harmer." The man drove his spurs into the loins of his horse, and in an instant was by the side of his master, which he signified by raising his hand to his cap with the palm opening outward.

"You must prepare to go to Spain when required, in attendance on Mrs. Fitzgerald."

The man received his order with the indifference of one used to adventures and movements, and having laconically dignified his assent, he drew his horse back again into his station in the rear.

Chapter XXXVIII

The day succeeding the arrival of the Moseleys at the seat of their ancestors, Mrs. Wilson observed Emily silently putting on her pelisse, and walking out unattended by either of the domestics or any of the family. There was a peculiar melancholy in her air and manner, which inclined the cautious aunt to suspect that her charge was bent on the indulgence of some ill-judged weakness; more particularly, as the direction she took led to the arbor, a theatre in which Denbigh had been so conspicuous an actor. Hastily throwing a cloak over her own shoulders, Mrs. Wilson followed Emily with the double purpose of ascertaining her views, and if necessary, of interposing her own authority against the repetition of similar excursions.

As Emily approached the arbor, whither in truth she had directed her steps, its faded vegetation and chilling aspect, so different from its verdure and luxuriance when she last saw it, came over her heart as a symbol of her own blighted prospects and deadened affections. The recollection of Denbigh's conduct on that spot, of his general benevolence and assiduity to please, being forcibly recalled to her mind at the instant, forgetful of her object in visiting the arbor, Emily yielded to her sensibilities, and sank on the seat weeping as if her heart would break.

She had not time to dry her eyes, and to collect her scattered thoughts, before Mrs. Wilson entered the arbor. Eyeing her niece for a moment with a sternness unusual for the one to adopt or the other to receive, she said,

"It is a solemn obligation we owe our religion and ourselves, to endeavor to suppress such passions as are incompatible with our duties; and there is no weakness greater than blindly adhering to the wrong, when we are convinced of our error. It is as fatal to good morals as it is unjust to ourselves to persevere, from selfish motives, in believing those innocent whom evidence has convicted as guilty. Many a weak woman has sealed her own misery by such wilful obstinacy, aided by the unpardonable vanity of believing herself able to control a man that the laws of God could not restrain."

"Oh, dear madam, speak not so unkindly to me," sobbed the weeping girl; "I--I am guilty of no such weakness, I assure you:" and looking up with an air of profound resignation and piety, she continued: "Here, on this spot, where he saved my life, I was about to offer up my prayers for his conviction of the error of his ways, and for the pardon of his too--too heavy transgressions."

Mrs. Wilson, softened almost to tears herself, viewed her for a moment with a mixture of delight, and continued in a milder tone,--

"I believe you, my dear. I am certain, although you may have loved Denbigh much, that you love your Maker and his ordinances more; and I have no apprehensions that, were he a disengaged man, and you alone in the world--unsupported by anything but your sense of duty--you would ever so far forget yourself as to become his wife But does not your religion, does not your own usefulness in society, require you wholly to free your heart from the power of a man who has so unworthily usurped a dominion over it?"

To this Emily replied, in a hardly audible voice, "Certainly--and I pray constantly for it."

"It is well, my love," said the aunt, soothingly; "you cannot fail with such means, and your own exertions, finally to prevail over your own worst enemies, your passions. The task our sex has to sustain is, at the best, an arduous one; but so much the greater is our credit if we do it well."

"Oh! how is an unguided girl ever to judge aright, if,--" cried Emily, clasping her hands and speaking with great energy, and she would have said, "one like Denbigh in appearance, be so vile!" Shame, however, kept her silent.

"Few men can support such a veil of hypocrisy as that with which I sometimes think Denbigh must deceive even himself. His case is an extraordinary exception to a very sacred rule--'that the tree is known by its fruits,'" replied her aunt. "There is no safer way of judging of character that one's opportunities will not admit of more closely investigating, than by examining into and duly appreciating early impressions. The man or woman who has constantly seen the practice of piety before them, from infancy to the noon of life, will seldom so far abandon the recollection of virtue as to be guilty of great enormities. Even Divine Truth has promised that his blessings or his curses shall extend to many generations. It is true, that with our most most guarded prudence we may be deceived." Mrs. Wilson paused and sighed heavily, as her own case, connected with the loves of Denbigh and her niece, occurred strongly to her mind. "Yet," she continued, "we may lessen the danger much by guarding against it; and it seems to me no more than what self-preservation requires in a young woman. But for a religious parent to neglect it, is a wilful abandonment of a most solemn duty."

As Mrs. Wilson concluded, her niece, who had recovered the command of her feelings pressed her hand in silence to her lips, and showed a disposition to retire from a spot which she found recalled too many recollections of a man whose image it was her imperious duty to banish, on every consideration of propriety and religion.

Their walk into the house was silent, and their thoughts were drawn from the unpleasant topic by finding a letter from Julia, announcing her intended departure from this country, and her wish to take leave of them in London before she sailed. As she had mentioned the probable day for that event, both the ladies were delighted to find it was posterior to the time fixed by Sir Edward for their own visit to the capital.

Had Jane, instead of Emily, been the one that suffered through the agency of Mrs. Fitzgerald, however innocently on the part of the lady, her violent and uncontrolled passions would have either blindly united the innocent with the guilty in her resentments; or, if a sense of justice had vindicated the lady in her judgment, yet her pride and ill-guided delicacy would have felt her name a reproach, that would have forbidden any intercourse with her or any belonging to her.

Not so with her sister. The sufferings of Mrs. Fitzgerald had taken a strong hold on her youthful feelings, and a similarity of opinions and practices on the great object of their lives, had brought them together in a manner no misconduct in a third person could weaken. It is true, the recollection of Denbigh was intimately blended with the fate of Mrs. Fitzgerald. But Emily sought support against her feeling from a quarter that rather required an investigation of them than a desire to *drown* care with thought.

She never indulged in romantic reflections in which the image of Denbigh was associated. This she had hardly done in her happiest moments; and his marriage, if nothing else had interfered, now absolutely put it out of the question. But, although a Christian, and an humble and devout one, Emily Moseley was a woman, and had loved ardently, confidingly, and gratefully. Marriage is the business of life with her sex,--with all, next to a preparation for a better world,--and it cannot be supposed that a first passion in a bosom like that of our heroine was to be suddenly erased and to leave no vestiges of its existence.

Her partiality for the society of Derwent, her meditations in which she sometimes detected herself drawing a picture of what Denbigh might have been, if early care had been taken to impress him with his situation in this world, and from which she generally retired to her closet and her knees, were the remains of feelings too strong and too pure to be torn from her in a moment.

The arrival of John, with Grace and Jane, enlivened not only the family but the neighborhood. Mr. Haughton and his numerous friends poured in on the young couple with their congratulations, and a few weeks stole by insensibly, previously to the commencement of the journeys of Sir Edward and his son--the one to Benfield Lodge and the other to St. James's Square.

On the return of the travellers, a few days before they commenced their journey to the capital, John laughingly told his uncle that, although he himself greatly admired the taste of Mr. Peter Johnson in dress, yet he doubted whether the present style of fashions in the metropolis would not be scandalized by the appearance of the honest steward.

John had in fact noticed, in their former visit to London, mob of mischievous boys eyeing Peter with indications of rebellious movements which threatened the old man, and from which he had retreated by taking a coach, and he now made the suggestion from pure good-nature, to save him any future trouble from a similar cause.

They were at dinner when Moseley made the remark, and the steward was in his place at the sideboard--for his master was his home. Drawing near at the mention of his name first, and casting an eye over his figure to see if all was decent, Peter respectfully broke silence, determined to defend his own cause.

"Why! Mr. John--Mr. John Moseley? if I might judge, for an elderly man, and a serving man," said the steward, bowing humbly, "I am no disparagement to my friends, or even to my honored master."

Johnson's vindication of his wardrobe drew the eyes of the family upon him, and an involuntary smile passed from one to the other, as they admired his starched figure and drab frock, or rather doublet with sleeves and skirts. Sir Edward, being of the same opinion with his son, observed--

"I do think, Uncle Benfield, there might be an improvement in the dress of your steward without much trouble to the ingenuity of his tailor."

"Sir Edward Moseley--honorable sir," said the steward, beginning to grow alarmed, "if I may be so bold, you young gentlemen may like gay clothes; but as for me and his honor; we are used to such as we wear, and what we are used to we love."

The old man spoke with earnestness, and drew the particular attention of his master to a review of his attire. After reflecting that no gentleman in the house had been attended by any servitor in such a garb, Mr. Benfield thought it time to give his sentiments on the subject.

"Why I remember that my Lord Gosford's gentleman never wore a livery, nor can I say that he dressed exactly after the manner of Johnson. Every member had his body servant, and they were not unfrequently taken for their masters. Lady Juliana, too, after the death of her nephew, had one or two attendants out of livery, and in a different fashion from your attire. Peter, I think with John Moseley there, we must alter you a little for the sake of appearances."

"Your honor!" stammered out Peter, in increased terror; "for Mr. John Moseley and Sir Edward, and youngerly gentlemen like, dress may do. Now, your honor, if--" and Peter, turning to Grace, bowed nearly to the floor--"I had such a sweet, most beautiful young lady to smile on me, I might wish to change; but, sir, my day has gone by." Peter sighed as the recollection of Patty Steele and his youthful love floated across his brain. Grace blushed and thanked him for the compliment, and gave her opinion that his gallantry merited a better costume.

"Peter," said his master, decidedly, "I think Mrs. Moseley is right. If I should call on the viscountess (the Lady Juliana, who yet survived an ancient dowager of seventy), I shall want your attendance, and in your present garb you cannot fail to shock her delicate feelings. You remind me now I think, every time I look at you, of old Harry, the earl's gamekeeper, one of the most cruel men I ever knew."

This decided the matter. Peter well knew that his master's antipathy to old Harry arose from his having pursued a poacher one day, in place of helping the Lady Juliana over a stile, in her flight from a bull that was playing his gambols in the same field; and not for the world would the faithful steward retain even a feature, if it brought unpleasant recollections to his kind master. He at one time thought of closing his innovations on his wardrobe, however, with a change of his nether garment; as after a great deal of study he could only make out the resemblance between himself and the obnoxious gamekeeper to consist in the leathern breeches. But fearful of some points escaping his memory in forty years, he tamely acquiesced in all John's alterations, and appeared at his station three days afterwards newly decked from head to foot in a more modern suit of snuff-color.

The change once made, Peter greatly admired himself in a glass, and thought, could he have had the taste of Mr. John Moseley in his youth to direct his toilet, that the hard heart of Patty Steele would not always have continued so obdurate.

Sir Edward wished to collect his neighbors round him once more before he left them for another four months; and accordingly the rector and his wife, Francis and Clara, the Haughtons, with a few others, dined at the Hall by invitation, the last day of their stay in Northamptonshire. The company had left the table to join the ladies, when Grace came into the drawing-room with a face covered with smiles and beaming with pleasure.

"You look like the bearer of good news, Mrs. Moseley," cried the rector, catching a glimpse of her countenance as she passed.

"Good! I sincerely hope and believe," replied Grace. "My letters from my brother announce that his marriage took place last week, and give us hopes of seeing them all in town within the month."

"Married!" exclaimed Mr. Haughton, casting his eyes unconsciously on Emily, "my Lord Chatterton married! May I ask the name of the bride, my dear Mrs. Moseley?"

"To Lady Harriet Denbigh--and at Denbigh Castle in Westmoreland; but very privately, as you may suppose from seeing Moseley and myself here," answered Grace, her cheeks yet glowing with surprise and pleasure at the intelligence.

"Lady Harriet Denbigh?" echoed Mr. Haughton; "what! a kinswoman of our old friend? *your* friend, Miss Emily?" The recollection of the service he had performed at the arbor still-fresh in his memory.

Emily commanded herself sufficiently to reply, "Brothers' children, I believe, sir."

"But a *lady*--how came she my lady?" continued the good man, anxious to know the whole, and ignorant of any reasons for delicacy where so great a favorite as Denbigh was in the question.

"She is the daughter of the late Duke of Derwent," said Mrs. Moseley, as willing as himself to talk of her new sister.

"How happens it that the death of old Mr. Denbigh was announced as plain Geo. Denbigh, Esq., if he was the brother of a duke?" said Jane, forgetting for a moment the presence of Dr. and Mrs. Ives, in her surviving passion for genealogy: "should he not have been called Lord George, or honorable?"

This was the first time any allusion had been made to the sudden death in the church by any of the Moseleys in the hearing of the rector's family; and the speaker sat in breathless terror at her own inadvertency. But Dr. Ives, observing that a profound silence prevailed as soon as Jane ended, answered, mildly, though in a way to prevent any further comments--

"The late Duke's succeeding a cousin-german in the title, was the reason, I presume. Emily, I am to hear from you by letter I hope, after you enter into the gaieties of the metropolis?"

This Emily cheerfully promised, and the conversation took another turn.

Mrs. Wilson had carefully avoided all communications with the rector concerning his youthful friend, and the Doctor appeared unwilling to commence anything which might lead to his name being mentioned. "He is disappointed in him as well as ourselves," thought the widow, "and it must be unpleasant to have his image recalled. He saw his attentions to Emily, and he knows of his marriage to Lady Laura of course, and he loves us all, and Emily in particular, too well not to feel hurt by his conduct."

"Sir Edward!" cried Mr. Haughton, with a laugh, "Baronets are likely to be plenty. Have you heard how near we were to have another in the neighborhood lately?" Sir Edward answered in the negative, and his neighbor continued--

"Why no less a man than Captain Jarvis, promoted to the bloody hand."

"Captain Jarvis!" exclaimed five or six at once; "explain yourself, Mr. Haughton."

"My near neighbor, young Walker, has been to Bath on an unusual business--his health--and for the benefit of the country he has brought back a pretty piece of scandal. It seems that Lady Jarvis, as I am told she is since she left here, wished to have her hopeful heir made a lord, and that the two united for some six months in forming a kind of savings' bank between themselves, to enable them at some future day to bribe the minister to honor the peerage with such a prodigy. After awhile the daughter of our late acquaintance, Sir William Harris, became an accessory to the plot, and a contributor too, to the tune of a couple of hundred pounds. Some circumstances, however, at length made this latter lady suspicious, and she wished to audit the books. The Captain prevaricated--the lady remonstrated, until the gentleman, with more truth than manners, told her that she was a fool--the money he had expended or lost at dice; and that he did not think the ministers quite so silly as to make him a lord, or that he himself was such a fool as to make her his wife; so the whole thing exploded."

John listened with a delight but little short of what he had felt when Grace owned her love, and anxious to know all, eagerly inquired--

"But, is it true? how was it found out?"

"Oh, the lady complained of part, and the Captain tells all to get the laugh on his side; so that Walker says the former is the derision and the latter the contempt of all Bath."

"Poor Sir William," said the baronet, with feeling; "he is much to be pitied."

"I am afraid he has nothing to blame but his own indulgence," remarked the rector.

"You don't know the worst of it," replied Mr. Haughton. "We poor people are made to suffer--Lady Jarvis wept and fretted Sir Timo out of his lease, which has been given up, and a new house is to be taken in another part of the kingdom, where neither Miss Harris nor the story is known."

"Then Sir William has to procure a new tenant," said Lady Moseley, not in the least regretting the loss of the old one.

"No! my lady!" continued Mr. Haughton, with a smile. "Walker is, you know, an attorney, and does some business occasionally for Sir William. When Jarvis gave up the lease, the baronet, who finds himself a little short of money, offered the deanery for sale, it being a useless place to him; and the very next day, while Walker was with Sir William, a gentleman called, and without higgling agreed to pay down at once his thirty thousand pounds for it."

"And who is the purchaser?" inquired Lady Moseley, eagerly.

"The Earl of Pendennyss."

"Lord Pendennyss!" exclaimed Mrs. Wilson in rapture.

"Pendennyss!" cried the rector, eyeing the aunt and Emily with a smile.

"Pendennyss!" echoed all in the room in amazement.

"Yes," said Mr. Haughton, "it is now the property of the earl, who says he has bought it for his sister."

Chapter XXXIX

Mrs. Wilson found time the ensuing day to ascertain before they left the hall, the truth of the tale related by Mr. Haughton. The deanery had certainly changed its master, and a new steward had already arrived to take possession in the name of his lord. What induced Pendennyss to make this purchase she was at a loss to conceive--most probably some arrangement between himself and Lord Bolton. But whatever might be his motive, it in some measure insured his becoming for a season their neighbor; and Mrs. Wilson felt a degree of pleasure at the circumstance that she had been a stranger to for a long time--a pleasure which was greatly heightened as she dwelt on the lovely face of the companion who occupied the other seat in her travelling chaise.

The road to London led by the gates of the deanery, and near them they passed a servant in the livery of those they had once seen following the equipage of the earl. Anxious to know anything which might hasten her acquaintance with this admired nobleman, Mrs. Wilson stopped her carriage to inquire.

"Pray, sir, whom do you serve?"

"My Lord Pendennyss, ma'am," replied the man, respectfully taking off his hat.

"The earl is not here?" asked Mrs. Wilson, with interest.

"Oh, no, madam; I am here in waiting on his steward. My lord is in Westmoreland, with his grace and Colonel Denbigh, and the ladies."

"Does he remain there long?" continued the anxious widow, desirous of knowing all she could learn.

"I believe not, madam; most of our people have gone to Annerdale-House, and my lord is expected in town with the duke and the colonel."

As the servant was an elderly man, and appeared to understand the movements of his master so well, Mrs. Wilson was put in unusual spirits by this prospect of a speedy termination to her anxiety to meet Pendennyss.

"Annerdale-House is the earl's town residence?" quietly inquired Emily.

"Yes; he got the fortune of the last duke of that title, but how I do not exactly know. I believe, however, through his mother. General Wilson did not know his family: indeed, Pendennyss bore a second title during his lifetime; but did you observe how very civil his servant was, as well as the one John spoke to before,--a sure sign their master is a gentleman?"

Emily smiled at the strong partialities of her aunt, and replied, "Your handsome chaise and attendants will draw respect from most men in his situation, dear aunt, be their masters who they may."

The expected pleasure of meeting the earl was a topic frequently touched upon between her aunt and Emily during their journey; the former beginning to entertain hopes she would have laughed at herself for, could they have been fairly laid before her; and the latter entertaining a profound respect for his character, but chiefly governed by a wish to gratify her companion.

The third day they reached the baronet's handsome house in St. James's Square, and found that the forethought of John had provided everything in the best and most comfortable manner.

It was the first visit of both Jane and Emily to the metropolis; and under the protection of their almost equally curious mother, and escorted by John, they wisely determined to visit the curiosities, while their leisure yet admitted of the opportunity. For the first two weeks their time was chiefly employed in the indulgence of this unfashionable and vulgar propensity, which, if it had no other tendency, served greatly to draw the thoughts of both the young women from the recollections of the last few months.

While her sister and nieces were thus employed, Mrs. Wilson, assisted by Grace, was occupied in getting things in preparation to do credit to the baronet's hospitality.

The second week after their arrival, Mrs. Moseley was delighted by seeing advance upon her unexpectedly through the door of the breakfast parlor, her brother, with his bride leaning on his arm. After the most sincere greetings and congratulations, Lady Chatterton cried out gaily,

"You see, my dear Lady Moseley, I am determined to banish ceremony between us, and so, instead of sending you my card, have come myself to notify you of my arrival. Chatterton would not suffer me even to swallow my breakfast, he was so impatient to show me off."

"You are placing things exactly on the footing I wish to see ourselves with all our connexions," replied Lady Moseley, kindly; "but what have you done with the duke? is he not in your train?"

"Oh! he is gone to Canterbury with George Denbigh, madam," cried the lady, shaking her head reproachfully though affectionately at Emily; "his grace dislikes London just now excessively, he says, and the Colonel being obliged to leave his wife, on regimental business, Derwent was good enough to keep him company during his exile."

"And Lady Laura, do we see her?" inquired Lady Moseley.

"She came with us. Pendennyss and his sister follow immediately; so, my dear madam, the dramatis personæ will all be on the stage soon."

Cards and visits now began to accumulate on the Moseleys, and their time no longer admitted of that unfettered leisure which they had enjoyed at their entrance on the scene. Mrs. Wilson, for herself and charge, adopted a rule for the government of her manner of living, which was consistent with her duties. They mixed in general society sparingly; and, above all, they rigidly adhered to the obedience to the injunction which commanded them to keep the Sabbath day holy; a duty of no trifling difficulty to perform in fashionable society in the city of London, or, indeed, in any other place, where the influence of fashion has supplanted the laws of God.

Mrs. Wilson was not a bigot; but she knew and performed her duty rigidly. It was a pleasure to her to do so. It would have been misery to do otherwise. In the singleness of heart and deep piety of her niece, she had a willing pupil to her system of morals, and a rigid follower of her religious practices. As they both knew that the temptations to go astray were greater in town than in country, they kept a strict guard over the tendency to err, and in watchfulness found their greatest security.

John Moseley, next to his friends, loved his bays: indeed, if the aggregate of his affections for these and Lady Herriefield had been put in opposite scales, we strongly suspect the side of the horses would predominate.

One Sunday, soon after being domesticated, John, who had soberly attended morning service with the ladies, came into a little room where the more reflecting part of the family were assembled, in search of his wife.

Grace, we have before mentioned, had become a real member of that church in which she had been educated, and had entered, under the direction of Dr. Ives and Mrs. Wilson, into an observance of its wholesome ordinances. Grace was certainly piously inclined, if not devout. Her feelings on the subject of religion had been sensibly awakened during their voyage to Lisbon; and at the period of which we write, Mrs. Moseley was as sincerely disposed to perform her duty as her powers admitted. To the request of her husband, that she would take a seat in his phaeton while he drove her round the park once or twice, Grace gave a mild refusal, by saying,

"It is Sunday, my dear Moseley."

"Do you think I don't know that?" cried John, gaily. "There will be everybody there, and, the better day, the better deed."

Now, Moseley, if he had been asked to apply this speech to the case before them, would have frankly owned his inability; but his wife did not make the trial: she was contented with saying, as she laid down her book to look on a face she so tenderly loved,

"Ah! Moseley, you should set a better example to those below you in life."

"I wish to set an example," returned her husband, with an affectionate smile, "to all above as well as below me, in order that they may find out the path to happiness, by exhibiting to the world a model of a wife, in yourself, dear Grace."

As this was uttered with a sincerity which distinguished the manner of Moseley, his wife was more pleased with the compliment than she would have been willing to make known; and John spoke no more than he thought; for a desire to show his handsome wife was the ruling passion for a moment.

The husband was too pressing and the wife too fond not to yield the point; and Grace took her seat in the carriage with a kind of half-formed resolution to improve the opportunity by a discourse on serious subjects--a resolution which terminated as all others do, that postpone one duty to discharge another of less magnitude; it was forgotten.

Mrs. Wilson had listened with interest to the efforts of John to prevail on his wife to take the ride, and on her leaving the room to comply she observed to Emily, with whom she now remained alone--

"Here is a consequence of a difference in religious views between man and wife, my child: John, in place of supporting Grace in the discharge of her duties, has been the actual cause of her going astray."

Emily felt the force of her aunt's remark, and saw its justice; yet her love for the offender induced her to say--

"John will not lead her openly astray for he has a sincere respect for religion, and this offence is not unpardonable, dear aunt."

"The offence is assuredly not unpardonable," replied Mrs. Wilson, "and to infinite mercy it is hard to say what is; but it is an offence, and directly in the face of an express ordinance of the Lord; it is even throwing off the *appearance* of keeping the Sabbath day holy, much less observing the substance of the commandment; and as to John's respect for holy things in this instance, it was injurious to his wife. Had he been an open deist she would have shrunk from the act in suspicion of its sinfulness. Either John must become Christian, or I am afraid Grace will fall from her undertaking."

Mrs. Wilson shook her head mournfully, while Emily offered up a silent petition that the first might speedily be the case.

Lady Laura had been early in her visit to the Moseleys; and as Denbigh had both a town residence and a seat in parliament, it appeared next to impossible to avoid meeting him or to requite the pressing civilities of his wife by harsh refusals; that might prove in the end injurious to themselves by creating a suspicion that resentment at his not choosing a partner from amongst them, governed the conduct of the Moseleys towards a man to whom they were under such a heavy obligation.

Had Sir Edward known as much as his sister and daughters he would probably have discountenanced the acquaintance altogether; but owing to the ignorance of the rest of her friends of what had passed, Mrs. Wilson and Emily had not only the assiduities of Lady Laura but the wishes of their own family to contend with, and consequently she submitted to the association with a reluctance that was in some measure counteracted by their regard for Lady Laura, and by compassion for her abused confidence.

A distant connexion of Lady Moseley's had managed to collect in her house a few hundred of her nominal friends, and as she had been particularly attentive in calling in person on her venerable relative, Mr. Benfield, soon after his arrival in town, out of respect to her father's cousin, or perhaps mindful of his approaching end, and remembering there were such things as codicils to wills, the old man, flattered by her notice, and yet too gallant to reject the favor of a lady, consented to accompany the remainder of the family on the occasion.

Most of their acquaintances were there, and Lady Moseley soon found herself engaged in a party at quadrille, while the young people were occupied by the usual amusements of their age in such scenes. Emily alone feeling but little desire to enter into the gaiety of general conversation with a host of gentlemen who had collected round her aunt and sisters, offered her arm to Mr. Benfield, on seeing him manifest a disposition to take a closer view of the company, and walked away with him.

They wandered from room to room, unconscious of the observation attracted by the sight of a man in the costume of Mr. Benfield, leaning on the arm of so young and lovely a woman as his niece; and many an exclamation of surprise, ridicule, admiration, and wonder had been made, unnoticed by the pair, until finding the crowd rather inconvenient to her companion, Emily gently drew him into one of the apartments where the card-tables, and the general absence of beauty, made room less difficult to be found.

"Ah! Emmy dear," said the old gentleman, wiping his face, "times are much changed, I see, since my youth. Then you would see no such throngs assembled in so small a space; gentlemen shoving ladies, and yes, Emmy," continued her uncle in a lower tone, as if afraid of uttering something dangerous, "the ladies themselves shouldering the men. I remember at a drum given by Lady Gosford, that although I may, without vanity, say I was one of the gallantest men in the rooms, I came in contact with but one of the ladies during the whole evening, with the exception of handing the Lady Juliana to a chair, and that," said her uncle, stopping short and lowering his voice to a whisper, "was occasioned by a mischance in the old duchess in rising from her seat when she had taken too much strong waters, as she was at times a little troubled with a pain in the chest."

Emily smiled at the casualty of her grace, and they proceeded slowly through the table until their passage was stopped by a party at the game of whist, which, by its incongruous mixture of ages and character, forcibly drew her attention.

The party was composed of a young man of five or six and twenty, who threw down his cards in careless indifference, and heedlessly played with the guineas which were laid on the side of the table as markers, or the fruits of a former victory: or by stealing hasty and repeated glances through the vista of the tables into the gayer scenes of the adjoining rooms, proved he was in duresse, and waited for an opportunity to make his escape from the tedium of cards and ugliness to the life of conversation and beauty.

His partner was a woman of doubtful age, and one whose countenance rather indicated that the uncertainty was likely to continue until the record of the tomb-stone divulged the so often contested circumstance to the world. Her eyes also wandered to the gayer scenes, but with an expression of censoriousness mingled with longings; nor did she neglect the progress of the game as frequently as her more heedless partner. A glance thrown on the golden pair which was placed between her and her neighbor on her right, marked the importance of the *corner*, and she shuffled the cards with a nervousness which plainly denoted her apprehension of the consequences of her partner's abstraction.

Her neighbor on the right was a man of sixty, and his vestments announced him a servant of the sanctuary. His intentness on the game proceeded no doubt from his habits of reflection; his smile at success, quite possibly from charity to his neighbors; his frown in adversity from displeasure at the triumphs of the wicked, for such in his heart he had set down Miss Wigram to be; and his unconquerable gravity in the employment from a profound regard to the dignity of his holy office.

The fourth performer in this trial of memories was an ancient lady, gaily dressed, and intently eager on the game. Between her and the young man was a large pile of guineas, which appeared to be her exclusive property, from which she repeatedly, during the play, tendered one to his acceptance on the event of a hand or a trick, and to which she seldom failed from inadvertence to add his mite, contributing to accumulate the pile.

"Two double and the rub, my dear doctor," exclaimed the senior lady, in triumph. "Sir William, you owe me ten."

The money was paid as easily as it had been won, and the dowager proceeded to settle some bets with her female antagonist.

"Two more, I fancy, ma'am," said she, closely scanning the contributions of the maiden.

"I believe it is right, my lady," was the answer, with a look that said pretty plainly, that or nothing.

"I beg pardon, my dear, here are but four; and you remember two on the corner, and four on the points. Doctor, I will trouble you for a couple of guineas from Miss Wigram's store, I am in haste to get to the Countess's route."

The doctor was coolly helping himself from the said store, under the watchful eyes of its owner, and secretly exulting in his own judgment in requiring the stakes, when the maiden replied in great warmth,

"Your ladyship forgets the two you lost to me at Mrs. Howard's."

"It must be a mistake, my dear, I always pay as I lose," cried the dowager, with great spirit, stretching over the table and helping herself to the disputed money.

Mr. Benfield and Emily had stood silent spectators of the whole scene, the latter in astonishment to meet such manners in such society, and the former under feelings it would have been difficult to describe; for in the face of the Dowager which was inflamed partly from passion and more from high living, he recognised the remains of his Lady Juliana, now the Dowager Viscountess Haverford.

"Emmy, dear," said the old man, with a heavy-drawn sigh, as if awaking from a long and troubled dream, "we will go."

The phantom of forty years had vanished before the truth and the fancies of retirement, simplicity, and a diseased imagination yielded to the influence of life and common sense.

Chapter XL

With Harriet, now closely connected with them by marriage as well as attachment, the baronet's family maintained a most friendly intercourse; and Mrs. Wilson, and Emily, a prodigious favorite with her new cousin, consented to pass a day soberly with her during an excursion of her husband to Windsor on business connected with his station. They had, accordingly, driven round to an early breakfast; and Chatterton, after politely regretting his loss, and thanking them for their consideration for his wife, made his bow.

Lady Harriet Denbigh had brought the Baron a very substantial addition to his fortune; and as his sisters were both provided for by ample settlements, the pecuniary distresses which had existed a twelvemonth before had been entirely removed. Chatterton's income was now large, his demands upon it small, and he kept up an establishment in proportion to the rank of both husband and wife.

"Mrs. Wilson," cried the hostess, twirling her cup as she followed with her eyes the retreating figure of her husband at the door, "I am about to take up the trade of Miss Harris, and become a match-maker."

"Not on your own behalf so soon, surely," rejoined the widow.

"Oh no, my fortune is made for life, or not at all," continued the other, gaily; "but in behalf of our little friend Emily here."

"Me," cried Emily, starting from a reverie, in which the prospect of happiness to Lady Laura was the subject; "you are very good, Harriet; for whom do you intend me?"

"Whom! Who is good enough for you, but my cousin Pendennyss? Ah!" she cried, laughing, as she caught Emily by the hand, "Derwent and myself both settled the matter long since, and I know you will yield when you come to know him."

"The duke!" cried the other, with a surprise and innocence that immediately brought a blush of the brightest vermillion into her face.

"Yes, the duke," said Lady Chatterton: "you may think it odd for a discarded lover to dispose of his mistress so soon, but both our hearts are set upon it. The earl arrived last night, and this day he and his sister dine with us in a sober way: now, my dear madam," turning to Mrs. Wilson, "have I not prepared an agreeable surprise for you?"

"Surprise indeed," said the widow, excessively gratified at the probable termination to her anxieties for this meeting; "but where are they from?"

"From Northamptonshire, where the earl has already purchased a residence, I understand, and in your neighborhood too; so, you perceive, *he* at least begins to think of the thing."

"A certain evidence, truly," cried Emily, "his having purchased the house. But was he without a residence that he bought the deanery?"

"Oh no! he has a palace in town, and three seats in the country; but none in Northamptonshire but this," said the lady, with a laugh. "To own the truth he did offer to let George Denbigh have it for the next summer, but the Colonel chose to be nearer Eltringham; and I take it, it was only a ruse in the earl to cloak his own designs. You may depend upon it, we trumpeted your praises to him incessantly in Westmoreland."

"And is Colonel Denbigh in town?" said Mrs. Wilson, stealing an anxious glance towards her niece, who, in spite of all her efforts, sensibly changed color.

"Oh, yes! and Laura is as happy--as happy--as myself," said Lady Chatterton, with a glow on her cheeks, as she attended to the request of her housekeeper, and left the room.

Her guests sat in silence, occupied with their own reflections, while they heard a summons at the door of the house. It was opened, and footsteps approached the door of their own room. It was pushed partly open, as a voice on the other side said, speaking to a servant without,--

"Very well. Do not disturb your lady. I am in no haste."

At the sound of its well known tones, both the ladies almost sprang from their seats. Here could be no resemblance, and a moment removed their doubts. The speaker entered. It was Denbigh.

He stood for a moment fixed as a statue: It was evident the surprise was mutual. His face was pale as death, and then instantly was succeeded by a glow of fire. Approaching them, he paid his compliments with great earnestness, and in a voice in which his softest tones preponderated.

"I am happy, very happy, to be so fortunate in again meeting with such friends, and so unexpectedly."

Mrs. Wilson bowed in silence to his compliment, and Emily, pale as himself, sat with her eyes fastened on the carpet, without daring to trust her voice with an attempt to speak.

After struggling with his mortified feelings for a moment, Denbigh rose from the chair he had taken, and drawing near the sofa on which the ladies were placed, exclaimed with fervor,

"Tell me, dear madam, lovely, too lovely Miss Moseley, has one act of folly, of wickedness if you please, lost me your good opinion for ever? Derwent had given me hopes that you yet retained some esteem for my character, lowered, as I acknowledge it to be, in my own estimation."

"The Duke of Derwent? Mr. Denbigh!"

"Do not; do not use a name, dear madam, almost hateful to me," cried he, in a tone of despair.

"If," said Mrs. Wilson, gravely, "you have made your own name disreputable, I can only regret it, but--"

"Call me by my title--oh! do not remind me of my folly; I cannot bear it, and from you."

"Your title!" exclaimed Mrs. Wilson, with a cry of wonder, and Emily turned on him a face in which the flashes of color and succeeding paleness were as quick, and almost as vivid, as the glow of lightning. He caught their astonishment in equal surprise.

"How is this? some dreadful mistake, of which I am yet in ignorance," he cried, taking the unresisting hand of Mrs. Wilson, and pressing it with warmth between both his own, as he added, "do not leave me in suspense."

"For the sake of truth, for my sake, for the sake of this suffering innocent, say, in sincerity, who and what you are," said Mrs. Wilson in a solemn voice, gazing on him in dread of his reply.

Still retaining her hand, he dropped on his knees before her, as he answered,--

"I am the pupil, the child of your late husband, the companion of his dangers, the sharer of his joys and griefs, and would I could add, the friend of his widow. I am the Earl of Pendennyss."

Mrs. Wilson's head dropped on the shoulders of the kneeling youth, her arms were thrown in fervor around his neck, and she burst into a flood of tears. For a moment, both were absorbed in their own feelings; but a cry from Pendennyss aroused the aunt to the situation of her niece.

Emily had fallen senseless on the sofa.

An hour elapsed before her engagements admitted of the return of Lady Chatterton to the breakfast parlor, where she was surprised to find the breakfast equipage yet standing, and her cousin, the earl. Looking from one to the other in surprise, she exclaimed,--

"Very sociable, upon my word; how long has your lordship honored my house with your presence, and have you taken the liberty to introduce yourself to Mrs. Wilson and Miss Moseley?"

"Sociability and ease are the fashion of the day. I have been here an hour, my dear coz, and *have* taken the liberty of *introducing myself* to Mrs. Wilson and Miss Moseley," replied the earl gravely, although a smile of meaning lighted his handsome features as he uttered the latter part of the sentence, which was returned by Emily with a look of archness and pleasure that would have graced her happiest moments of juvenile joy.

There was such an interchange of looks, and such a visible alteration in the appearance of her guests, that it could not but attract the notice of Lady Chatterton. After listening to the conversation between them for some time in silence; and wondering what could have wrought so sudden a change below stairs, she broke forth with saying,--"Upon my word, you are an incomprehensible party to me. I left you ladies alone, and find a gentleman with you. I left you grave, if not melancholy, and find you all life and gaiety. I find you with a stranger, and you talk with him about walks, and rides, and scenes, and acquaintances. Will *you*, madam, or *you*, my lord, be so kind as to explain these seeming inconsistencies?"

"No," cried the earl, "to punish your curiosity, I will keep you in ignorance; but Marian is in waiting for me at your neighbor's, Mrs. Wilmot, and I must hasten to her--- you will see us both by five." Rising from his seat he took the offered hand of Mrs. Wilson and pressed it to his lips. To Emily he also extended his hand, and received hers in return, though with a face suffused with the color of the rose. Pendennyss held it to his heart for a moment with fervor, and kissing it, precipitately left the room. Emily concealed her face with her hands, and, dissolving in tears, sought the retirement of an adjoining apartment.

All these unaccountable movements filled Lady Chatterton with amazement, that would have been too painful for further endurance; and Mrs. Wilson, knowing that further concealment with so near a connexion would be impossible, if not unnecessary, entered into a brief explanation of the earl's masquerade (although ignorant herself of its cause, or of the means of supporting it), and his present relation with her niece.

"I declare it is provoking," cried Lady Chatterton, with a tear in her eye, "to have such ingenious plans as Derwent and I had made lost from the want of necessity in putting them in force. Your demure niece has deceived us all handsomely; and my rigid cousin, too--I will rate him soundly for his deception."

"I believe he already repents sincerely of his having practised it," said Mrs. Wilson, "and is sufficiently punished for his error by its consequence. A life of misery for four months is a serious penalty to a lover."

"Yes," said the other; "I am afraid his punishment was not confined to himself alone: he has made others suffer from his misconduct. I will rate him famously, depend upon it I will."

If anything, the interest felt by Lady Chatterton for her friend was increased by this discovery of the affections of Pendennyss, and a few hours were passed by the three, in we will not say sober delight, for transport would be a better word. Lady Chatterton frankly declared that she would rather see Emily the wife of the earl than of her brother, for *he* alone was good enough for her; and Mrs. Wilson felt an exhilaration of spirits, in the completion of her most sanguine wishes, that neither her years, her philosophy, nor even her religion, could entirely restrain. The face of Emily was a continued blush, her eye sparkled with the lustre of renewed hope, and her bosom was heaving with the purest emotions of happiness.

At the appointed hour the rattling of wheels announced the approach of the earl and his sister.

Pendennyss came into the room with a young woman of great personal beauty and extremely feminine manners, leaning on his arm. He first announced her to Mrs. Wilson as his sister, Lady Marian Denbigh, who received her with a frank cordiality that made them instantly acquainted. Emily, although confiding in the fullest manner in the truth and worth of her lover, had felt an inexplicable sensation of pleasure, as she heard the earl speak of his sister by the name of Marian; love is such an unquiet, and generally such an engrossing passion, that few avoid unnecessary uneasiness while under its influence, unless so situated as to enjoy a mutual confidence.

As this once so formidable Marian approached to salute her with an extended hand, Emily rose, with a face illumined with pleasure, to receive her. Marian viewed her for a moment intently, and folding her arms around her, whispered softly as she pressed her to her heart,

"My sister, my only sister."

Our heroine was affected to tears, and Pendennyss gently separating the two he loved best in the world, they soon became calm.

Lady Marian was extremely like her brother, and had a family resemblance to her cousin Harriet; but her manners were softer and more retiring, and she had a slight tinge of a settled melancholy. When her brother spoke she was generally silent, not in fear, but in love. She evidently regarded him amongst the first of human beings, and all her love was amply returned.

Both the aunt and niece studied the manners of the earl closely, and found several shades of distinction between what he was and what he had been. He was now the perfect man of the world, without having lost the frank sincerity which caused you to believe all he said. Had Pendennyss once told Mrs. Wilson, with his natural air and manner, "I am innocent," she would have believed him, and an earlier investigation would have saved them months of misery; but the consciousness of his deception had oppressed him with the curse of the wicked.

Pendennyss had lost that air of embarrassment and alarm which had so often startled the aunt, even in her hours of greatest confidence, and which had their original in the awkwardness of disguise. But he retained his softness, his respect, his modest diffidence of his opinions, although somewhat corrected now by his acknowledged experience and acquaintance with man.

Mrs. Wilson thought these decided trifling alterations in manner were improvements; but it required some days and a few tender speeches to reconcile Emily to any change in the appearance of Denbigh.

Lady Marian had ordered her carriage early, as she had not anticipated the pleasure she found, and was engaged to accompany her cousin, Lady Laura, to a fashionable rout that evening. Unwilling to be torn from ins newly found friends, the earl proposed that the three ladies should accompany his sister to Annerdale House, and then accept himself as an escort to their own residence. To this Harriet assented, and leaving a message for Chatterton, they entered the coach of Marian, and Pendennyss, mounting the dickey, drove off.

Annerdale House was amongst the best edifices of London. It had been erected in the preceding century, and Emily for a moment felt, as she went through its splendid apartments, that it threw a chill around her domestic affections; but the figure of Pendennyss by her side reconciled her to a magnificence she had been unused to, which looked the lord indeed; but with so much modesty and softness, and so much attention to herself, that before she left the house, Emily began to think it very possible to enjoy happiness even in the lap of splendor.

The names of Colonel Denbigh and Lady Laura were soon announced, and this formidable gentleman made his appearance, He resembled Pendennyss more than even the duke, and appeared about the same age.

Mrs. Wilson soon saw that she had no grounds for pitying Lady Laura. The colonel was a polished, elegant man, of evident good sense and knowledge of the world, and apparently devoted to his wife. He was called George frequently by all his relatives, and he, not unfrequently, used the same term himself in speaking to the earl. Something was said of a much admired bust, and the doors of a large library were opened to view it. Emily was running over the backs of a case of books, until her eye rested on one; and half smiling and blushing she turned to Pendennyss, who watched every movement, as she said, playfully,

"Pity me, my lord, and lend me this volume."

"What is it you read?" he asked, as he bowed his cheerful assent.

But Emily hid the book in her handkerchief. Pendennyss noticing an unwillingness, though an extremely playful one, to let him into the secret, examined the case, and perceiving her motive, smiled, as he took down another volume and said--

"I am not an Irish, but an English peer, Emily. You have the wrong volume."

Emily laughed, with deeper blushes, when she found her wishes detected, while the earl, opening the volume he held--the first of Debrett's Peerage--pointed with his finger to the article concerning his own family, and said to Mrs. Wilson, who had joined them at the instant--

"To-morrow, dear madam, I shall beg your attention to a melancholy tale, and which may, in some slight degree, extenuate the offence I was guilty of in assuming, or rather in maintaining an accidental disguise."

As he ended, he went to the others, to draw off their attention, while Emily and her aunt examined the paragraph. It was as follows:

"George Denbigh--Earl of Pendennyss--and Baron Lumley, of Lumley Castle--- Baron Pendennyss--Beaumaris, and Fitzwalter, born----, of----, in the year of----; a bachelor." The list of earls and nobles occupied several pages, but the closing article was as follows:

"George, the 21st earl, succeeded his mother Marian, late Countess of Pendennyss, in her own right, being born of her marriage with George Denbigh, Esq., a cousin-german to Frederick, the 9th Duke of Derwent."

"Heir apparent. The titles being to heirs general, will descend to his lordship's sister, Lady Marian Denbigh, should the present earl die without lawful issue."

As much of the explanation of the mystery of our tales, involved in the foregoing paragraphs, we may be allowed to relate in our own language, what Pendennyss made his friends acquainted with at different times, and in a manner suitable to the subject and his situation.

Chapter XLI

It was at the close of that war which lost this country the wealthiest and most populous of her American colonies, that a fleet of ships were returning from their service amongst the islands of the New World, to seek for their worn out and battered hulks, and equally weakened crews, the repairs and comforts of England and home.

The latter word, to the mariner the most endearing of all sounds, had, as it were, drawn together by instinct a group of sailors on the forecastle of the proudest ship of the squadron, who gazed with varied emotions on the land which gave them birth, but with one common feeling of joy that the day of attaining it was at length arrived.

The water curled from the bows of this castle of the ocean, in increasing waves and growing murmurs, that at times drew the attention of the veteran tar to their quickening progress, and having cheered his heart with the sight, he cast his experienced eye in silence on the swelling sails, to see if nothing more could be done to shorten the distance between him and his country.

Hundreds of eyes were fixed on the land of their birth, and hundreds of hearts were beating in that one vessel with the awakening delights of domestic love and renewed affections; but no tongue broke the disciplined silence of the ship into sounds that overcame the propitious ripple of the water.

On the highest summit of their towering mast floated a small blue flag, the symbol of authority, and beneath it paced a man to and fro the deck, who was abandoned by his inferiors to his more elevated rank. His square-built form and careworn features, which had lost the brilliancy of an English complexion, and hair whitened prematurely, spoke of bodily vigor, and arduous services which had put that vigor to the severest trials.

At each turn of his walk, as he faced the land of his nativity, a lurking smile stole over his sun-burnt features, and then a glance of his eye would scan the progress of the far-stretched squadron which obeyed his orders, and which he was now returning to his superiors, undiminished in numbers, and proud with victory.

By himself stood an officer in a uniform differing from all around him. His figure was small, his eye restless, quick, and piercing, and bent on those shores to which he was unwillingly advancing, with a look of anxiety and mortification, that showed him the late commander of those vessels around them, which, by displaying their double flags, manifested to the eye of the seaman a recent change of masters.

Occasionally the conqueror would stop, and by some effort of well meant, but rather uncouth civility, endeavor to soften the hours of captivity; efforts which were received with the courtesy of the most punctilious etiquette, but a restraint which showed that they were unwelcome.

It was, perhaps, the most unlucky moment that had occurred within the two months of their association, for an exchange of their better feelings. The honest heart of the English tar dilated with ill-concealed delight at his approach to the termination of labors performed with credit and honor, and his smiles and good humor, which partly proceeded from the feelings of a father and a friend, were daggers to the heart of his discomfited rival.

A third personage now appeared from the cabin of the vessel, and approached the spot where the adverse admirals at the moment were engaged in one of these constrained conferences.

The appearance and dress of this gentleman differed widely from the two just described. He was tall, graceful, and dignified; he was a soldier, and clearly of high rank. His carefully dressed hair concealed the ravages of time and on the quarter-deck of a first-rate his attire and manners were suited to a field-day in the park.

"I really insist, monsieur," cried the admiral, good-naturedly, "that you shall take part of my chaise to London. You are a stranger, and it will help to keep up your spirits by the way."

"You are very good, Monsieur Howell," replied the Frenchman, with a polite bow and forced smile, misconstruing ill-judged benevolence into a wish for his person to grace a triumph--"but I have accepted the offer Monsieur le General Denbigh was so good as to make me."

"The comte is engaged to me, Howell," said the general, with a courtly smile, "and, indeed, you must leave the ship to night, or as soon as we anchor.--But I shall take daylight and to-morrow."

"Well--well--Denbigh," exclaimed the other, rubbing his hands with pleasure as he viewed the increasing power of the wind, "only make yourselves happy, and I am contented."

A few hours intervened before they reached the Bay of Plymouth, and round the table, after their dinner, were seated the general and English admiral. The comte, under the pretence of preparing his things for a removal, had retired to his apartment to conceal his feelings;--and the captain of the ship was above, superintending the approach of the vessel to her anchorage. Two or three well emptied bottles of wine yet remained; but as the healths of all the branches of the House of Brunswick had been propitiated from their contents, with a polite remembrance of Louis XVI. and Marie Antoinette from General Denbigh, neither of the superiors was much inclined for action.

"Is the Thunderer in her station?" said the admiral to the signal lieutenant, who at that moment came below with a report.

"Yes, sir, and has answered."

"Very well; make the signal to prepare to anchor."

"Aye, aye, sir."

"And here, Bennet," to the retiring lieutenant--"call the transports all in shore of us."

"Three hundred and eighty-four, sir," said the officer, looking at his signal-book.

The admiral cast his eye at the book, and nodded an assent.

"And let the Mermaid--Flora--Weasel--Bruiser, and all the sloops lie well off, until we have landed the soldiers: the pilot says the channel is full of luggers, and Jonathan has grown very saucy."

The lieutenant made a complying bow, and was retiring to execute these orders, as Admiral Howell, taking up a bottle not yet entirely deserted by its former tenant, cried stoutly--"Here, Bennet--I forgot--take a glass of wine; drink success to ourselves, and defeat to the French all over the world."

The general pointed significantly to the adjoining cabin of the French admiral, as he pressed his hand on his lips for silence.

"Oh!" cried Admiral Howell, recollecting himself, continuing in a whisper, "you can drink it in your heart, notwithstanding."

The signal officer nodded, and drank the liquor. As he smacked his lips while going on deck, he thought to himself, these nabobs drink famous good wine.

Although the feelings of General Denbigh were under much more command and disciplined obedience than those of his friend, yet was he too unusually elated with his return to home and expected honors. If the admiral had captured a fleet, *he* had taken an island;--and hand in hand they had co-operated in unusual harmony through the difficulties of an arduous campaign. This rather singular circumstance was owing to their personal friendship. From their youth they had been companions, and although of very different characters and habits, chance had cemented their intimacy in more advanced life. While in subordinate stations, they had been associated together in service; and the general and admiral, in command of an army and fleet, had once before returned to England with less renown, as a colonel and a captain of a frigate. The great family influence of the soldier, with the known circumstance of their harmony, had procured them this later command, and home, with its comforts and rewards, was close before them. Pouring out a glass of Madeira, the general, who always calculated what he said, exclaimed,

"Peter--we have been friends from boys."

"To be sure we have," said the admiral, looking up in a little surprise at this unexpected commencement--"and it will not be my fault if we do not die such, Frederick."

Dying was a subject the general did not much delight in although of conspicuous courage in the field; and he proceeded to his more important purpose--"I could never find, although I have looked over our family tree so often, that we are in any manner related, Howell."

"I believe it is too late to mend that matter now," said the admiral, musing.

"Why no--hem--I think not, Howell; take a glass of this Burgundy."

The admiral shook his head with a stubborn resolution to taste nothing French, but he helped himself to a bountiful stock of Madeira, as he replied--

"I should like to know how you can bring it about this time of day, Denbigh."

"How much money will you be able to give that girl of yours, Peter?" said his friend, evading the point.

"Forty thousand down, my good fellow, and as much more when I die," cried the open-hearted sailor, with a nod of exultation.

"George, my youngest son, will not be rich--but Francis will be a duke, and have a noble estate; yet," said the general; meditating, "he is so unhappy in his disposition and uncouth in his manners, I cannot think of offering him to your daughter as a husband."

"Isabel shall marry a good-natured man, like myself, or not at all," said the admiral, positively, but not in the least suspecting the drift of his friend, who was influenced by anything but a regard for the lady's happiness.

Francis, his first born, was, in truth, as he had described; but his governing wish was to provide for his favorite George. Dukes could never want wives, but unportioned captains in the guards might.

"George is one of the best tempers in the world," said his father, with strong feeling, "and the delight of us all. I could wish he had been the heir to the family honors."

"*That* it is certainly too late to help," cried the admiral, wondering if the ingenuity of his friend could devise a remedy for this evil too.

"Too late, indeed," said the other, with a heavy sigh, "but Howell, what say you to matching Isabel with my favorite George?"

"Denbigh," cried the sailor, eyeing him keenly, "Isabel is my only child, and a dutiful, good girl; one that will obey orders if she breaks owners, as we sailors say. Now I did think of marrying her to a seaman, when a proper man came athwart my course; yet your son is a soldier, and that is next to being in the navy: if-so-be you had made him come aboard me, when I wanted you to, there would have been no objection at all: however, when occasion offers. I will overhaul the lad, and if I find him staunch he may turn in with Bell and welcome."

This was uttered in perfect simplicity, and with no intention of giving offence, partaking partly of the nature of a soliloquy; so the general, greatly encouraged, was about to push the point, when a gun was fired from their own ship.

"There's some of them lubberly transports won't mind our signals; they have had these soldiers so long on board, they get as clumsy as the red-coats themselves," muttered the admiral, hastening on deck to enforce his commands.

A shot or two, sent significantly in the direction of the wanderers, but so as not to hit them, restored order; and within an hour forty line of battle ships and a hundred transports were disposed in the best manner for convenience and safety.

On their presentation to their sovereign, both veterans were embellished with the riband of the Bath; and as their exploits filled the mouths of the newsmongers, and the columns of the public prints of the day, the new knights began to think more seriously of building a monument to their victories, in a union between their children. The admiral, however, determined to do nothing with his eyes shut, and he demanded a scrutiny.

"Where is the boy who is to be a duke?" exclaimed he, one day, when his friend had introduced the point with a view to a final arrangement. "Bell has good blood in her veins--is a tight built little vessel--clean heel'd and trim, and would make as good a duchess as the best of them; so Denbigh, I will begin by taking a survey of the senior." To this the general had no objection, as he well knew that Francis would be wide of pleasing the tastes of an open-hearted, simple man, like the sailor. They met, accordingly, for what the general facetiously called the review, and what the admiral innocently termed his survey, at the house of the former, when the young gentlemen were submitted to his inspection.

Francis Denbigh was about four and twenty, of a feeble body, and with a face marked with the small-pox, to approaching deformity; his eye was brilliant and piercing, but unsettled, and at times wild--his manner awkward, constrained, and timid. There would be seen, it is true, an intelligence and animation, which occasionally lighted his countenance into gleams of sunshine, that caused you to overlook the lesser accompaniments of complexion and features in the expression; but they were transient, and inevitably vanished whenever his father spoke or in any manner mingled in his pursuits.

An observer close as Mrs. Wilson, would have said that the feelings of the father and son were not such as ought to exist between parent and child.

But the admiral, who regarded model and rigging a good deal, satisfied himself with muttering, as he turned his eye on the junior--

"He may do for a duke--but I would not have him for a cockswain."

George was a year younger than Francis; in form, stature, and personal grace, the counterpart of his father; his eye was less keen but more attractive than that of his brother; his air open, polished, and manly.

"Ah!" thought the sailor, as he ended a satisfactory survey of the youth, "what a thousand pities Denbigh did not send him to sea!"

The thing was soon settled, and George was to be the happy man. Sir Peter concluded to dine with his friend, in order to settle preliminaries over the bottle by themselves; the young men and their mother being engaged to their uncle the duke.

"Well, Denbigh," cried the admiral, as the last servant withdrew, "when do you mean to have the young couple spliced?"

"Why," replied the wary soldier, who knew he could not calculate on obedience to his mandate with as great a certainty as his friend--"the better way is to bring the young people together, in order that they may become acquainted, you know."

"Acquainted--together--" cried his companion, in a little surprise, "what better way is there to bring them together, than to have them up before a priest, or to make them acquainted by letting them swing in the same hammock?"

"It might answer the end, indeed," said the general, with a smile, "but somehow or other, it is always the best method to bring young folks together, to let them have their own way in the affair for a time."

"Own way!" rejoined Sir Peter, bluntly, "did you ever find it answer to let a woman have her own way, Sir Frederick?"

"Not common women certainly, my good friend," said the general, "but such a girl as my intended daughter is an exception."

"I don't know that," cried the sailor; "Bell is a good girl, but she has her quirks and whims like all the sex."

"You have had no trouble with her as yet, I believe, Howell," said Sir Frederick cavalierly, throwing an inquiring glance on his friend at the same time.

"No, not yet--nor do I think she will ever dare to mutiny; but there has been one wishing to take her in tow already since we got in."

"How!" said the other in alarm, "who--what is he? some officer in the navy, I suppose."

"No, he was a kind of chaplain, one Parson Ives, a good sort of a youth enough, and a prodigious favorite with my sister, Lady Hawker."

"Well, what did you answer, Peter?" said his companion in increasing uneasiness; "did you put him off?"

"Off! to be sure I did--do you think I wanted a barber's clerk for a son-in-law? No, no, Denbigh; a soldier is bad enough, without having a preacher."

The general compressed his lips at this direct attack on a profession that he thought the most honorable of any in the world, in some resentment; but remembering the eighty thousand pounds, and accustomed to the ways of the other, he curbed his temper, and inquired--

"But Miss Howell--your daughter--how did she stand affected to this priest?"

"How--why--how?--why I never asked her."

"Never asked her?"

"No, never asked her: she is my daughter, you know, and bound to obey my orders, and I did not choose she should marry a parson; but, once for all, when is the wedding to take place?"

General Denbigh had indulged his younger son too blindly and too fondly to expect that implicit obedience the admiral calculated to a certainty on, and with every prospect of not being disappointed, from his daughter. Isabel Howell was pretty, mild, and timid, and unused to oppose any of her father's commands; but George Denbigh was haughty, positive, and self-willed, and unless the affair could be so managed as to make him a willing assistant in the courtship, his father knew it might be abandoned at once. He thought his son might be led, but not driven; and, relying on his own powers for managing, the general saw his only safety in executing the scheme was in postponing his advances for a regular siege to the lady's heart.

Sir Peter chafed and swore at this circumlocution: the thing could be done as well in a week as in a year; and the veterans, who, for a miracle, had agreed in their rival stations, and in doubtful moments of success, were near splitting on the point of marrying a girl of nineteen.

As Sir Peter both loved his friend, and had taken a prodigious fancy to the youth, he however was fain to submit to a short probation.

"You are always for going a round-about way to do a thing," said the admiral, as he yielded the point. "Now, when you took that battery, had you gone up in front, as I advised you, you would have taken it in ten minutes, instead of five hours."

"Yes," said the other, with a friendly shake of the hand at parting, "and lost fifty men in place of one by the step."

Chapter XLII

The Honorable General Denbigh was the youngest of three sons. His seniors, Francis and George, were yet bachelors. The death of a cousin had made Francis a duke while yet a child, and both he and his favorite brother George, had decided on lives of inactivity and sluggishness.

"When I die, brother," the oldest would say, "you will succeed me, and Frederick can provide heirs for the name hereafter."

This arrangement had been closely adhered to, and the two elder brothers reached the ages of fifty-five and fifty-six, without altering their condition. In the mean time, Frederick married a young woman of rank and fortune; the fruits of their union being the two young candidates for the hand of Isabel Howell.

Francis Denbigh, the eldest son of the general, was naturally diffident, and, in addition, it was his misfortune to be the reverse of captivating in external appearance. The small-pox sealed his doom;--ignorance, and the violence of the attack, left him indelibly impressed with the ravages of that dreadful disorder. Oh the other hand, his brother escaped without any vestiges of the complaint; and his spotless skin and fine open countenance, met the gaze of his mother, after the recovery of the two, in striking contrast to the deformed lineaments of his elder brother. Such an occurrence is sure to excite one of two feelings in the breast of every beholder--pity or disgust; and, unhappily for Francis, maternal tenderness, in his case, was unable to counteract the latter sensation. George become a favorite, and Francis a neutral. The effect was easy to be seen, and it was rapid, as it was indelible.

The feelings of Francis were sensitive to an extreme. He had more quickness, more sensibility, more real talent than George; which enabled him to perceive, and caused him to feel more acutely, the partiality of his mother.

As yet, the engagements and duties of the general had kept his children and, their improvements out of his sight; but at the ages of eleven and twelve, the feelings of a father, began, to take pride in the possession of his sons.

On his return from a foreign station, after an absence of two years, his children were ordered from school to meet him. Francis had improved in stature, but not in beauty; George had flourished in both.

The natural diffidence of the former was increased, by perceiving that he was no favorite, and the effect began to show itself on manners at no time engaging. He met his father with doubt, and he saw with anguish, that the embrace received by his brother much exceeded in warmth that which had been bestowed on himself.

"Lady Margaret," said the general to his wife, as he followed the boys as they retired from the dinner table, with his eyes, "it is a thousand pities George had not been the elder. *He* would have graced a dukedom or a throne. Frank is only fit for a parson."

This ill-judged speech was uttered sufficiently loud to be overheard by both the sons: on the younger, it made a pleasurable sensation for the moment. His father--his dear father, had thought him fit to be a king; and his father must be a judge, whispered his native vanity; but all this time the connexion between the speech and his brother's rights did not present themselves to his mind. George loved this brother too well, too sincerely, to have injured him even in thought; and so far as Francis was concerned, his vanity was as blameless as it was natural.

The effect produced on the mind of Francis was different both in substance and in degree. It mortified his pride, alarmed his delicacy, and wounded his already morbid sensibility to such an extent, as to make him entertain the romantic notion of withdrawing from the world, and of yielding a birthright to one so every way more deserving of it than himself.

From this period might be dated an opinion of Francis's, which never afterwards left him; he fancied he was doing injustice to another, and that other, a brother whom he ardently loved, by continuing to exist. Had he met with fondness in his parents, or sociability in his playfellows, these fancies would have left him as he grew into life. But the affections of his parents were settled on his more promising brother; and his manners daily increasing in their repulsive traits, drove his companions to the society of others, more agreeable to their own buoyancy and joy.

Had Francis Denbigh, at this age, met with a guardian clear-sighted enough to fathom his real character, and competent to direct his onward course, he would yet have become an ornament to his name and country, and a useful member of society. But no such guide existed. His natural guardians, in his particular case, were his worst enemies; and the boys left school for college four years afterwards, each advanced in his respective properties of attraction and repulsion.

Irreligion is hardly a worse evil in a family than favoritism. When once allowed to exist, in the breast of the parent, though hid apparently from all other eyes, its sad consequences begin to show themselves. Effects are produced, and we look in vain for the cause. The awakened sympathies of reciprocal caresses and fondness are mistaken for uncommon feelings, and the forbidding aspect of deadened affections is miscalled native sensibility.

In this manner the evil increases itself, until manners are formed, and characters created, that must descend with their possessor to the tomb.

In the peculiar formation of the mind of Francis Denbigh, the evil was doubly injurious. His feelings required sympathy and softness, and they met only with coldness and disgust. George alone was an exception to the rule. *He* did love his brother; but even his gaiety and spirits finally tired of the dull uniformity of the diseased habits of his senior.

The only refuge Francis found in his solitude, amidst the hundreds of the university, was in his muse and in the powers of melody. The voice of his family has been frequently mentioned in these pages; and if, as Lady Laura had intimated, there had ever been a siren in the race, it was a male one. He wrote prettily, and would sing these efforts of his muse to music of his own, drawing crowds around his windows, in the stillness of the night, to listen to sounds as melodious as they were mournful. His poetical efforts partook of the distinctive character of the man, being melancholy, wild, and sometimes pious.

George was always amongst the most admiring of his brother's auditors, and would feel a yearning of his heart towards him, at such moments, that was painful. But George was too young and too heedless, to supply the place of a monitor, or to draw his thoughts into a more salutary train. This was the *duty* of his parents, and should have been their *task*. But the world, his rising honors, and his professional engagements, occupied the time of the father; and fashion, parties, and pleasure, killed the time of his mother. When they did think of their children, it was of George; the painful image of Francis being seldom admitted to disturb their serenity.

George Denbigh was open-hearted without suspicion, and a favorite. The first quality taxed his generosity, the second subjected him to fraud, and the third supplied him with the means. But these means sometimes failed. The fortune of the general, though handsome, was not more than competent to support his style of living. He expected to be a duke himself one day, and was anxious to maintain an appearance now that would not disgrace his future elevation. A system of strict but liberal economy had been adopted in the case of his sons. They had, for the sake of appearances, a stated and equal allowance.

The duke had offered to educate the heir himself, and under his own eye. But to this Lady Margaret had found some ingenious excuse, and one that seemed to herself and the world honorable to her natural feeling; but had the offer been made to George, these reasons would have vanished in the desire to advance his interests, or to gratify his propensities. Such decisions are by no means uncommon; parents having once decided on the merits and abilities of their children, frequently decline the interference of third persons, since the improvement of their denounced offspring might bring their own judgment into question, if it did not convey an indirect censure on their justice.

The heedlessness of George brought his purse to a state of emptiness. His last guinea was gone, and two months were wanting to the end of the quarter. George had played and been cheated. He had ventured to apply to his mother for small sums, when his dress or some trifling indulgence required an advance; and always with success. But here were sixty guineas gone at a blow, and pride, candor, forbade his concealing the manner of his loss, if he made the application. This was dreadful; his own conscience reproached him, and he had so often witnessed the violence of his mother's resentments against Francis, for faults which appeared to him very trivial, not to stand in the utmost dread of her more just displeasure in the present case.

Entering the apartment of his brother, in this disturbed condition, George threw himself into a chair, and with his face concealed between his hands, sat brooding over his forlorn situation.

"George!" said his brother, soothingly, "you are in distress; can I relieve you in any way?"

"Oh no--no--no--Frank; it is entirely out of your power."

"Perhaps not, my dear brother," continued the other, endeavoring to draw his hand into his own.

"Entirely! entirely!" said George. Then springing up in despair, he exclaimed, "But I must live--I cannot die."

"Live! die!" cried Francis, recoiling in horror. "What do you mean by such language? Tell me, George, am I not your brother? Your only brother and best friend?"

Francis felt he had no friend if George was not that friend, and his face grew pale while the tears flowed rapidly down his cheeks.

George could not resist such an appeal. He caught the hand of his brother and made him acquainted with his losses and his wants.

Francis mused some little time over his narration, ere he broke silence.

"It was all you had?"

"The last shilling," cried George, beating his head with his hand.

"How much will you require to make out the quarter?"

"Oh I must have at least fifty guineas, or how can I live at all?"

The ideas of life in George were connected a good deal with the manner it was to be enjoyed. His brother appeared struggling with himself, and then turning to the other, continued,

"But surely, under present circumstances, you could make less do."

"Less, never--hardly that"--interrupted George, vehemently. "If Lady Margaret did not inclose me a note now and then, how could we get along at all? don't you find it so yourself, brother?"

"I don't know," said Francis, turning pale--

"Don't know!" cried George, catching a view of his altered countenance--"you get the money, though?"

"I do not remember it," said the other, sighing heavily.

"Francis," cried George, comprehending the truth, "you shall share every shilling I receive in future--you shall--indeed you shall."

"Well, then," rejoined Francis with a smile, "it is a bargain; and you will receive from me a supply in your present necessities."

Without waiting for an answer, Francis withdrew into an inner apartment, and brought out the required sum for his brother's subsistence for two months. George remonstrated, but Francis was positive; he had been saving, and his stock was ample for his simple habits without it.

"Besides, you forget we are partners, and in the end I shall be a gainer."

George yielded to his wants and his brother's entreaties, and he gave him great credit for the disinterestedness of the act. Several weeks passed without any further allusion to this disagreeable subject, which had at least the favorable result of making George more guarded and a better student.

The brothers, from this period, advanced gradually in those distinctive qualities which were to mark the future men; George daily improving in grace and attraction, Francis, in an equal ratio, receding from those very attainments which it was his too great desire to possess. In the education of his sons, General Denbigh had preserved the appearance of impartiality; his allowance to each was the same: they were at the same college, they had been at the same school; and if Frank did not improve as much as his younger brother, it was unquestionably his own obstinacy and stupidity, and surely not want of opportunity or favor.

Such, then, were the artificial and accidental causes, which kept a noble, a proud, an acute but a diseased mind, in acquirements much below another every way its inferior, excepting in the happy circumstance of wanting those very excellences, the excess and indiscreet management of which proved the ruin instead of the blessing of their possessor.

The duke would occasionally rouse himself from his lethargy, and complain to the father, that the heir of his honors was far inferior to his younger brother in acquirements, and remonstrate against the course which produced such an unfortunate inequality. On these occasions a superficial statement of his system from the general met the objection; they cost the same money, and he was sure he not only wished but did everything an indulgent parent could, to render Francis worthy of his future honors. Another evil of the admission of feelings of partiality, in the favor of one child, to the prejudice of another, is that the malady is contagious as well as lasting: it exists without our own knowledge, and it seldom fails to affect those around us. The uncle soon learnt to distinguish George as the hope of the family, yet Francis must be the heir of its honors, and consequently of its wealth.

The duke and his brother were not much addicted to action, hardly to reflection; but if anything could rouse them to either, it was the reputation of the house of Denbigh. Their ideas of reputation, it is true, were of their own forming.

The hour at length drew near when George expected a supply from the ill-judged generosity of his mother; it came, and with a heart beating with pleasure, the youth flew to the room of Francis with a determination to force the whole of his twenty pounds on his acceptance. On throwing open his door, he saw his brother evidently striving to conceal something behind his books. It was at the hour of breakfast, and George had intended for a novelty to share his brother's morning repast. They always met at dinner, but the other meals were made in their own rooms. George looked in vain for the usual equipage of the table; suspicion flashed upon him; he threw aside the books, and a crust of bread and a glass of water met his eye; the truth now flashed upon him in all its force.

"Francis, my brother, to what has my extravagance reduced you!" exclaimed the contrite George with a heart nearly ready to burst. Francis endeavored to explain, but a sacred regard to the truth held him tongue-tied, until dropping his head on the shoulder of George, he sobbed out--

"It is a trifle; nothing to what I would do for you, my brother."

George felt all the horrors of remorse, and was much too generous to conceal his error any longer; he wrote a circumstantial account of the whole transaction to Lady Margaret.

Francis for a few days was a new being. He had acted nobly, his conscience approved of his motives, and of his delicate concealment of them; he in fact began to think there were in himself the seeds of usefulness, as his brother, who from this moment began to understand his character better, attached himself more closely to him.

The eye of Francis met that of George with the look of acknowledged affection, his mind became less moody, and his face was sometimes embellished with a smile.

The reply of their mother to the communication of George threw a damp on the revived hopes of the senior, and drove him back into himself with tenfold humility.

"I am shocked, my child, to find that you have lowered yourself, and forgot the family you belong to, so much as to frequent those gambling-houses, which ought not to be suffered in the neighborhood of the universities: when at a proper age and in proper company, your occasional indulgence at cards I could not object to, as both your father and myself sometimes resort to it as an amusement, but never in low company. The consequence of mingling in such society is, that you were cheated, and such will always be your lot unless you confine yourself to associates more becoming your rank and illustrious name.

"As to Francis, I see every reason to condemn the course he has taken. Being the senior by a year, he should have taken the means to prevent your falling into such company; and he should have acquainted me immediately with your loss, in place of wounding your pride by subjecting you to the mortification of receiving a pecuniary obligation from one so little older than yourself, and exposing his own health by a diet on bread and water, as you wrote me, for a whole month. Both the general and myself are seriously displeased with him, and think of separating you, as you thus connive at each other's follies."

George was too indignant to conceal this letter and the reflections of Francis were dreadful.

For a short time he actually meditated suicide, as the only method of removing himself from before the advancement of George. Had not George been more attentive and affectionate than formerly, the awful expedient might have been resorted to.

From college the young men went, one into the army and the other to the mansion of his uncle. George became an elegant, gay, open-hearted, admired captain in the guards; and Francis stalked through the halls of his ancestors, their acknowledged future lord, but a misanthrope; hateful to himself and disagreeable to all around him.

This picture may be highly wrought, but the effects, in the case of Francis, were increased by the peculiar tone of his diseased state of mind. The indulgence of favoritism, nevertheless, always brings its own sad consequences, in a greater or less degree, while it seldom fails to give sorrow and penitence to the bosom of the parents.

Chapter XLIII

No little art and management had been necessary to make the admiral auxiliary to the indirect plan proposed by his friend to bring George and Isabel together. This, however, effected, the general turned his whole strategy to the impression to be made on the heart of the young gentleman.

Sir Frederick Denbigh had the same idea of the virtue of management as the Dowager Lady Chatterton, but he understood human nature better.

Like a prudent officer, his attacks were all masked, and, like a great officer, they seldom failed of success.

The young couple were thrown in each other's way, and as Isabel was extremely attractive, somewhat the opposite to himself in ardor of temperament and vivacity, modest, and sensible, it cannot be expected that the association was maintained by the youth with perfect impunity. Within a couple of months he fancied himself desperately in love with Isabel Howell; and, in truth, he had some reason for the supposition.

The general watched every movement of his son with a wary and vigilant eye--occasionally adding fuel to the flame, by drawing his attention to projects of matrimony in other quarters, until George began to think he was soon to undergo a trial of his constancy, and in consequence he armed himself with a double portion of admiration for his Isabel, in order to enable himself to endure the persecution; while the admiral several times endangered the success of the whole enterprise by volunteer contributions to the hopes of the young man, which only escaped producing an opposite effect to that which was intended, by being mistaken for the overflowings of good nature and friendship.

After suffering his son to get, as he thought, sufficiently entangled in the snares of Cupid, Sir Frederick determined to fire a volley from one of his masked batteries, which he rightly judged would bring on a general engagement. They were sitting at the table after dinner, alone, when the general took the advantage of the name of Miss Howell being accidentally mentioned, to say--

"By the by, George, my friend the admiral said something yesterday on the subject of your being so much with his daughter. I wish you to be cautious, and not to give the old sailor offence in any way, for he is my particular friend."

"He need be under no violent apprehensions," cried George, coloring highly with shame and pride, "I am sure a Denbigh is no unworthy match for a daughter of Sir Peter Howell."

"Oh! to be sure not, boy, we are as old a house as there is in the kingdom, and as noble too; but the admiral has queer notions, and, perhaps, he has some cub of a sailor in his eye for a son-in-law. Be prudent, my boy, be prudent; that is all I ask of you."

The general, satisfied with the effect he had produced, carelessly arose from his seat, and joined Lady Margaret in her drawing-room.

George remained for several minutes musing on his father's singular request, as well as the admiral's caution, when he sprang from his seat, caught up his hat and sword, and in ten minutes rang at Sir Peter's door in Grosvenor Square. He was admitted, and ascending to the drawing-room, he met the admiral on his way out. Nothing was further from the thoughts of the veteran than a finesse like the general's; and, delighted to see George on the battle-ground, he pointed significantly over his shoulder towards the door of the room Isabel was in, and exclaimed, with a good-natured smile,

"There she is, my hearty; lay her aside, and hang me if she don't strike. I say, George, faint heart never won fair lady: remember that, my boy; no, nor a French ship."

George would have been at some loss to have reconciled this speech to his father's caution, if time had been allowed him to think at all; but the door being open he entered, and found Isabel endeavoring to hide her tears.

The admiral, dissatisfied from the beginning with the tardy method of despatching things, thought he might be of use in breaking the ice for George, by trumpeting his praises on divers occasions to his daughter. Under all circumstances, he thought she might be learning to love the man, as he was to be her husband; and speeches like the following had been frequent of late from the parent to the child:

"There's that youngster, George Denbigh: now, Bell, is he not a fine looking lad? Then I know he is brave. His father before him, was good stuff and a true Englishman. What a proper husband he would make for a young woman, he loves his king and country so; none of your new-fangled notions about religion and government, but a sober, religious churchman; that is, as much so, girl, as you can expect in the guards. No Methodist, to be sure;--it's a great pity he wasn't sent to sea, don't you think so? But cheer up, girl, one of these days he may be taking a liking to you yet."

Isabel, whose fears taught her the meaning of these eloquent praises of Captain Denbigh, listened to these harangues in silence, and often meditated on their import by herself in tears.

George approached the sofa on which the lady was seated before she had time to conceal the traces of her sorrow, and in a voice softened by emotion, he took her hand gently as he said,--

"What can have occasioned this distress to Miss Howell. If anything in my power to remove, or which a life devoted to her service can mitigate, she has only to command me to find a cheerful obedience."

"The trifling causes of sorrow in a young woman," replied Isabel, endeavoring to smile, "will hardly require such serious services to remove them."

But the lady was extremely interesting at the moment. George was goaded by his father's caution, and urged on by his own feelings, with great sincerity, and certainly much eloquence, he therefore proffered his love and hand to the acceptance of his mistress.

Isabel heard him in painful silence. She respected him, and dreaded his power over her father; but, unwilling to abandon hopes to which she yet clung as to her spring of existence, with a violent effort she determined to throw herself on the generosity of her lover.

During her father's late absence Isabel had, as usual, since the death of her mother, been left with his sister, and had formed an attachment for a young clergyman, a younger son of a baronet, and the present Dr. Ives. The inclination had been mutual; and as Lady Hawker knew her brother to be perfectly indifferent to money, she could see no possible objection to its indulgence.

On his return, Ives made his proposals, as related; and although warmly backed by the recommendations of the aunt, he was refused. Out of delicacy the wishes of Isabel had not been mentioned by her clerical lover, and the admiral supposed he had only complied with his agreement with the general, without in any manner affecting the happiness of his daughter by his answer. But the feelings which prompted the request still remained in full vigor in the lovers; and Isabel now, with many blushes and some hesitation of utterance, made George fully acquainted with the state of her heart, giving him at the same time to understand that he was the only obstacle to her happiness.

It cannot be supposed that George heard her without pain or mortification. The struggle with self-love was a severe one, but his better feelings prevailed, and he assured the anxious Isabel that from his importunities she had nothing to apprehend in future. The grateful girl overwhelmed him with thanks, and George had to fly ere he repented of his own generosity.

Miss Howell intimated, in the course of her narrative, that a better understanding existed between their parents than the caution of the general had discovered to his unsuspecting child, and George was determined to know the worst at once.

At supper he mentioned, as if in remembrance of his father's injunction, that he had been to take his leave of Miss Howell, since he found his visits gave uneasiness to her friends. "On the whole," he added, endeavoring to yawn carelessly, "I believe I shall visit there no more."

"Nay, nay," returned Sir Frederick, a little displeased at his son's obedience, "I meant no such thing. Neither the admiral nor myself, has the least objection to your visiting in moderation; indeed, you may marry the girl with all our hearts, if you can agree."

"But we can't agree, I take it," said George, looking up at the wall.

"Why not? what hinders?' cried his father unguardedly.

"Only--only I don't like her," said the son, tossing off a glass of wine, which nearly strangled him.

"You don't," cried the general with great warmth, thrown entirely off his guard by this unexpected declaration "and may I presume to ask the reason why you do not like Miss Howell, sir?"

"Oh! you know, one never pretends to give a reason for this sort of feeling, my dear sir."

"Then," cried his father with increasing heat, "you must allow me to say, my dear sir, that the sooner you get rid of these sort of feelings the better. I choose you shall not only like, but love Miss Howell; and this I have promised her father."

"I thought that the admiral was displeased with my coming to his house so much--or did I not understand you this morning?"

"I know nothing of his displeasure, and care less. He has agreed that Isabel shall be your wife, and I have passed my word to the engagement; and if, sir, you wish to be considered as my son, you will prepare to comply."

George was expecting to discover some management on the part of his father, but by no means so settled an arrangement, and his anger was in proportion to the deception.

To annoy Isabel any further was out of the question; to betray her, base; and the next morning he sought an audience with the Duke. To him he mentioned his wish for actual service, but hinted that the maternal fondness of Lady Margaret was averse to his seeking it. This was true, and George now pressed his uncle to assist him in effecting an exchange.

The boroughs of the Duke of Derwent were represented by loyal members of parliament, his two brothers being contemporary with Mr. Benfield in that honor; and a request from a man who sent six members to the Commons, besides having a seat in the Lords in his own person, must be listened to.

Within the week George ceased to be a captain in the guards, and became lieutenant-colonel of a regiment under orders for America.

Sir Frederick soon became sensible of the error his warmth had led him into, and endeavored, by soothing and indulgence, to gain the ground he had so unguardedly lost. But terrible was his anger, and bitter his denunciations, when his son acquainted him with his approaching embarkation with his new regiment for America. They quarrelled; and as the favorite child had never, until now, been thwarted or spoken harshly to, they parted in mutual disgust. With his mother George was more tender; and as Lady Margaret never thought the match such as the descendant of two lines of dukes was entitled to form, she almost pardoned the offence in the cause.

"What's this here?" cried Sir Peter Howell, as he ran over a morning paper at the breakfast table: "Captain Denbigh, late of the guards, has been promoted to the Lieutenant-Colonelcy of the ---- Foot, and sails to-morrow to join that regiment, now on its way to America."

"It's a lie, Bell!--it's all a lie! not but what he ought to be there, too, serving his king and country; but he never would serve you so."

"Me?" said Isabel, with a heart throbbing with the contending feelings of admiration for George's generosity, and delight at her own deliverance. "What have I to do with the movements of Mr. Denbigh?"

"What!" cried her father in astonishment; "a'n't you to be his wife, a'n't it all agreed upon--that is, between Sir Frederick and me, which is the same thing, you know--"

Here he was interrupted by the sudden appearance of the general himself, who had just learnt the departure of his son and hastened, with the double purpose of breaking the intelligence to his friend, and of making his own peace.

"See here, Denbigh," exclaimed the admiral, pointing to the paragraph, "what do you say to that?"

"Too true--too true, my dear friend," replied the general shaking his head mournfully.

"Hark ye, Sir Frederick Denbigh," cried the admiral fiercely; "did you not say that your son George was to marry my daughter?"

"I certainly did, Sir Peter, and am sorry to say that, in defiance of my entreaties and commands, he has deserted his home, and, in consequence, I have discarded him for ever."

"Now, Denbigh," said the admiral, a good deal mollified by this declaration, "have I not always told you, that in the army you know nothing of discipline? Why, sir, if he was a son of mine, he should marry blindfolded, if I chose to order it. I wish, now, Bell had an offer, and dared to refuse it."

"There is the barber's clerk, you know," said the general, a good deal irritated by the contemptuous manner of his friend.

"And what of that, Sir Frederick?" said the sailor sternly; "if I choose her to marry a quill-driver, she shall comply."

"Ah! my good friend," said the general, willing to drop the disagreeable subject, "I am afraid we shall both find it more difficult to control the affections of our children than we at first imagined."

"You do, General Denbigh?" said the admiral, with a curl of contempt on his lip; and ringing the bell violently, he bid the servant send his young lady to him.

On the appearance of Isabel, her father inquired with an air of settled meaning where young Mr. Ives resided. It was only in the next street, and a messenger was sent to him, with Sir Peter Howell's compliments, and a request to see him without a moment's delay.

"We'll see, we'll see, my old friend, who keeps the best discipline," muttered the admiral, as he paced up and down the room, in eager expectation of the return of his messenger.

The wondering general gazed on his friend, to ascertain if he was out of his senses. He knew he was quick to decide, and excessively obstinate, but he did not think him so crazy as to throw away his daughter in a fit of spleen. It never occurred to Sir Frederick, however, that the engagement with himself was an act of equal injustice and folly, because it was done with more form and deliberation, which, to the eye of sober reason, would rather make the matter worse. Isabel sat in trembling suspense for the issue of the scene, and Ives in a few minutes made his appearance in no little alarm.

On entering, the admiral addressed him abruptly, by inquiring if he still wished to marry that girl, pointing to his daughter. The reply was an eager affirmative. Sir Peter beckoned to Isabel, who approached, covered with blushes; and her father having placed her hand in that of her lover, with an air of great solemnity he gave them his blessing. The young people withdrew to another room at Sir Peter's request, when he turned to his friend, delighted with his own decision and authority, and exclaimed,

"There, Fred. Denbigh, that is what I call being minded."

The general had penetration enough to see that the result was agreeable to both the young people, a thing he had long apprehended; and being glad to get rid of the affair in any way that did not involve him in a quarrel with his old comrade, he gravely congratulated the admiral on his good fortune and retired.

"Yes, yes," said Sir Peter to himself, as he paced up and down his room, "Denbigh is mortified enough, with his joy, and felicity, and grand-children. I never had any opinion of their manner of discipline at all; too much bowing and scraping. I'm sorry, though, he is a priest; not but what a priest may be as good a man as another, but let him behave ever so well, he can only get to be a bishop at the most. Heaven forbid he should ever get to be a Pope! After all, his boys may be admirals if they behave themselves;" and he went to seek his daughter, having in imagination manned her nursery with vice and rear admirals in embryo by the half dozen.

Sir Peter Howell survived the marriage of his daughter but eighteen months; yet that was sufficient time to become attached to his invaluable son-in-law. Mr. Ives insensibly led the admiral, during his long indisposition, to a more correct view of sacred things, than he had been wont to entertain; and the old man breathed his last, blessing both his children for their kindness, and with an humble hope of future happiness. Some time before his death, Isabel, whose conscience had always reproached her with the deception practised on her father, and with the banishment of George from his country and home, threw herself at the feet of Sir Peter and acknowledged her transgression.

The admiral heard her in astonishment, but not in anger. His opinions of life had sensibly changed, and his great cause of satisfaction with his new son removed all motives for regret for anything but for the fate of poor George. With the noble forbearance and tenderness of the young man to his daughter, the hardy veteran was sensibly touched; and his entreaties with

Sir Frederick made his peace with a father already longing for the return of his only hope.

The admiral left Colonel Denbigh his blessing, and his favorite pistols, as a remembrance of his esteem; but he did not live to see the reunion with his family.

George had soon learnt, deprived of hope and in the midst of novelty, to forget a passion which could no longer be prosperous; and two years from his departure returned to England, glowing in health, and improved in person and manners by a more extensive knowledge of the world and mankind.

Chapter XLIV

During the time occupied by the foregoing events, Francis continued a gloomy inmate of his uncle's house. The duke and his brother George were too indolent and inactive in their minds to pierce the cloud that mortification and deadened affections had drawn around the real character of their nephew; and although he was tolerated as the heir, he was but little loved as a man.

In losing his brother, Francis lost the only human being with whom he possessed any sympathies in common; and he daily drew more and more into himself, in gloomy meditation on his forlorn situation, in the midst of wealth and expected honors. The attentions he received were paid to his rank, and Francis had penetration enough to perceive it. His visits to his parents were visits of ceremony, and in time all parties came to look to their termination with pleasure, as to the discontinuance of heartless and forced civilities.

Affection, even in the young man, could not endure, repulsed as his feelings were, for ever; and in the course of three years, if his attachments were not alienated from his parents, his ardor had become much abated.

It is a dreadful truth, that the bonds of natural affection can be broken by injustice and contumely; and it is yet more to be deplored, that when from such causes we loosen the ties habit and education have drawn around us, a reaction in our feelings commences; we seldom cease to love, but we begin to hate. Against such awful consequences it is one of the most solemn duties of the parent to provide in season; and what surer safeguard is there, than to inculcate those feelings which teach the mind to love God, and in so doing induce love to the whole human family?

Sir Frederick and Lady Margaret attended the church regularly, repeated the responses with much decency, toasted the church next to the king, even appeared at the altars of their God, and continued sinners. From such sowings, no good fruit could be expected to flourish: yet Francis was not without his hours of devotion; but his religion was, like himself, reserved, superstitious, ascetic, and gloomy. He never entered into social worship: if he prayed it was with an ill-concealed wish to end this life of care. If he returned thanks, it was with a bitterness that mocked the throne before which he was prostrate. Such pictures are revolting; but their originals have and do exist; for what enormity is there of which human frailty, unchecked by divine assistance, may not be guilty?

Francis received an invitation to visit a brother of his mother's at his seat in the country, about the time of the expected return of George from America; and in compliance with the wishes of his uncles he accepted it. The house was thronged with visitors, and many of them were ladies. To these, the arrival of the unmarried heir of the house of Derwent was a subject of no little interest. His character had, however, preceded him, and a few days of his awkward and, as they conceived, sullen deportment, drove them back to their former beaux, with the exception of one; and she was not only amongst the fairest of the throng, but decidedly of the highest pretensions on the score of birth and fortune.

Marian Lumley was the only surviving child of the last Duke of Annerdale, with whom had expired the higher honors of his house. But the Earldom of Pendennyss, with numerous ancient baronies, were titles in fee; and together with his princely estates had descended to his daughter as heir-general of the family. A peeress in her own right, with an income far exceeding her utmost means of expenditure, the lovely Countess of Pendennyss was a prize aimed at by all the young nobles of the empire.

Educated in the midst of flatterers and dependants she had become haughty, vain, and supercilious; still she was lovely, and no one knew better how to practise the most winning arts of her sex, when whim or interest prompted her to the trial.

Her host was her guardian and relative; and through his agency she had rejected, at the age of twenty, numerous suitors for her hand. Her eyes were fixed on the ducal coronet; and unfortunately for Francis Denbigh, he was, at the time, the only man of the proper age who could elevate her to that enviable distinction in the kingdom; and an indirect measure of her own had been the means of his invitation to the country.

Like the rest of her young companions, Marian was greatly disappointed on the view of her intended captive, and for a day or two she abandoned him to his melancholy and himself. But ambition was her idol; and to its powerful rival, love, she was yet a stranger. After a few struggles with her inclinations the consideration that their united fortunes and family alliances would make one of the wealthiest and most powerful houses in the kingdom, prevailed. Such early sacrifices of the inclinations in a woman of her beauty, youth and accomplishments, may excite surprise; but where the mind is left uncultivated by the hand of care, the soul untouched by the love of goodness, the human heart seldom fails to set up an idol of its own to worship. In the Countess of Pendennyss this idol was pride.

The remainder of the ladies, from ceasing to wonder at the manners of Francis, had made them the subject of their mirth; and nettled at his apparent indifference to their society, which they erroneously attributed to his sense of his importance, they overstepped the bounds of good-breeding in manifesting their displeasure.

"Mr. Denbigh," cried one of the most thoughtless and pretty of the gay tribe to him one day, as Francis sat in a corner abstracted from the scene around him, "when do you mean to favor the world with your brilliant ideas in the shape of a book?"

"Oh! no doubt soon," said a second; "and I expect they will be homilies, or another volume to the Whole Duty of Man."

"Rather," cried a third, with bitter irony, "another canto to the Rape of the Lock, his ideas are so vivid and full of imagery."

"Or, what do you think," said a fourth, speaking in a voice of harmony, and tones of the most soothing tenderness, "of pity and compassion, for the follies of those inferior minds, who cannot enjoy the reflections of a good sense and modesty peculiarly his own?"

This might also be irony; and Francis thought it so; but the tones were so soft and conciliating, that with a face pale with his emotions, he ventured to look up and met the eye of Marian, fixed on him in an expression that changed his death-like hue into the color of vermillion.

He thought of this speech; he reasoned on it; he dreamt on it. But for the looks which accompanied it, like the rest of the party, he would have thought it the cruellest cut of them all. But that look, those eyes, that voice, what a commentary on her language did they not afford!

Francis was not long in suspense; the next morning an excursion was proposed, which included all but himself in its arrangements. He was either too reserved or too proud to offer services which were not required.

Several gentlemen had contended for the honor of driving the countess in a beautiful phaeton of her own. They grew earnest in their claims: one had been promised by its mistress with an opportunity of trying the ease of the carriage; another was delighted with the excellent training of her horses; in short, all had some particular claim to the distinction, which was urged with a warmth and pertinacity proportionate to the value of the prize to be obtained. Marian heard the several claimants with an ease and indifference natural to her situation, and ended the dispute by saying--

"Gentlemen, as I have made so many promises from the dread of giving offence, I must throw myself on the mercy of Mr. Denbigh, who alone, with the best claims, does not urge them; to you then," continued she, approaching him with the whip which was to be given the victor, "I adjudge the prize, if you will condescend to accept it."

This was uttered with one of her most attractive smiles, and Francis received the whip with an emotion that he with difficulty could control.

The gentlemen were glad to have the contest decided by adjudging the prize to one so little dangerous, and the ladies sneered at her choice as they left the house.

There was something so soothing in the manners of Lady Pendennyss, she listened to the little he said with such a respectful attention, was so anxious to have him give his opinions, that the unction of flattery, thus sweetly applied, and for the first time, could not fail of its wonted effects.

The communications thus commenced were continued. It was so easy to be attentive, by being simply polite to one unused to notice of any kind, that Marian found the fate of the young man in her hands almost as soon as she attempted to control it.

A new existence opened upon Francis, as day after day she insensibly led him to a display of powers he was unconscious until now of possessing himself. His self-respect began to increase, his limited pleasures to multiply, and he could now look around him with a sense of participation in the delights of life, as he perceived himself of consequence to this much admired woman.

Trifling incidents, managed on her part with consummate art, had led him to the daring inference that he was not entirely indifferent to her; and Francis returned the incipient affection of his mistress with a feeling but little removed from adoration. Week flew by after week, and still he lingered at the residence of his kinsman, unable to tear himself from the society of one so worshipped, and yet afraid to take a step by making a distinct declaration which might involve him in disgrace or ridicule.

The condescension of the countess increased, and she had indirectly given him the most flattering assurances of his success, when George, just arrived from America, having first paid his greetings to his reconciled parents, and the happy couple of his generosity, flew to the arms of his brother in Suffolk.

Francis was overjoyed to see George, and George delighted in the visible improvement of his brother. Still Francis was far, very far behind his junior in graces of mind and body; indeed, few men in England were more adapted by nature and education for female society than was Colonel Denbigh at the period of which we write.

Marian witnessed all his attractions, and deeply felt their influence; for the first time she felt the emotions of the gentle passion; and after having sported in the gay world, and trifled with the feelings of others for years, the countess in her turn became an unwilling victim to its power. George met her flame with a corresponding ardor, and the struggle between ambition and love became severe; the brothers unconsciously were rivals.

Had George for a moment suspected the situation of the feelings of Francis, his very superiority in the contest would have induced him to retreat from the unnatural rivalry. Had the elder dreamt of the views of his junior, he would have abandoned his dearest hopes in utter despair. Francis had so long been accustomed to consider George as his superior in everything, that a competition with him would have appeared desperate. Marian contrived to keep both in hopes, undecided herself which to choose, and perhaps ready to yield to the first applicant. A sudden event, however, removed all doubts, and decided the fate of the three.

The Duke of Derwent and his bachelor brother became so dissatisfied with the character of their future heir, that they as coolly set about providing themselves with wives as they had performed any other ordinary transaction of life, They married cousins, and on the same day the choice of the ladies was assigned between them by lots; and if his grace got the prettier, his brother certainly got the richest; under the circumstances a very tolerable distribution of fortune's favors.

These double marriages dissolved the charm of Francis, and Lady Pendennyss determined to consult her wishes; a little pointed encouragement brought out the declaration of George, and he was accepted.

Francis, who had never communicated his feelings to any one but the lady, and that only indirectly, was crushed by the blow. He continued in public until the day of their union; was present, composed and silent; but it was the silence of a mountain whose volcanic contents had not reached the surface. The same day he disappeared, and every inquiry after him proved fruitless; search was baffled, and for seven years it was not known what had become of the general's eldest son.

George on marrying resigned his commission, at the earnest entreaties of his wife, and retired to one of her seats, to the enjoyment of ease and domestic love. The countess was enthusiastically attached to him; and as motives for the indulgence of coquetry were wanting, her character became gradually improved by the contemplation of the excellent qualities of her generous husband.

A lurking suspicion of the cause of Francis's sudden disappearance rendered her uneasy at times; but Marian was too much beloved, too happy, in the enjoyment of too many honors, and of too great wealth, to be open to the convictions of conscience. It is in our hours of pain and privation that we begin to feel its sting: if we are prosperous, we fancy we reap the fruits of our own merit; but if we are unfortunate, the voice of truth seldom fails to remind us that we are deserving of our fate:--a blessed provision of Providence that often makes the saddest hours of our earthly career the morn of a day that is to endure for ever.

General Denbigh and Lady Margaret both died within five years of the marriage of their favorite child, although both lived to see their descendant, in the person of the infant Lord Lumley.

The duke and his brother George were each blessed with offspring, and in these several descendants of the different branches of the family of Denbigh may be seen the different personages of our history. On the birth of her youngest child, the Lady Marian, the Countess of Pendennyss sustained a shock in her health from which she never wholly recovered: she became nervous, and lost most of her energy both of mind and body. Her husband was her solace; his tenderness remaining unextinguished, while his attentions increased.

As the fortune of Ives and Isabel put the necessity of a living out of the question, and no cure offering for the acceptance of the first, he was happy to avail himself of an offer to become domestic chaplain to his now intimate friend, Mr. Denbigh. For the first six years they were inmates of Pendennyss Castle. The rector of the parish was infirm, and averse to a regular assistant; but the unobtrusive services of Mr. Ives were not less welcome to the pastor than to his parishioners.

Employed in the duties which of right fell to the incumbent, and intrusted with the spiritual guardianship of the dependants of the castle, our young clergyman had ample occupation for all his time, if not a sufficient theatre for his usefulness. Isabel and himself remained the year round in Wales, and the first dawnings of education received by Lord Lumley were those he acquired conjointly with Francis from the care of the latter's father. They formed, with the interval of the time spent by Mr. Denbigh and Lady Pendennyss in town in winter, but one family. To the gentleman, the attachment of the grateful Ives was as strong as it was lasting. Mrs. Ives never ceased to consider him as a self-devoted victim to her happiness; and although a far more brilliant lot had awaited him by the change, yet her own husband could not think it a more happy one.

The birth of Lady Marian had already, in its consequences, begun, to throw a gloom round the domestic comforts of Denbigh, when he was to sustain another misfortune in a separation from his friends.

Mr., now Dr. Ives, had early announced his firm intention, whenever an opportunity was afforded him, to enter into the fullest functions of his ministry, as a matter of duty. Such an opportunity now offered at B----, and the doctor became its rector about the period Sir Edward became possessor of his paternal estate.

Denbigh tried every inducement within his power to keep the doctor in his own society. If as many thousands as his living would give him hundreds could effect it, they would have been at his service; but Denbigh understood the character of the divine too well to offer such an inducement: he however urged the claims of friendship to the utmost, but without success. The doctor acknowledged the hold both himself and family had gained upon his affections, but he added--

"Consider, my dear Mr. Denbigh, what we would have thought of one of the earlier followers of our Saviour, who from motives of convenience or worldly-mindedness could have deserted his sacred calling. Although the changes in the times may have rendered the modes of conducting them different, necessarily the duties remain the same. The minister of our holy religion who has once submitted to the call of his divine Master, must allow nothing but ungovernable necessity to turn him from the path he has entered on; and should he so far forget himself, I greatly fear he would plead, when too late to remedy the evil, his worldly duties, his cares, or even his misfortunes, in vain. Solemn and arduous are his obligations to labor, but when faithfully he has discharged these duties, oh! how glorious must be his reward."

Before such opinions every barrier must fall, and the doctor entered into the cure of his parish without further opposition, though not without unceasing regret on the part of his friend. Their intercourse was, however, maintained by letter, and they also frequently met at Lumley Castle, a seat of the countess's, within two days' ride of the doctor's parish, until her increasing indisposition rendered journeying impossible; then, indeed, the doctor extended his rides into Wales, but with longer intervals between his visits, though with the happiest effects to the objects of his journey.

Mr. Denbigh, worn down with watching and blasted hopes, under the direction of the spiritual watchfulness of the rector of B----, became an humble, sincere, and pious Christian.

Chapter XLV

It has been already mentioned, that the health of Lady Pendennyss suffered a severe shock, in giving birth to a daughter. Change of scene was prescribed as a remedy for her disorder, and Denbigh and his wife were on their return from a fruitless excursion amongst the northern lakes, in pursuit of amusement and relief for the latter when they were compelled to seek shelter from the fury of a sudden gust in the first building that offered. It was a farm-house of the better sort; and the attendants, carriages, and appearance of their guests, caused no little confusion to its simple inmates. A fire was lighted in the best parlor, and every effort was made by the inhabitants to contribute to the comforts of the travellers.

The countess and her husband were sitting in that kind of listless melancholy which had been too much the companion of their later hours, when in the interval of the storm, a male voice in an adjoining room commenced singing the following ballad, the notes being low, monotonous, but unusually sweet, and the enunciation so distinct, as to rende every syllable intelligible:

> Oh! I have lived in endless pain,
> And I have lived, alas! in vain,
>   For none regard my woe--
> No father's care conveyed the truth,
> No mother's fondness blessed my youth,
>   Ah! joys too great to know--
>
> And Marian's love, and Marian's pride,
> Have crushed the heart that would have died.
>   To save my Marian's tears--
> A brother's hand has struck the blow
> Oh! may that brother never know
>   Such madly sorrowing years!
>
> But hush my griefs--and hush my song,
> I've mourned in vain--I've mourned too long;
>   When none have come to soothe--
> And dark's the path, that lies before,

> And dark have been the days of yore,
> And all was dark in youth.

The maids employed around the person of their comfortless mistress, the valet of Denbigh engaged in arranging a dry coat for his master--all suspended their employments to listen in breathless silence to the mournful melody of the song.

But Denbigh himself had started from his seat at the first notes, and he continued until the voice ceased, gazing in vacant horror in the direction of the sounds. A door opened from the parlor to the room of the musician; he rushed through it, and there, in a kind of shed to the building, which hardly sheltered him from the fury of the tempest, clad in the garments of the extremest poverty, with an eye roving in madness, and a body rocking to and fro from mental inquietude, he beheld seated on a stone the remains of his long lost brother, Francis.

The language of the song was too plain to be misunderstood. The truth glared around George with a violence that dazzled his brain; but he saw it all, he felt it all, and rushing to the feet of his brother, he exclaimed in horror, pressing his hands between his own,--

"Francis--my own brother--do you not know me?"

The maniac regarded him with a vacant gaze, but the voice and the person recalled the compositions of his more reasonable moments to his recollection; pushing back the hair of George, so as to expose his fine forehead to view, he contemplated him for a few moments, and then continued to sing, in a voice still rendered sweeter than before by his faint impressions:

> His raven locks, that richly curled,
> His eye, that proud defiance hurled.
> Have stol'n my Marian's love!
> Had I been blest by nature's grace,
> With such a form, with such a face,
> Could I so treacherous prove?
>
> And what is man--and what is care--
> That he should let such passions tear
> The bases of the soul!
> Oh! you should do, as I have done--
> And having pleasure's summit won,
> Each bursting sob control!

On ending the last stanza, the maniac released his brother, and broke into the wildest laugh of madness.

"Francis!--Oh! Francis, my brother," cried George, in bitterness. A piercing shriek drew his eye to the door he had passed through--on its threshold lay the senseless body of his wife. The distracted husband forgot everything in the situation of his Marian, and raising her in his arms, he exclaimed,--

"Marian--my Marian, revive--look up--know me."

Francis had followed him, and now stood by his side, gazing intently on the lifeless body; his looks became more soft--his eye glanced less wildly--he too cried,--

"Marian--*My* Marian."

There was a mighty effort; nature could endure no more, he broke a blood-vessel and fell at the feet of George. They flew to his assistance, giving the countess to her women; but he was dead.

For seventeen years Lady Pendennyss survived this shock: but having reached her own abode, during that long period she never left her room.

In the confidence of his surviving hopes, Doctor Ives and his wife were made acquainted with the real cause of the grief of their friend, but the truth went no further. Denbigh was the guardian of his three young cousins, the duke, his sister, and young George Denbigh; these, with his son, Lord Lumley, and daughter, Lady Marian, were removed from the melancholy of the Castle to scenes better adapted to their opening prospects in life. Yet Lumley was fond of the society of his father, and finding him a youth endowed beyond his years, the care of his parent was early turned to the most important of his duties in that sacred office; and when he yielded to his wishes to go into the army, he knew he went a youth of sixteen, possessed of principles and self-denial that would become a man of five-and-twenty.

General Wilson completed the work which the father had begun; and Lord Lumley formed a singular exception to the character of most of his companions.

At the close of the Spanish war, he returned home, and was just in time to receive the parting breath of his mother.

A few days before her death, the countess requested that her children might be made acquainted with her history and misconduct; and she placed in the hands of her son a letter; with directions for him to open it after her decease. It was addressed to both children, and after recapitulating generally the principal events of her life, continued:

"Thus, my children, you perceive the consequences of indulgence and hardness of heart, which made me insensible to the sufferings of others, and regardless of the plainest dictates of justice. Self was my idol. The love of admiration, which was natural to me, was increased by the flatterers who surrounded me; and had the customs of our country suffered royalty to descend in their unions to a grade in life below their own, your uncle would have escaped the fangs of my baneful coquetry.

"Oh! Marian, my child, never descend so low as to practise those arts which have degraded your unhappy mother. I would impress on you, as a memorial of my parting affection, these simple truths--that coquetry stands next to the want of chastity in the scale of female vices; it is in fact a kind of mental prostitution; it is ruinous to all that delicacy of feeling which gives added lustre to female charms; it is almost destructive to modesty itself. A woman who has been addicted to its practice, may strive long and in vain to regain that singleness of heart, which can bind her up so closely in her husband and children as to make her a good wife or a mother; and if it should have degenerated into habit, it may lead to the awful result of infidelity to her marriage vows.

"It is vain for a coquette to pretend to religion; its practice involves hypocrisy, falsehood, and deception--everything that is mean--everything that is debasing. In short, as it is bottomed on selfishness and pride, where it has once possessed the mind, it will only yield to the truth-displaying banners of the cross. This, and this only, can remove the evil; for without it she, whom the charms of youth and beauty have enabled to act the coquette, will descend into the vale of life, altered, it is true, but not amended. She will find the world, with its allurements, clinging around her parting years, in vain regrets for days that are flown, and in mercenary views for her descendants. Heaven bless you, my children, console and esteem your inestimable father while he yet remains with you; and place your reliance on that Heavenly Parent who will never desert those who seek him in sincerity and love. Your dying mother,

"M. PENDENNYSS."

This letter, evidently written under the excitement of deep remorse, made a great impression on both her children. In Lady Marian it was pity, regret, and abhorrence of the fault which had been the principal cause of the wreck of her mother's peace of mind; but in her brother, now Earl of Pendennyss, these feelings were united with a jealous dread of his own probable lot in the chances of matrimony.

His uncle had been the supposed heir to a more elevated title than his own, but he was now the actual possessor of as honorable a name, and of much larger revenues. The great wealth of his maternal grandfather, and the considerable estate of his own father, were, or would soon be, centred in himself; and if a woman as amiable, as faultless, as affection had taught him to believe his mother to be, could yield in her situation to the lure of worldly honors, had he not great reason to dread, that a hand might be bestowed at some day upon himself, when the heart would point out some other destination, if the real wishes of its owner were consulted?

Pendennyss was modest by nature, and humble from principle, though by no means distrustful; yet the shock of discovering his mother's fault, the gloom occasioned by her death and his father's declining health, sometimes led him into a train of reflections which, at others, he would have fervently deprecated.

A short time after the decease of the countess, Mr. Denbigh, finding his constitution fast giving way, under the wasting of a decline he had been in for a year, resolved to finish his days in the abode of his Christian friend, Doctor Ives. For several years they had not met; increasing duties and infirmities on both sides having interrupted their visits.

By easy stages he left the residence of his son in Wales, and accompanied by both his children he reached Lumley Castle much exhausted; here he took a solemn and final leave of Marian, unwilling that she should so soon witness again the death of another parent, and dismissing the earl's equipage and attendants a short day's ride from B----, they proceeded alone to the rectory.

A letter had been forwarded acquainting the doctor of his approaching visit, wishing it to be perfectly private, but not alluding to its object, and naming a day, a week later than the one on which he arrived. This plan was altered on perceiving the torch of life more rapidly approaching the socket than he had at first supposed. His unexpected appearance and reception are known. Denbigh's death and the departure of his son followed; Francis having been Pendennyss's companion to the tomb of his ancestors in Westmoreland.

The earl had a shrinking delicacy, under the knowledge of his family history, that made him anxious to draw all eyes from the contemplation of his mother's conduct; how far the knowledge of it had extended in society he could not know, but he wished it buried with her in the tomb. The peculiar manner of his father's death would attract notice, and might recall attention to the prime cause of his disorder; as yet all was veiled, and he wished the doctor's family to let it remain so. It was, however, impossible that the death of a man of Mr. Denbigh's rank should be unnoticed in the prints, and the care of Francis dictated the simple truth without comments, as it appeared. As regarded the Moseleys, what was more natural than that the son of *Mr. Denbigh* should also be *Mr. Denbigh?*

In the presence of the rector's family no allusions were made to their friends, and the villagers and the neighborhood spoke of them as old and young Mr. Denbigh.

The name of Lord Lumley, now Earl of Pendennyss, was known to the whole British nation; but the long retirement of his father and mother had driven them almost from the recollection of their friends. Even Mrs. Wilson supposed her favorite hero a Lumley. Pendennyss Castle had been for centuries the proud residence of that family; and the change of name in its possessor was forgotten with the circumstances that had led to it.

When, therefore, Emily met the earl so unexpectedly the second time at the rectory, she, of course, with all her companions, spoke of him as Mr. Denbigh. On that occasion, Pendennyss had called in person, in expectation of meeting his kinsman, Lord Bolton; but, finding him absent, he could not resist his desire to visit the rectory. Accordingly, he sent his carriage and servants on to London, leaving them at a convenient spot, and arrived on foot at the house of Dr. Ives. From the same motives which had influenced him before--a wish to indulge, undisturbed by useless ceremony, his melancholy reflections--he desired that his name might not be mentioned.

This was an easy task. Both Doctor and Mrs. Ives had called him, when a child, George or Lumley, and were unused to his new appellation of Pendennyss; indeed, it rather recalled painful recollections to them all.

It may be remembered that circumstances removed the necessity of any introduction to Mrs. Wilson and her party; and the difficulty in that instance was happily got rid of.

The earl had often heard Emily Moseley spoken of by his friends, and in their letters they frequently mentioned her name as connected with their pleasures and employments, and always with an affection Pendennyss thought exceeding that which they manifested for their son's wife; and Mrs Ives, the evening before, to remove unpleasant thoughts, had given him a lively description of her person and character. The earl's curiosity had been a little excited to see this paragon of female beauty and virtue; and, unlike most curiosity on such subjects, he was agreeably disappointed by the examination. He wished to know more, and made interest with the doctor to assist him to continue the incognito with which accident had favored him.

The doctor objected on the ground of principle, and the earl desisted; but the beauty of Emily, aided by her character, had made an impression not to be easily shaken off, and Pendennyss returned to the charge.

His former jealousies were awakened in proportion to his admiration; and, after some time, he threw himself on the mercy of the divine, by declaring his new motive, but without mentioning his parents. The doctor pitied him, for he scanned his feelings thoroughly, and consented to keep silent, but laughingly declared it was bad enough for a divine to be accessory to, much less aiding in a deception; and that he knew if Emily and Mrs. Wilson learnt his imposition, he would lose ground in their favor by the discovery.

"Surely, George," said the doctor with a laugh, "you don't mean to marry the young lady as Mr. Denbigh?"

"Oh, no! it is too soon to think of marrying her at all," replied the earl with a smile; "but, somehow, I should like to see what my reception in the world will be as plain Mr. Denbigh, unprovided for and unknown."

"No doubt, my lord," said the rector archly, "in proportion to your merits, very unfavorably indeed; but then your humility will be finally elevated by the occasional praises I have heard Mrs. Wilson lavish on your proper character of late."

"I am much indebted to her partiality," continued the earl mournfully; then throwing off his gloomy thoughts he added, "I wonder, my dear doctor, your goodness did not set her right in the latter particular."

"Why, she has hardly given me an opportunity; delicacy and my own feelings have kept me very silent on the subject of your family to any of that connexion. They think, I believe, I was a rector in Wales, instead of your father's chaplain; and somehow," continued the doctor, smiling on his wife, "the association with your late parents was so connected in my mind with my most romantic feelings, that although I have delighted in it, I have seldom alluded to it in conversation at all. Mrs. Wilson has spoken of you but twice in my hearing, and that since she has expected to meet you; your name has doubtless recalled the remembrance of her husband."

"I have many, many reasons to remember the general with gratitude," cried the earl with fervor; "but doctor, do not forget my incognito: only call me George; I ask no more."

The plan of Pendennyss was put in execution. Day after day he lingered in Northamptonshire, until his principles and character had grown upon the esteem of the Moseleys in the manner we have mentioned.

His frequent embarrassments were from the dread and shame of a detection. With Sir Herbert Nicholson he had a narrow escape, and Mrs. Fitzgerald and Lord Henry Stapleton he of course avoided; for having gone so far, he was determined to persevere to the end. Egerton he thought knew him, and he disliked his character and manners.

When Chatterton appeared most attentive to Emily, the candor and good opinion of that young nobleman made the earl acquainted with his wishes and his situation. Pendennyss was too generous not to meet his rival on fair grounds. His cousin and the duke were requested to use their united influence secretly to obtain the desired station for the baron. The result is known, and Pendennyss trusted his secret to Chatterton; he took him to London, gave him in charge to Derwent, and returned to prosecute his own suit. His note from Bolton Castle was a *ruse* to conceal his character, as he knew the departure of the baronet's family to an hour, and had so timed his visit to the earl as not to come in collision with the Moseleys.

"Indeed, my lord," cried the doctor to him one day, "your scheme goes on swimmingly, and I am only afraid when your mistress discovers the imposition, you will find your rank producing a different effect from what you have apprehended."

Chapter XLVI

But Dr. Ives was mistaken. Had he seen the sparkling eyes and glowing cheeks of Miss Moseley, the smile of satisfaction and happiness which played on the usually thoughtful face of Mrs. Wilson, when the earl handed them into his own carriage, as they left his house on the evening of the discovery, the doctor would have gladly acknowledged the failure of his prognostics. In truth, there was no possible event that, under the circumstances, could have given both aunt and niece such heartfelt pleasure, as the knowledge that Denbigh and the earl were the same person.

Pendennyss stood holding the door of the carriage in his hand, irresolute how to act, when Mrs. Wilson said--

"Surely, my lord, you sup with us."

"A thousand thanks, my dear madam, for the privilege," cried the earl, as he sprang into the coach; the door was closed, and they drove off.

"After the explanations of this morning, my lord," said Mrs. Wilson, willing to remove all doubts between him and Emily, and perhaps anxious to satisfy her own curiosity, "it will be fastidious to conceal our desire to know more of your movements. How came your pocket-book in the possession of Mrs. Fitzgerald?"

"Mrs. Fitzgerald!" cried Pendennyss, in astonishment "I lost the book in one of the rooms of the Lodge, and supposed it had fallen into your hands, and betrayed my disguise by Emily's rejection of me, and your own altered eye. Was I mistaken then in both?"

Mrs. Wilson now, for the first time, explained their real grounds for refusing his offers, which, in the morning, she had loosely mentioned as owing to a misapprehension of his just character, and recounted the manner of the book falling into the hands of Mrs. Fitzgerald.

The earl listened in amazement, and after musing with himself, exclaimed--

"I remember taking it from my pocket, to show Colonel Egerton some singular plants I had gathered, and think I first missed it when returning to the place where I had then laid it; in some of the side-pockets were letters from Marian, addressed to me, properly; and I naturally thought they had met your eye."

Mrs. Wilson and Emily immediately thought Egerton the real villain, who had caused both themselves and Mrs. Fitzgerald so much uneasiness, and the former mentioned her suspicions to the earl.

"Nothing more probable, dear madam," cried he, "and this explains to me his startled looks when we first met, and his evident dislike to my society, for he must have seen my person, though the carriage hid *him* from my sight."

That Egerton was the wretch, and that through his agency the pocket-book had been carried to the cottage, they all now agreed, and turned to more pleasant subjects.

"Master!--here--master," said Peter Johnson, as he stood at a window of Mr. Benfield's room, stirring a gruel for the old gentleman's supper, and stretching his neck and straining his eyes to distinguish objects by the light of the lamps--"I do think there is Mr. Denbigh, handing Miss Emmy from a coach, covered with gold, and two footmen, all dizened with pride like."

The spoon fell from the hands of Mr. Benfield. He rose briskly from his seat, and adjusting his dress, took the arm of the steward, and proceeded to the drawing-room. While these several movements were in operation, which consumed some time, the old bachelor relieved the tedium of Peter's impatience by the following speech:--

"Mr. Denbigh!--what, back?--I thought he never could let that rascal John shoot him and forsake Emmy after all; (here the old gentleman suddenly recollected Denbigh's marriage) but now, Peter, it can do no good either.--I remember, that when my friend the Earl of Gosford "--(and again he was checked by the image of the card-table and the viscountess) "but, Peter," he said with great warmth, "we can go down and see him, notwithstanding."

"Mr. Denbigh!" exclaimed Sir Edward, in astonishment, when he saw the companion of his sister and child enter the drawing-room, "you are welcome once more to your old friends: your sudden retreat from us gave us much pain; but we suppose Lady Laura had too many attractions to allow us to keep you any longer in Norfolk."

The good Baronet sighed, as he held out his hand to the man whom he had once hoped to receive as a son.

"Neither Lady Laura nor any other lady, my dear Sir Edward," cried the earl, as he took the baronet's hand, "drove me from you, but the frowns of your own fair daughter; and here she is, ready to acknowledge her offence, and, I hope, to atone for it."

John, who knew of the refusal of his sister, and was not a little displeased with the cavalier treatment he had received at Denbigh's hands, felt indignant at such improper levity in a married man, and approached with--

"Your servant, Mr. Denbigh--I hope my Lady Laura is well."

Pendennyss understood his look, and replied very gravely--

"Your servant, Mr. John Moseley--my Lady Laura is, or certainly ought to be, very well, as she has this moment gone to a rout, accompanied by her husband."

The quick eye of John glanced from the earl to his aunt, to Emily; a lurking smile was on all their features. The heightened color of his sister, the flashing eyes of the young nobleman, the face of his aunt, all told him that something uncommon was about to be explained; and, yielding to his feelings, he caught the hand which Pendennyss extended to him, and cried,

"Denbigh, I see--I feel--there is some unaccountable mistake--we are--"

"Brothers!" said the earl, emphatically. "Sir Edward--dear Lady Moseley, I throw myself on your mercy. I am an impostor: when your hospitality received me into your house, it is true you admitted George Denbigh, but he is better known as the Earl of Pendennyss."

"The Earl of Pendennyss!" exclaimed Lady Moseley, in a glow of delight, as she saw at once through some juvenile folly a deception which promised both happiness and rank to one of her children. "Is it possible, my dear Charlotte, that this is your unknown friend?"

"The very same, Anne," replied the smiling widow, "and guilty of a folly that, at all events, removes the distance between us a little, by showing that he is subject to the failings of mortality. But the masquerade is ended, and I hope you and Edward will not only treat him as an earl, but receive him as a son."

"Most willingly--most willingly," cried the baronet, with great energy; "be he prince, peer, or beggar, he is the preserver of my child, and as such he is always welcome."

The door now slowly opened, and the venerable bachelor appeared on its threshold.

Pendennyss, who had never forgotten the good will manifested to him by Mr. Benfield, met him with a look of pleasure, as he expressed his happiness at seeing him again in London.

"I never have forgotten your goodness in sending honest Peter such a distance from home, on the object of his visit. I now regret that a feeling of shame occasioned my answering your kindness so laconically:" turning to Mrs. Wilson, he added, "for a time I knew not how to write a letter even, being afraid to sign my proper appellation, and ashamed to use my adopted."

"Mr. Denbigh, I am happy to see you. I did send Peter, it is true, to London, on a message to you--but it is all over now," the old man sighed--"Peter, however, escaped the snares of this wicked place; and if you are happy, I am content. I remember when the Earl of--"

"Pendennyss!" exclaimed the other, "imposed on the hospitality of a worthy man, under an assumed appellation, in order to pry into the character of a lovely female, who was only too good for him, and who now is willing to forget his follies, and make him not only the happiest of men, but the nephew of Mr. Benfield."

During this speech, the countenance of Mr. Benfield had manifested evident emotion: he looked from one to another, until he saw Mrs. Wilson smiling near him. Pointing to the earl with his finger, he stood unable to speak, as she answered simply,--

"Lord Pendennyss."

"And Emmy dear--will you--will you marry him?" cried Mr. Benfield, suppressing his feelings, to give utterance to his question.

Emily felt for her uncle, and blushing deeply, with great frankness she put her hand in that of the earl, who pressed it with rapture again and again to his lips.

Mr. Benfield sank into a chair, and with a heart softened by emotion, burst into tears.

"Peter," he cried, struggling with his feelings, "I am now ready to depart in peace--I shall see my darling Emmy happy, and to her care I shall commit you."

Emily, deeply affected with his love, threw herself into his arms, in a torrent of tears, and was removed from them by Pendennyss, in consideration for the feelings of both.

Jane felt no emotions of envy for her sister's happiness; on the contrary, she rejoiced in common with the rest of their friends in her brightening prospects, and they all took their seats at the supper table, as happy a group as was contained in the wide circle of the metropolis. A few more particulars served to explain the mystery sufficiently, until a more fitting opportunity made them acquainted with the whole of the earl's proceedings.

"My Lord Pendennyss," said Sir Edward, pouring out a glass of wine, and passing the bottle to his neighbor: "I drink your health--and happiness to yourself and my darling child."

The toast was drunk by all the family, and the earl replied to the compliments with his thanks and smiles, while Emily could only notice them with her blushes and tears.

But this was an opportunity not to be lost by the honest steward, who, from affection and long services, had been indulged in familiarities exceeding any other of his master's establishment. He very deliberately helped himself to a glass of wine, and drawing near the seat of the bride-elect, with an humble reverence, commenced his speech as follows:

"My dear Miss Emmy:--Here's hoping you'll live to be a comfort to your honored father, and your honored mother, and my dear honored master, and yourself, and Madam Wilson." The steward paused to clear his voice, and profited by the delay to cast his eye round the table to collect the names; "and Mr. John Moseley, and sweet Mrs. Moseley, and pretty Miss Jane" (Peter had lived too long in the world to compliment one handsome woman in the presence of another, without the qualifying his speech a little); "and Mr. Lord Denbigh--earl like, as they say he now is, and"--Peter stopped a moment to deliberate, and then making another reference, he put the glass to his lips; but before he had got half through its contents, recollected himself, and replenishing it to the brim, with a smile acknowledging his forgetfulness, continued, "and the Rev. Mr. Francis Ives, and the Rev. Mrs. Francis Ives."

Here the unrestrained laugh of John interrupted him; and considering with himself that he had included the whole family, he finished his bumper. Whether it was pleasure at his own eloquence in venturing on so long a speech, or the unusual allowance, that affected the steward, he was evidently much satisfied with himself, and stepped back behind his master's chair, in great good humor.

Emily, as she thanked him, noticed a tear in the eye of the old man, as he concluded his oration, that would have excused a thousand breaches of fastidious ceremony. But Pendennyss rose from his seat, and took him kindly by the hand, and returned his own thanks for his good wishes.

"I owe you much good will, Mr. Johnson, for, your two journeys in my behalf, and trust I never shall forget the manner in which you executed your last mission in particular. We are friends, I trust, for life."

"Thank you--thank your honor's lordship," said the steward, almost unable to utter; "I hope you may live long, to make dear little Miss Emmy as happy--as I know she ought to be."

"But really, my lord," cried John, observing that the steward's affection for his sister had affected her to tears, "it was a singular circumstance, the meeting of the four passengers of the stage so soon at your hotel."

Moseley explained his meaning to the rest of the company.

"Not so much so as you imagine," said the earl in reply; "yourself and Johnson were in quest of me. Lord Henry Stapleton was under an engagement to meet me that evening at the hotel, as we were both going to his sister's wedding--I having arranged the thing with him by letter previously; and General M'Carthy was also in search of me, on business relating to his niece, the Donna Julia. He had been to Annerdale House, and, through my servants, heard I was at an hotel. It was the first interview between us, and not quite as amicable a one as has since been had in Wales. During my service in Spain, I saw the Conde, but not the general. The letter he gave me was from the Spanish ambassador, claiming a right to require Mrs. Fitzgerald from our government, and deprecating my using an influence to counteract his exertions"--

"Which you refused," said Emily, eagerly.

"Not refused," answered the earl, smiling at her warmth, while he admired her friendly zeal, "for it was unnecessary: there is no such power vested in the ministry. But I explicitly told the general, I would oppose any violent measures to restore her to her country and a convent. From the courts, I apprehended nothing for my fair friend."

"Your honor--my lord," said Peter, who had been listening with great attention, "if I may presume just to ask two questions, without offence."

"Say on, my good friend," said Pendennyss, with an encouraging smile.

"Only" continued the steward--hemming, to give proper utterance to his thoughts--"I wish to know, whether you stayed in that same street after you left the hotel--for Mr. John Moseley and I had a slight difference in opinion about it."

The earl smiled, having caught the arch expression of John, and replied--

"I believe I owe you an apology, Moseley, for my cavalier treatment; but guilt makes us all cowards. I found you were ignorant of my incognito, and I was equally ashamed to continue it, or to become the relater of my own folly. Indeed," he continued, smiling on Emily as he spoke, "I thought your sister had pronounced the opinion of all reflecting people on my conduct. I went out of town, Johnson, at day-break. What is the other query?"

"Why, my lord," said Peter, a little disappointed at finding his first surmise untrue, "that outlandish tongue your honor used--"

"Was Spanish," cried the earl.

"And not Greek, Peter," said his master, gravely. "I thought, from the words you endeavored to repeat to me, that you had made a mistake. You need not be disconcerted, however, for I know several members of the parliament of this realm who could not talk the Greek language, that is, fluently. So it can be no disgrace to a serving-man to be ignorant of it."

Somewhat consoled to find himself as well off as the representatives of his country, Peter resumed his station in silence, when the carriages began to announce the return from the opera. The earl took his leave, and the party retired to rest.

The thanksgivings of Emily that night, ere she laid her head on her pillow, were the purest offering of mortal innocence. The prospect before her was unsullied by a cloud and she poured out her heart in the fullest confidence of pious love and heartfelt gratitude.

As early on the succeeding morning as good-breeding would allow, and much earlier than the hour sanctioned by fashion, the earl and Lady Marian stopped in the carriage of the latter at the door of Sir Edward Moseley. Their reception was the most flattering that could be offered to people of their stamp; sincere, cordial, and, with a trifling exception in Lady Moseley, unfettered with any useless ceremonies.

Emily felt herself drawn to her new acquaintance with a fondness which doubtless grew out of her situation with her brother; which soon found reasons enough in the soft, lady-like, and sincere manners of Lady Marian, to justify her attachment on her own account.

There was a very handsome suite of drawing-rooms in Sir Edward's house, and the communicating doors were carelessly open. Curiosity to view the furniture, or some such trifling reasons, induced the earl to find his way into the one adjoining that in which the family were seated. It was unquestionably a dread of being lost in a strange house, that induced him to whisper a request to the blushing Emily, to be his companion; and lastly, it must have been nothing but a knowledge that a vacant room was easier viewed than one filled with company, that prevented any one from following them. John smiled archly at Grace, doubtless in approbation of the comfortable time his friend was likely to enjoy, in his musings on the taste of their mother. How the door became shut, we have ever been at a loss to imagine.

The company without were too good-natured and well satisfied with each other to miss the absentees, until the figure of the earl appeared at the reopened door, beckoning, with a face of rapture, to Lady Moseley and Mrs. Wilson. Sir Edward next disappeared, then Jane, then Grace--then Marian; until John began to think a tête-à-tête with Mr. Benfield was to be his morning's amusement.

The lovely countenance of his wife, however, soon relieved his ennui, and John's curiosity was gratified by an order to prepare for his sister's wedding the following week.

Emily might have blushed more than common during this interview, but it is certain she did not smile less; and the earl, Lady Marian assured Sir Edward, was so very different a creature from what he had recently been, that she could hardly think it was the same sombre gentleman with whom she had passed the last few months in Wales and Westmoreland.

A messenger was dispatched for Dr. Ives and their friends at B----, to be witnesses to the approaching nuptials; and Lady Moseley at length found an opportunity of indulging her taste for splendor on this joyful occasion.

Money was no consideration; and Mr. Benfield absolutely pined at the thought that the great wealth of the earl put it out of his power to contribute in any manner to the comfort of his Emmy. However, a fifteenth codicil was framed by the ingenuity of Peter and his master, and if it did not contain the name of George Denbigh, it did that of his expected second son, Roderick Benfield Denbigh, to the qualifying circumstance of twenty thousand pounds, as a bribe for the name.

"And a very pretty child, I dare say, it will be," said the steward, as he placed the paper in its repository. "I don't know that I ever saw, your honor, a couple that I thought would make a handsomer pair like, except--" Peter's mind dwelt on his own youthful form coupled with the smiling graces of Patty Steele.

"Yes! they are as handsome as they are good!" replied his master. "I remember now, when our Speaker took his third wife, the world said that they were as pretty a couple as there was at court. But my Emma and the earl will be a much finer pair. Oh! Peter Johnson; they are young, and rich, and beloved; but, after all, it avails but little if they be not good."

"Good!" cried the steward in astonishment; "they are as good as angels."

The master's ideas of human excellence had suffered a heavy blow in the view of his viscountess, but he answered mildly,

"As good as mankind can well be."

Chapter XLVII

The warm weather had now commenced; and Sir Edward, unwilling to be shut up in London at a time the appearance of vegetation gave the country a new interest, and accustomed for many years of his life to devote an hour in his garden each morn, had taken a little ready furnished cottage a short ride from his residence, with the intention of frequenting it until after the birthday. Thither then Pendennyss took his bride from the altar, and a few days were passed by the newly married pair in this little asylum.

Doctor Ives, with Francis, Clara, and their mother, had obeyed the summons with an alacrity in proportion to the joy they felt on receiving it, and the former had the happiness of officiating on the occasion. It would have been easy for the wealth of the earl to procure a license to enable them to marry in the drawing-room; the permission was obtained, but neither Emily nor himself felt a wish to utter their vows in any other spot than at the altar, and in the house of their Maker.

If there was a single heart that felt the least emotion of regret or uneasiness, it was Lady Moseley, who little relished the retirement of the cottage on so joyful an occasion; but Pendennyss silenced her objections by good-humoredly replying--

"The fates have been so kind to me, in giving me castles and seats, you ought to allow me, my dear Lady Moseley, the only opportunity I shall probably ever have of enjoying love in a cottage."

A few days, however, removed the uneasiness of the good matron, who had the felicity within the week of seeing her daughter initiated mistress of Annerdale House.

The morning of their return to this noble mansion the earl presented himself in St. James's Square, with the intelligence of their arrival, and smiling as he bowed to Mrs. Wilson, he continued--

"And to escort you, dear madam, to your new abode."

Mrs. Wilson started with surprise, and with a heart beating quick with emotion, she required an explanation of his words.

"Surely, dearest Mrs. Wilson--more than aunt--my mother--you cannot mean, after having trained my Emily through infancy to maturity in the paths of duty, to desert her in the moment of her greatest trial. I am the pupil of your husband," he continued, taking her hands in his own with reverence and affection; "we are the children of your joint care, and one home, as there is but one heart, must in future contain us."

Mrs. Wilson had wished for, but hardly dared to expect this invitation. It was now urged from the right quarter, and in a manner that was as sincere as it was gratifying. Unable to conceal her tears, the good widow pressed the hand of Pendennyss to her lips as she murmured out her thanks. Sir Edward was prepared also to lose his sister; but unwilling to relinquish the pleasure of her society, he urged her making a common residence between the two families.

"Pendennyss has spoken truth, my dear brother," cried she, recovering her voice; "Emily is the child of my care and my love--the two beings I love best in this world are now united--but," she added, pressing Lady Moseley to her bosom, "my heart is large enough for you all; you are of my blood, and my gratitude for your affection is boundless. There shall be but one large family of us; and although our duties may separate us for a time, we will, I trust, ever meet in tenderness and love, though with George and Emily I will take up my abode."

"I hope your house in Northamptonshire is not to be vacant always," said Lady Moseley to the earl, anxiously.

"I have no house there, my dear madam," he replied; "when I thought myself about to succeed in my suit before, I directed a lawyer at Bath, where Sir William Harris resided most of his time, to endeavor to purchase the deanery, whenever a good opportunity offered: in my discomfiture," he added, smiling, "I forgot to countermand the order, and he purchased it immediately on its being advertised. For a short time it was an incumbrance to me, but it is now applied to its original purpose. It is the sole property of the Countess of Pendennyss, and I doubt not you will see it often and agreeably tenanted."

This intelligence gave great satisfaction to his friends, and the expected summer restored to even Jane a gleam of her former pleasure.

If there be bliss in this life, approaching in any degree to the happiness of the blessed, it is the fruition of long and ardent love, where youth, innocence, piety, and family concord, smile upon the union. And all these were united in the case of the new-married pair; but happiness in this world cannot or does not, in any situation, exist without alloy.

The peace of mind and fortitude of Emily were fated to receive a blow, as unlooked for to herself as it was unexpected to the world. Bonaparte appeared in France, and Europe became in motion.

From the moment the earl heard the intelligence his own course was decided. His regiment was the pride of the army, and that it would be ordered to join the duke he did not entertain a doubt.

Emily was, therefore, in some little measure prepared for the blow. It is at such moments as our own acts, or events affecting us, get to be without our control, that faith in the justice and benevolence of God is the most serviceable to the Christian. When others spend their time in useless regrets he is piously resigned: it even so happens, that when others mourn he can rejoice.

The sound of the bugle, wildly winding its notes, broke on the stillness of the morning in the little village in which was situated the cottage tenanted by Sir Edward Moseley. Almost concealed by the shrubbery which surrounded its piazza, stood the forms of the Countess of Pendennyss and her sister Lady Marian, watching eagerly the appearance of those whose approach was thus announced.

The carriage of the ladies, with its idle attendants, was in waiting at a short distance; and the pale face but composed resignation of its mistress, indicated a struggle between conflicting duties.

File after file of heavy horse passed them in military pomp, and the wistful gaze of the two females had scanned them in vain for the well known, much-beloved countenance of the leader. At length a single horseman approached them, riding deliberately and musing: their forms met his eye, and in an instant Emily was pressed to the bosom of her husband.

"It is the doom of a soldier," said the earl, dashing a tear from his eye; "I had hoped that the peace of the world would not again be assailed for years, and that ambition and jealousy would yield a respite to our bloody profession; but cheer up, my love--hope for the best--your trust is not in the things of this life, and your happiness is without the power of man."

"Ah! Pendennyss--my husband," sobbed Emily, sinking on his bosom, "take with you my prayers--my love--everything that can console you--everything that may profit you. I will not tell you to be careful of your life; your duty teaches you that. As a soldier, expose it; as a husband guard it; and return to me as you leave me, a lover, the dearest of men, and a Christian."

Unwilling to prolong the pain of parting, the earl gave his wife a last embrace, held Marian affectionately to his bosom, and mounting his horse, was out of sight in an instant.

Within a few days of the departure of Pendennyss, Chatterton was surprised with the entrance of his mother and Catharine. His reception of them was that of a respectful child, and his wife exerted herself to be kind to connexions she could not love, in order to give pleasure to a husband she adored. Their tale was soon told. Lord and Lady Herriefield were separated; and the dowager, alive to the dangers of a young woman in Catharine's situation, and without a single principle on which to rest the assurance of her blameless conduct in future, had brought her to England, in order to keep off disgrace, by residing with her child herself.

There was nothing in his wife to answer the expectations with which Lord Herriefield married. She had beauty, but with that he was already sated; her simplicity, which, by having her attention drawn elsewhere, had at first charmed him, was succeeded by the knowing conduct of a determined follower of the fashions, and a decided woman of the world.

It had never struck the viscount as impossible that an artless and innocent girl would fall in love with his faded and bilious face, but the moment Catharine betrayed the arts of a manager, he saw at once the artifice that had been practised; of course he ceased to love her.

Men are flattered for a season with notice that has been unsought, but it never fails to injure the woman who practises it in the opinion of the other sex, in time. Without a single feeling in common, without a regard to anything but self, in either husband or wife, it could not but happen that a separation must follow, or their days be spent in wrangling and misery. Catharine willingly left her husband; her husband more willingly got rid of her.

During all these movements the dowager had a difficult game to play. It was unbecoming her to encourage the strife, and it was against her wishes to suppress it; she therefore moralized with the peer, and frowned upon her daughter.

The viscount listened to her truisms with the attention of a boy who is told by a drunken father how wicked it is to love liquor, and heeded them about as much; while Kate, mistress at all events of two thousand a year, minded her mother's frowns as little as she regarded her smiles; both were indifferent to her.

A few days after the ladies left Lisbon, the viscount proceeded to Italy in company with the repudiated wife of a British naval officer; and if Kate was not guilty of an offence of equal magnitude, it was more owing to her mother's present vigilance than to her previous care.

The presence of Mrs. Wilson was a great source of consolation to Emily in the absence of her husband; and as their longer abode in town was useless, the countess declining to be presented without the earl, the whole family decided upon a return into Northamptonshire.

The deanery had been furnished by order of Pendennyss immediately on his marriage; and its mistress hastened to take possession of her new dwelling. The amusement and occupation of this movement, the planning of little improvements, her various duties under her increased responsibilities, kept Emily from dwelling unduly upon the danger of her husband. She sought out amongst the first objects of her bounty the venerable peasant whose loss had been formerly supplied by Pendennyss on his first visit to B----, after the death of his father. There might not have been the usual discrimination and temporal usefulness in this instance which generally accompanied her benevolent acts; but it was associated with the image of her husband, and it could excite no surprise in Mrs. Wilson, although it did in Marian, to see her sister driving two or three times a week to relieve the necessities of a man who appeared actually to be in want of nothing.

Sir Edward was again amongst those he loved, and his hospitable board was once more surrounded with the faces of his friends and neighbors. The good-natured Mr. Haughton was always a welcome guest at the hall, and met, soon after their return, the collected family of the baronet, at a dinner given by the latter to his children and one or two of his most intimate neighbors--

"My Lady Pendennyss," cried Mr. Haughton, in the course of the afternoon, "I have news from the earl, which I know it will do your heart good to hear."

Emily smiled at the prospect of hearing in any manner of her husband, although she internally questioned the probability of Mr. Haughton's knowing anything of his movements, of which her daily letters did not apprise her.

"Will you favor me with the particulars of your intelligence, sir?" said the countess.

"He has arrived safe with his regiment near Brussels; heard it from a neighbor's son who saw him enter the house occupied by Wellington, while he was standing in the crowd without, waiting to get a peep at the duke."

"Oh!" said Mrs. Wilson with a laugh, "Emily knew that ten days ago. Could your friend tell us anything of Bonaparte? We are much interested in his movements just now."

Mr. Haughton, a good deal mortified to find his news stale, mused a moment, as if in doubt to proceed or not; but liking of all things to act the part of a newspaper, he continued--

"Nothing more than you see in the prints; but I suppose your ladyship has heard about Captain Jarvis too?"

"Why, no," said Emily, laughing; "the movements of Captain Jarvis are not quite as interesting to me as those of Lord Pendennyss--has the duke made him an aide-de-camp?"

"Oh! no," cried the other, exulting at his having something new: "as soon as he heard of the return of Boney, he threw up his commission and got married."

"Married!" cried John; "not to Miss Harris, surely."

"No; to a silly girl he met in Cornwall, who was fool enough to be caught with his gold lace. He married one day, and the next told his disconsolate wife and panic-stricken mother that the honor of the Jarvises must sleep until the supporters of the name became sufficiently numerous to risk them in the field of battle."

"And how did Mrs. Jarvis and Sir Timo's lady relish the news?" inquired John, expecting something ridiculous.

"Not at all," rejoined Mr. Haughton; "the former sobbed, and said she had only married him for his bravery and red coat, and the *lady* exclaimed against the destruction of his budding honors."

"How did it terminate?" asked Mrs. Wilson.

"Why, it seems while they were quarrelling about it, the War-Office cut the matter short by accepting his resignation, I suppose the commander-in-chief had learned his character; but the matter was warmly contested: they even drove the captain to a declaration of his principles."

"And what kind of ones might they have been, Haughton?" said Sir Edward, drily.

"Republican."

"Republican!" exclaimed two or three in surprise.

"Yes, liberty and equality, he contended, were his idols, and he could not find it in his heart to fight against Bonaparte."

"A somewhat singular conclusion," said Mr. Benfield, musing. "I remember when I sat in the House, there was a party who were fond of the cry of this said liberty; but when they got the power they did not seem to me to suffer people to go more at large than they went before; but I suppose they were diffident of telling the world their minds after they were put in such responsible stations, for fear of the effect of example."

"Most people like liberty as servants but not as masters, uncle," cried John, with a sneer.

"Captain Jarvis, it seems, liked it as a preservative against danger," continued Mr. Haughton; "to avoid ridicule in his new neighborhood, he has consented to his father's wishes, and turned merchant in the city again."

"Where I sincerely hope he will remain," cried John, who since the accident of the arbor, could not tolerate the unfortunate youth.

"Amen!" said Emily, in an under tone, heard only by her brother.

"But Sir Timo--what has become of Sir Timo--the good, honest merchant?" asked John.

"He has dropt the title, insists on being called plain Mr. Jarvis, and lives entirely in Cornwall. His hopeful son-in-law has gone with his regiment to Flanders; and Lady Egerton, being unable to live without her father's assistance, is obliged to hide her consequence in the west also."

The subject became now disagreeable to Lady Moseley, and it was changed. Such conversations made Jane more reserved and dissatisfied than ever. She had no one respectable excuse to offer for her partiality to her former lover, and when her conscience told her the mortifying fact, was apt to think that others remembered it too.

The letters from the continent now teemed with preparations for the approaching contest; and the apprehensions of our heroine and her friends increased, in proportion to the nearness of the struggle, on which hung not only the fates of thousands of individuals, but of adverse princes and mighty empires. In this confusion of interests, and of jarring of passions, there were offered prayers almost hourly for the safety of Pendennyss, which were as pure and ardent as the love which prompted them.

Chapter XLVIII

Napoleon had commenced those daring and rapid movements, which for a time threw the peace of the world into the scale of fortune, and which nothing but the interposition of a ruling Providence could avert from their threatened success. As the the ----th dragoons wheeled into a field already deluged with English blood, on the heights of Quatre Bras, the eye of its gallant colonel saw a friendly battalion falling beneath the sabres of the enemy's cuirassiers. The word was passed, the column opens, the sounds of the quivering bugle were heard for a moment above the roar of the cannon and the shouts of the combatants; the charge, sweeping like a whirlwind, fell heavily on those treacherous Frenchmen, who to-day had sworn fidelity to Louis, and to-morrow intended lifting their hands in allegiance to his rival.

"Spare my life in mercy," cried an officer, already dreadfully wounded, who stood shrinking from the impending blow of an enraged Frenchman. An English dragoon dashed at the cuirassier, and with one blow severed his arm from his body.

"Thank God," sighed the wounded officer, sinking beneath the horse's feet.

His rescuer threw himself from the saddle, and raising the fallen man inquired into his wounds. It was Pendennyss, and it was Egerton. The wounded man groaned aloud, as he saw the face of him who had averted the fatal blow; but it was not the hour for explanations or confessions, other than those with which the dying soldiers endeavored to make their tardy peace with their God.

Sir Henry was given in charge to two slightly wounded British soldiers, and the earl remounted: the scattered troops were rallied at the sound of the trumpet, and again and again, led by their dauntless colonel, were seen in the thickest of the fray, with sabres drenched in blood, and voices hoarse with the shouts of victory.

The period between the battles of Quatre Bras and Waterloo was a trying one to the discipline and courage of the British army. The discomfited Prussians on their flank had been routed and compelled to retire, and in their front was an enemy, brave, skilful, and victorious, led by the greatest captain of the age. The prudent commander of the English forces fell back with dignity and reluctance to the field of Waterloo; here the mighty struggle was to terminate, and the eye of every experienced soldier looked on those eminences as on the future graves for thousands.

During this solemn interval of comparative inactivity the mind of Pendennyss dwelt on the affection, the innocence, the beauty and worth of his Emily, until the curdling blood, as he thought on her lot should his life be the purchase of the coming victory, warned him to quit the gloomy subject, for the consolations of that religion which only could yield him the solace his wounded feelings required. In his former campaigns the earl had been sensible of the mighty changes of death, and had ever kept in view the preparations necessary to meet it with hope and joy; but the world clung around him now, in the best affections of his nature, and it was only as he could picture the happy reunion with his Emily in a future life, that he could look on a separation in this without despair.

The vicinity of the enemy admitted of no relaxation in the strictest watchfulness in the British lines: and the comfortless night of the seventeenth was passed by the earl, and his Lieutenant Colonel, George Denbigh, on the same cloak, and under the open canopy of Heaven.

As the opening cannon of the enemy gave the signal for the commencing conflict, Pendennyss mounted his charger with a last thought on his distant wife. With a mighty struggle he tore her as it were from his bosom, and gave the remainder of the day to duty.

Who has not heard of the events of that fearful hour, on which the fate of Europe hung as it were suspended in the scale? On one side supported by the efforts of desperate resolution, guided by the most consummate art; and on the other defended by a discipline and enduring courage almost without a parallel.

The indefatigable Blucher arrived, and the star of Napoleon sank.

Pendennyss threw himself from his horse, on the night of the eighteenth of June, as he gave way by orders, in the pursuit, to the fresher battalions of the Prussians, with the languor that follows unusual excitement, and mental thanksgivings that this bloody work was at length ended. The image of his Emily again broke over the sterner feelings of the battle, like the first glimmerings of light which succeed the awful darkness of the eclipse of the sun: and he again breathed freely, in the consciousness of the happiness which would await his speedy return.

"I am sent for the colonel of the ----th dragoons," said a courier in broken English to a soldier, near where the earl lay on the ground, waiting the preparations of his attendants "have I found the right regiment, my friend?"

"To be sure you have," answered the man, without looking up from his toil on his favorite animal, "you might have tracked us by the dead Frenchmen, I should think. So you want my lord, my lad, do you? do we move again to-night?" suspending his labor for a moment in expectation of a reply.

"Not to my knowledge," rejoined the courier; "my message is to your colonel, from a dying man. Will you point out his station?"

The soldier complied, the message was soon delivered, and Pendennyss prepared to obey its summons immediately. Preceded by the messenger as a guide, and followed by Harmer, the earl retraced his steps over that ground on which he had but a few hours before been engaged in the deadly strife of man to man, hand to hand.

How different is the contemplation of a field of battle during and after the conflict! The excitement, suspended success, shouts, uproar, and confusion of the former, prevent any contemplation of the nicer parts of this confused mass of movements, charges, and retreats; or if a brilliant advance is made, a masterly retreat effected, the imagination is chained by the splendor and glory of the act, without resting for a moment on the sacrifice of individual happiness with which it is purchased. A battle-ground from which the whirlwind of the combat has passed, presents a different sight; it offers the very consummation of human misery.

There may occasionally be an individual, who from station, distempered mind, or the encouragement of chimerical ideas of glory, quits the theatre of life with at least the appearance of pleasure in his triumphs. If such there be in reality, if this rapture of departing glory be anything more than the deception of a distempered excitement, the subject of its exhibition is to be greatly pitied. To the Christian, dying in peace with both God and man, can it alone be ceded in the eye of reason, to pour out his existence with a smile on his quivering lip.

And the warrior, who falls in the very arms of victory, after passing a life devoted to the world; even, if he sees kingdoms hang suspended on his success, may smile indeed, may utter sentiments full of loyalty and zeal, may be the admiration of the world, and what is his reward? a deathless name, and an existence of misery, which knows no termination.

Christianity alone can make us good soldiers in any cause, for he who knows how to live, is always the least afraid to die.

Pendennyss and his companions pushed their way over the ground occupied before the battle by the enemy; descended into and through that little valley, in which yet lay, in undistinguished confusion, masses of the dead and dying of either side; and again over the ridge, on which could be marked the situation of those gallant squares which had so long resisted the efforts of the horse and artillery by the groups of bodies, fallen where they had bravely stood, until even the callous Harmer sickened with the sight of a waste of life that he had but a few hours before exultingly contributed to increase.

Appeals to their feelings as they rode through the field had been frequent, and their progress was much retarded by attempts to contribute to the ease of a wounded or a dying man; but as the courier constantly urged speed, as the only means of securing the object of their ride, these halts were reluctantly abandoned.

It was ten o'clock before they reached the farm-house, where, in the midst of hundreds of his countrymen, lay the former lover of Jane.

As the subject of his confession must be anticipated by the reader, we will give a short relation of his life, and of those acts which more materially affect our history.

Henry Egerton had been turned early on the world, hundreds of his countrymen, without any principle to counteract the arts of infidelity, or resist the temptations of life. His father held a situation under government, and was devoted to his rise in the diplomatic line. His mother was a woman of fashion, who lived for effect and idle competition with her sisters in weakness and folly. All he learnt in his father's house was selfishness, from the example of one, and a love of high life and its extravagance from the other.

He entered the army young, and from choice. The splendor and reputation of the service caught his fancy; and, by pride and constitution, he was indifferent to personal danger. Yet he loved London and its amusements better than glory; and the money of his uncle, Sir Edgar, whose heir he was reputed to be, raised him to the rank of lieutenant colonel, without his spending an hour in the field.

Egerton had some abilities, and a good deal of ardor of temperament, by nature. The former, from indulgence and example, degenerated into acquiring the art to please in mixed society; and the latter, from want of employment, expended itself at the card table.

The association between the vices is intimate. There really appears to be a kind of modesty in sin that makes it ashamed of good company. If we are unable to reconcile a favorite propensity to our principles, we are apt to abandon the unpleasant restraint on our actions, rather than admit the incongruous mixture. Freed entirely from the fetters of our morals, what is there that our vices will not prompt us to commit? Egerton, like thousands of others, went on from step to step, until he found himself in the world; free to follow all his inclinations, so he violated none of the decencies of life.

When in Spain, in his only campaign, he was accidentally, as has been mentioned, thrown in the way of the Donna Julia, and brought her off the ground under the influence of natural sympathy and national feeling; a kind of merit that makes vice only more dangerous, by making it sometimes amiable. He had not seen his dependant long before her beauty, situation, and his passions decided him to effect her ruin.

This was an occupation that his figure, manners, and propensities had made him an adept in, and nothing was further from his thoughts than the commission of any other than the crime that, according to his code, a gentleman might be guilty of with impunity.

It is, however, the misfortune of sin, that from being our slave it becomes a tyrant; and Egerton attempted what in other countries, and where the laws ruled, might have cost him his life.

The conjecture of Pendennyss was true. He saw the face of the officer who interposed between him and his villanous attempt, but was hid himself from view. He aimed not at his life, but at his own escape. Happily his first shot succeeded, for the earl would have been sacrificed to preserve the character of a man of honor; though no one was more regardless of the estimation he was held in by the virtuous than Colonel Egerton.

In pursuance of his plans on Mrs. Fitzgerald, the colonel had sedulously avoided admitting any of his companions into the secret of his having a female in his care.

When he left the army to return home, he remained until a movement of the troops to a distant part of the country enabled him to effect his own purposes, without incurring their ridicule; and when he found himself obliged to abandon his vehicle for a refuge in the woods, the fear of detection made him alter his course; and under the pretence of wishing to be in a battle about to be fought, he secretly rejoined the army, and the gallantry of Colonel Egerton was mentioned in the next despatches.

Sir Herbert Nicholson commanded the advanced guard, at which the earl arrived with the Donna Julia; and like every other brave man (unless guilty himself) was indignant at the villany of the fugitive. The confusion and enormities daily practised in the theatre of the war prevented any close inquiries into the subject, and circumstances had so enveloped Egerton in mystery, that nothing but an interview with the lady herself was likely to expose him.

With Sir Herbert Nicholson, he had been in habits of intimacy, and on that gentleman's alluding in a conversation in the barracks at F---- to the lady brought into his quarters before Lisbon, he accidentally omitted mentioning the name of her rescuer. Egerton had never before heard the transaction spoken of, and as he had of course never mentioned the subject himself, was ignorant who had interfered between him and his views; also of the fate of Donna Julia; indeed, he thought it probable that it had not much improved by a change of guardians.

In coming into Northamptonshire he had several views; he wanted a temporary retreat from his creditors. Jarvis had an infant fondness for play, without an adequate skill, and the money of the young ladies, in his necessities, was becoming of importance; but the daughters of Sir Edward Moseley were of a description more suited to his taste, and their portions were as ample as the others. He had become in some degree attached to Jane; and as her imprudent parents, satisfied with his possessing the exterior and requisite recommendations of a gentleman admitted his visits freely, he determined to make her his wife.

When he met Denbigh the first time, he saw that chance had thrown him in the way of a man who might hold his character in his power. He had never seen him as Pendennyss, and, it will be remembered, was ignorant of the name of Julia's friend: he now learnt for the first time that it was Denbigh. Uneasy at he knew not what, fearful of some exposure he knew not how, when Sir Herbert alluded to the occurrence, with a view to rebut the charge, if Denbigh should choose to make one, and with the near-sightedness of guilt, he pretended to know the occurrence, and under the promise of secresy, mentioned that the name of the officer was Denbigh. He had noticed Denbigh avoiding Sir Herbert at the ball; and judging others from himself, thought it was a wish to avoid any allusions to the lady he had brought into the other's quarters that induced the measure; for he was in hopes that if Denbigh was not as guilty as himself, he was sufficiently so to wish to keep the transaction from the eyes of Emily. He was, however, prepared for an explosion or an alliance with him, when the sudden departure of Sir Herbert removed the danger of a collision. Believing at last that they were to be brothers-in-law, and mistaking the earl for his cousin, whose name he bore, Egerton became reconciled to the association; while Pendennyss, having in his absence heard, on inquiring, some of the vices of the colonel, was debating with himself whether he should expose them to Sir Edward or not.

It was in their occasional interchange of civilities that Pendennyss placed his pocket-book upon a table, while he exhibited the plants to the colonel: the figure of Emily passing the window drew him from the room, and Egerton having ended his examination, observing the book, put it in his own pocket, to return it to its owner when they next met.

The situation, name, and history of Mrs. Fitzgerald were never mentioned by the Moseleys in public; but Jane, in the confidence of her affections, had told her lover who the inmate of the cottage was. The idea of her being kept there by Denbigh immediately occurred to him, and although he was surprised at the audacity of the thing, he was determined to profit by the occasion.

To pay this visit, he stayed away from the excursion on the water, as Pendennyss had done to avoid his friend, Lord Henry Stapleton. An excuse of business, which served for his apology, kept the colonel from seeing Denbigh to return the book, until after his visit to the cottage. His rhapsody of love, and offers to desert his intended wife, were nothing but the common-place talk of his purposes; and his presumption in alluding to his situation with Miss Moseley, proceeded from his impressions as to Julia's real character. In the struggle for the bell, the pocket-book of Denbigh accidentally fell from his coat, and the retreat of the colonel was too precipitate to enable him to recover it.

Mrs. Fitzgerald was too much alarmed to distinguish nicely, and Egerton proceeded to the ball-room with the indifference of a hardened offender. When the arrival of Miss Jarvis, to whom he had committed himself, prompted him to a speedy declaration, and the unlucky conversation of Mr. Holt brought about a probable detection of his gaming propensities, the colonel determined to get rid of his awkward situation and his debts by a coup-de-main. He accordingly eloped with Miss Jarvis.

What portion of the foregoing narrative made the dying confession of Egerton to the man he had so lately discovered to be the Earl of Pendennyss, the reader can easily imagine.

Chapter XLIX

The harvest had been gathered, and the beautiful vales of Pendennyss were shooting forth a second crop of verdure. The husbandman was turning his prudent forethought to the promises of the coming year, while the castle itself exhibited to the gaze of the wondering peasant a sight of cheerfulness and animation which had not been seen in it since the days of the good duke. Its numerous windows were opened to the light of the sun, its halls teemed with the faces of its happy inmates. Servants in various liveries were seen gliding through its magnificent apartments and multiplied passages. Horses, grooms, and carriages, with varied costumes and different armorial bearings, crowded its spacious stables and offices. Everything spoke society, splendor, and activity without; everything denoted order, propriety, and happiness within.

In a long range of spacious apartments were grouped in the pursuit of their morning employments, or in arranging their duties and pleasures of the day, the guests and owners of the princely abode.

In one room was John Moseley, carefully examining the properties of some flints which were submitted to his examination by his attending servant; while Grace, sitting at his side, playfully snatches the stones from his hand, as she cries half reproachfully, half tenderly---

"You must not devote yourself to your gun so incessantly, Moseley; it is cruel to kill inoffensive birds for your amusement only."

"Ask Emily's cook, and Mr. Haughton's appetite," said John, coolly extending his hand towards her for the flint--"whether no one is gratified but myself. I tell you, Grace, I seldom fire in vain."

"That only makes the matter worse; the slaughter you commit is dreadful."

"Oh!" cried John, with a laugh, "the ci-devant Captain Jarvis is a sportsman to your mind. He would shoot a month without moving a feather; he was a great friend to," throwing an arch look to his solitary sister, who sat on a sofa at a distance perusing a book, "Jane's feathered songsters."

"But now, Mosely," said Grace, yielding the flints, but gently retaining the hand that took them, "Pendenyss and Chatterton intend driving their wives, like good husbands, to see the beautiful waterfall in the mountains; and what am I to do this long tedious morning?"

John stole an enquiring glance, to see if his wife was very anxious to join the party--cast one look of regret on a beautiful agate that he had selected, and inquired--

"Do you wish to go very much, Mrs. Mosely?"

"Indeed--indeed I do," said the other, eagerly, "if--"

"If what?"

"You will drive me?" continued she, with a cheek slightly tinged with color.

"Well, then," answered John, with deliberation, and regarding his wife with affection "I will go on one condition."

"Name it!" cried Grace, with still increasing color.

"That you will not expose your health again in going to the church on a Sunday, if it rains."

"The carriage is so close, Mosely," answered Grace, with a paler cheek than beforehand eyes fixed on the carpet, "it is impossible I can take cold: you see the earl, and countess, and aunt Wilson never miss public worship, when possibly within their power."

"The earl goes with his wife; but what becomes of poor me at such times!" said John, taking her hand and pressing it kindly. "I like to hear a good sermon, but not in bad weather. You must consent to oblige me, who only live in your presence."

Grace smiled faintly, as John, pursuing the point, said--"What do you say to my condition?"

"Well then, if you wish," replied Graces without the look of gaiety her hopes had first inspired, "I will not go if it rain."

John ordered his phaeton, and his wife went to her room to prepare for the trip, and to regret her own resolution.

In, the recess of a window, in which bloomed a profusion of exotics, stood the figure of Lady Marian Denbigh, playing with a half-blown rose of the richest colors; and before her, leaning against the angle of the wall, stood her kinsman the Duke of Derwent.

"You heard the plan at the breakfast table," said his Grace, "to visit the little falls in the hills. But I suppose you have seen them too often to undergo the fatigue?"

"Oh no! I love that ride dearly, and should wish to accompany the countess in her first visit to it. I had half a mind to ask George to take me in his phaeton."

"My curricle would be honored with the presence of Lady Marian Denbigh," cried the duke with animation, "if, she would accept me for her knight on the occasion."

Marian bowed an assent, in evident satisfaction, as the duke proceeded--

"But if you take me as your knight I should wear your ladyship's colors;" and he held out his hand towards the budding rose. Lady Marian hesitated a moment--looked out at the prospect--up at the wall--turned, and wondered where her brother was; and still finding the hand of the duke extended, while his eye rested on her in admiration, she gave him the boon with a cheek that vied with the richest tints of the flower. They separated to prepare, and it was on their return from the falls that the duke seemed uncommonly gay and amusing, and the lady silent with her tongue, though her eyes danced in every direction but towards her cousin.

"Really, my dear Lady Mosely," said the dowager, as, seated by the side of her companion, her eyes roved over the magnificence within, and widely extended domains without--"Emily is well established indeed--better even than my Grace."

"Grace has an affectionate husband," replied the other, gravely, "and one that I hope will make her happy."

"Oh! no doubt happy!" said Lady Chatterton, hastily: "but they say Emily has a jointure of twelve thousand a year--by-the-by," she added, in a low tone, though no one was near enough to hear what she said, "could not the earl have settled Lumley Castle on her instead of the deanery?"

"Upon my word I never think of such gloomy subjects as provisions for widowhood," cried Lady Mosely: "you have been in Annerdale House--is it not a princely mansion?"

"Princely, indeed," rejoined the dowager, sighing: "don't the earl intend increasing the rents of this estate as the leases fall in? I am told they are very low now!"

"I believe not," said the other. "He has enough, and is willing others should prosper. But there is Clara, with her little boy--is he not a lovely child?" cried the grandmother, rising to take the infant in her arms.

"Oh! excessively beautiful!" said the dowager, looking the other way, and observing Catharine making a movement towards Lord Henry

Stapleton, she called to her. "Lady Herriefield--come this way, my dear--I wish to speak to you."

Kate obeyed with a sullen pout of her pretty lip, and entered into some idle discussion about a cap, though her eyes wandered round the rooms in listless vacancy.

The dowager had the curse of bad impressions in youth to contend with, and labored infinitely harder now to make her daughter act right, than formerly she had ever done to make her act wrong.

"Here! uncle Benfield," cried Emily, with a face glowing with health and animation, as she approached his seat with a glass in her hands. "Here is the negus you wished; I have made it myself, and you will praise it of course."

"Oh! my dear Lady Pendennyss," said the old gentleman, rising politely from his seat to receive the beverage: "you are putting yourself to a great deal of trouble for an old bachelor like me; too much indeed, too much."

"Old bachelors are sometimes more esteemed than young one," cried the earl gaily, joining them in time to hear this speech. "Here is my friend, Mr. Peter Johnson; who knows when we may dance at his wedding?"

"My lord, and my lady, and my honored master," said Peter gravely, in reply, bowing respectfully where he stood, waiting to take his master's glass--"I am past the age to think of a wife: I am seventy-three coming next 'lammas, counting by the old style."

"What do you intend to do with your three hundred a year," said Emily with a smile, "unless you bestow it on some good woman, for making the evening of your life comfortable?'

"My lady--hem--my lady," said the steward, blushing, "I had a little thought, with your kind ladyship's consent, as I have no relations, chick or child in the world, what to do with it."

"I should be happy to hear your plan," said the countess, observing that the steward was anxious to communicate something.

"Why, my lady, if my lord and my honored master's agreeable, I did think of making another codicil to master's will in order to dispose of it."

"Your master's will," said the earl laughing; "why not to your own, good Peter?"

"My honored lord," said the steward, with great humility, "it don't become a poor serving-man like me to make a will."

"But how will you prove it?" said the earl, kindly, willing to convince him of his error; "you must be both dead to prove it."

"Our wills," said Peter, gulping his words, "will be proved on the same day."

His master looked round at him with great affection, and both the earl and Emily were too much struck to say anything. Peter had, however, the subject too much at heart to abandon it, just as he had broken the ice. He anxiously wished for the countess's consent to the scheme, for he would not affront her, even after he was dead.

"My lady--Miss Emmy," said Johnson, eagerly, "my plan is, if my honored master's agreeable--to make a codicil, and give my mite to a little--Lady Emily Denbigh."

"Oh! Peter, you and uncle Benfield are both too good," cried Emily, laughing and blushing, as she hastened to Clara and her mother.

"Thank you, thank you," cried the delighted earl, following his wife with his eyes, and shaking the steward cordially by the hand; "and, if no better expedient be adopted by us, you have full permission to do as you please with your money.

"Peter," said his master to him in a low tone, "you should never speak of such things prematurely; now I remember when the Earl of Pendennyss, my nephew, was first presented to me, I was struck with the delicacy and propriety of his demeanor, and the Lady Pendennyss, my niece, too; you never see any thing forward, or--Ah! Emmy, dear," said the old man, tenderly interrupting himself, "you are too good to remember your old uncle," taking one of the fine peaches she handed him from a plate.

"My lord," said Mr. Haughton to the earl, "Mrs. Ives and myself have had a contest about the comforts of matrimony; she insists she may be quite as happy at Bolton Parsonage as in this noble castle, and with this rich prospect in view."

"I hope," said Francis, "you are not teaching my wife to be discontented with her humble lot--if so, both hers and your visit will be an unhappy one."

"It would be no easy task, if our good friend intended any such thing by his jests," said Clara, smiling. "I know my true interests, I trust, too well, to wish to change my fortune."

"You are right," said Pendennyss; "it is wonderful how little our happiness depends on a temporal condition. When here, or at Lumley Castle, surrounded by my tenantry, there are, I confess, moments of weakness, in which the loss of my wealth or rank would be missed greatly; but when on service, subjected to great privations, and surrounded by men superior to me in military rank, who say unto me--go, and I go--come, and I come--I find my enjoyments intrinsically the same."

"That," said Francis, "may be owing to your Lordship's tempered feelings, which have taught you to look beyond this world for pleasures and consolation."

"It has, doubtless, an effect," said the earl, "but there is no truth of which I am more fully persuaded, than that our happiness here does not depend upon our lot in life, so we are not suffering for necessaries--even changes bring less real misery than they are supposed to do."

"Doubtless," cried Mr. Haughton, "under the circumstances, I would not wish to change even with your lordship--unless, indeed," he continued, with a smile and bow to the countess, "it were the temptation of your lovely wife."

"You are quite polite," said Emily laughing, "but I have no desire to deprive Mrs. Haughton of a companion she has made out so well with these twenty years past."

"*Thirty*, my lady, if you please."

"And thirty more, I hope," continued Emily, as a servant announced the several carriages at the door. The younger part of the company now hastened to their different engagements, and Chatterton handed Harriet; John, Grace; and Pendennyss, Emily, into their respective carriages; the duke and Lady Marian following, but at some little distance from the rest of the party.

As the earl drove from the door, the countess looked up to a window, at which were standing her aunt and Doctor Ives. She kissed her hand to them, with a face, in which glowed the mingled expression of innocence, love, and joy.

Before leaving the Park, the party passed Sir Edward; with his wife leaning on one arm and Jane on the other, pursuing their daily walk. The baronet followed the carriages with his eyes, and exchanged looks of the fondest love with his children, as they drove slowly and respectfully by him; and if the glance which followed on Jane, did not speak equal pleasure, it surely denoted its proper proportion of paternal love.

"You have much reason to congratulate yourself on the happy termination of your labors," said the doctor, with a smile, to the widow; "Emily is placed, so far as human foresight can judge, in the happiest of all stations a female can be in: she is the pious wife of a pious husband, beloved, and deserving of it."

"Yes," said Mrs. Wilson, drawing back from following the phaeton with her eyes, "they are as happy as this world will admit, and, what is better, they are well prepared to meet any reverse of fortune which may occur, as well as to discharge the duties on which they have entered. I do not think," continued she, musing, "that Pendennyss can ever doubt the affections of such a woman as Emily."

"I should think not" said the doctor, "but what can excite such a thought in your breast, and one so much to the prejudice of George?"

"The only unpleasant thing I have ever observed in him," said Mrs. Wilson gravely, "is the suspicion which induced him to adopt the disguise in which he entered our family."

"He did not adopt it, madam--- chance and circumstances drew it around him accidentally; and when you consider the peculiar state of his mind from the discovery of his mother's misconduct--his own great wealth and rank--- it is not so surprising that he should yield to a deception, rather harmless than injurious."

"Dr. Ives," said Mrs. Wilson, "is not wont to defend deceit."

"Nor do I now, madam;" replied the doctor with a smile; "I acknowledge the offence of George, myself, wife, and son. I remonstrated at the time upon principle; I said the end would not justify the means; that a departure from ordinary rules of propriety was at all times dangerous, and seldom practised with impunity."

"And you failed to convince your hearers," cried Mrs. Wilson, gaily; "a novelty in your case, my good rector."

"I thank you for the compliment," said the doctor; "I did convince them as to the truth of the principle, but the earl contended that his case might make an innocent exception. He had the vanity to think, I believe, that by concealing his real name, he injured himself more than any one else, and got rid of the charge in some such way. He is however, thoroughly convinced of the truth of the position, by practice; his sufferings, growing out of the mistake of his real character, and which could not have happened had he appeared in proper person, having been greater than he is ready to acknowledge."

"If they study the fate of the Donna Julia, and his own weakness," said the widow, "they will have a salutary moral always at hand, to teach them the importance of two cardinal virtues at least--obedience and truth."

"Julia has suffered much," replied the doctor; "and although she has returned to her father, the consequences of her imprudence are likely to continue. When once the bonds of mutual confidence and respect are broken, they may be partially restored, it is true, but never with a warmth and reliance such as existed previously. To return, however, to yourself, do you not feel a sensation of delight at the prosperous end of your exertions in behalf of Emily?"

"It is certainly pleasant to think we have discharged our duties, and the task is much easier than we are apt to suppose," said Mrs. Wilson; "it is only to commence the foundation, so that it will be able to support the superstructure. I have endeavored to make Emily a Christian. I have endeavored to form such a taste and principles in her, that she would not be apt to admire an improper suitor and I have labored to prepare her to discharge her continued duties through life, in such a manner and with such a faith, as under the providence of God will result in happiness far exceeding anything she now enjoys. In all these, by the blessing of Heaven, I have succeeded, and had occasion offered, I would have assisted her inexperience through the more delicate decisions of her sex, though in no instance would I attempt to control them."

"You are right, my dear madam," said the doctor, taking her kindly by the hand, "and had I a daughter, I would follow a similar course. Give her delicacy, religion, and a proper taste, aided by the unseen influence of a prudent parent's care, and the chances of a woman for happiness would be much greater than they are; and I am entirely of your opinion--'That prevention is at all times better than cure.'"